Shadow Killers
&
Deathwalk

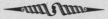

Shadow Killers

Shadow Killers

Previously Published as *Bloodstorm*

MATT BRAUN

St. Martin's Paperbacks

This is a work of fiction. All of the characters, organizations, and events portrayed in this novel are either products of the author's imagination or are used fictitiously.

SHADOW KILLERS / DEATHWALK

Shadow Killers copyright © 1985 by Matt Braun.
Deathwalk copyright © 2000 by Winchester Productions, Ltd.

All rights reserved.

For information address St. Martin's Press, 175 Fifth Avenue, New York, NY 10010.

ISBN: 978-1-250-30854-2

Our books may be purchased in bulk for promotional, educational, or business use. Please contact your local bookseller or the Macmillan Corporate and Premium Sales Department at 1-800-221-7945, ext. 5442, or by e-mail at MacmillanSpecialMarkets@macmillan.com.

Printed in the United States of America

Shadow Killers St. Martin's Paperbacks edition / February 2000
Deathwalk St. Martin's Paperbacks edition / September 2000

St. Martin's Paperbacks are published by St. Martin's Press, 175 Fifth Avenue, New York, NY 10010.

10 9 8 7 6 5 4 3 2

CHAPTER ONE

The three men reined their horses to a halt. High overhead, the sun beat down with a brassy glare. The landscape was barren, with windswept boulders dotted randomly among stunted trees. Westward, the Sangre de Cristo Mountains stood framed against a cloudless sky.

Ahead, the terrain sloped sharply upward. The men dismounted and one of them remained behind with the horses. Then, without a word, the other two pulled Winchester carbines from their saddle scabbards. The larger man was swarthy, with hawklike features and a droopy mustache. His companion was also dark-skinned, but clean shaven and somewhat less formidable in appearance. Their spurs jangled in the morning stillness as they walked forward.

The slope ended abruptly on a rocky escarpment. Some distance below was a narrow canyon, bisected by a small stream and a worn trail. The terrain rose steeply on the opposite side, sheltering the canyon north and south with sheer palisades. Only the faint gurgle of the stream broke the silence, and nothing moved. There was a foreboding sense of quiet, with time and motion stilled in a frozen tableau. The men stood there a moment, staring down.

Finally the larger one motioned to a craggy outcrop. His manner had about it an air of authority, and the second man moved as though on command. They seated themselves behind jagged boulders and dropped their sombreros on the ground. From his shirt pocket the clean-shaven one pulled out cigarette papers and tobacco. The leader hissed a sharp warning and shook his head. With a weak smile the man stuffed the makings back into his pocket. They settled down to wait.

An hour or so later the men suddenly tensed, their eyes alert. The sound of hoofbeats, growing steadily louder, echoed off the canyon walls. A rider appeared only a short distance downstream, his horse now held to a walk as the grade steepened westward toward the mountains. The men scrambled to their feet, staring intently into the gorge below. A moment passed while the larger one studied the rider with a look of watchful concentration. Then, as though in silent affirmation, he nodded to his companion. They shouldered their carbines, sighting on the rider.

Their shots cracked almost in unison. The rider seemed to jerk upright in the saddle, twin puffs of dust spurting from his broadcloth coat. Like a prolonged drumroll, the sound of gunfire reverberated endlessly along the rocky corridor. An instant later the rider toppled out of the saddle and his horse bolted, clattering away upstream. He hit the ground with a muffled thud, arms splayed outward. A shaft of sunlight reflected off what appeared to be the starched brilliance of a minister's dog collar. The darkish vermilion of blood slowly stained his shirtfront.

Grinning, the leader barked a command in guttural Spanish. The other man left his carbine behind and gingerly made his way down the face of the outcrop. On the canyon floor, he crossed the stream and knelt beside the body. He took the dead man's wallet, which contained less than twenty dollars in greenbacks, and a cheap pocket watch. As a final touch, he turned the dead man's coat and trousers pockets inside out. Then he rose and hurried back across the stream.

On top of the escarpment, he obediently handed over the wallet and pocket watch. The larger man examined the watch with a cautious expression, then he tossed it into the rocks. His mustache lifted in a sardonic smile as he thumbed through the wallet. He laughed and walked off toward the horses.

"Vamos! Hemos acabado el trabajo."

CHAPTER TWO

Braddock scanned the letter. So far he'd answered none of today's correspondence. The letter in hand, which was from a midwestern bank, was no exception. He dropped it into the wastebasket.

There was a light rap and the door to his office opened. Verna Potter, his secretary, stepped inside. Her pince-nez eyeglasses were perched on the end of her nose, and her expression was properly formal. She closed the door behind her.

"A Mr. Kirkland to see you."

"Frank Kirkland?" Braddock asked. "New Mexico?"

"I believe so."

Braddock checked his pocket watch. "Nothing like a punctual client. In fact, he's a little early."

Verna sniffed. "Perhaps Mr. Kirkland could teach you his secret."

"Spare me the lecture." Braddock grinned, pushing the correspondence aside. "C'mon. Chop, chop, Verna! Let's not keep him waiting."

Verna opened the door and motioned. "Won't you come this way, Mr. Kirkland?"

The man who entered was a natty dresser. Somewhere in his late thirties, he had pleasant features and dark hair that was flecked through with gray. He carried himself with a military bearing, and the immediate impression was of someone both distinguished and forceful, a man accustomed to issuing orders.

Braddock rose, extending his hand. "Welcome to Denver, Mr. Kirkland."

"Thank you." Kirkland shook hands with a firm grasp. "I presume you received my wire."

"Late yesterday." Braddock nodded. "Have a seat."

Kirkland took a wooden armchair. "Fortunately, my train was on time. I came straightaway from the depot."

Braddock lowered himself into the swivel chair behind his desk. He shook a cigarette from a half-empty pack and lit up in a wreath of smoke. He blew out the match, tossing it into an ashtray. His gaze was speculative.

"Your wire mentioned an emergency."

"Correct," Kirkland acknowledged. "Sorry the wording was so vague, but I had no choice. I couldn't afford to let anyone in Santa Fe know the purpose of our meeting."

"And what would that be exactly?"

"Murder."

Braddock slowly exhaled. "Tell me about it."

"Four days ago," Kirkland said grimly, "the Reverend John Tolby was killed. Someone ambushed him and shot him down in cold blood."

"Where?"

"Outside Cimarron," Kirkland replied. "That's the county seat of Colfax County. Reverend Tolby was the Methodist minister there."

"Is Cimarron near Santa Fe?"

"It's eighty miles or so to the northeast."

"Up somewhere around Raton Pass?"

"Yes."

"Which puts it fairly close to the Colorado border?"

"Colfax County abuts the Colorado line."

"Your wire said you're a lawyer."

Kirkland stiffened. "Are you questioning my credentials?"

"No," Braddock said quietly. "I was wondering why a lawyer from Santa Fe would be concerned with the murder of a preacher from Cimarron."

"I'm the attorney for the Cimarron Coalition. Reverend Tolby was one of the founders of the coalition. He was also a friend."

"Uh-huh." Braddock flicked an ash off his cigarette. "What's the Cimarron Coalition?"

"A citizens' organization," Kirkland informed him. "Businessmen and ranchers, even some small homesteaders. The better element of Colfax County."

"Why would they retain a lawyer so far away?"

"As you know, Santa Fe is the territorial capital. I represent their legal interests and lobby on their behalf."

"If you lobby for them"—Braddock paused with a quizzical look—"then you must lobby against someone or something."

"I do indeed."

"Who?"

"The Santa Fe Ring."

Braddock's ice-blue eyes were suddenly alert. "How come I get the feeling we just stopped talking about murder?"

"We haven't," Kirkland assured him. "There's every reason to believe the Santa Fe Ring was behind Reverend Tolby's death."

"I'd like a straight answer," Braddock said woodenly. "You didn't pick my name out of a hat, did you?"

"No."

"So," Braddock said, watching him carefully, "why me?"

"You were there the night Pat Garrett killed Billy the Kid."

"I'm still listening."

"By all accounts, the Kid was indirectly linked to Judge Owen Hough. Some people believe Judge Hough was the ring's man in Lincoln County. I understand you killed him."

Braddock had killed many men. He was regarded as the foremost manhunter on the frontier. Among others, he'd been involved in the downfall of such noted badmen as Dutch Henry Horn and Jesse James. His fame as a private detective had spread throughout the West, and the attendant publicity had destroyed his anonymity forever. These days he operated undercover, and always in disguise.

One of the first cases to bring him notoriety had occurred in Lincoln County, New Mexico Territory. There, working with Pat Garrett, he had been instrumental in the death of Billy the Kid. By happenstance, the case had pitted him against Judge Owen Hough. While no proof existed, Braddock had always believed that Hough was a political underling of the Santa Fe Ring. There was definite proof, however, that Hough had been responsible for the murder of a witness in the case. Her name was Ellen Nesbeth, and she'd been someone special in Braddock's life. He hadn't let her death go unavenged.

"You heard wrong," he said at length. "I killed Hough for personal reasons. It had nothing to do with the Santa Fe Ring."

"Perhaps," Kirkland allowed. "But one fact remains inescapable. He was their man, and you killed him. So far, that's the closest anybody has come to penetrating the ring."

"Wrong again." Braddock blew a plume of smoke into the air. "I linked Hough to a man by the name of Warren Mitchell. At the time, he was president of the Santa Fe Land and Development Company."

"He's still the president."

"Good for him," Braddock commented dryly. "But I never established any connection between the ring and Mitchell. It was pure supposition—no proof."

Kirkland leaned forward, staring earnestly at him.

"Nonetheless, you *believed* he was part of the ring, didn't you?"

"Let's get something straight," Braddock said flatly. "A man I respected told me about the ring. Other than his word, I have no knowledge that it even exists. Not a scrap of evidence."

"Oh, it exists all right!"

"Then you tell me," Braddock asked bluntly, "who belongs to the ring?"

"A great many men," Kirkland said, evasively. "Businessmen and politicians, bankers and lawyers and judges. The list would be endless."

"What are their names?"

"I have no idea."

"Who's the leader?"

"I don't know."

"Then what makes you so certain there is a ring?"

"Someone has an economic stranglehold on the territory. I'm talking about land and railroads, virtually every form of commerce. That wouldn't be possible without an organized conspiracy."

"Now you're dealing in supposition."

"To an extent," Kirkland admitted. "However, the people I represent are willing to pay to turn supposition into proof. We'd like to retain your services."

"I don't work for committees," Braddock said, no irony in his tone. "It only takes one loose lip to put my fat in the fire."

"You would report solely to me."

"That's another problem," Braddock remarked. "I don't make reports. I do the job my own way and at my own speed. The result speaks for itself."

Kirkland regarded him somberly. "Are you stating conditions or turning me down, Mr. Braddock?"

"Depends," Braddock said idly. "You started off talking about murder. Then you leapfrogged to the Santa Fe Ring. Which is it?"

"Both!" Kirkland's voice was heated and vindictive. "The

murder of Reverend Tolby is part and parcel of the greater problem. I'm convinced his killer will lead you to whoever's behind the conspiracy."

"Why was he killed?"

"Reverend Tolby used the pulpit as a public forum. He spoke out against the injustices visited on the people of Colfax County. His death was a warning to those who oppose the Santa Fe Ring."

"In other words, the Cimarron Coalition."

"Precisely."

Braddock stubbed out his cigarette in the ashtray. "You said his murder was part of a greater problem. Would you care to spell that out?"

"Of course," Kirkland said gravely. "At bottom, it amounts to a land-grabbing scheme by the Santa Fe Land and Development Company. Warren Mitchell performed the miraculous feat of transforming ninety-seven thousand acres into two million acres. And he did it virtually overnight!"

"How'd he manage that?"

"By outright bribery and political hocus-pocus!"

"Try to be a little more specific."

"To understand, you'll need some background information."

"The floor's all yours, Counselor."

"Very well."

Kirkland quickly warmed to his subject. Following the war with Mexico, all land north of the Rio Grande had been ceded to the United States. By the Treaty of Guadalupe Hidalgo, the American government agreed to respect the holdings of Mexican landowners. Yet the title to all property in New Mexico Territory had evolved from ancient land grants; the issue of who owned what was clouded by a convoluted maze of documents. At various times, land grants had been awarded by the King of Spain, the Republic of New Mexico, and the provincial governor. Ownership was often nine points physical possession and having the force to back the claim.

To compound the problem, many of the grants overlapped one another. Fraudulent land surveys further added to the confusion, and long legal battles seemingly resolved nothing. One such grant, the Beaubien-Miranda claim, was eventually acquired by the Santa Fe Land and Development Company. All too aware of the vagueness of the grant, the company hired the U.S. Deputy Surveyor to conduct an official survey. By virtue of the survey, the original 97,000-acre grant was swiftly converted into a 2,000,000-acre claim. At the same time, the company acquired other huge tracts of land throughout the territory. None was as large as the Beaubien-Miranda grant, which occupied a major portion of Colfax County. Overall, however, these holdings gave the company economic leverage in every county of New Mexico.

The company's position was strengthened when a deal was struck with the Santa Fe Railroad. The track line, which roughly followed the old Santa Fe Trail, traversed the land grant on the northern edge of Colfax County and proceeded on to the territorial capital. Yet there still remained the legal question of the original grant. In an audacious move, the company persuaded the U.S. Land Commissioner to establish an extraordinary precedent. Henceforth, a court decision based on an official survey would determine the validity of a claim. Shortly thereafter, a favorable court ruling declared the grant to be two million acres. The company had perfected a method by which New Mexico could be profitably, and legally, exploited.

Still, despite these devious maneuvers, trouble quickly erupted in Colfax County. Scores of settlers and ranchers had already staked out claims in the vicinity of Cimarron. By court edict, they were now declared trespassers on private property. The situation was further aggravated by the presence of several mining camps. The nearby mountains were rich with gold, and the miners now found themselves in the position of encroaching on company land. All the parties involved—ranchers, settlers, and miners—were ordered to vacate their claims or pay an exorbitant price for valid title. Colfax County quickly became a battleground between those with established roots and an organization that claimed prior ownership of the land.

The Santa Fe Land & Development Company was widely considered the offspring of the Santa Fe Ring. Warren Mitchell, president of the company, was thought to be a little more than a front man. Speculation and rumor fueled the belief that a powerful clique operated behind the scenes. The identity of the members was unknown, but their goal was obvious from the outset. Like feudal lords of ancient times, the Santa Fe Ring sought to control the economic lifeblood of an entire territory. The immediate response of ordinary citizens was the formation of the Cimarron Coalition, and open revolt in Colfax County began.

"We won't be budged," Kirkland concluded. "We've ignored the court order to vacate and we have no intention of paying them for the land. We're there to stay."

Braddock looked at him without expression. "I'd say you've got them convinced. Otherwise they wouldn't have resorted to gunplay."

"Assassins!" Kirkland said in an aggrieved tone. "We won't be intimidated either! Reverend Tolby's murder merely strengthened our resolve to hold out."

"What's the political situation?" Braddock ventured. "Any luck with your lobbying efforts?"

"I'm afraid not," Kirkland said glumly. "Territorial legislators have either been bought off or they're reluctant to oppose the ring. Our influence at the capital is practically nil."

"And in Colfax County?"

"Even worse!" Kirkland said with bitterness. "The courthouse crowd openly supports the land company."

"How do you explain that?" Braddock persisted. "Doesn't the coalition control enough votes to swing an election?"

"Not yet," Kirkland conceded. "We've been organized only a short time, and the next elections are still a year away."

"Sounds pretty bleak." Braddock paused, giving him an

evaluating glance. "So what're you asking me to do, Mr. Kirkland?"

"Find Reverend Tolby's murderer!" Kirkland said hotly. "And break the back of the Santa Fe Ring!"

"Let's be clear." Braddock's voice dropped. "Are you after evidence that will overturn the land grant? Or do you want an eye for an eye?"

Kirkland sensed the conversation was at a critical juncture. Braddock's reputation as a mankiller was unrivaled anywhere on the frontier. No lawman, certainly no outlaw, commanded such respect or outright fear. Yet it was common knowledge that Cole Braddock was not a gun for hire. He killed in the line of duty—or self-defense—but never for blood money. So now, acutely aware of what he'd been asked, Kirkland warned himself to proceed cautiously. He chose his words with care.

"There's no profit in revenge. Of course, considering the men we're up against, you may find it necessary to fight fire with fire. However, I would much prefer live witnesses, talkative witnesses. I want a case that will result in grand jury indictments."

Braddock stared at him for a time. He'd learned never to place any faith in a lawyer's double-talk. But the assignment intrigued him, for it was both broad in scope and something of a professional challenge. All the more so since his last encounter with the Santa Fe Ring had ended in a stalemate.

"I don't work cheap," he finally said. "The fee's five thousand out front and five thousand on delivery."

"Perfectly acceptable," Kirkland agreed. "I'll give you a bank draft on the coalition account."

"No," Braddock said slowly. "Write it out to yourself and let me have the cash. That way nobody in your bank will accidentally on purpose put out the word in Santa Fe."

"Very clever," Kirkland chortled. "I like the way you think, Mr. Braddock."

Braddock merely nodded reflectively. "I'll need a contact in Cimarron."

"Orville McMain," Kirkland said without hesitation. "He's publisher of the *Cimarron Beacon* and a moving force behind the coalition."

"How far can I trust him?"

"Completely," Kirkland observed. "McMain won't breathe a word to anyone. He's in some personal danger himself."

"Oh?"

"His editorials," Kirkland explained. "He's denounced the ring in no uncertain terms. We feel quite certain he's next on the assassins' death list."

"I guess he'll do," Braddock said, suddenly abstracted. "Have they hired a new preacher yet?"

"In Cimarron?"

"Yeah."

Kirkland shrugged. "Not to my knowledge. Why?"

"Have McMain put an announcement in the paper. Tell everybody a new parson's on the way." Braddock smiled cryptically. "The Reverend Titus Jacoby."

"Who's he?"

"You're looking at him."

"I—" Kirkland was bemused. "You intend to impersonate a minister?"

"A Bible thumper and a detective aren't all that different. We both listen to confessions and save souls—in our own ways."

"I see your point," Kirkland noted wryly. "One might even say you both perform the last rites."

"Your words, not mine."

"No offense meant."

"None taken."

"Well, now," Kirkland began, sensing he'd overstepped himself, "how shall we proceed?"

"How soon can you get your draft cashed?"

"No later than tomorrow."

"I'll leave when I see the money."

"Will you and I have any further contact?"

Braddock stood. "Not till the job's done."

Kirkland realized he'd been dismissed. He rose to his feet and shook hands. Then he walked out the door with a slightly dazed expression. He thought it ironic that Braddock would pose as a man of God.

And he wondered what sermon the Reverend Titus Jacoby would preach in Cimarron.

CHAPTER THREE

—◆—

Braddock waited until the door closed. Then he moved to a large safe positioned against the far wall. He spun the combination knob and cranked the handle. From an inside shelf, he removed one of four ledgers. The cover was stenciled, "M–R."

The ledgers were a Who's Who of western outlaws and badmen. The contents were compiled from wanted posters, newspaper articles, and voluminous correspondence with peace officers throughout the West. A page was assigned to each desperado, and the dossier detailed every known fact regarding his past activities. The ledgers were cross-referenced by name and alias, as well as state and territory. Virtually everyone who was anyone, from horse thieves to gunslicks, was listed therein. The result was a comprehensive rogues' gallery.

The page on New Mexico Territory was a quick read. With the end of the Lincoln County War, a relative calm had settled over the territory. The names of Billy the Kid and most of his gang had been lined out, indicating they were no longer among the living. Yet New Mexico was not altogether a land of peace and brotherly love. One name stood out, and his place of residence was of immediate interest. He lived outside the town of Cimarron.

The man's name was Clay Allison. His dossier was a brief chronicle of violence and bloodletting. No outlaw, Allison was instead one of the more successful ranchers in Colfax County. Yet his quarrelsome nature, abetted by a hair-trigger temper, often put him afoul of the law. His first entry in the ledger involved a particularly brutal vigilante action. Allison led a mob which stormed the jail and lynched an accused murderer. Following the hanging, Allison then decapitated the man and put the head on public display in a saloon.

There were two other entries in the dossier. The first involved an argument over a horse race, resulting in a shootout. Allison killed his opponent and then exchanged insults with a friend of the dead man. The friend mysteriously disappeared and Allison was charged with murder. However, no body was recovered, and he was released for lack of evidence. Scarcely two years later, Allison went on a drunken rampage and terrorized the patrons of a dance hall. A deputy sheriff was summoned, and Allison killed him in a blazing gunfight. Although arrested and charged with murder, Allison was released. Witnesses swore the deputy had fired first.

Braddock closed the ledger. He lit a cigarette and stared off into space. From what Kirkland had told him, the Cimarron Coalition was composed of various factions. One of the factions mentioned was ranchers, and it was therefore logical to assume that Clay Allison was a member of the coalition. The dossier indicated that Allison was a violent hothead who seldom, if ever, considered the consequences of his acts. Such a man was dangerous to himself and anyone associated with him. He might fly off the handle at any moment, provoking trouble at an inopportune time. Or his temper might cause him to blurt out secrets when the situation demanded silence. In short, he was not to be trusted.

Normally when operating undercover, Braddock kept his own counsel. He told the client nothing of his plans and undertook the assignment in the most covert manner possible. All the more so since his notoriety—along with his photo in newspapers—made it necessary for him to operate in disguise. Yet, on the spur of the moment, he'd decided to take Kirkland into his confidence. Cimarron was a small town, and a stranger would immediately draw attention. A local contact was therefore essential; the publisher, Orville McMain, would introduce him into the community and lend credibility to his cover story. The danger was that McMain might reveal his actual identity to other members of the coalition. It was a calculated risk, and he'd weighed it against the advantages of arriving in Cimarron under the guise of a preacher. But now he made a mental note to warn McMain to keep his lip buttoned and, in particular, to say nothing whatever to Clay Allison.

Crushing out his cigarette, Braddock rose and moved to the door. Verna Potter looked up from her desk as he entered the outer office. She was a spinster with plain features and hair pulled back in a tight chignon. His work as a detective was the focal point of her life, and she took a certain vicarious satisfaction in the number of outlaws he'd killed. His personal life, on the other hand, left her mortified. He spent his evenings in Denver's sporting district, and the woman who shared his bed was the feature attraction at a variety theater. Verna considered it all quite reprehensible for a man in his position.

Braddock paused at her desk. "I took the case. When you have a minute, check out the train schedules to New Mexico. I want the nearest stop to a place called Cimarron."

"Very well." Verna jotted it down on her notepad. "When will you leave?"

"In a day or so," Braddock said absently. "Kirkland's supposed to drop off five thousand in cash. Hold out a thousand for my expenses and deposit the rest."

"Why cash?" Verna peered over her pince-nez glasses. "I thought Mr. Kirkland appeared quite respectable."

"He's a regular prince," Braddock deadpanned. "But a

check leaves a paper trail. I'd prefer to keep the arrangement to ourselves."

Verna gave him an apprehensive glance. "Is the assignment that much more dangerous than normal?"

"Yes and no," Braddock said equably. "The stakes are bigger, and that tends to make people play rougher. I guess it all evens out in the end, though."

"In what way?"

Braddock grinned. "I'm not exactly a tyro myself."

"Don't brag!" Verna said sharply. "Everyone knows it brings bad luck."

"Are you superstitious"—Braddock cocked one eyebrow—"or just a worrywart?"

"Humph!" Verna averted her gaze. "Have you finished with today's correspondence?"

"There's nothing of interest," Braddock replied. "I dumped it in the wastebasket."

"I wonder that you read it at all!"

"Lock up for me." Braddock speared his hat off a hat tree. "The safe's open and a couple of ledgers are on the desk."

"Of course," Verna said with frosty disapproval. "I assume you won't return today?"

"You know what they say," Braddock called over his shoulder. "All work and no play . . ."

Verna watched him go out the door. Her waspish expression slowly dissolved into a faint smile. She thought him a devil and a roué, thoroughly incorrigible, yet late at night, alone in her cold spinster's bed, she forgave him everything.

He was her forbidden fruit, untasted.

Braddock walked toward the sporting district. Not without certain qualms, he had decided to approach the underworld czar of Denver. On occasion, they had been of service to one another. And while they were not colleagues, he'd nonetheless established an understanding of sorts with Lou Blomger.

On Larimer Street, he crossed into another world. The

Tenderloin represented a brand of civic betterment unique to westerners. Every imaginable vice, from the ordinary to the bizarre, was contained within an area of several square blocks. By municipal ordinance, all gambling dives, dance halls, bordellos, and saloons were restricted to the Tenderloin. Easterners found the concept at once fascinating and morally unconscionable. But to Braddock, who'd migrated to Denver by way of Texas, it seemed a wise and farsighted policy. Everyone benefited when whores and high rollers knew their place and stayed there.

As he strolled along Larimer, Braddock's thoughts turned to the town itself. Like many western settlements, its origins were linked to an enterprising form of avarice. Gold was discovered on Cherry Creek in 1858, and within a matter of months thousands of reasonably sane men hocked their worldly possessions and lit out for Colorado Territory. Some struck it rich, but most went away bedraggled and footsore, their quest for the mother lode a bitter memory. That same year a land speculator founded a town along the banks of Cherry Creek. He called it Denver.

Over the years, the town had reproduced itself a hundred-fold. What was once a sad collection of log huts had spread and grown until finally a glittering metropolis had been created amidst the gold fields. By the early 1880s, Denver had become a cosmopolitan beehive, with theaters, opera, plush hotels, six churches, four newspapers, three railroads, and an entire street devoted to nothing but whorehouses. Vice was an organized industry in Denver, and the town's sporting district, known locally as the Tenderloin, was controlled by one man. His name was Lou Blomger.

Denver was also a peaceful, law-abiding town. By Lou Blomger's edict, no crimes of violence were tolerated within the Tenderloin. What highwaymen and robbers did outside the city limits was their own business. But those reckless enough to practice their craft in Denver proper were dealt a swift, brutal lesson in obeying the law. It was a lesson that exacted absolute and final justice, without appeal or clemency. Blomger's enforcers were skilled at performing neat, workmanlike executions.

There was no sense of civic virtue behind Blomger's edict. He was simply a pragmatic businessman, and the rackets were his business. He meant to insure that the Tenderloin operated without undue publicity or needless acts of violence. Experience had taught him that the public was blindly apathetic to almost any form of vice, so long as it was conducted quietly and out of sight. The man in the street wanted to know he could visit a cathouse or drop a few dollars at the faro tables in the evening. Yet he also wanted assurance that he wouldn't be waylaid by some hardcase on his way home.

Whores and crooked gaming dens, even bunco games, were condoned by Blomger. Still, he drew the line at spilling citizens' blood or forcibly separating them from their wallets. He declared that any man who stepped over that line would be judged an outlaw even among his own kind. With his rise to power, peace had settled over Denver. The public viewed the Tenderloin as a tawdry playground, and the rackets operated with blissful tranquility. Gunslingers, highwaymen, and thieves were welcome for as long as they cared to sample the delights of Denver's heady atmosphere. But only if they minded their manners and weren't tempted to molest the local residents. Otherwise they were found floating facedown in Cherry Creek.

Politicians and police alike hailed Blomger as a civic benefactor. The foundation of his power, of course, was in the fact that he controlled the rackets. The decision of who got paid off, and how much, was his alone. Yet there was more to it than mere payoffs. The Tenderloin cast the swing vote in any election. Without Blomger's support a politician never attained office, much less participated in the corruption and graft. Slowly, always from behind the scenes, the tentacles of his power reached outward and upward. When the votes were counted after the most recent elections, the results came as no surprise to Denver's political hierarchy. Lou Blomger owned city hall and the courthouse, and his name was spoken with reverence in the halls of the state capitol. His influence, however insidiously, extended to every level of government.

Braddock's visit was prompted by that very thought. He reasoned that a man with such widespread influence would have political connections beyond Colorado's borders. Since New Mexico joined Colorado on the south, it was conceivable that those connections extended all the way to Santa Fe. Or perhaps to the Santa Fe Ring itself. All of which raised the specter of yet another calculated risk. Lou Blomger might prove to be a valuable source of information. He might also represent a hazard, one with deadly consequences. Everything hinged on whether or not it was Blomger's ox that got gored.

Entering the Progressive Club, Braddock reminded himself to proceed with caution. Upstairs, where Blomger's office was located, he rapped on the door. The man who opened it was short and wiry, with the features of a ferret and a disposition to match. His name was Slats Drago and he was Blomger's personal bodyguard. He carried twin Colts snugged down tight in shoulder holsters, and his reputation was that of a cold-blooded killer. His attitude toward Braddock was one of amiable, albeit wary, respect. He nodded.

"Long time no see, Braddock."

"Hello, Slats. I'd like a word with Lou."

"Business or social?"

"Would it make a difference?"

Drago hesitated, then stepped aside. "Mr. Blomger, it's Cole Braddock."

Lou Blomger sat behind a massive walnut desk. He was a man of considerable bulk, with a rounded paunch and sagging jowls. His hair was flecked with gray and his eyes were deceptively humorous. His handshake was perfunctory, but he seemed genuinely pleased by the unexpected visit. He motioned Braddock to a chair.

"Have a seat, Cole. You ought to drop around more often."

"Well, you know how it is, Lou. No rest for the weary."

Blomger chuckled. "I know the feeling all too well. What can I do for you?"

"It's personal."

"Pay no mind to Slats. He's deaf and dumb where my affairs are concerned."

"No offense, but this time . . ." Braddock shrugged.

Blomger regarded him thoughtfully. After a moment, he glanced across at Drago. "Wait outside, Slats. I'll call if I need you."

Drago shot Braddock a dirty look. Then he opened the door and stepped into the hallway. When the latch clicked, Blomger slowly shook his head. "I think you hurt Slats's feelings. He considers himself a professional."

"No way around it. What I have to say has to be said to you alone."

"Oh? Why is that?"

"If it's repeated," Braddock said deliberately, "I'll hold you accountable."

Blomger's expression was impassive. He understood that the threat was made in earnest. Braddock was in effect offering him a chance to end the conversation, for once he gave his word, any breach of confidence would be taken as personal betrayal. No one, including Slats Drago, would then be able to protect him. Somewhere, somehow, Braddock would kill him.

"All right, Cole. Whatever you say stops here."

Braddock lit a cigarette. As he exhaled the smoke, he decided on the direct approach. "Have you got connections in New Mexico?"

"Political or otherwise?"

"Political."

"Not with anybody who carries any clout."

"How about a fellow named Warren Mitchell?"

"Never heard of him."

"I'm surprised," Braddock said casually. "He's rumored to be the head of the Santa Fe Ring."

Blomger loosed a rumbling laugh. "You've been hired to investigate the Santa Fe Ring?"

"I didn't say—"

"And you're asking me for the inside dope?"

"Yeah, something like that."

"Well, I'm sorry to disappoint you, Cole. I can tell you that the Santa Fe Ring exists, but nothing more."

"Why not?"

"Politics in New Mexico is a closed club. Outsiders aren't allowed to join, and insiders never talk."

"Then what makes you so sure the ring exists?"

"Because everybody's lips are sealed tight. When that many people get lockjaw, you can bet the rumors are true."

"That's it, nothing else?"

"A bit of friendly advice," Blomger replied. "Whoever operates the ring plays rough—damned rough. You'd do well to stay out of New Mexico."

Braddock smiled. "I've been there before."

"And lived to tell the tale. So you obviously intend to ignore my advice."

"I'll let you know—sometime."

"Fair enough. Until then, I'll just assume we never had this conversation."

"I'm obliged, Lou."

"Of course you are. I'm in the business of obligating people. And I always call the marker!"

Blomger's laugh followed him out the door. In the hallway, he traded a curt nod with Slats Drago. Then he turned toward the stairs and emerged a moment later on the street. Walking back uptown, he slowly put the day's business from his mind. His thoughts centered instead on tonight.

He wondered how Lise would react when he told her. And within a few steps, he stopped wondering. He knew.

CHAPTER FOUR

Braddock arrived at the Alcazar Variety Theater early that evening. The owner, Jack Brady, greeted him with effusive warmth. He was escorted to his usual table down front, and a waiter materialized with a chilled bottle of champagne. The bubbly, as always, was on the house.

In the sporting district, Braddock was looked upon as a celebrity. He was Denver's resident mankiller and as much an attraction as the stage show. The fact that he slept with Lise Hammond, the Alcazar's headliner, merely enhanced his reputation. Speculation among the theater's clientele was evenly divided between his affair with the girl and the actual number of men he'd killed. Still, for all their curiosity, no one broached such matters in his presence. He was a private man and tolerated few questions.

Apart from his reputation with a gun, his physical appearance also gave men pause. He was lean and tough, a strapping six-footer with shoulders like a singletree. His eyes were smoky blue and impersonal, set off by squared features and light chestnut hair. He had the look of a loner, and he did nothing to correct the impression. A similar streak of independence extended to his professional life. Shrewd investments, which included a diverse portfolio of stocks and real estate, allowed him to pick and choose his assignments. He accepted a case for the challenge, because he took pride in his craft. The money was simply the gauge of his worth as an investigator.

"Good evening, Cole."

"Hello there, Daniel."

"Sorry I'm so late."

"Forget it." Braddock gestured to a chair. "Sit down and pour yourself a drink."

Daniel Cameron was one of the few men Braddock invited to his table. A master gunsmith, he was stooped and gray-haired, almost gnomelike in appearance. He kept Braddock's guns in perfect working order and often suggested innovations calculated to give the manhunter an edge. One such innovation was the cartridges Braddock carried in his Colt.

The bullets sold over the counter were notoriously poor man-stoppers. Though mortally wounded in a gunfight, an outlaw would often live long enough to kill his adversary. What Braddock needed was a bullet that would neutralize the other man on the spot, stop him instantly. Daniel Cameron's innovation provided true stopping power.

The standard factory loading utilized a round pug-nosed bullet. Cameron's design was a molded lead slug which gradually tapered to a flat nose. Going a step farther, he then reversed the slug and loaded it upside down. The nose of the slug was now seated inside the cartridge case, crimped tight well above the sloping shoulders. The base, which was blunt and truncated, was thereby positioned at the front of the cartridge.

The factory load normally achieved deep penetration. It was not unusual for a standard pug-nosed bullet to plow through a man, exiting virtually unmarred and still very much in its original shape. What resulted was that the bullet expended the greater part of its energy drilling a clean, somewhat symmetrical hole. The effect was not at all what Braddock wanted. A man dead on his feet frequently emptied his gun before dropping.

Cameron's imaginative innovation rather neatly solved the problem. The reverse-loaded slug achieved scarcely one-third the penetration of a factory load. Upon impact, the truncated base expanded, squashing the entire slug, from front to rear, into a mushroom-shaped chunk of lead. The result was that the mushroomed slug imparted its energy with massive shock, delivering a horrendous wound rather than drilling a clean hole. The effect was instantaneous, literally a man-stopper that halted an opponent dead in his tracks. On more than one occasion, the reverse-loaded slug had saved Cole Braddock's life.

"Happy days!" Cameron smiled over the rim of his glass. "You might be interested in why I was late."

"You'll tell me anyway," Braddock said genially. "So go ahead and get it off your chest."

A sly look crossed Cameron's face. "Tonight I put the finishing touches on a new Smith and Wesson forty-four."

"So?"

"Cole, it's unbelievable!" Cameron's eyes gleamed with pride. "I've honed the double-action trigger pull down to nothing. It almost goes off by itself!"

"C'mon, Daniel," Braddock groaned. "You tried the same thing on me when Colt came out with a double-action."

"This one's different," Cameron protested. "It's smooth as silk—smoother! And I still contend a double-action will shave time off your draw."

"Not with a cross-draw holster." Braddock patted the left side of his coat. "Figure it out for yourself, Daniel. By the time I pull and bring it up to fire, I've already got the hammer cocked. And a single-action trigger is a hell of a lot lighter than a double-action."

"Why cock the hammer?" Cameron insisted. "You could be squeezing a double-action as you align the sights. I say it would make you faster—much faster!"

Braddock shook his head. "Fast doesn't win gunfights. Take my word for it, Daniel. A quick man who's dead-on accurate will beat a speed demon every time."

"How about reloading?" Cameron countered. "A Smith and Wesson breaks at the top and ejects all the spent shells at once. The loading gate on a Colt takes twice as long, maybe longer."

"Well, I'll tell you," Braddock said with a sardonic smile, "I've never had occasion to reload. Your trick bullets stop the fight before it goes that far."

Cameron spread his hands in an exaggerated gesture. "It's 1882, Cole. Time marches on, and you, my friend, you're falling behind!"

"I'm still fogging a mirror." Braddock laughed and motioned toward the stage. "Drink your champagne and watch the show."

The orchestra thumped to life and the curtain swished open. Lise pranced onstage, her skirts flashing and her breasts jiggling over the top of her gown. At a signal from the maestro, the orchestra segued into a rousing dance number.

A line of chorus girls exploded out of the wings. Lise hoisted her skirts higher, exposing her magnificent legs, and led them in a high-stepping cakewalk. The tempo of the music quickened and the girls squealed and Lise wigwagged her underdrawers with bouncy exuberance. A spate of jubilant shouts erupted from men around the room.

In the midst of the routine, Lise moved downstage. Her bloomers were revealed in a showy step, and a spotlight enveloped her with dazzling brilliance. As the chorus line romped and cavorted behind her, she halted before the footlights. She dimpled her lips in a bee-stung pucker and blew Braddock a kiss.

The crowd went wild.

A shaft of light from the parlor lamp streamed through the bedroom door. Braddock lay sprawled on the bed, hands locked behind his head. His gaze was fixed on the ceiling and his expression was pensive. He pondered on the easiest way to tell her.

The bathroom door opened. Lise wore only a sheer peignoir and high-heeled slippers. She moved sinuously across the room and halted beside the bed. Her eyes were bright with excitement and a vixenish smile touched her lips. She shrugged out of the peignoir, letting it drop to the floor.

She was naked. The streamer of lamplight framed her in an amber glow, making her a vision of loveliness. She stood before him with sculptured legs and jutting breasts, her body rounded and supple. Her golden hair hung long and unbound, spilling down over her shoulders. A moment slipped past while she teased and tantalized, posing in the slatted light. Then, with a low, throaty laugh, she stepped out of the slippers and joined him in bed.

Braddock enfolded her in a tight embrace. Her arms went around his neck, and she kissed him with fiery passion. Her tongue darted into his mouth, and she shuddered convulsively, squirming closer. His hand went to the delta between her legs, and a murmur of feverish urgency escaped her throat. He rolled on top of her and entered her. Their mouths locked in union, his stroke gradually quickened and she drove at him until her body was wracked by jolting shudders. Her nails taloned his shoulders as she surged with violent contractions. Her mouth opened in an explosive cry.

"Oooh—oh, Cole. Oh, my God!"

Breathing heavily, they separated and his arm slipped around her waist. She clung to his hard-muscled frame, and for a long while time lost all meaning. Satiated with the musky smell of love, they rested, and after a period of silence, they kissed again, their bodies warm and their legs intertwined. Then she snuggled closer, her mouth pressed to his ear in a low whisper.

"Mmm. That was scrumptious, lover."

Braddock patted her bottom. "It'll have to last awhile."

"Oh?" She nuzzled his earlobe. "Why?"

"I accepted an assignment today."

"Damn!" She scooted around and sat upright. "When do you leave?"

"Tomorrow," Braddock said casually. "Maybe the day after."

"Where to this time?"

"New Mexico."

Her gaze sharpened. "What sort of job?"

Braddock was by nature a cynic. He trusted no one completely and he accepted nothing at face value. With time, however, he'd learned that his secrets were safe with Lise. What began as a sexual liaison had slowly ripened into an emotional bond. She shared his suite at the Brown Palace Hotel and she shared his innermost thoughts. She was his sole confidante.

"Someone was murdered," he said matter-of-factly. "Somebody else thinks the Santa Fe Ring was behind it. I've been hired to take a look-see."

"What's the Santa Fe Ring?"

"Good question." Braddock raised up on one elbow. "Some people believe it's an organized conspiracy involving politicians and crooked businessmen. It's so hush-hush nobody's proved it yet."

"You will!" She jiggled with excitement. "I just know you will!"

"I aim to do my damnedest."

She eyed him keenly. "It's big, isn't it? I mean really big—your biggest case."

"Yeah." Braddock gave her a wary look. "I suppose you could say that."

"Well, then"—she paused with a beguiling grin—"how about some help? I'm ready, willing, and available."

"No soap," Braddock said stolidly. "It's too dangerous."

"You need a new line!" She tweaked the hairs on his chest. "That's what you said last time, remember?"

"Save your breath," Braddock advised her. "You won't con me into it this trip out."

"Why not?" She mocked him with a minxlike smile.

"I had those lunkheads in Virginia City eating out of my hand. Without me, you wouldn't have solved the case! You said so yourself."

Braddock couldn't argue the point. She was a blond sexpot, a bawdy nymph with a body like mortal sin. She possessed a kind of bursting vitality, and she was the mental equal of any man he'd ever met. On his last case, she had accompanied him to Montana and played a one-week engagement at a Virginia City variety theater. Her natural talent for undercover work had quickly unearthed a vital lead in the investigation, a lead that he would never have turned up by himself. So her statement tonight was no idle boast. She had a flair for the detective business.

"Sorry," he said firmly. "New Mexico's a powder keg and somebody's already lit the fuse. I won't risk it."

"C'mon, lover!" She fluttered her eyelashes. "I handled myself all right in Virginia City, didn't I? And those boys weren't exactly kindergarten stuff!"

"No, they weren't," Braddock granted. "But you were offered a job there, and that gave you a legitimate front. We couldn't work the same dodge twice in a row, especially where I'm headed. It's a one-horse burg smack dab in the middle of nowhere."

"Excuses, excuses!" She lifted her chin defiantly. "Where there's a will, there's a way. And we both know it!"

Braddock wagged his head. "You might as well call it quits. The answer's no, and that's final."

"Jesus Christ!"

Lise bounced out of bed. She scooped up her peignoir and went storming into the parlor. Braddock listened to the clatter of glass on glass as she poured herself a shot from the brandy decanter. He'd never seen her lose her temper, and it bothered him more than he cared to admit. He slipped on a robe and walked from the bedroom.

Seated on the sofa, Lise looked like a sulky child. She took a slug of brandy and refused to meet his gaze. He moved forward and sat down beside her. Some things were difficult for him to articulate, and he now had to struggle for words. At last he let out his breath with a heavy sigh.

"Here's the score," he said softly. "If it was anyone else, I wouldn't give it a second thought. But it's not anyone else. It's you, and that makes a hell of a difference, from where I sit."

A lump formed in Lise's throat. Any open display of affection was foreign to his character, and she knew the words had cost him dearly. All his life he'd been an emotional nomad, allowing no strings and asking none in return. Tonight, in his own way he'd told her that his wanderlust was a thing of the past. He cared for her too deeply to put her in harm's way. Her eyes suddenly glistened and a tear rolled down her cheek.

"You must think I'm a spoiled brat."

"You're worth spoiling—in some ways."

"Are you mad at me?"

"One way to find out."

Braddock took her in his arms. He squeezed her in a crushing bear hug and the brandy glass dropped to the floor. She pulled his head down and kissed him with fierce abandon. When they finally parted, her tears were gone and the vixenish look had returned. Her eyes sparkled with a mischievous glitter.

"Cole."

"Hmmm?"

"If you should change your mind—"

"Holy crucified Christ!"

"—I'm still available, lover."

Her laugh was like wind chimes in a gentle breeze.

CHAPTER FIVE

Lise studied herself in the mirror.

Her mind was elsewhere as she slowly applied her stage makeup. Somewhat mechanically, she colored her cheeks with a magenta shade of rouge. Then she darkened her eyelids with kohl, spreading it in a fan-shaped pattern until her eyes seemed to blaze like opals set in dusky onyx. The last step was the tint on her mouth, which was accomplished with the same methodical motions. She painted her lips into a scarlet bee-stung pucker.

By now her evening ritual was performed largely by rote. She had spent a thousand nights, perhaps more, seated before a dressing-room mirror. As a stagestruck young girl, she'd hooked up with a traveling variety troupe. She began as a hoofer. Eager and naive, she had been determined to escape her family and the quaint boredom of midwestern life. From St. Louis she had toured virtually any city of consequence west of the Mississippi. Slowly she'd acquired stage presence, cultivated her voice, and moved out of the chorus. A headliner when the troupe finally folded, she had gone out on her own. And now, scarcely a year later, she had star billing at the Alcazar.

Tonight the glamor and excitement of her stage life somehow seemed trivial, even threadbare. Only an hour ago, Cole Braddock had caught the evening southbound train. Their parting had been short, without any great ceremony, for he hated good-byes. He'd simply kissed her with his usual look-for-me-when-you-see-me farewell, and walked from the hotel suite. She had only the vaguest notion of his destination and absolutely no idea when he might return. Sometimes an assignment ended quickly, but other times he'd be gone a month or longer. Worse, there would be no means of contacting him while he was away. Nor would he write her or even attempt to pass along a message through his secretary. She was effectively in a state of limbo for however long his assignment lasted.

For all his good intentions, she was still miffed about his current case. She appreciated his protective attitude and she understood that his concern was solely for her welfare, but she was nonetheless upset by the thought of being left behind. She'd said nothing more last night, and all day she had bitten her tongue in an effort to remain silent. She was determined that nothing would spoil their last few hours together. Further, she was resolved that he wouldn't leave with bad memories of their parting. Still, she felt piqued and just the least bit offended. All his logic in no way offset the substance of her argument. Working undercover, she could have rendered valuable assistance in New Mexico. And she could have done it without endangering herself or his precious assignment!

Staring into the mirror, she wondered if her anger stemmed from hurt pride. For despite the bond between them, she understood that he was still his own man. Her only assurance of holding him was in allowing him the freedom to come and go as he pleased. And to let him stay away, without so much as a note, for however long it suited his purpose.

Somehow the arrangement seemed a little lopsided. Yet she possessed the wisdom to understand that it would end if she ever attempted to smother him with demands. She genuinely believed that he never slept with other women, and while he wanted no strings attached to his life, he always returned to her. Not that he ever spoke of their relationship, for he was a man who seldom revealed his innermost emotions. He was more apt to cover his feelings with an offhand remark or a casual gesture of tenderness. When they were together, he *was* attentive and thoughtful and an ardent lover, but these damnable separations were sometimes more than she could bear. And she knew that her foul mood wouldn't improve with the passing of time. She was going to be very bitchy until he returned.

There were three sharp raps and the door opened. Jack Brady, owner of the Alcazar, stuck his head inside the dressing room. He was a florid-faced Irishman with a genial manner and a fondness for pretty women. Not without reason, he pampered Lise and treated her with the diplomacy befitting Denver's star songbird. He lived in constant dread that a competitor would pirate her away, and with her, the bulk of the evening trade. Her three shows a night made the Alcazar a veritable money tree. Now his face split in a broad grin as he jerked his head toward the stage.

"Five minutes till show time."

"Don't worry, Jack, I'll make it."

Brady's grin dissolved. "You look a little piqued. Anything wrong?"

"No. Everything's just hunky-dory."

"You sure don't sound like it."

"How I sound in here doesn't matter, Jack. It's how I sound onstage."

"Yeah, of course. I just thought if there was anything I could do. You know . . ."

"What you can do is shut the door on your way out. I'll be there when the curtain goes up, Jack."

"Uh—" Brady cleared his throat. "Well, give 'em a good show tonight. We've got a big crowd out front."

"Scram!"

Brady hastily closed the door. Lise regretted her tone the instant he'd gone, and almost called him back. But then on second thought, she changed her mind. She felt bitchy and she'd probably stay that way for the foreseeable future, and Jack Brady would just have to live with it!

She stood and slipped out of her dressing robe. Quickly she stepped into a spangled gown that was cut low on top and ended above her knees. After fastening the hooks, she checked her makeup one last time. Then she squared her shoulders and marched out the door.

Her face lit up with a bright, theatrical smile.

The curtain rang down on the first show. Lise walked offstage to thunderous applause. She moved through a bevy of chorus girls crowding the wings and started toward her dressing room. Then, on the spur of the moment, she reversed directions.

As a rule, Lise remained backstage between shows. She had learned long ago that mingling with the customers was more bother than it was worth. But in the midst of her last number, she'd noticed Daniel Cameron sitting at one of the tables down front. And now, somewhat impulsively she decided to join the gunsmith for a drink. However loath she was to admit it, she simply couldn't stand her own company tonight.

A moment later she emerged from a door beside the orchestra pit. All the tables were full, and a buzz swept through the crowd when she started across the room. Hurriedly, ignoring a drunk who shouted her name, she made her way to Cameron's table. He was alone and pleasantly surprised by her sudden appearance. He scrambled to his feet.

"Good evening, Lise."

"Hello, Daniel. May I join you?"

"By all means."

Cameron held out a chair. Lise seated herself, and a waiter materialized at her elbow. She ordered a brandy, then turned back to Cameron. His wizened features were split in a wide smile.

"I can't tell you how delighted I am. I'm the envy of every man in the room."

"Aren't you the flatterer?"

"No, it's true. Frankly, I can't imagine why you'd pick an old reprobate like me. But I'm delighted all the same."

"To tell you the truth"—Lise cut her eyes around the room—"you're the only friend I see here tonight."

"Uh-huh." Cameron regarded her with a somber expression. "Forced to guess, I'd say Cole left town today. Would that be a safe bet?"

"You must be reading my mind."

"Hardly that. I'm just familiar with the symptoms."

"Symptoms?"

"Loneliness mixed with a dab of anxiety. Quite natural, given the circumstances."

Lise appeared puzzled. "I plead guilty to lonely. But what makes you think I'm suffering anxiety?"

"Cole," Cameron said reasonably. "I assume he's accepted another assignment. And knowing him, I would imagine it entails an element of danger."

The waiter reappeared with her brandy. When he walked away, she took a sip, watching Cameron over the rim of the glass. After a moment, she slowly shook her head.

"You're wrong, Daniel. I miss him, and when he stays away too long, I even begin to resent his work. But I never worry about him."

"Never?"

"Oh, I did at first. I suppose anyone would. After a while, though, I realized it was actually a little silly."

"Why?"

"For one thing, he's not the sort to get himself killed. I'm not saying he's infallible or walks on water. I just happen to believe he'll die with his boots off."

Cameron nodded. "I suspect you're probably right."

"And for another thing"—Lise paused, staring into her brandy—"Cole and I will never grow old together anyway. So why give myself heartburn?"

"Offhand I would say it's heartache rather than heartburn. Or else you're much more fatalistic than you appear."

"You're right on both counts, Daniel."

"How so?"

"I'm the one with heartache and Cole's the fatalist. He's not the least bit afraid of getting killed. And because he isn't, it'll never happen."

"Then why do you say you'll never grow old together?"

"Do you think Cole will ever make an honest woman of me?"

Cameron looked embarrassed. "Well, I'm hardly the one to answer that."

"We both know the answer, Daniel. He wouldn't stand to have his wings clipped, and I wouldn't try. Quite frankly, it's one of the reasons I fell for him."

"I see."

Cameron was clearly uncomfortable with the drift of the conversation. He swigged his drink, unable to meet her eyes. She laughed gaily and patted his hand.

"Oh, forgive me, Daniel. I'm making you play father confessor."

"No, no! Not at all."

"Let's talk about you. What's new in the gun business?"

"Well, I wouldn't want to bore you."

"Perish the thought. Go ahead, tell me all your secrets."

Cameron launched into the details of the experimental cartridge he had under development. He believed it would increase the knock-down power of the over-under Derringer which she always carried. Lise pretended rapt interest, listening attentively, but her thoughts, like windblown smoke, kept drifting back to personal matters.

She imagined herself returning alone to the hotel later that night to a cold, empty bed.

CHAPTER SIX

———◦◦◦———

A brisk October wind whipped through Raton Pass. The town, which was just south of the pass, had been a way station on the old Santa Fe Trail. With the arrival of the railroad, Raton experienced a building boom, and its population doubled virtually overnight. It was now a mountain gateway to the far Southwest.

Braddock emerged from a ramshackle hotel. He'd arrived last night on the evening southbound from Denver. Now, with the sun barely an hour high, his appearance had undergone a startling transformation. His hair was dyed a dark brown, and fake muttonchop side-whiskers were plastered to his jaws with spirit gum. He wore a black frock coat and trousers and the stiff, turned-around collar of a minister. His greatcoat was equally drab, and the outfit was topped off by a flat-brimmed Quaker hat.

The frock coat was generously cut, and no telltale bulge betrayed the Colt .45 snug in its cross-draw holster. He was, to all outward appearances, a man of the cloth. And he called himself the Reverend Titus Jacoby.

Over the years Braddock had played a wide variety of

roles. Early on in his career, he'd discovered he possessed a streak of the actor. As his reputation spread, the gift had served him well. His face was known wherever he traveled, and so his very survival dictated that he operate in disguise. Every assignment differed, and his threatrical flair enabled him to create a character suitable to every occasion. By turn, he'd posed as a grifter and tinhorn, whoremonger and con man, and a veritable stock company of outlaws. He was, by necessity, a man of many faces, none of them his own.

Outward trappings, however, were merely an illusion. A magician employs sleight of hand to misdirect the eye, and Braddock used disguise in much the same way. For complete deception, the character he portrayed was rounded out with quirks and mannerisms and whatever lingo or speech pattern best fit the role. Experience had taught him that a touch of the bizarre enhanced the overall plausibility of the performance. A man who stood out in the crowd was somehow more believable than one who appeared ordinary and common. The final twist was to add a credible cover story to the disguise. So it was that he'd mastered the trick of submerging himself totally in the character of the moment. In these disguises Cole Braddock simply ceased to exist.

Reverend Titus Jacoby was no figment of the imagination. Braddock had grown to manhood in Texas, where religion was an everyday part of life. He'd worked his way up from cowhand to ranch foreman to range detective. From there, he had drifted almost by happenstance into the field of general investigation. In those early days, prior to the Civil War, he'd been exposed to the fire-and-brimstone brand of religion. Tent revivals and circuit preachers represented both salvation and entertainment to those who inhabited the re-mote backlands. The recollection of one evangelist was burned into his memory like a long-healed brand.

Titus Jacoby had been a man given to florid speech and thunderous quotes from the Scripture. The character Braddock had fashioned in his mind's eye was modeled on the good reverend. He remembered the bombast and the wild harangues, and he even recalled a fair amount of the Scripture. He thought it would make a whale of a performance in Cimarron.

All the same, a couple of things about the role gave him pause. Braddock enjoyed a sociable drink and a good smoke, but tobacco and demon rum were strictly taboo for any self-respecting member of the clergy. Along with blasphemous language and chasing women, these were strictures no minister would break lightly. So Braddock perceived a crown of thorns in the role he'd undertaken. While in Cimarron, he couldn't curse or drink, smoke the weed, or ogle the ladies. Any backsliding would be an instant tipoff that he didn't truly have the Lord's calling. He reminded himself never to play a preacher on future assignments.

Still, as of today he'd stepped into character. He looked the part, and henceforth he would act the part. He reminded himself that a minister seldom had two nickels to rub together. But unlike priests, no vow of poverty was involved. Protestant clergymen were simply underpaid, and the majority eventually turned into professional moochers. While none carried a beggar's cup, a handout or a free meal was never refused. The idea was to play on other people's sympathy, and talk poor-mouth.

Outside the hotel, Braddock walked south along the main street. He'd traveled through Raton several times before, both on personal business and while on assignment. Yet now he was struck anew by the natural wonder of the pass and the part it had played in the settling of the West. The Santa Fe Trail was pioneered some sixty years past by explorers turned traders. The jump-off point, where traders were outfitted for the trek westward, was Independence, Missouri. The initial leg of the journey led across boundless prairies to where the trail forded the Arkansas River. From there, it meandered on to Bent's Old Fort and then dropped into New Mexico through Raton Pass.

By 1824 caravans of freight wagons were crossing the plains. Fully half the trade goods hauled overland were funneled through Santa Fe and on south into Old Mexico. In 1846, with the advent of the Mexican War, Santa Fe became a frontier outpost of the United States. The volume of business along the trail increased enormously as freighters rushed to supply the government and private companies with contract goods. Then in 1878 the Santa Fe Railroad finally surmounted Raton Pass. Shortly thereafter, by way of Glorieta Pass, the end-of-track reached the New Mexico capital. With the coming of the Iron Horse, the Santa Fe Trail ceased to exist. Yet Raton Pass, the Trail's gateway through the mountains, prospered as never before. Once a remote stopover westward, it was now a major north-south artery on the railway line.

Walking past the depot, Braddock tipped his Quaker hat to a couple of ladies waiting on the platform. He was carrying a tattered carpetbag, which further enhanced the image of an itinerant preacher. But he was a preacher afoot and in need of transportation, for the railway didn't connect with Cimarron. Hopping a stagecoach was an option he'd already considered and rejected. He needed mobility, and a circuit rider could poke around almost anywhere without arousing suspicion. A horse was the logical solution, and he found what he was looking for on the edge of town. He turned into a combination livery stable and livestock dealer.

The owner was thick around the paunch and smelled of manure. He greeted Braddock with a slow once-over and a cautious smile. His name was Walt Suggs, and his attitude indicated he'd previously had bad experiences with preachers. He shook hands with studied reluctance.

"What can I do for you, parson?"

"I'm in the market for a horse, Mr. Suggs."

"How much was you aimin' to spend?"

"Well, not much," Braddock said lamely. "I might go as high as ten dollars."

"Ten—" Suggs stopped and shook his head with a pained expression. "You've come to the wrong place if you're lookin' for charity."

"God's work demands sacrifices of us all!"

"Mebbe so," Suggs grumped, "but I ain't no rich man tryin' to squeeze through the eye of a needle. And ten dollars won't get you nothin' but shank's mare."

"Perhaps. I could go twenty—with a saddle included."

"Tell you what," Suggs said testily. "If you ain't lookin' for speed, I got an old crowbait I'll let go cheap. Whereabouts you headed?"

"Cimarron," Braddock informed him. "I'm the new pastor for the Methodist church."

Suggs inspected him more closely. "Hope you're in real thick with the Lord, because the fellow you're replacin' got himself killed—and it weren't no accident."

"Yes, I heard." Braddock rolled his eyes heavenward. "But, then, we're all soldiers in the army of Christ. We go where we're called."

"Yeah, I reckon so," Suggs said without interest. "How's thirty bucks sound for the horse and a used saddle? I couldn't do no better."

"You are indeed a man of generous spirit, Mr. Suggs."

"Don't mention it, parson."

A few minutes later Braddock stepped aboard a dun gelding. The horse was swaybacked, with one walleye and the conformation of a mule. With his carpetbag strapped behind the cantle of the saddle, Braddock looked even more itinerant than he'd intended. His mount was fit for a pauper who traveled light.

Outside town, he turned onto a rutted wagon road. To the southeast lay Llano Estacado—the Staked Plains—and due east was the territorial juncture of New Mexico, Colorado, Texas, and no-man's-land. The wagon road dropped southwestward from mountainous terrain to a high, rolling plateau. A latticework of rivers and streams wound through grassland studded with rocky gorges and wooded canyons. Yet it was a land of sun and solitude, evoking a sense of something lost forever. The vast emptiness swept westward to where the spires of the Sangre de Cristo range towered awesomely against the horizon. Nothing moved as far as the eye could see, and the deafening silence was broken only by the low moan of the wind. There was an eerie sense that man was the intruder here. He felt like an alien presence, unwanted and uninvited, entering into a hostile land. It seemed to Braddock a presentiment of what lay ahead.

He reined his horse toward Cimarron.

The Sangre de Cristo range stood like a column of majestic sentinels. Several of the peaks topped 13,000 feet, and even those at lower elevations were capped with snow. Upper New Mexico was split by the range, which extended roughly on a north-south line. A few miles to the east, Cimarron was cloaked in the shadows of the mountains.

The town was small but prosperous. The countryside was dotted with ranches and small farms, and mining ventures were scattered throughout the nearby mountains. Stores and business establishments were ranked along either side of the town's main thoroughfare. The courthouse was situated in the heart of the downtown area, directly across from a bank and a hotel. Civic boosters were quick to brag that Cimarron was a hub of trade and commerce. Lately, however, its chief claim to fame was the Cimarron Coalition.

Braddock rode into town shortly before sunset. Upstreet from the hotel, he spotted the *Cimarron Beacon*. He reined to a halt before a hitch rack and swung down from the saddle. Someone lit a lamp inside the newspaper office as Braddock looped the reins around the post. His clothes were covered with grime from the long ride, and he took a moment to dust himself off. Then he mounted the boardwalk, moving to the door. He opened it and stepped inside.

There were two men in the outer office. One sat behind a desk, scribbling furiously on a sheet of foolscap. The other stood before a counter that ran the width of the room. He was attired in range clothes, with a Stetson tugged low on his forehead. A pistol was strapped to his hip and a shotgun was cradled across the crook of his arm. Braddock noted that the pistol was a Colt .41 Thunderer and the shotgun a lever-action Winchester, one of the latest innovations in firearms. He thought it a rather peculiar armament for a man who appeared to be a cowhand.

Closing the door, Braddock walked toward the counter. He nodded to the man with the shotgun, but the only response was a stoic watchfulness. Upon closer examination, he detected a certain strangeness about the man. An inch or so shorter than Braddock, he was lean and wiry and thickly corded with muscle. There was a tawny cast to his skin, set off by high cheekbones and a brushy mustache and jet-black hair. Yet his eyes were pale gray, which was somehow out of place with his overall appearance. He looked oddly like an Indian—except for his eyes.

"Good afternoon." Braddock stopped at the counter. "I'm looking for Mr. Orville McMain."

The man behind the desk glanced up from his scribbling. His eyes narrowed and he inspected Braddock's manner of dress. Then he rose and hurried forward with an outstretched hand.

"You must be the Reverend Titus Jacoby."

Braddock accepted his handshake. "And you must be Mr. McMain?"

"Call me Orville." McMain motioned him around the counter. "Come on back and have a seat. I've been expecting you."

Braddock took a wooden armchair beside the desk. McMain settled into a creaky swivel chair and leaned forward. His gaze burned with intensity.

"I don't mind saying you're a welcome sight, Mr. Braddock."

"Hold it!" Braddock halted him with an upraised palm. "Forget you ever heard that name. From now on, I'm Titus Jacoby—nobody else."

"I'll remember," McMain promised. "It won't happen again."

"Before we go any farther"—Braddock jerked a thumb over his shoulder—"who's your friend up front?"

McMain's face grew overcast. "The word's around that I'm next on the ring's death list. So the coalition members decided I should have a bodyguard. Buck got tapped for the job."

"Buck?" Braddock was bemused. "Is that a nickname?"

"I don't believe so," McMain said vaguely. "He goes by the name of Buck Colter. He's a hand on Isaac Coleman's spread."

"How'd he get picked for your bodyguard?"

"Because he's tough as nails," McMain confided. "Of course, I've never seen him pick a fight. He's quiet-spoken, real pleasant until he's pushed. Then he comes unwound like a buzz saw, and he never loses. Folks tend to give him lots of elbow room."

"Any idea how he came by that shotgun?"

"No." McMain looked puzzled. "Why all the questions?"

"Professional interest," Braddock said with a shrug. "Have you told anyone I'm on the case?"

"Frank Kirkland advised me to keep it quiet."

"Some people don't take advice," Braddock observed dryly. "Let's try the question again—have you told anyone?"

"No, I haven't." McMain made an empty gesture with his hands. "Not even my wife."

"Good," Braddock said with a measured smile. "Suppose you fill me in on the political situation. According to Kirkland, the ring pretty well controls the courthouse."

"That's true," McMain confirmed. "Top to bottom."

"Every county office?"

"The whole crowd," McMain said miserably. "Sheriff, county judge, tax collector—all bought and paid for."

"Who's the local kingfish?" Braddock asked. "The ring's front man?"

"Florencio Donaghue," McMain said scornfully. "He's part Mexican, part Irish. He walks both sides of the street, and that enables him to control the ballot box. Very crafty fellow."

"What's he do for a living?"

"He owns the hardware store."

"Have you been able to link him to Reverend Tolby's murder?"

"Fat chance!" McMain's tone was severe. "The sheriff investigated and said it was the work of robbers. The coroner's jury ruled it 'death at the hands of parties unknown.' Case closed."

"Where was Tolby killed?"

"Cimarron Canyon," McMain said gloomily. "It's the main road through the mountains. He made it a regular practice to visit the mining camps and hold services. Somebody bushwhacked him about twenty miles west of town."

"Somebody?" Braddock mused out loud. "Any idea who?"

"Only a guess," McMain said bitterly. "A good-for-nothing named Cruz Vega works for Donaghue. His principal job is to turn out the Mexican vote come election time. I'd say he's your man."

"But you've got no proof?"

"None."

"And there's nothing that connects Donaghue to the Santa Fe Ring?"

"Correct."

"One big mystery and no leads."

"That's why we hired you—Reverend Jacoby."

"So it is."

Braddock was silent for a time. He pulled thoughtfully at his earlobe and stared off into space. A stillness settled over the office while he weighed everything he'd heard. At length his gaze shifted back to McMain.

"Here's the way I see it," he said almost idly. "The whole ball of wax comes down to finding Tolby's killers. We have to catch them before we'll get a line on Donaghue or the Santa Fe Ring. So we'll take it one step at a time."

"Where do you propose to start?"

"I'll pick up where Tolby left off."

McMain raised an uncertain eyebrow. "I don't follow you."

"It's simple enough," Braddock remarked. "The killers have to be lured out into the open."

"I—" McMain hesitated, cleared his throat. "Are you saying you mean to use yourself as bait?"

"That's about the size of it."

"But how will you force them into the open?"

Braddock smiled. "Spread the word in your newspaper. The new preacher's arrived and he'll deliver his first sermon on Sunday."

McMain stared at him incredulously. "You plan to denounce them from the pulpit?"

"See you in church, Orville."

Braddock stood and walked around the end of the counter. He swapped nods with Colter as he moved to the door. Then, with his hand on the knob, he paused. He looked back over his shoulder.

"I'm curious about your shotgun."

Colter regarded him evenly. "What about it?"

"Why a lever-action?"

"Holds five shots," Colter said simply. "That's three more than a double-barrel."

"I notice you also carry a Colt Thunderer."

"Yeah?"

"Same question." Braddock angled his head critically. "Why?"

"It's double action and that saves cocking the hammer."

"You feel it's faster, then?"

"Wouldn't carry it otherwise."

"How about accuracy?"

Colter gave him a slow, dark smile. "I generally put 'em where they're meant to go. Why do you ask?"

"Curiosity." Braddock fixed him with a speculative gaze. "It's a lot of hardware—for a cowhand."

"Maybe." Colter returned his look steadily. "Course, you ask a lot of questions—for a preacher."

"I reckon that makes us even."

"How so?"

"Come to church Sunday and find out."

The door opened and closed. Outside, Braddock unhitched his horse and led it downstreet toward the livery stable. He now had a new mystery to add to the pot.

Why would a half-breed killer masquerade as a cowhand?

CHAPTER SEVEN

On Sunday the buggies and farm wagons began arriving early. An article in the newspaper, along with word of mouth, had spread the news throughout the countryside. Reverend Titus Jacoby would officiate at today's services.

The Methodist Church was located at the end of Main Street. It was the only Protestant house of worship in Cimarron, and therefore the pride of the community. The congregation was roughly half townspeople and half ranchers and farmers. Their economic and political interests were not always in harmony, but they were nonetheless united by their views on two very dissimilar topics. First, God and religion were central to their lives. And second, they considered the Santa Fe Ring an abomination, the spawn of Lucifer himself.

By ten o'clock the church was packed. All the pews were full and the crowd spilled out onto the front steps. The organ wheezed to life and the choir went into a stirring rendition of "The Old Rugged Cross." The deacons and their wives occupied a pew down front, and the remainder of the congregation seemed on the edge of their seats. An almost palpable sense of expectation filled the church, as though some momentous event was about to occur. Then, as the choir segued into another hymn, the door to an anteroom opened. The crowd strained forward for a better look.

Braddock walked to a chair midway between the pulpit and the choir box. He seated himself and crossed his legs, hands folded in his lap. His suit was freshly sponged and pressed, and a starchy collar encircled his neck like a white band of iron. His expression was somber but not sad, somewhat similar to an undertaker overseeing a high-priced funeral. His gaze was fixed on the middle distance, as if he were contemplating some profound matter known only to himself and God. He sat perfectly still and allowed the congregation to inspect their new pastor.

The last two days had been a time of preparation. Braddock had taken a room in the hotel and closeted himself with a Bible. He meant to deliver a stemwinder of a sermon, one that would singe the hair of anyone even vaguely connected with the Santa Fe Ring. Thus, he had read and reread both the Old Testament and the New Testament. Finally, after long deliberation, he'd chosen evil as his theme. His purpose was to incite anger in the ring leaders, and instill in them a dread that he would rally the coalition. He wanted someone to make an attempt on his life, and today's sermon was designed to set the stage. He would portray a zealot begging to be spiked to the cross.

Insofar as the congregation was concerned, Braddock hardly gave them a second thought. Orville McMain was a deacon as well as the moving force behind the coalition, and therefore a power in the church. No one would seriously question his selection of a new minister or the rather hurried fashion in which it had been arranged. Yet Braddock was all too aware that everyone present was there to hear the Reverend Titus Jacoby deliver his first sermon. Their former pastor had been brutally slain for openly challenging the Santa Fe Ring. They would expect his replacement to take up the standard and sound a similar battle cry. Braddock thought no one here today would go away disappointed.

The hymn ended and the choir took their seats. A hush settled over the church and the crowd sat motionless. Braddock rose from his chair and walked to the pulpit. He stood there a moment, staring out across the frozen tableau of faces. Then he squared himself up and raised his arms high overhead.

"Woe unto them that call evil good, and good evil!"

The crowd stared at him, instantly mesmerized. He paused, allowing the suspense to mount, and abruptly stepped away from the pulpit. His voice flooded the church, deep and resonant. His words hammered at them with a drumroll cadence.

"I say to you today what Paul said to the Ephesians. We wrestle not against flesh and blood, but against principalities . . . against powers . . . against the rulers of the darkness of this world . . . *against spiritual wickedness in high places!*"

Braddock strode back and forth in a tempest of oratory. He slammed his fist into his palm and punctuated his speech with wildly exaggerated gestures. He summoned up the specters of evil and injustice and innocent blood spilled. His eulogy to Reverend Tolby, most foully murdered!, left hardly a dry eye in the house. His damnation of the Santa Fe Ring sent a buzz of righteous anger sweeping back over the crowd. His fiery denunciation of land-grabbing rascals and corrupt politicians actually brought cheers. He combined demagogy with theatrics, and he held the congregation spellbound for nearly a half hour. At last, his voice raised in an orotund bellow, he marched back to the pulpit. He thrust his arms heavenward and shook his clenched fists.

"Take unto you the armor of God, that ye may withstand evil! Be strong and of good courage; be not afraid, for the Lord thy God is with thee. Glory hallelujah, brothers and sisters. Amen!"

A chorus of amens reverberated from the congregation. The choir broke out in "Onward Christian Soldiers," and Braddock stepped down from the pulpit. The three church deacons, one of them Orville McMain, joined him and soberly shook hands. The symbolism of their gesture was plain to read: the Reverend Titus Jacoby had been accepted as the new leader of the flock. Then, solemn-faced as owls, the deacons trailed Braddock up the aisle. Outside the church, McMain positioned himself beside Braddock on the steps. The congregation slowly filed out the door, and McMain performed introductions. Braddock shook every hand and modestly accepted their praise. The overall reaction confirmed what he was already thinking to himself. He'd put on a hell of a show.

When the crowd thinned out, McMain steered him toward a couple of men waiting off to one side. Their dress pegged them as ranchers, and their size commanded immediate respect. McMain, who was short and stocky, appeared dwarfed in their presence. The men were tall and rawboned, and looked tough as whang leather. Their features were pleasant enough and their smiles seemed genuine. Yet, curiously, there was no humor in their eyes.

"Reverend Jacoby," McMain announced, "I'd like you to meet Isaac Coleman and Clay Allison. These boys are the top cattlemen in Colfax County."

"Gentlemen." Braddock exchanged handshakes. "I hope you found the sermon worth the ride."

"A real barn-burner!" Allison beamed. "Goddamnedest thing I ever heard—if you'll pardon my French."

"Pay him no mind," Coleman interjected. "He's just tryin' to say you've earned your welcome, parson."

"I appreciate the sentiment." Braddock smiled politely. "Would I be correct in assuming that you men are members of the coalition?"

"Quite correct," McMain broke in smoothly. "Clay and Isaac were the first to join, and they helped me organize the coalition. Apart from Reverend Tolby, no one has contributed more in our fight with the ring."

"Some fight!" Coleman snorted. "All we've got to show for it so far is one dead preacher."

"Sonsabitches," Allison said viciously. "I'd shore like to lay my hands on whoever done it. We'd turn him into worm pudding muy damn pronto!"

"I wonder," Braddock said in a reflective tone. "Would killing him be the best policy? Or would we further our cause by persuading him to talk?"

"No harm in that!" Allison laughed. "We'll just string him up after he talks."

Braddock shook his head ruefully. "Vengeance is mine, sayeth the Lord. Not to mention the fact that a live witness might open all sorts of doors. Don't you agree, Mr. Allison?"

"Well, I'll tell you, parson." Allison studied him with a frown. "After that sermon, you oughtn't to feel so charitable. You're liable to need a bodyguard yourself."

"Amen to that," Coleman added seriously. "Whether you know it or not, you made yourself a target today. And we don't need another dead preacher."

Braddock exchanged a quick glance with McMain. Then he waved his hand in a casual gesture. "I'm gratified by your concern, gentlemen. But it's very unlikely I'm in any great jeopardy. The ring wouldn't risk public censure by murdering another—"

"Don't bet on it!" Allison cut him short. "Public opinion don't mean do-diddily to them. Otherwise they wouldn't've killed Tolby."

"Clay's right," Coleman pointed out. "Why d'you think we assigned one of my men to look after Orville? You'd be wise to listen, parson. No two ways about it."

"Have no fear," Braddock replied loftily. "The Lord will not forsake me in my hour of trial. I entrust myself into His hands."

Allison grunted sharply. "Orville gave us pretty much the

same argument. But he shore changed his tune after somebody drygulched Reverend Tolby."

"Which reminds me." Braddock turned to McMain with a quizzical look. "Where's young Colter today? I don't recall seeing him at services."

"Oh, he was around," McMain said lightly. "Not much on religion, but he sticks to me like glue. He's waiting right over there."

Braddock followed the direction of McMain's gaze. He saw Colter standing beneath the shade of a tree near the street. The barrel of the shotgun gleamed dully in sunlight filtering through the leaves. Colter dipped his head in a sign of acknowledgment and smiled. Braddock understood that the smile was something more than a courtesy. It had to do with respect, mutual recognition.

He and Buck Colter were birds of a feather.

The pale light of a sickle moon bathed the Mexican quarter of town. Late Monday night the central street was nearly deserted. Only a few horses lined the hitch rails, standing hip-shot in the shadowed darkness. The faint strains of a guitar drifted from inside a lamplit cantina.

Florencio Donaghue appeared, walking swiftly along the street, looking neither right nor left. A large man, his features were hawklike and tawny brown, indicating a fair degree of Mexican blood. Yet he wore a vested business suit, with glossy half boots and a brushed Stetson. He looked prosperous, and troubled.

Outside the cantina, Donaghue halted and peered through the window. Three men, dressed in native clothing, stood talking quietly at the bar. Off to one side, the guitar player was perched on a stool, strumming a soft melody. At the rear of the room, a lone man was seated by himself at a table. Beneath a worn sombrero, his droopy mustache glinted in the lamplight. He was drinking tequila.

Satisfied with the look of things, Donaghue entered the cantina. He ignored the three men and nodded brusquely to the bartender. Walking to the rear of the room, he stopped at the table. As he took a chair, the man seated there poured tequila into a clean glass. Donaghue waved it away with an abrupt gesture.

"For once, I see you're on time."

"Buenas noches, mi jefe."

Cruz Vega spoke in a raspy, low-pitched voice. His mouth seemed curled in a perpetual smirk and his eyes were insolent. He took a swig of tequila and wiped his mustache with a thorny forefinger. He appeared sanguine, almost carefree.

"Listen closely," Donaghue informed him. "I have a job for you."

"I serve at your pleasure, *mi jefe*."

Donaghue considered the flippant tone a moment. Then, deciding to overlook it, he went on. "You've heard of the new preacher, Reverend Jacoby?"

"But of course! Everyone knows of his sermon yesterday."

"What do they say about what he preaches?"

Vega smiled. "They say he speaks the truth. Now, me, I dunno. I never saw no conspiracy around here."

"Are you trying to be funny?"

"No, *mi jefe*! I am a very sincere man."

Donaghue frowned. "I could always find someone else to handle—these things."

"But never so well. I am very good at such work, is it not true?"

"Then save your humor for another time. I'm here to talk business."

"As you wish. I meant no disrespect."

"Very wise," Donaghue grunted. "Can you get hold of Cardenas tonight?"

"Sí."

"Then see to it. I want you both on the job by tomorrow morning."

Vega cocked his head in a sly look. "Who are we to kill?"

"Who else?" Donaghue shrugged. "Reverend Jacoby."

"Madre de Dios! You want us to kill another holy man?"

"I want you to do as you're told."

"Have your superiors ordered this thing?"

Donaghue stiffened and gave him a hard look. "What do you mean by that?"

"Oh, nothing."

"Speak up. I asked you a question."

"Well, this Reverend Jacoby talks of a conspiracy. A great conspiracy, controlled by men in Santa Fe. It seems natural that they would order his death."

"Does it?"

"*Sí.* After all, it was they who ordered the death of the other one. The preacher called Tolby. Is it not so?"

"What makes you think that?"

"You do me a disservice, *mi jefe*. I am more than a simple *asesino*. I am a man of experience."

"Perhaps. But it is the assassin I pay. And I do not pay him to nose into my affairs. Is that clear?"

Vega realized he'd gone too far. He spread his hands in an elaborate gesture of deference. "Pardon my inquisitive nature, *mi jefe*. It was curiosity, nothing more."

Donaghue nodded. "Just keep your mind on business. Your business."

"Have no fear. I will make this Jacoby my personal business."

"I want it attended to quickly."

"Where do you wish him killed?"

"Outside town, if possible. But however it's done, it has to be done before next Sunday. We can't have him taking the pulpit again."

"Should it be made to appear a robbery, like the last one?"

"If time permits. Just don't let it drag on till the end of the week."

"Of course. And our arrangement will be as usual?"

"It will," Donaghue confirmed. "A hundred dollars for you and Cardenas. Payable when the job's finished."

"Consider him dead, *mi jefe*."

"Don't disappoint me."

"Have I ever?"

Vega grinned and tossed off his tequila. Donaghue stared at him a moment, on the verge of saying something more. Then, with a heavy sigh, he hitched back his chair. He walked from the cantina into the dappled moonlight. His face was still troubled.

Early Tuesday morning, Braddock rode out of town. He turned the walleyed dun west and proceeded toward the mountains. Ostensibly he was off on his first tour of the backcountry circuit. His true destination was Cimarron Canyon.

Since church services on Sunday, he'd devoted considerable thought to his next move. The lapse of two days had provided sufficient time for word of his sermon to reach Santa Fe. By now a message would have been passed back in the opposite direction. Whether it had gone directly to Florencio Donaghue was open to conjecture. But there was every reason to believe that someone in Cimarron had been ordered to act. And it would be the same someone who had silenced Reverend John Tolby.

Braddock understood the mentality of killers. He also possessed a strong insight into the minds of those who ordered the killing done. His years as a manhunter had given him an uncanny sixth sense for the way they thought and how they would react when provoked. To a degree, he was able to put himself in their boots and view the situation from their perspective. While it was a warped perspective, it nonetheless lent a certain predictability to those who issued the orders. Violence, from their standpoint, was merely an instrument. A tool of business.

The Santa Fe Ring had embarked on a campaign of intimidation. The ultimate goal was to force the ranchers and homesteaders to abandon their landholdings. To that end, the leaders of the Cimarron Coalition were to be used as object lessons. Those who spoke out in open forum—such as Orville McMain and Reverend Tolby—were slated for death. Their untimely demise would serve notice that no one, whether a prominent newspaperman or a man of God, was immune to harm. And the ring, having killed once, would have no choice but to kill again. Otherwise their campaign of intimidation would simply fizzle out to nothing.

So Braddock felt confident he was now a marked man. Within the town limits he was relatively safe. Bloodshed on the streets of Cimarron was clearly a complication the ring wanted to avoid. Along with Buck Colter's shotgun, that was the major factor in McMain's continued good health. But outside Cimarron it was open season on coalition leaders. A murder in the high country could be rigged to look like robbery, even though the true motive was apparent to everyone. Hired killers were generally men of limited imagination, and Braddock had little doubt the same ploy would be used again. As he rode west, some inner conviction told him that Cimarron Canyon was where it would happen. Someone waited there to silence Reverend Titus Jacoby.

The noonday sun was at its zenith when Braddock entered Cimarron Canyon. In the west the snowcapped peaks of the Sangre de Cristo range loomed against an azure sky. According to his cover story, the first stop on his backcountry circuit would be Elizabethtown. The mining camp, located high in the mountains, was New Mexico's major gold producer. By all accounts, the camp was a scene of depravity and immorality, populated largely by whores and saloonkeepers. Quite apart from being a den of iniquity, Elizabethtown was also an outpost of opposition to the Santa Fe Ring. It seemed a logical forum for a preacher-turned-crusader.

Yet, as he moved deeper into Cimarron Canyon, Braddock thought the odds of reaching Elizabethtown were somewhere between slim and none. The canyon zigzagged through the heart of the mountains, with walls sweeping upward in craggy palisades. Here in the high country the landscape was forested with piñon pines and junipers, and rocky outcrops thrust skyward as the trail steadily steepened. Hummingbirds and goldfinches darted among the trees, and lazy dragonflies hovered over a swift-running stream that cut through the gorge. Overhead a sparrow hawk floated past on outspread wings, a dead rattler gripped in its talons. The bird settled on a boulder and cocked its head with a fierce glare at the horse and rider. Then, with lordly hauteur, it began feeding on the snake.

Braddock's nerves were strung tight. His every sense was alerted and his eyes were in constant motion. The clatter of the dun's hoofbeats echoed off the canyon walls, and the sound aggravated his feeling of being exposed and vulnerable to attack. The terrain was made to order for bushwhackers, and every switchback along the snaky trail was a natural ambush site. Yet, beneath the relentless tension, some inward composure steeled him to the task ahead. He'd set himself up as the lure with the express purpose of capturing a murderer. And he somehow knew today wasn't his day to die.

An hour or so later, as Braddock rounded a bend on a sharp upgrade, something caught his eye—a glint of sunlight on metal from a jagged outcrop directly in front of him. All thought suspended, he reacted on sheer reflex and threw himself sideways out of the saddle. A slug whistled past his ear, and in the same instant he heard the simultaneous crack of two rifle shots. He rolled toward a pile of boulders, pulling the Colt as he slammed up against the canyon wall. Spooked by the gunfire, the dun bolted and whirled away downstream.

Tossing his hat aside, Braddock thumbed the hammer on the Colt and inched his head around a boulder. Some thirty yards distant, twin puffs of smoke billowed from an outcrop near the top of the gorge. One slug pocked the dirt and the other whanged off the boulder, showering him with rocky shards. He saw two men, partially hidden behind the outcrop, frantically working the levers on their saddle guns. He picked the man on the left and drew a fine bead, laying the front sight shoulder-high. His finger touched the trigger and the Colt roared.

The man was jerked upright by the impact of the slug. He dropped his rifle and lurched sideways, arms windmilling like a scarecrow in a high wind. Then he lost his balance, teetering a moment on the edge of the outcrop, and tumbled into space. He bounced off the canyon wall and cartwheeled down the sheer slope. He landed headfirst and pitched forward on his back, the heels of his boots in the stream. He lay perfectly still.

A bullet plucked the sleeve of Braddock's coat, and he turned his attention to the second man. He thumbed the hammer and feathered the trigger, no more than a heartbeat between shots. He got off three rounds in the time it took the bushwhacker to jack a fresh cartridge into his saddle gun. The first and second shots, within a handspan of one another, kicked flinty sparks in the man's face. The third shot whumped into the stock of the rifle and blew it to splinters. The man yelped and let go of the rifle as though he'd taken hold of a hot poker. Then, seemingly galvanized, he took off in a wild scramble toward the top of the gorge. Braddock's last shot nicked his pants leg a moment before he vanished over the rim of the wall.

Stillness descended on the canyon. Nothing moved and the silence was tomblike, broken only by the gurgle of the stream. Braddock shucked empties out of the Colt and rapidly reloaded. All told, perhaps ten or twelve seconds had elapsed between the time he fired the last shot and the instant he stuffed the fifth shell into the cylinder. But as he snapped the loading gate shut, he realized there was no longer any need to hurry. From somewhere above, he heard the faint sound of hoofbeats and then nothing. The bushwhacker apparently knew the mountains and was by now long gone over some remote back trail. Any thought of pursuit was futile.

Braddock stood and moved around the boulders. Warily, the pistol cocked, he approached the fallen man. A single glance told the story, and he lowered the hammer with a sharp curse. His shot had gone where he'd aimed, shattering the man's collarbone. But the fall from the outcrop had undone his handiwork. The man's neck was broken, and his eyes stared sightlessly into the void of afterdeath. Instead of a witness, there was only a corpse. A crooked-necked dead man who would tell no tales.

For a moment Braddock examined the body with clinical interest. The man was Mexican, somewhere in his early thirties, with an old knife scar along his right jawbone. He would be easily identified, and his name might be linked to other names. Yet he was stone-cold, and by whatever name he was known, he would reveal nothing about the one who had escaped. Braddock jammed the Colt into its holster and turned away.

He walked off in search of the walleyed dun.

CHAPTER EIGHT

———⟊⟊⟊〰〰〰———

Sheriff Floyd Mather tilted back in his chair. He was a large man, with stern features and a sweeping handlebar mustache. His eyes were hard and his mouth was set in a dour expression. He stared across the desk at Braddock.

"Let's go through it again."

"Don't you believe me, Sheriff?"

"What I believe don't mean a hill of beans. I'm paid to get the facts, and we're gonna stick with it till I'm satisfied with your story."

"A commendable point of view."

"You tryin' to get smart?"

"Perish the thought!"

Braddock was walking a tightrope. Shortly before dusk, he'd ridden into Cimarron, the body draped across the back of his horse. By the time he halted outside the courthouse, word had spread along the street, and a large crowd quickly gathered. Several people identified the dead man as Manuel Cardenas, a familiar figure among the town's Mexican population. The sheriff was summoned, and he had immediately ordered the crowd to disperse. After inspecting the body, he waited until the local undertaker arrived. Then he'd marched Braddock into the courthouse.

The sheriff's attitude was one of ill-disguised skepticism. In his office, he had proceeded to interrogate Braddock at some length. The answers he got merely raised more questions in his mind. A look of disgruntled suspicion slowly settled over his features. For his part, Braddock hoped to learn more than he revealed. He was an old hand at the art of interrogation: he thought it quite possible the sheriff could be tricked into disclosing vital information. Yet his position was tenuous, for any slip-up would immediately destroy his cover story. And now, pinned by the sheriff's harsh stare, he warned himself to proceed with caution. A preacher who appeared too slick would only arouse further suspicion.

"All right," Mather demanded. "You say you were headed for the mining camps?"

"That's correct."

"What was your rush?" Mather persisted. "You'd barely took over as pastor."

"Where sin flourishes," Braddock said breezily, "there's not a moment to spare. I take my ministry where it's needed most—and miners are notorious sinners."

"Do tell?" Mather gave him the fish-eye. "So you're ridin' along and suddenly you get jumped out of the clear blue?"

"Exactly," Braddock affirmed. "No warning whatever."

"Who fired first?"

"Why, my assailants!" Braddock stared back at him with round, guileless eyes. "It's a miracle I wasn't killed outright."

"Some miracle," Mather grunted. "You've got two men takin' potshots at you, and you kill one and drive the other off. How'd you manage that?"

"Strictly the Lord's doing," Braddock replied innocently. "He stood beside me in my moment of peril."

"Sounds more like fast and fancy shootin' to me."

"On the contrary," Braddock corrected him. "The dead

man died from a broken neck. I was fortunate merely to wound him."

"What'd you wound him with?"

"I beg your pardon?"

"You weren't throwin' rocks, were you?"

"No, of course not."

"Then lemme see your gun."

Braddock sensed his troubles were about to multiply. He pulled the Colt from inside his jacket and handed it across the desk. The Peacemaker was chambered for .45 caliber, with standard sights and a 4 ¾-inch barrel. The finish was lustrous indigo blue and the grips were gutta-percha, custom-made, and deep brown in color. Apart from its distinctive appearance, the guts of the gun had been completely overhauled by Daniel Cameron. The sear had been honed, resulting in a trigger pull of scarcely three pounds, and a specially tempered mainspring had been installed. The end product was a weapon of incomparable artistry and silky-smooth action.

Floyd Mather's gaze narrowed. He hefted the gun, critically judging its balance. Then he unloaded it, dumping the shells on his desk, and closed the loading gate. He studied one of the blunt-nosed shells a moment, his brow wrinkled in a puzzled frown. At last he earred the Colt's hammer to full cock and gingerly touched the trigger. The hammer dropped with a crisp, metallic snap. He let out a low whistle under his breath.

"Judas priest," he said softly. "A hair trigger, hand-loaded shells, and a cross-draw holster. When you go heeled, you don't mess around, do you?"

"I'm pleased you approve."

"It's a lotta gun." Mather carefully laid the Colt on the desk top. "Why would a preacher carry a slick article like that?"

"Come now, Sheriff." Braddock kept his tone light. "Under the circumstances, it seems a normal precaution."

"What circumstances?"

"For one thing, my predecessor was murdered."

"He was killed by robbers. That's not exactly the same thing as murder."

"Would you characterize today's incident as the work of bandits?"

"Has all the earmarks." Mather looked him straight in the eye. "Why, you figure it was something else?"

"Oh, yes indeed!" Braddock said briskly. "I would say it fairly reeks of assassination."

"Why the blue-billy hell would anybody want to assassinate a preacher?"

"For the same reason Reverend Tolby was murdered."

"And what was that?"

"Are we playing cat and mouse, Sheriff?"

"I'm the one askin' the questions here!"

"Very well." Braddock spread his hands in a bland gesture. "Reverend Tolby was murdered because he publicly denounced the Santa Fe Ring."

"Bullfeathers!" Mather growled. "You've been listening to Orville McMain and his pipe dreams. There's no such thing as the Santa Fe Ring and never was!"

"How curious." Braddock deliberately goaded him. "Some people say this entire courthouse is controlled by the ring."

Mather flushed. "Are you accusing me of political shenanigans?"

"Are you denying it, Sheriff?"

"Goddammit!" Mather rasped. "I asked you a question. Are you accusing me or not?"

"If the shoes fits," Braddock said with a shrug, "wear it."

"Cute, aren't you?" Mather said with a flare of annoyance. "I suppose McMain's the one that told you all this hogwash?"

"Please, no names." Braddock paused with a smug grin. "Let us say the allegation has widespread currency throughout the community."

"That a fact?" Mather said gruffly. "Well, if you're so

smart, who's behind this so-called Santa Fe Ring? Suppose you tell me that."

Braddock took a chance. "I do keep hearing one name—Warren Mitchell."

Mather unwittingly blinked. His features screwed up in a tight grimace and his eyes went cold. "Who the hell are you anyway?"

"A servant of Christ," Braddock said humbly. "I spread the gospel and offer salvation to those who have strayed from the fold."

"You don't act like no preacher I ever met."

"Perhaps not." A smile shadowed Braddock's lips. "And all the more reason to look to your own salvation."

"That sounds the least bit like a threat."

"No," Braddock said without inflection. "It's more on the order of a prophecy."

"What's that supposed to mean?"

"A smart man abandons ship before it sinks."

"Get lost," Mather rumbled. "Take your fancy gun and don't let the door hit you in the ass."

Braddock retrieved the Colt and loaded it without a word. Then he holstered it and walked to the door. Abruptly, as though struck by an afterthought, he turned back.

"Oh, by the way," he asked casually, "the dead man, Manuel Cardenas, who was he?"

"Nobody special," Mather noted. "Handyman, jack-of-all-trades. He did odd jobs around town."

"Odd jobs indeed," Braddock commented wryly. "Who were his associates or friends?"

"Beats me."

"Does it really?"

"You callin' me a liar?"

"If the shoe fits . . ."

Braddock laughed and stepped through the door. On his way out of the courthouse, he mentally patted himself on the back. Floyd Mather had by no means told him all he wanted to know. But actions spoke louder than words, and for a moment the sheriff had been visibly unnerved. A telltale blink was brought on by the mention of a name.

Warren Mitchell.

A few minutes later Braddock strolled into the newspaper office. The pressmen were gone for the day and McMain was scribbling at his desk. Colter was stationed at his usual spot by the front counter.

"Howdy, parson."

"Good evening, Buck."

Colter smiled. "Hear you had a busy day."

"The Lord's work is never done."

Braddock moved around the counter and walked toward the rear of the room. McMain looked up and suddenly dropped his pen. His features were etched with concern.

"What happened?" he inquired nervously. "By the time I got to the courthouse, you were already inside with the sheriff. Were you really ambushed? How many were there?"

"All in good time," Braddock said as he got himself seated. "I'll tell you all about it later. But right now I need some information."

"Yes, of course," McMain agreed. "How can I help?"

"I got waylaid by two men. One of them got away and I sort of half-ass killed the other one. His name was Manuel Cardenas."

"I know," McMain said in a shaky voice. "It's all over town. People are talking about a preacher who carries a gun, and they're asking questions. I hope you have a good story in mind."

Braddock brushed aside the objection. "We'll worry about that later. What can you tell me about Cardenas?"

"Nothing." McMain gave him a blank look. "Oh, I've seen him around town. But Mexicans tend to stick to themselves. I've never so much as spoken to him."

"Who would know him?" Braddock insisted. "Someone we could trust to keep quiet?"

"I don't understand your urgency."

"Just humor me and put your thinking cap on."

"Well," McMain said, considering for a moment, "there's Bud Grant, the town marshal. He'd probably know more than anyone else."

"Would he keep his mouth shut?"

"I believe so," McMain said hesitantly. "In fact, I'm certain he would. Bud's always been neutral and never took sides, but he's a decent man. I respect him."

"All right." Braddock nodded. "Why don't you send Colter to fetch him? A town jail isn't much on privacy."

While they waited, Braddock recounted the day's events. He briefly described the shootout in Cimarron Canyon and related how Cardenas had died. Then he outlined the interrogation by Sheriff Mather, touching only on the highlights. But he declined to mention anything about Warren Mitchell or the sheriff's startled reaction. Some inner voice told him to stop short of the full truth.

Ten minutes later Colter walked through the door with Bud Grant. The marshal was a beefy man, with broad shoulders and the gnarled hands of someone accustomed to physical labor. He looked as though he would be more at home behind a plow than wearing a star. Colter resumed his post up front and Grant lumbered on back to the desk. After a round of handshakes, the men seated themselves.

McMain took an oblique approach. "Bud, we'd like your help on a certain matter. I've assured Reverend Jacoby"—his gaze shifted briefly to Braddock—"that you're no loose talker. So anything said here would be off the record and confidential."

"Sounds serious." Grant's features creased with worry. "I've always done my best not to take sides. I wouldn't want anybody to get the wrong idea."

"And no one will," Braddock cut in earnestly. "We wouldn't compromise your position, Marshal. All we want to do is ask a question."

The worry lines on Grant's forehead deepened. "Has it got to do with you being drygulched today?"

"You've already heard about that?"

"Cimarron's a small town, Reverend."

"Then you're probably aware I was jumped by two men. One of them was Manuel Cardenas."

"Are you fixin' to ask me something about Cardenas?"

"Yes." Braddock's eyes gave away nothing. "I understand you know most of the Mexicans in town."

"That'd be a fair statement."

"How familiar were you with Cardenas?"

"No more'n most," Grant said frankly. "He loafed a little and he worked a little. Sometimes he'd get likkered up and I'd have to put him in the cooler overnight. Not what you'd call a real troublemaker."

"No record of robbery or violence?"

"Nope." Grant met his gaze with an amused expression. "Course that don't include a few personal disagreements. Mexicans tend to settle things like that with knives. I generally overlook it, unless there's a killin'."

"Has he ever killed anyone?"

"Not so far as I know."

"Was there anyone in particular he chummed around with?"

Grant massaged his jaw. "I can't say as there was. Leastways, not outside of family."

"Are you talking about immediate family?"

"Yeah, sort of," Grant allowed. "He didn't have any brothers; just a passel of sisters. But he was pretty thick with one of his cousins, Cruz Vega."

Braddock swapped glances with McMain. "One last question, Marshal. Some folks believe Cruz Vega was behind the murder of Reverend Tolby. Have you heard anything that would link Cardenas to the killing?"

"Not a peep."

"There's speculation," Braddock ventured, "that Vega handles the dirty work for Florencio Donaghue. Would you have any information to that effect?"

"Well, I'll tell you, parson." Grant climbed to his feet.

"You've just crossed the line from fact to gossip. I try to steer clear of such talk."

"Anything else you would talk about, Marshal?"

"Nothin' I'd swear to."

The conversation ended on a cordial note. Bud Grant shook hands and walked from the newspaper office. McMain and Braddock watched in silence until he passed through the front door. Then McMain let out a gusty sigh.

"I guess we know who the second bushwhacker was."

"Knowing it and proving it," Braddock pointed out, "aren't one and the same. I couldn't place Vega at Cimarron Canyon today. Things were happening a little too fast for me to stop and take a look at his face."

"But it's obvious!" McMain protested. "Vega and Cardenas were there on Donaghue's orders. Who else would have sent them?"

"You ask tough questions, Orville."

"There's one way to find out."

"How?"

"Take Vega prisoner," McMain said sternly. "Threaten to hang him and he'll confess fast enough."

"What if he doesn't?"

"Then hang him!" McMain grated. "At least we'll have gotten Tolby's murderer."

"No dice." Braddock shook his head firmly. "For one thing, I don't deal in lynch law. For another, we're liable to spook Donaghue and force him to run. I want him handy when the right time comes."

"The right time for what?"

"When we need a songbird to whistle a tune on the ring."

"Are you saying we just wait—do nothing?"

"You wait," Braddock said, getting up. "I think I'll take myself a trip."

"Where to?"

"Santa Fe."

"Nonsense!" McMain grouched. "You won't learn anything in Santa Fe. It's *their* town!"

"Nothing ventured, nothing gained."

McMain rose as Braddock turned away. "I tell you it's madness!"

"Hold down the fort, Orville."

"But," McMain sputtered, "when will you return?"

"Look for me when you see me."

Braddock walked toward the front of the office. As he rounded the counter, Colter regarded him with an odd, steadfast look. Their eyes locked in a moment of silent assessment. Then the younger man cracked a smile.

"Off to convert some more sinners, parson?"

"Yea, verily, I give light to them that sit in darkness."

"Funny how they end up with powder burns too."

"God moves in a mysterious way, His wonders to perform."

"You performed a puredee wonder on Cardenas!"

Braddock let the remark pass. He grinned and waved and moved through the door. Colter clearly wasn't fooled by his masquerade or his glib way with Scripture. He reminded himself that he was already overdue for a talk with the young half-breed. But tonight his priorities were elsewhere, and he hurried off in the direction of the hotel. His thoughts turned immediately to Santa Fe.

And Warren Mitchell.

Isaac Coleman rode into town the following morning. His features were set in a tight scowl as he reined up before the newspaper. He dismounted and left his horse hitched out front.

Entering the newspaper, he greeted Colter with a dour nod. The stormy look on his face discouraged any attempt at conversation. So Colter merely watched as he marched toward the rear of the office. From the back of the shop, the pressmen barely glanced around.

Orville McMain braced himself. One look at Coleman's expression told him the reason behind the visit. He briefly wondered whether he was capable of carrying the charade any further. Then, remembering his promise to Braddock, he decided there was no choice in the matter. It was not yet time to reveal the detective's true identity.

"Good morning, Isaac."

"Mornin'."

"What brings you to town?"

"Our new parson."

Coleman took a chair. He tipped his hat to the back of his head and stared across the desk. McMain tried to look innocent.

"I see you've heard."

"Damn right I've heard! News like that travels faster'n scat."

"An unfortunate incident. But very much as you and Clay predicted. The reverend should have heeded your warning."

"Quit dancin' me around, Orville."

"I beg your pardon?"

Coleman jabbed the air with a finger. "You know god-damn well I'm not talkin' about them taking a shot at Jacoby. I wanna hear about him."

"Isaac, please." McMain darted a look toward the press-room. "I suggest you lower your voice."

"The hell with 'em. You just gimme some answers— now!"

"What is it you want to know?"

"For openers, how come a preacher packs a gun?"

"Wouldn't you?" McMain gave him a conspiratorial smile. "Under the circumstances?"

"We're not discussin' me. We're talkin' about a minister."

"Are you saying a man of God forfeits the right to self-defense? No, Isaac, I think not."

"You're twistin' my words."

"Perhaps I didn't understand the question."

"All right," Coleman said testily. "I'll spell it out for you. Where'd a preacher get so good with a gun? Way I heard it, he did some mighty fancy shootin'."

McMain shrugged. "I suppose it was just one of those

things. Reverend Jacoby told me it was providential, a matter of luck."

"Bullshit!" Coleman snorted. "Takes more'n luck to walk away from that. The bastards had him cold."

"Maybe God was on his side after all. Stranger things have happened."

"And I suppose it didn't bother him the least bit, lettin' daylight through Cardenas. What happened to 'Thou shalt not kill'?"

"Are you condemning Reverend Jacoby for protecting himself?"

"Nope," Coleman said, wagging his head. "I'm just sayin' there's something funny here. None of it makes any sense."

"Aren't you being overly skeptical? After all, the Bible doesn't forbid any man—even a minister—the right to preserve his life."

Coleman pondered a moment. "What the hell was he doing out at Cimarron Canyon anyway?"

"As I gather it, he was on his way to Elizabethtown. He's a circuit rider as well as our parson, you know."

"Still goddamn curious." Coleman paused, staring at him intently. "You'd almost think he dared 'em to bushwhack him. Hell, he knew that's where they killed Tolby."

McMain willed himself to remain calm. A film of sweat popped out on his forehead and his mouth tasted dry. He forced a rueful smile. "You're imagining things, Isaac. Reverend Jacoby just happens to be a very determined man. He won't allow anyone to interfere with his mission."

Coleman hitched back his chair. He stood, tugging down his hat, silent a moment. Then he looked at McMain.

"Maybe I'll walk down to the hotel. I'd like to hear that story from the reverend himself."

"You're too late. I told you he's a determined man."

"What d'you mean?"

"I mean he won't be stopped. He rode out to complete the circuit. He plans to spread the word of God, no matter the risk to himself."

Coleman slowly shook his head. "You reckon he's a fool, Orville?"

"You've met him. You tell me."

"Looks to me like he wants people to think he's a fool. You know what I think?"

"What?"

"I think he's a goddamn liar."

"What's there to lie about?"

"I dunno. But I'm sure as hell gonna ask him when he gets back."

"Well, he won't return for a week or so. A backcountry circuit does take time."

"I can wait, Orville."

Coleman hesitated, as though about to say something more. Then he gave McMain an odd smile and walked away. Up front, he swapped nods with Colter and went through the door. A moment later he rode north out of town.

Orville McMain appeared shaken. He knew he'd been granted a short reprieve and nothing more. Sometime soon the truth would come out. And he dreaded that day.

Above all things, Isaac Coleman detested a liar.

CHAPTER NINE

Santa Fe was located on the banks of a stream that flowed southwesterly from the Sangre de Cristos. Its altitude was above seven thousand feet and the town itself was surrounded by several mountain ranges. The railway entered the valley from the southeast, through Glorieta Pass.

Braddock stepped off the train two days following the assassination attempt. Before departing Cimarron, he had arranged for McMain to publish a story in the *Beacon*. The Reverend Titus Jacoby, undaunted by his brush with death, was off on another tour of the circuit. With his absence explained, he'd then mounted the dun and ridden directly to Raton. There he had laid the good preacher to rest and spent the afternoon putting together another disguise. Late yesterday evening he had boarded the overnight train for Santa Fe.

Today, crossing the depot platform, Braddock looked anything but a preacher. He was attired in a broadcloth coat and striped trousers, with a flashy brocaded vest and a high-crowned Stetson. A pearl stickpin decorated his tie, and the pocket watch nestled in his vest was attached to a heavy gold chain. The muttonchop whiskers were gone, and his upper lip was now covered by a luxuriant soup-strainer of a mustache. His appearance was that of a wealthy high roller, and he had adopted the lexicon peculiar to Texans. His cover name was Elmer Boyd.

From the train station, Braddock walked uptown to the plaza. A broad square dominated by a cathedral and the governor's palace, the plaza was the town's center of activity. Built on commerce and politics, the territorial capital was the major trade center between Mexico and the United States. Formerly the terminus for the Santa Fe Trail, it was now served by railroad instead of wagon caravans. Trade goods were off-loaded there and stored for transshipment to all points of the compass. The plaza was crowded with shops and businesses and several open-air markets. The architecture was predominantly adobe, and the scene had a quaint atmosphere. For all its growth, Santa Fe still retained much of its native charm.

Approaching the plaza, Braddock was struck by a sharp sense of déjà vu. Not quite two years ago he had crossed the same plaza on his way to the territorial prison. There he had interrogated William Bonney—alias Billy the Kid—with regard to a murder and a gang of cattle rustlers. On that same day, he had happened across a secret meeting between Judge Owen Hough and Warren Mitchell. Only later had he come to suspect a connection between Mitchell and the Santa Fe Ring. The object of his investigation had proved to be Owen Hough, the political kingpin of Lincoln County. After killing Hough, he'd had no reason to delve further into the machinations of the ring. Nor had he ever met Warren Mitchell face-to-face. Today he planned to remedy that oversight.

One thought led to another as he walked toward the Capitol Hotel. He was reminded that he'd learned a vital lesson while investigating Judge Hough. At the time, he was still operating openly, using his own name. He'd made no great effort to conceal his movements or his whereabouts during the course of his stay in Lincoln County. Nor had he kept back any secrets from those allied with him in the investigation. The upshot was an attempt on his own life and the murder of several innocent people. One of those killed was a girl, and he'd never quite forgiven himself for her death. Yet he had profited by the mistake. Thereafter he operated on the principle that it was wiser not to let the left hand know what the right hand was doing. So he'd told McMain where he was headed, but nothing of what he planned. And not a word about the Texan named Elmer Boyd.

Braddock engaged a suite at the hotel. His manner was loud and vulgar, the perfect embodiment of a swaggering Texican. He overtipped the bellboy and went out of his way to act the part of a big spender. After lunch in the hotel dining room, where he pinched the waitress's fanny, he felt confident he would be remembered. Anyone inquiring about Elmer Boyd would be told of a brassy wild man who threw money to the winds. The tale would further bolster his cover story, for it contained a dash of the bizarre. He was just outrageous enough to be the genuine article.

Shortly after noon hour, Braddock crossed the plaza to the Mercantile National Bank. A long cigar jutted from his mouth, and he trailed a cloud of smoke as he entered a stairwell to the second floor. On the upper landing, several offices were ranged along a central corridor. He walked to the end of the passageway, where a suite of offices occupied one corner of the building. The top half of the door was frosted glass and the name of the firm was inscribed in gilt letters.

THE SANTA FE LAND & DEVELOPMENT CO.
WARREN F. MITCHELL
PRESIDENT

Braddock barged through the door like a conquering hero. A receptionist looked up from her desk with a polite smile. After introducing himself, Braddock demanded an interview with the head of the firm. His bluff air of assurance left her disconcerted, and she hurried off to an inner office.

Several moments passed, then the door opened and the receptionist reappeared. She beckoned him inside.

"Please come this way, Mr. Boyd."

"Thank you kindly, little lady."

Warren Mitchell rose to greet him as he entered. Braddock had the immediate impression of someone who was accustomed to having his own way and who was very seldom thwarted. Mitchell was tall and lean, quite distinguished-looking in a cutaway coat and a stiff wing collar covered by a black cravat. His gray mustache was neatly trimmed and waxed, and the overall effect was of confidence mixed with personal magnetism. He extended his hand in a firm grasp.

"Won't you have a seat, Mr. Boyd?"

"Call me Elmer. Everybody does!"

The office was furnished in dark walnut and lush chocolate leather. Braddock took a wing-backed chair, and Mitchell resumed his seat behind a massive desk. He gave Braddock's outfit a swift once-over, his appraisal cool and deliberate. A brief interval elapsed before he spoke.

"Well, now," he said pleasantly, "what can I do for you—Elmer?"

Braddock chortled, "Nobody does nothin' for nobody. Leastways not unless one hand washes the other. You follow my drift?"

"Vaguely." Mitchell gave him a blank stare. "Would you care to elaborate?"

"Glad to," Braddock said, munching on his cigar. "I came all the way from Fort Worth to offer you a proposition. You might say it's an everybody-wins proposition."

"I see," Mitchell said tentatively. "What did you have in mind, specifically?"

"The word around Texas," Braddock said with an oily grin, "is that you've got the Midas touch. I hear you make lots of money for your investors—tons of the stuff."

A fleeting look of puzzlement crossed Mitchell's face, then his expression became flat and guarded. "By investors, who do you mean?"

"Well, there was that deal you worked with the railroad. An acre for them and an acre for you and your crowd. Mighty slick little operation. And mighty profitable too."

Braddock had done his homework. Through a Colorado railroad baron, who owed him a favor, he had learned the details of the Santa Fe line's expansion into New Mexico. Warren Mitchell had been instrumental in obtaining the necessary right-of-way, part of which passed through Colfax County. Later it was whispered that, in return, the railroad had deeded to the ring a sizable portion of the federal land grant. Whatever the truth, the ultimate goal became apparent when the Santa Fe began laying track toward Los Angeles. Quite soon it would be the only railroad in the country with line extending from Chicago to the West Coast.

"Anyone else?" Mitchell asked. "Or are you just repeating rumors?"

"Don't believe me, huh?" Braddock's smile broadened. "How about that consortium you put together? The one with all them English and Dutch high rollers. I understand you made a hell of a killing!"

Mitchell's stare betrayed nothing. "You seem very well informed."

"I've got my sources." Braddock admired the tip of his cigar. "Course, what's important is what we can do for each other. I think you big financiers call it the quid pro quo."

"Hmmm." Mitchell considered a moment, then nodded. "I presume that brings us to your proposition."

"Yessir, it does!" Braddock said with cheery vigor. "You see, I made myself a right nice fortune in the cow business. But it's gotten to seem sorta boring, too easy. I'm ready to try my hand in a no-limit game."

"For the sake of argument," Mitchell replied, returning his gaze steadily, "let us say I was receptive to outside investors. What type of return would you expect on your money?"

"A fifty-fifty split on the profits."

"Aren't your terms overly generous?"

"A mite." Braddock blew a plume of smoke into the air. "But don't think you're dealin' with some addle-brained shit-kicker from Texas. I want to buy into your game and I'm willin' to make it worth your while. I'll settle for a divvy down the middle."

"Very astute," Mitchell said reasonably. "What size investment are we talking about?"

"Three million," Braddock said with a gravelly chuckle. "In case you think you heard wrong, that's a three with six big zeroes behind it."

A pinpoint of greed surfaced in Mitchell's eyes. "You talk extremely tempting figures, Elmer."

"I do more'n talk," Braddock told him jovially. "You show me a deal I like and I'll write you a check for three million simoleons. I come to play and I'm willin' to pony up for a piece of the action."

"I do believe you are." Mitchell regarded him thoughtfully. "I wonder if you'd care to join me for dinner tonight?"

"Why, I'd be downright honored, Mr. Mitchell."

"And, please," Mitchell said affably, "do call me Warren."

Braddock's grin was so wide it was almost a laugh. "Warren, I think we're gonna get along like a couple of turds in a teacup."

Mitchell winced. "I've no doubt of it, Elmer. None whatever."

After setting a time, Mitchell agreed to call for him at the hotel that evening. Braddock left the office in a jubilant mood, immensely pleased with himself. He'd salted the bait and it had proved an irresistible lure.

All that remained was to spring the trap.

Clay Allison dismounted in front of the newspaper. He looped the reins around the hitch rack, then stepped onto the boardwalk. Through the door he caught Colter's eye. He jerked his head for the other to come outside.

Colter hesitated a moment. After glancing toward the rear of the office, he leaned the shotgun in a corner. His gaze was neutral as he moved outside and crossed to the hitch rack. He nodded to Allison.

"What's up?"

"Want to ask you something."

"Yeah?"

"What d'you think of the new preacher, Jacoby?"

Colter pulled out some makings. He methodically built himself a smoke, saying nothing. At last he lit up and flicked the match into the street.

"I don't think about him too much. What makes you ask?"

"Isaac was here yesterday."

Colter exhaled slowly. "I saw him."

"Then you know he talked to McMain about the preacher."

"News to me. Isaac didn't say boo about nothin'. Same goes for McMain."

Allison gave him a sideways look. "How'd McMain act afterwards?"

"I don't get you."

"Well, you know. Did he act different? Do anything out of the ordinary?"

"Not so far as I saw. He went on back to work after Isaac left. Looked pretty ordinary to me."

"What about last night?"

"Same old routine. I saw him home and then went on to the hotel. Why all the questions?"

"Isaac thinks he lied."

Allison watched for a reaction. Even at the best of times, he found it difficult to be civil toward Colter. Something in the man's indifferent attitude rubbed him the wrong way. He was accustomed to a show of respect from hired hands.

Still, Coleman had warned him to go slow. Colter was not a man to be pushed or ordered about. Watching him now, Allison was nonetheless irked by his evasive manner. Some more direct method seemed in order.

"I get the feeling"—Colter paused, blew the ash off his cigarette—"you're askin' me if McMain lied."

"What if I was?"

"I'd tell you to go ask McMain. I don't even know what him and Isaac talked about."

"They talked about the preacher."

"Like I said, it's news to me."

Allison stared at him. "Lemme put it another way. What's your opinion of Jacoby?"

"I've got no opinion one way or the other."

"Why the hell not? You've been standin' around every time he comes to see McMain."

Colter smiled. "I try not to overhear other people's conversation. The less I know, the better I like it."

"All the same," Allison growled, "you're not deaf, dumb, and blind. You must've got some idea about him."

"Like what?"

"Well, for one thing, he's goddamn handy with a gun. 'Specially for a preacher."

"So?"

"So hasn't he ever said nothin' to you? Anything that'd give you a clue?"

"Nope. It's 'Hello, Buck,' and 'Howdy, parson.' We let it go at that."

"And you never eavesdropped on him and McMain? Just out of curiosity?"

"I reckon I ain't that curious."

"Goddamn peculiar, if you ask me. Only natural you'd wonder."

Colter took a long pull on his cigarette. He exhaled, eyes cold as glass. "You callin' me a liar?"

There was a moment of strained silence. Allison seemed to measure the other man with an appraising look. Then, for whatever reason, he let the remark pass.

"Nobody called you nothin'. But you could do me and Isaac a big favor."

"What's that?"

"Keep your ears open. We'd like to hear anything you hear."

"I'll let you know."

Allison started to question the cryptic comment. Then, on second thought, he decided to leave it there. He nodded, walking to his horse, and mounted. Without looking around, he rode out of town.

Colter grinned and turned back to the newspaper.

Warren Mitchell proved to be a genial host. He was urbane and witty, with a droll sense of humor. He was also a raconteur with a taste for the good life.

The meal that evening was meant to impress Braddock. Mitchell took him to Santa Fe's most exclusive restaurant, obviously a gathering spot for those of wealth and power. The maître d' greeted Mitchell effusively, escorting them to a reserved table. Several diners waved to Mitchell, and others stopped by the table to shake hands. Their attitude was at once friendly and servile, even though they were clearly men of substance themselves. There was a sense of nobles paying homage to a liege lord.

Fine cuisine was high on Mitchell's list of priorities. The dinner was a seven-course affair built around a superb trout almandine. From the wine cellar, Mitchell selected a delicate Chablis imported from the vineyards of France. Over dinner he pointed out various dignitaries seated around the room, mainly politicians and influential businessmen.

Then, with several glasses of wine under his belt, he related amusing anecdotes about their personal and professional lives. After the meal he ordered *aguardiente*, a fiery native brandy brewed by Franciscan monks. His stories about Santa Fe's elite soon took on a note of sardonic contempt.

Braddock was a rapt listener, suitably wide-eyed and attentive. Yet he slowly formed a new and disturbing impression of his host. He'd crossed paths with many of the West's most notable robber barons and political overlords. The experience had taught him a crucial lesson, one of his ironclad rules of conduct. A true overlord, a man secure in his own power, never stooped to petty criticism. Mitchell's anecdotes and catty stories were the stamp of an envious man, not a man who had ascended to the top rung of the ladder. But he was a man, nonetheless, who plainly commanded the respect of Santa Fe's upper class. All of which led Braddock to a conclusion too compelling to ignore. Some complex of deduction and gut instinct told him that Warren Mitchell was not the leader of the Santa Fe Ring. There was someone higher, a power behind the scenes. A czar who worked his will from the shadows.

The sudden realization brought Braddock up short. Then, from some dim corner of his mind, he recalled a lesson of a different sort. In conversation, a master bunco artist had once used an analogy to illustrate the art of fleecing a mark. He'd compared a con game to fishing for a wise old bass on the bottom of a lake. The idea was to dangle the bait until the bass was tempted to leave the safety of deep water. The next step was to jiggle the bait and pretend to withdraw it altogether. As the bait disappeared into shallow water, the bass would believe his meal was about to vanish for good. Finally, unable to resist the temptation, the bass would forsake the bottom for a quick strike. And presto! The bass was hooked and landed before he realized he'd outsmarted himself. A properly rigged confidence game operated on the same principle, and $3 million was very enticing bait. Braddock decided to try his luck in deeper water.

Mitchell avoided any mention of investments throughout the meal. Only when they were on their second glass of *aguardiente* did he broach the subject. He raised his brandy snifter in a toast.

"Here's to happy days," he said genially. "And a mutually profitable association."

"You damn betcha!" Braddock quaffed his brandy. "Course, I'm still waitin' to hear your deal. You got something against mixin' grub with business?"

"Not at all." Mitchell gave him a sly, conspiratorial look. "As a matter of fact, I've been considering several possibilities. The one that strikes me as most promising is Guadalupe County. I'm dickering right now on a land grant that covers almost ninety square miles. You could get in on the ground floor."

"Where's Guadalupe County?"

"Southeast of here, fifty or sixty miles."

"What makes this land grant worth buyin'?"

"Prime cattle country," Mitchell explained. "Watered by the Pecos River and perfect for leasing to some big rancher. Or we could split it into smaller parcels and sell it off."

"I dunno," Braddock said doubtfully. "I was lookin' to get out of the cow business. Guess I sorta had my mind set on something a little more civilized."

"How do you mean?"

"Well, for one thing, there's no railroad down that way. No towns to speak of either. It's just common, ordinary grassland."

"Hardly ordinary," Mitchell rejoined. "Cattlemen always need graze, and they're willing to pay top dollar. I visualize a quick turnover and enormous profits."

"Mebbe," Braddock allowed. "All the same, it don't set my mouth to waterin'."

"What would?"

"Like I said, something closer to civilization. Towns and people and a railroad. Something that's gonna grow."

"Elmer, you disappoint me. I thought you were a gambler."

"I am!"

"But you're asking to buy in on property that's already developed. The game doesn't work that way."

"And you're askin' me to buy a pig in a poke!"

"I beg your pardon?"

"Guadalupe County!" Braddock said hotly. "That land grant's likely got more holes than a sieve. You're liable to spend years proving it out in court."

"I assure you that won't happen. I've laid the groundwork with all the right people. The deal will go through without a snag, Elmer. You can take my word on it."

"Uh-huh," Braddock grunted. "So we're talkin' about connections. And where there's *right* people, there's a *right* man. Somebody that calls the tune."

"Your point escapes me."

"Well, looky here, Warren. I'm not questionin' your word, understand. But I'd just like to hear it straight from the horse's mouth. Suppose you set it up and lemme have a talk with the man himself."

"I'm afraid not," Mitchell informed him stiffly. "You'll have to rely on the assurances I've already given you."

"In that case"—Braddock tossed his napkin on the table—"why don't we shake hands and forget the whole thing? I'm plumb snake-bit when it comes to operatin' on blind faith."

Mitchell saw the three million vanishing before his eyes. There was a moment's calculation while he debated something within himself. Then he followed the bait into shallow water.

"All right," he said grudgingly. "I'll arrange a meeting."

"When?"

"In the next day or so."

"No money passes hands till I've met the *man*."

"Agreed."

"What's his name?"

"You'll have to wait for that, Elmer."

Braddock decided to push no further. He'd worked the con with finesse and time was on his side. He had played the gullible Texan with a fortune in cash, and the role insured that the meeting would actually take place. He counseled himself to patience, and raised his glass in a toast. His mouth split in a lopsided grin.

"Here's to you and me, Warren. And Guadalupe County!"

CHAPTER TEN

The next couple of days passed uneventfully. Warren Mitchell stalled, asking for time, and Braddock curbed his impatience. The only option was to walk away empty-handed.

Braddock nonetheless put the time to good use. He was reluctant to contact Frank Kirkland for fear of blowing his cover. But he spent several hours a day lounging about in saloons, playing the well-heeled Texan. He was quick to order a round of drinks, and the men he engaged in conversation never knew they'd been subjected to a subtle form of interrogation. He learned that the political climate in the capital was volatile, sometimes explosive. There was active, open opposition to the Santa Fe Ring.

The most vocal opposition was from the *New Mexican*, a small newspaper with limited circulation. The publisher, Max Flagg, used his editorials to blast the Republicans, currently the party in power. He branded everyone from the governor on down as tools of the ring, and his editorials fairly sizzled with righteous indignation. Yet his allegations were long on verbiage and short on substance. He wrote of cabals and conspiracies, but he offered nothing in the way of documentation. More than anything else, his newspaper appeared to be an organ for the opposition party. The Democrats were led by Francisco Chavez, a *jefe* within the Mexican community. He had the support of Flagg and the *New Mexican*, as well as the Anglo Democrats. Still, he was seldom quoted as saying anything of lasting significance. All of which was interesting, if not particularly enlightening. Braddock filed the names away for future reference.

On a personal note, he found Warren Mitchell a welcome diversion. In fact, their second evening together proved to be something of a revelation. Fashionable restaurants and the world of the social elite were Mitchell's natural habitat. Yet, for all his polished manner, there was a darker side to his nature. He was a womanizer, a connoisseur of the flesh, and he made no attempt to disguise it. Instead, he promptly introduced Braddock to Santa Fe's nightlife.

Though married, Mitchell seldom spent a night at home. He maintained a suite at the hotel, ostensibly for the purpose of entertaining business clients. Practically every evening he dined out and afterward strolled down to the sporting district. There he was a regular at the Tivoli Variety Theater, the town's swankiest dive. He had a fondness for roulette, and he generally spent an hour or so wagering modest bets. Then he retired to a table directly below the footlights and devoted the balance of the night to ogling showgirls. But even then, he was selective in his choice of company. He picked only the prettiest and the most voluptuous from the chorus line, and his invitations were never refused. He treated his guests to champagne and charmed them with his debonair manner. And he bedded them almost as a matter of routine.

Braddock thought this behavior revealed much about Mitchell's character. Here was a man of prominence and stature who took his pleasure with tawdry showgirls. A trait common to all libertines was that they were both self-destructive and not all that secure in their manhood. The fact that Mitchell found his sexual outlet on the wrong side of town indicated that his character was flawed in much the same way. There was, moreover, the element of moral bankruptcy. A pillar of the community by day, he became a randy satyr at night. All in all, it tagged him as a man of questionable scruples.

Still, Mitchell made no effort to hide his debauchery, and therein lay the problem. Braddock saw no immediate way to exploit the weakness. Nor would he have tried while awaiting a meeting with the leader of the Santa Fe Ring. Any overt move on his part would merely jeopardize the progress he'd made thus far. So he catalogued the information for some future time.

The wait ended late the third evening in Santa Fe. Braddock was seated with Mitchell at his usual table in the Tivoli. The curtain rang down on the final show, and Braddock assumed they would shortly be joined by a couple of girls. Quite unexpectedly, Mitchell paid the bill and suggested they take a walk. His manner was cryptic, and he offered nothing by way of an explanation. Outside the theater he turned uptown and led Braddock toward the plaza. Some minutes later they rounded a corner onto a side street and halted before a storefront office. A sign on the window was dimly visible in the glow of a nearby street lamp.

STEPHEN B. ELKTON
ATTORNEY AT LAW

Mitchell entered without knocking. The outer office was dark, but a shaft of light streamed from a door across the room. He closed and locked the street door and removed his hat. Then, nodding to Braddock, he led the way to the inner office. The interior was utilitarian by any standards, furnished with a plain oak desk and two wooden armchairs. The walls were covered with law books from floor to ceiling.

The man behind the desk was short and thick-set. Somewhere in his late forties, he had the girth of one who indulged himself in all the good life had to offer. He was clean-shaven, with round features and thin hair combed back over his head.

His eyes were deep-set and shrewd, and his smile was patently bogus. He rose as they entered the office.

"Elmer Boyd," Mitchell said as he motioned Braddock forward, "permit me to introduce Stephen Elkton."

"A pleasure, Mr. Boyd." Elkton pumped his arm warmly. "Warren has told me a great deal about you."

"You're one up on me," Braddock announced. "He hasn't said do-diddily about you."

Elkton laughed a fat man's laugh. "Warren does carry discretion to extremes. Won't you have a seat?"

Braddock doffed his Stetson and took one of the armchairs. Mitchell sat down beside him and Elkton lowered himself into a squeaky swivel chair behind the desk. There was an awkward moment of silence, then Elkton smiled.

"Warren tells me you're from Fort Worth."

"Thereabouts," Braddock said easily. "I do my bankin' in Forth Worth. My spread's southwest of there, down on the Brazos."

"Would I be familiar with your brand?"

Braddock was instantly alert. "You a cattleman?"

"No," Elkton said, a bit too quickly. "But from what Warren says, you've made quite a name for yourself."

"Circle B, that's my brand." Braddock regarded him with a level gaze. "Anybody that knows cows will tell you it's registered to Elmer Boyd. Now, lemme ask you one."

"By all means."

"You makin' small talk?" Braddock said bluntly. "Or are you questionin' my credentials?"

Elkton laughed indulgently. "We simply like to know who we're dealing with, Mr. Boyd. After all, we are discussing a very substantial investment."

"Only one trouble," Braddock said, a note of irritation in his tone. "You got the order of things all ass backwards. It's me puttin' up the three million, and that ain't exactly pocket change. So you've got to convince me—not the other way round!"

"A point well taken." Elkton smiled benignly. "I assume you're referring to Guadalupe County?"

"Betcher boots!" Braddock nodded soberly. "Warren claims there won't be no hitch with the land grant. He says we'll get valid title to ninety square miles."

"Quite true."

"To guarantee that"—Braddock's voice dropped—"you gotta have somebody real damn important in your hip pocket."

"True again."

"Who?"

Elkton favored him with a patronizing smile. "I hardly think that concerns you, Mr. Boyd. Nor could you reasonably expect me to be so —forthcoming."

"Wrong on all counts!" Braddock said brusquely. "You're asking me to bet without lookin' at the hole card. Nobody ever accused me of playin' dumb poker, Mr. Elkton."

"All I can say is that a court decision, based on a surveyor's recommendation, establishes valid title under the law. We have a survey and it coincides exactly with the original land grant. And we will—let me stress that again, Mr. Boyd—we *will* obtain a favorable court ruling."

"That a fact?" Braddock said skeptically. "You talkin' about a federal judge or what?"

"I've told you all you need to know, Mr. Boyd."

"Not by a damn sight!" Braddock croaked. "All that legal jabbering don't guarantee me nothin'."

"Then let me phrase it another way." Elkton smiled without warmth. "I've told you all I'm going to tell you. Some things must be taken on trust."

Braddock flipped a palm back and forth. "No offense, but why should I trust you? Warren tells me you're the he-wolf around these parts. So far, though, I haven't heard nothin' that'd make it a fact."

"I could pose the same question," Elkton replied succinctly. "Why should I trust you, Mr. Boyd? You're an absolute stranger."

"Hell's bells!" Braddock said with a baroque sweep of his arm. "Three million dollars buys a whole shitload of trust!"

Elkton gave him a frosty smile. "We haven't seen your money so far, Mr. Boyd."

"Don't worry," Braddock assured him earnestly. "I'm willin' to put my money where my mouth is and no two ways about it. But I'd sure like to hear something besides double-talk before I do."

"I regret there's nothing more I can say."

"Lemme ask you this," Braddock pressed him. "What's your part in Warren's land company?"

An indirection came into Elkton's eyes. "Suffice it to say I am an interested party."

"Yeah, but have you got any of your own money on the line?"

"You obviously have more questions than I have answers, Mr. Boyd. I suggest you use your own judgment as to whether or not it's a sound investment. Warren will be happy to accommodate you in any way possible."

Braddock knew he'd pushed it to the limit. Further questions would simply antagonize Elkton and accomplish nothing. Far better to leave the door open and play for a break. He looked from Elkton to Mitchell and back again. Then he slapped his knee and laughed.

"You would've made a hell of a horse trader, Mr. Elkton."

"I'll take that as a compliment, Mr. Boyd."

"Don't misunderstand me," Braddock said evenly. "I haven't bought into the game yet. I'll need a little time to study on it."

"Very well." Elkton stared at him like a stuffed owl. "I trust we can rely on your discretion. A word in the wrong ear might create problems for everyone."

"I get your drift," Braddock said with a waggish grin. "Nobody'll hear a peep out of Elmer Boyd."

"We'll wait to hear from you, then."

"Depend on it, Mr. Elkton."

Mitchell and Elkton exchanged a look. Something unspoken passed between them, and Mitchell moved his head in an imperceptible nod. Braddock caught the byplay as he turned toward the door, and he needed no explanation. The meaning was clear.

He would be watched while he was in Santa Fe.

Braddock departed with a cheery wave, and Elkton waited until he heard the front door close. Then he stood and peered into the outer office, satisfying himself it was empty. He resumed his seat.

"Boyd is hardly the bumpkin you described."

Mitchell shrugged. "I admit I'm surprised. He's sharper than I thought."

"Perhaps too sharp."

"In what way?"

"Every way," Elkton replied. "For example, he was very inquisitive about our judicial connections. How do you suppose he found out?"

"Not from me!" Mitchell said quickly.

"If not from you, then from whom?"

"All I said was that there would be no problem in obtaining a valid title. He apparently put the rest together for himself."

"Are you saying he inferred all that from a single statement?"

"How else would he figure it out?"

"How, indeed?" Elkton mused. "We seem to have underestimated Mr. Boyd all the way round."

"I don't follow you."

"Come now, Warren! He obviously knows a good deal about our operation. You said yourself that he'd somehow learned of the railroad deal and the European consortium. Isn't that so?"

"Well, yes, I did."

"Which means he's looked into our affairs rather thoroughly."

"Nothing wrong with that," Mitchell countered. "Anyone

who intends to invest three million would do the same thing.
Besides, everything he's learned has been rumored for years.
And printed in the newspapers, I might add."

"Perhaps," Elkton conceded. "But something about
Mr. Boyd still bothers me. I distrust a man who has nothing
to hide."

"Hide?"

"A man with no secrets. He seemed entirely too open
about himself and his money."

"Some of that was an act. I've never met a wealthy Texan
who didn't have larceny in his heart. They like to think of
themselves as part buccaneer, part bunco man."

"Even so," Elkton remarked, "where does the act end and
the man begin?"

"Hard to say."

"And all the more reason to check him out."

"We don't want to risk offending him. Why not wait until
he gives us a draft for the three million? Then I'll put through
a routine inquiry to his bank."

"Yes, that should suffice. Meanwhile, I want him followed. See to it."

"I'll talk with Johnson and Ortega."

"No rough stuff."

"Of course."

"Unless," Elkton went on, "we discover that Mr. Boyd
does have secrets. Then, as the saying goes, he's fair game."

Mitchell nodded grimly. "I understand."

Early the next morning Braddock emerged from the hotel.
His thumbs were hooked in his vest and a cigar was wedged
into the corner of his mouth. He halted on the veranda and
stood for a moment surveying the plaza. Then he went down
the steps and strolled off at a leisurely pace.

Once across the plaza, Braddock turned onto a side street.
His stride quickened and he walked rapidly to the distant
corner. There he moved to the other side of the intersecting
street and ducked into an alleyway. For the next half hour he

followed a twisting path, frequently doubling back on himself, always looking over his shoulder. Finally, satisfied he wasn't being tailed, he headed for the west side of town.

Shortly before nine o'clock, Braddock walked through the door of the *New Mexican*. Overnight he'd concluded there was little chance of obtaining more information from either Mitchell or Elkton. In his own mind, he felt confident that Mitchell was indeed the front man for the Santa Fe Ring. He was equally convinced that Elkton was the shadowy mastermind who operated from behind the scenes. Yet it was apparent that the relationship was similar to a ventriloquist manipulating a dummy. On important matters, Mitchell only spoke when Elkton moved his lips, and the words were seldom his own. Therefore, Mitchell was unlikely to divulge anything of an incriminating nature.

All things considered, Braddock had decided there was nothing to lose by talking with Max Flagg. The publisher of the *New Mexican* was the avowed enemy of the Santa Fe Ring. His knowledge of the territorial capital and its inner political workings was undoubtedly first-rate. A Johnny-on-the-spot news hound was generally privy to all the juicy tidbits so seldom made public. The publisher might very well reveal something that would dovetail with what Braddock had already learned. In particular, Braddock was looking for inside dope on Stephen Elkton. The man was still very much a cipher, an unknown quantity.

Max Flagg appeared dubious from the outset. He was on the sundown side of forty, with a widow's peak hairline and a nose veined red from liquor. He wore steel-rimmed spectacles and his eyes had the canny look of a man who was surprised by nothing. His expression was unreadable when Braddock introduced himself as "a friend of Frank Kirkland." He closed the door of his cubbyhole office and offered Braddock a chair. Then he steepled his fingers and peered across the desk.

"What can I do for you, Mr.—?"

Braddock smiled. "The name isn't important."

"No?" Flagg squinted querulously. "You walk in off the street and tell me you're pals with Kirkland. Why should I take the word of a man who won't even give me his name?"

"The next time you see Frank"—Braddock paused to light a cigar—"ask him about the Gospel according to Saint Cole. He won't tell you my name either, but he'll vouch for the fact that we're all working toward the same end—the downfall of the Santa Fe Ring."

Frost's eyes were still veiled with caution. "How do I know you're not working for the ring?"

"Simple." Braddock took a draw on the cigar and his face toughened. "You mention me to anyone but Frank Kirkland and the ring will try to kill me. I'll look you up if that happens—and you'll wish I hadn't."

Flagg scrutinized him closely. Whatever he saw in Braddock's gaze, it convinced him the statement was no idle threat. Some swift-felt impulse also told him he was in the presence of an ally. He decided to accept the man with no name at face value.

"All right," he said at last, "mum's the word. How can I help you?"

"What do you know about Warren Mitchell?"

"Everything and nothing," Frost commented morosely. "He's the lightning rod for the ring. By that, I mean his land company provides a legitimate front for their schemes. He does the dirty work and he's very good at it. I would say he's indispensable to their operation."

"Who are 'they'—the ring members?"

"Do you want cold facts or warm gossip?"

"What's the difference?"

"In terms of cold facts," Flagg said in an aggrieved tone, "there's not an iota of proof against anybody. We're dealing with a secretive organization, and their methods are utterly ruthless. No one talks—ever!"

Braddock shrugged. "I guess I'll have to settle for gossip."

"The list is endless," Flagg confided. "The governor, the attorney general, the chief federal court judge, the surveyor general. Shall I go on?"

"You're saying all those men are members of the ring?"

"Not entirely." Flagg's voice was soft and troubled. "I believe the governor and the attorney general are almost certainly members. The others either accept payoffs or cooperate for political reasons. I've never been able to determine where one leaves off and the other begins."

"So far, all I've heard are allegations. Have you got anything concrete?"

Frost briefly outlined the turbulent nature of Santa Fe politics. Following the Civil War, local Republicans had gained control of the political apparatus. The White House, in concert with Congress, had initiated a program designed to punish pro-southern Democrats. Even now, almost twenty years later, the Democrats were still battling to restore a balance of power. But it was an uphill fight conducted largely against men who operated from the shadows. Only last year the territorial governor had been forced to resign when he fell into disfavor with the ring. The new governor, by all reports, had been selected principally for his amicable manner and his lack of curiosity. Allegations or not, Flagg concluded, the pattern of backroom politics was undeniable. New Mexico reeked of corruption.

"In other words," Braddock said pointedly, "you have no proof."

"If I did, I'd print it in banner headlines."

Braddock puffed on his cigar and blew a smoke ring. "Why do you place so much stock in rumors?"

"Stop and think about it," Flagg said grimly. "A single land company—presumably owned by one man—controls the economic lifeblood of New Mexico Territory. How is that possible?"

"I'm asking you."

Flagg gave him a weak smile. "The rumors say it's

possible because Warren Mitchell either owns or black-mails every politician in Santa Fe. I see no other conceivable explanation."

Braddock's eyes turned hard, questing. "Who owns Warren Mitchell?"

"I'm not sure I understand."

"Would you say Mitchell has the brains and the balls to pull all that off by himself?"

"To my knowledge"—Flagg lifted his hands in a lame gesture—"Mitchell has done exactly that. He's the power to be reckoned with, and he's the power broker. No one in public office got there without his stamp of approval."

"So I've heard." Braddock fixed him with a piercing look. "What do you know about Stephen Elkton?"

"Elkton?" Flagg repeated hollowly. "He's a widely respected lawyer and something of an intellect. I understand he's a student of Plato and Aristotle. The Greek school of thought."

"Wonder if he ever read Machiavelli."

"Pardon me?"

"A private joke," Braddock said woodenly. "Has Elkton ever been actively involved in politics?"

"Never," Flagg responded. "Apparently he's a very private man who devotes himself to his law practice. Why do you ask?"

"No reason." Braddock rose to his feet. "Just a shot in the dark."

Flagg eyed him keenly. "Should I inquire further? Perhaps I've overlooked something."

"Suit yourself," Braddock said with a tight smile. "When you see Frank, tell him I said hello."

"I still don't know your name."

"Let's leave it that way—for now."

Braddock nodded and stepped through the door. Once outside, he walked off with the cigar stuck in his mouth and his hands stuffed in his pockets. The conversation with Flagg had been a complete washout, and he mocked himself with sardonic bitterness. He'd played out his string in Santa Fe, and he was now at an impasse. Worse, he was assailed by a sense of time running ahead of him like an hourglass almost emptied of sand.

A short walk across town brought him to the train depot. He entered the station house and asked the telegrapher for a message form. Then he wrote out his instructions in a code known only to himself and one other person.

The wire was addressed to Verna Potter.

Slim Johnson tailed Braddock back to the hotel. He waited on the veranda, watching through a window as Braddock crossed the lobby to the stairs. Then he took off upstreet at a brisk pace.

Several moments later Johnson entered Warren Mitchell's office. In the anteroom, the secretary greeted him with a disapproving look. He was tall and lean, roughly dressed, and she thoroughly mistrusted him. But her boss kept him on the payroll and apparently valued his services. She showed him into the inner office.

Mitchell looked up from a stack of documents. He nodded to Johnson and then waited until his secretary closed the door. He didn't offer the other man a chair.

"What is it?"

"I followed Boyd," Johnson said, "like you told me."

"So?"

"I lost him."

"You dimwit!"

"And then I found him."

"Explain yourself," Mitchell ordered. "From the beginning."

"Well, he come out of the hotel a little before nine. He walks off, easy as you please, puffin' on a cigar. Acted like he had all day and nowhere to go."

"Get to the point."

"Sure thing, boss," Johnson said, hurrying on. "A couple of blocks from the hotel he turned a corner and *poof!*, he flat disappeared."

Mitchell gave him a withering look. "What happened then?"

"Nothin'. Leastways not for a while. Half hour or so later, I spotted him hotfootin' it across the plaza. So I tailed—"

"Wait," Mitchell interrupted. "Any idea at all where he might have been during that half hour?"

"Beats me, boss. Like I said, he gimme the slip."

"Where was Ortega? Why wasn't he helping you?"

"Well," Johnson began, hanging his head, "it didn't look to be that big of a job. Never figgered some peckerhead Texan would pull a fast one."

Mitchell suppressed a curse. He realized, not for the first time, that initiative was in scarce supply in his men.

Johnson and Ortega were hardened toughnuts, skilled killers, but there wasn't an ounce of imagination between them. He catalogued the thought for future reference.

"All right, go on."

"So anyway," Johnson resumed, "I tailed him down to the depot, waited till he sent a wire, then I followed him back to the hotel. He's there now."

"You saw him send a wire?" Mitchell demanded.

"Big as life."

"To whom?"

"Huh?"

"Who was it sent to?"

"I dunno. If you want, I'll go lean on the depot agent. He'd tell me pretty quick."

"No, never mind. Boyd might find out, and we can't risk that."

"Anything you say, boss."

"Stick with him, Slim. Don't lose him again."

"You damn betcha I won't!"

After Johnson left, Mitchell considered what he'd heard. None of it was particularly incriminating in itself. Losing a tail and sending a telegram were hardly grounds for pulling out of the deal with Boyd. Still, it was something to flag and file away for further study.

Upon reflection, Mitchell thought it wiser to keep his own counsel. He saw no reason to advise Elkton of the day's events.

Not just yet.

CHAPTER ELEVEN

Braddock was seated in the lobby. The chair he'd selected faced the hotel entrance and was within earshot of the registration desk. He idly leafed through the morning newspaper.

Three days had passed since he'd wired Verna Potter. Yesterday, with Mitchell pressing for a decision, he had finally agreed to the Guadalupe County land deal. Contracts were now being drawn, and he had promised a check upon formal signing. He figured he had a couple of weeks, perhaps less, before the check bounced from the Fort Worth bank. The timing was critical, but he wasn't overly concerned. Verna had responded by wire, and her decoded message was very much as he'd expected. A new element would shortly be introduced into the game.

Braddock's vigil ended late that morning. His mouth sagged open in amazement as Lise Hammond sailed through the hotel entrance. Her hair, normally golden blond, had been dyed with henna. She was now something of a strawberry roan, the shade coppery red with auburn highlights.

Her coiffure had been changed as well; the style was now upswept with finger-puffs on top and masses of curls clustered high on her forehead. The dye job was professionally done and provided a startling contrast to her usual appearance. She looked brassy and brazen, an impression accentuated by her gaudy emerald-green dress. She had quite completely become someone else.

Lise spotted him the moment she entered the lobby. She lowered one eyelid in a quick wink and marched directly to the desk. A bellboy trailed along with her luggage, and the room clerk perked up noticeably when she requested accommodations with a bathtub. Braddock listened while she registered as Dora Kimble, and overheard the clerk announce her room number. Then, with the bellboy in the lead, she mounted the broad flight of stairs to the second floor. Braddock went back to his newspaper, waiting until the bellboy returned several minutes later. Then he rose and sauntered casually upstairs.

A worm of doubt still gnawed at Braddock. His wire summoning Lise to Santa Fe had been a last-ditch measure. Ever the icy realist, he knew he would uncover nothing more on his own. His investigation was at a dead end, and some bolder approach was needed to break the case. So he'd hatched a scheme whereby Lise would flimflam Warren Mitchell with sexual allure. Yet, despite her gift for guile and subterfuge, he remained more apprehensive than he cared to admit. Nor were his qualms wholly dispelled by the dye job and the striking change in her physical appearance. His concern centered on the man who orchestrated every facet of the ring's activities. One slip-up and Stephen Elkton would order her killed.

Upstairs, Braddock checked the hallway in both directions. No one was around and he walked swiftly to room 226. The door opened to his knock and he stepped inside. Lise closed it behind him, twisting the key. Then she threw herself into his arms. As she cupped his face between her hands, her kiss was warm and hungry. At last, with a final peck on the lips, she disengaged from his embrace and struck a pose, one hand to her hair.

"Hope you like redheads, lover."

"Well," Braddock began as he tossed his hat on the bureau, "I've always been partial to the cake, not the frosting."

"You old smoothy!" Her eyes gleamed with pleasure. "How do you think it will play in Santa Fe?"

"Pretty good," Braddock said, inspecting her closer. "You look like yourself and yet you don't. It'd fool anybody who doesn't know you personally."

"How about someone who's seen me onstage?"

"No problem," Braddock reassured her. "The color and the new hairdo turn the trick. I'm impressed."

"So am I." She tweaked his false mustache. "You're a regular chameleon when it comes to disguise."

"All part of the trade."

She looked at him with impudent eyes. "Your wire was something of a surprise."

"Yeah, well," Braddock mugged, hands outstretched, "things haven't gone exactly the way I'd planned."

"See?" Her lips curved in a teasing smile. "You needed me after all!"

"Don't rub it in."

"I'm just happy you sent for me, lover. And happier to be here!"

"Any trouble getting away from your job?"

"Not a bit." She threw back her head and laughed. "I told Jack Brady he could like it or lump it."

"How long have you got off?"

"However long it takes," she replied airily. "Brady couldn't replace me and he knows it! As you'll recall, I do tend to draw a crowd."

"No argument there," Braddock said absently. "Now all you've got to do is convince Ned Ingram. He owns the biggest dive in town, the Tivoli."

"I'm all ears."

Braddock took a chair and Lise seated herself on the edge of the bed. He briefed her on the assignment, starting with his impersonation of a minister in Cimarron. Then, step by step, he recounted what he'd unearthed during the course of the investigation. He frankly admitted he was stymied, with nowhere left to turn. A whole new dodge was needed to expose the Santa Fe Ring—something shifty and sly, perhaps even seductive. Which was why he'd sent for her.

"So that's it," he concluded. "I want you to put the whammy on Warren Mitchell."

A devilish smile played at the corners of her mouth. "What's he like?"

"A charmer," Braddock observed. "Educated, fancy manners, what the ladies call suave. He likes to think of himself as one of the big muckamucks, top-hat variety."

"Mmm." She uttered a low, gloating laugh. "Just my speed! The swells never could resist my brand of catnip."

"He's no dimdot," Braddock warned her. "So don't treat him lightly. You'll have to watch yourself every minute."

"Consider it done." Her eyes seemed to glint with secret amusement. "I'll have him eating out of my hand in no time."

"Overconfidence"—Braddock paused to underscore the word—"leads to mistakes. Keep that in mind or he'll tumble to you before you get started."

"Oh, pooh!" She lifted her chin slightly. "You said he likes naughty ladies, didn't you?"

"He likes them vulgar and cheap. The cruder, the better."

"Well, honey, you've never seen me at my wickedest. I can talk dirty with the best of them."

Braddock eyed her in silence for a moment. "He does more than talk. None of the girls at the Tivoli say no to him. You'll have to figure a way to hook him and hold him off—without losing his interest."

"You're looking at an expert." She wrinkled her nose and gave him a sassy grin. "I know every trick in the lechers' book. And I know how to string them along too!"

"You won't have any choice." Braddock opened his

hands and shrugged. "You'll have to buy time and somehow pump him for information. And you'll have to do it without mentioning Stephen Elkton. That would be a dead giveaway."

"But it's Elkton we're really after! How do I get the goods on him without using his name?"

"Good question," Braddock conceded. "And I wish I had the answer. What I do know is that Elkton plays for all the marbles. The least little tip-off and you won't get a second chance. Understand?"

Lise looked pensive. "Tell me a little more about Elkton."

"For openers, he's dangerous as hell. Mitchell had the jitters the entire time we were in his office."

"Maybe Mitchell scares easily."

"No." Braddock shook his head. "Elkton qualifies for the term 'sinister.' He's smart and he's a cold fish. No emotion at all. That's the worst possible combination."

"C'mon, lover. Don't tell me he got to you!"

"Let's just say I came away a believer."

"How do you mean?"

"I've been grilled by experts, but Elkton knows all the tricks and then some. He damn near pinned me to the wall."

"But you convinced him, didn't you?"

"I bought a little time, that's all. He's having me shadowed, and he warned me in no uncertain terms to keep my lip buttoned. Like I said, he plays for keeps."

"Are you saying he actually threatened you?"

"Not in so many words. He left it to my imagination what would happen if I spoke out of turn. I got the general drift."

"So you think he really would . . ."

"Kill me?"

"Yes."

"I don't think he'd bat an eye. To him, things tally out in dollars—not lives."

"I guess you're right. I mean, after all he did have a preacher killed."

"Exactly. And if you get careless, he'll kill you too."

"You sound like you're trying to scare me."

"I am." Braddock lifted a questioning eyebrow. "Just in case things go wrong, do you have your Derringer handy?"

"Handy enough," she said, patting her thigh. "I keep it stuck in my garter."

"Use it if push comes to shove."

"When do you want me to start at the Tivoli?"

"Tonight."

"Then we haven't a moment to spare."

Lise stretched voluptuously and held out her arms. He grinned and rose from his chair, moving to the bed. She pulled him down beside her and snuggled close in his arms. Her mouth found his and eagerly sought his tongue, and she kissed him with a fierce, passionate urgency. His arms tightened, strong and demanding, and she whimpered deep in her throat.

Her hand touched his belt buckle. . . .

Some two hours later Lise entered the Tivoli Variety Theater. One of the barkeeps pointed her in the right direction, and the afternoon crowd watched with appreciative stares as she sashayed toward the rear. She crossed from the barroom to the theater, switching her hips for their benefit. She went through a door to the left of a small orchestra pit.

The backstage area was empty and dimly lighted. Lise saw the glow of a lamp from a door near the alley entrance. She walked forward and halted in the open doorway. The office was small and musty and furnished somewhat like a monk's cell. There was a battered desk, flanked by a double file cabinet, and one straight-backed chair for visitors.

Up against the far wall was an overstuffed reclining divan. It was worn and threadbare and seemed perfectly suited for casting chorus girls. The man seated behind the desk looked nothing like a monk.

Ned Ingram was lean and wiry, with jutting cheekbones and sleek, glistening hair. His features were pasty and splotched with gray, and his eyes were opaque and curiously without expression. He glanced up from an accounting ledger and fixed her with a lusterless gaze. He slowly looked her up and down. He mentally undressed her and apparently liked what he saw. His mouth creased in a thin smile.

"Do something for you, girlie?"

"Are you Mr. Ingram?"

"No," Ingram said tonelessly. "My pa was Mr. Ingram. Most everybody calls me Ned."

"Pleased to meet you," Lise said brightly. "I'm Dora Kimble. I'd like to talk to you about a job."

"You a hoofer?"

"Only when I'm hungry," Lise quipped. "My specialty is ballads."

"A canary, huh?" Ingram shook his head back and forth. "Never had much luck with singers. The boys like to see the hot stuff—legs and bloomers."

"That's because they haven't heard my ballads."

"What's different about you?"

"I sing risqué," Lise said with a bawdy smile. "Or I sing dirty. All depends on the quality of your trade."

"Mostly low lifes." Ingram hesitated, considering. "Where've you worked before?"

"Pick a spot!" Lise said merrily. "Abilene, Dodge City, Leadville, Deadwood. I've played 'em all!"

"What brings you to Santa Fe?"

Lise regarded him with brash impudence. "I've always had my eye on San Francisco—the big time. So I'm working my way west."

"Uh-huh." Ingram nailed her with a stern look. "You're not in trouble with the law, are you?"

"Christ, no!" Lise yelped. "I'm strictly legit, Mr. Ingram!"

"Ned."

"Okay, Ned." Lise gave him a bright little nod. "Well anyway, like I was saying, I stay straight with the law."

"Lemme hear you sing something."

"What?"

"You said you're a singer, so sing."

"Without accompaniment?"

"The piano player don't come on till six."

"Oh." Lise cleared her throat. "You want it dirty or risqué?"

"Something in between."

Lise composed herself. The next few moments represented an acid test. She had started out as a hoofer and worked her way up from the chorus to a star headliner. Her husky alto voice was her trademark, and the way she belted out a ballad had brought her a degree of celebrity. Unlike her physical appearance, her singing style would be quite difficult to disguise. Early on in her career, however, she had conquered a pronounced nasal tone with the aid of a voice coach. By concentrating, she was confident she could again introduce that flaw into her style and still sing well enough to land the job.

The ballad she sang was a naughty ditty about an Indian maiden and a cowboy. The lyrics were ripe with sexual innuendo and peppered here and there with four-letter words. Once she began, she found she was actually enjoying it. A lady would never use such explicit language, but she was playing a wicked woman, and the taboos no longer applied. She sang through her nose, and while it offended her ear, the tonal quality masked her normal voice. To add sizzle to the ballad, she performed a simple dance routine, wiggling and jiggling in concert with the tune. She ended with her arms flung wide and her breasts thrust high.

"Not bad," Ingram remarked when she finished. "You ought to get rid of that twang, but I've heard worse. Besides, my band plays so loud nobody'll notice it anyway."

"I've got the job?" Lise squealed. "You're hiring me?"

"Hold your horses." Ingram's mouth lifted in a tight grin. "There's more to the job than what you do onstage. I've got certain rules."

Lise darted a glance at the divan. "What sort of rules?"

"Between shows, all my girls mingle with the customers and push drinks. Course, I don't allow no hanky-panky on the premises. But whatever arrangements they make after hours, that's their business."

"I've got nothing against pushing drinks."

"One other thing."

"Yeah?"

"Before I hire a girl"—Ingram's grin widened—"I generally get a little something on account. A sample of the wares."

"Well, Ned," Lise said in a teasing lilt, "I don't sell it and I don't sleep around. Not that I'm any lily of the valley! I just don't hop into bed with strangers, that's all."

"How long before somebody stops being a stranger?"

"Depends on the somebody." Lise laughed, her eyes dancing merrily. "A man who treats me nice wouldn't be sorry. I'm a regular wildcat when I do let go."

Ingram burst out laughing. "All right, you got yourself a job. But let's have it understood there's a condition attached."

"You and me?"

"One week," Ingram said with a smarmy grin. "Come across in one week or go back to working your way west."

"Ned, you're looking less like a stranger all the time!"

Ingram told her to report for work at six o'clock. She could then plan her act with the band and put together a costume from the stockroom. Lise thanked him profusely and wigwagged her hips as she went out the door. The condition he'd placed on the job bothered her not at all. One week or a hundred was immaterial.

Ned Ingram would be a stranger till hell froze over!

"There once was an Indian maid
Who said she wasn't afraid
To lay on her back
In a cowboy's shack . . ."

Lise stood center stage. She was bathed in a ruby-hued spotlight, and her smile was like naked sin itself. Her sumptuous figure was emphasized by a gown that was cut low on the top and high on the bottom. Her breasts threatened to spill out of the gown and her lissome legs flashed as she performed a cakewalk in tempo with the music. The song was the last number in her act and the raunchiest of the lot. Beyond the footlights, the theater was packed. Even the serious drinkers from the barroom were ganged around the entranceway. The band thumped louder as she ended the ballad with the dirtiest stanza yet.

Thunderous applause broke out even before the music stopped. The audience cheered and whistled and stamped their feet, all the while yelling for more. Lise took four curtain calls, bowing low enough each time to give the crowd a quick peek down the top of her dress. The last time out she let her gaze linger a moment on Warren Mitchell, who was seated at his usual table. She caught open lechery in his look during the instant their eyes met. Then she backed off stage, throwing kisses with both hands as a final wave of applause flooded the theater. The curtain closed only momentarily before the band segued into an upbeat number. A line of chorus girls pranced out of the wings.

Backstage Lise found a waiter with a message from Warren Mitchell. He explained that Mitchell was a Tivoli regular, a very big spender, and that she'd been invited to share a bottle of champagne. She looked properly impressed and followed him out front. From the back of the house, Ned Ingram caught her attention and signaled his congratulations with a circled thumb and forefinger. His expression was that of a cat spitting feathers, and she reminded herself to hit him up for a private dressing room. Then the waiter halted at Mitchell's table and pulled out a chair. She sat down with a vivacious smile.

"Thanks for the invite, Mr. Mitchell."

"I'm honored you accepted." Mitchell promptly filled her glass. "Allow me to toast your bravura performance."

Lise clinked glasses. "Here's mud in your eye! You really liked it, huh?"

"Yes, indeed," Mitchell said, leaning closer. "You're the hit of the evening, Miss Kimble."

"Why don't you call me Dora?"

"And you may call me Warren."

"Good!" Lise held out her glass for a refill. "Life's too short for starchy ways, right, Warren?"

"Quite so." Mitchell stared down the front of her dress while he poured. "Ned Ingram tells me you're new to Santa Fe."

"Fresh off the train," Lise said pertly. "And so far it's a pisser of a town. What an audience! Did you hear that applause?"

"I led the pack, my dear. Your performance deserved the warmest possible reception."

"Say, you're all right! I was afraid you'd be some kind of stuffed shirt. But you're a regular sport, aren't you?"

"Very regular," Mitchell said with a raffish smile. "Among my vices are wine and games of chance. And of course I have a congenital weakness for the ladies."

"I'm sort of partial to men myself."

"How nice." Mitchell cocked one ribald eye at her. "Tell me, are you as naughty as the songs you sing?"

"Sometimes," Lise said with a lewd wink. "It all depends on how the mood strikes me."

"Fascinating," Mitchell murmured. "And how would you characterize your mood tonight?"

"Well, you see, Warren, I'm not a one-nighter. I tend to pick a man and stick with him as long as I'm in town."

"And how does this process of selection occur?"

"Oh, I just *know*!" Lise simpered. "It might take a couple of nights to decide, but I always know when I've met Mr. Right."

"And does Mr. Right find the wait worth his while?"

"Why not find out for yourself?"

"An excellent suggestion," Mitchell said with a sanguine look. "As some philosopher once noted, anticipation is half the pleasure."

Lise knew then she had him gaffed. He was accustomed to girls who wilted before his glib line and urbane manner.

A girl who set a higher price on herself was clearly a novelty and a challenge. She touched both his vanity and his male pride. He would wait for the simplest of reasons.

He had to be the first man in Santa Fe to bed Dora Kimble.

CHAPTER TWELVE

The Tivoli was packed with a rowdy crowd. Braddock stood at the bar, elbows on the counter and one boot heel hooked over the brass rail. He was nursing a whiskey and brooding on Lise Hammond. His expression was troubled.

Dora Kimble was now the toast of Santa Fe's sporting district. Her opening-night act had created a sensation, and everyone was talking about the lady who sang dirty ballads. On the second evening, Ned Ingram had wisely moved her into the headliner's spot. Her act had become the finale for each of the three shows presented nightly. The crowds had steadily grown larger as word of her racy performance spread through town. Tonight, which was her fourth night at the Tivoli, the turnout was little short of a mob scene. She was playing to standing room only.

Braddock watched her performance in the back-bar mirror. It was the last show of the evening, and she held the audience enthralled with the verve of her stage presence and the off-color lyrics of her songs. Yet Braddock scarcely heard the words, and his eyes followed her movements with only dulled awareness. His mind was focused instead on the events of the past few days. He found nothing to encourage him and a great deal to prompt his concern. He thought the risk to Lise was mounting at an alarming rate.

So far, Lise had uncovered nothing of value to the investigation. After the last show every evening, Warren Mitchell took her to his suite at the hotel for a nightcap. His sexual advances were rather mild in nature, and he'd made no attempt to force himself on her. To all appearances, he seemed content to bide his time. The platonic company of Santa Fe's newest stage sensation was, for the moment, a balm to his randier designs. He was attentive and entertaining, and it was obvious he reveled in squiring her around town. Her sudden fame also put him in the limelight, anointing him with a mark of distinction. For he was widely assumed to be Dora Kimble's lover.

Lise skillfully played on his vanity. She allowed him a kiss here and a squeeze there, and kept his ardor under control with promises of more to come. Her public display of affection also promoted the belief that she was his latest conquest. The envy of every man in town, he had arranged to show her off to some of his uptown friends. Only last night, he'd invited several of the chorus girls to an after-hours party at his suite. The gentlemen they were there to entertain included the attorney general, the territorial delegate to Congress, and a federal court judge. The party was a smashing success, with the politicos well oiled by the end of the night. One by one, they had disappeared with the girls to their own private hideaways.

Seizing opportunity, Lise had attempted to capitalize on the moment. Mitchell was mellowed by liquor and immensely pleased with the impression she'd made on his cohorts. She too had appeared impressed and exhibited a natural curiosity about his high connections in government. Her questions were subtle and worded in such a way as to appeal to his pride. Still, for all his mellow mood, Mitchell hadn't consumed enough whiskey to indulge in careless talk. His answers were limited to vague generalities, and he'd revealed nothing about his business or personal relationships with the men. Lise dared not press too far, and she had finally let the subject drop. Pleading the late hour, she'd then bid him good night.

Upon entering her room, Lise had found Braddock dozing on the bed. For the past three nights, he'd let himself into the room and awaited her return. The purpose was an exchange of information, and last night, like the nights before, had proved dismally unrewarding. Lise identified the men who had attended the party and went on to relate her later conversation with Mitchell. The upshot, as they'd both agreed, was of little consequence. That Mitchell entertained politicians with girls and booze proved nothing. Nor was there any hint of corruption or direct ties to the Santa Fe Ring. Their investigation, for all practical purposes, was going nowhere. But Lise had expressed a determination to stick with their original plan. She still believed she could dupe Mitchell into exposing his hand and establish a case against Stephen Elkton.

Braddock was no longer all that certain. Three nights in Mitchell's company had left Lise little to show for her efforts. It was possible, after introducing her to his cronies, that Mitchell might confide in her over a period of time. But Braddock secretly felt that he'd underestimated Mitchell's resolve and overestimated Lise's seductive powers. To compound matters, his own access to Mitchell had undergone a severe change. The land contract had been signed yesterday. With his check for three million in hand, Mitchell apparently saw no need to court him further. While he wasn't being snubbed, the dinner invitations had stopped and he was no longer Mitchell's guest at the Tivoli. Which pretty much eased him out of the picture. To see Mitchell, he now needed an appointment.

Tonight, as Lise finished her number Braddock was gripped by a sense of unease. He watched her take her bows and downed his drink as she hurried off stage. His gaze automatically shifted to Mitchell, who was seated at the table down front. His unease was suddenly replaced by a sharp stab of apprehension. He'd learned never to ignore his instincts, and some visceral compulsion told him it was time to try another tack. The feeling was reinforced when Lise appeared in her street clothes and joined Mitchell at his table. A moment later they walked from the Tivoli arm in arm.

Braddock watched them go out the door. His brooding abruptly ceased, and he decided that the danger to Lise had grown great enough for him to take action. Unless there was some sort of breakthrough, her charade would end tonight. Tomorrow he'd put her on the first train bound for Denver.

He rapped the bar for another drink.

"I really must insist, my dear."

"Honestly, Warren!" Lise shook a roguish finger at him. "You've been such a perfect gentleman. What's come over you?"

"Three nights of thinking about you—and gritting my teeth."

Lise was seated beside him on the sofa. When they'd entered the suite, she noticed there was something strange about his attitude. He had fixed their usual nightcap, but he'd been curiously silent. After a few sips of brandy, he had taken her glass and placed it beside his own on the coffee table. Then without a word he had wrapped her in a tight embrace and begun pawing her body. She'd wiggled loose only after a brief wrestling match.

"Why spoil things?" she said, looking at him now. "You agreed to let me decide in my own good time. Are you going to break your word?"

"Your own good time has the smell of forever."

"Oh, piddle!" She laughed and wagged her head. "Three nights isn't forever and you know it!"

"Haven't I treated you like a lady?"

"Yes."

"And haven't I exhibited both patience and restraint?"

"Of course."

"Then it's my turn for some consideration."

"Warren, all I'm asking for is a little more time."

"I need you now! Tonight!"

Mitchell seemed paralyzed by lust. His expression was somehow reminiscent of a tethered ram, and he stared at her with a look of glassy-eyed longing. He moistened his lower lip and the spell was suddenly broken. He grabbed her arms and pinned her to the corner of the sofa. She struggled, hammering at him with her fists in a vain attempt to escape. His hand slipped down the bodice of her dress and closed over one of her breasts.

A knock sounded at the door. Mitchell froze, his hand still cupping her breast. Then he sat erect and darted a glance at the door as the knock became louder. Lise straightened her disheveled dress and brushed a lock of hair off her forehead. He put a finger to his lips, signaling silence.

"Who is it?"

"It's me." A muffled male voice carried through the door. "Open up."

The voice galvanized Mitchell to action. He pulled Lise off the sofa and hustled her into the bedroom. He again cautioned her to silence and closed the door. The bedroom was dark, and as he turned away, Lise impulsively opened the door a crack. She put her eye to the slit and saw him tug his jacket straight as he crossed the parlor. He opened the hall door.

"Stephen!"

"You took your time about letting me in."

"Sorry."

"Are you alone?"

"Why, yes." Mitchell hastily closed the hall door. "What's wrong?"

"You're sure you don't have a woman in the bedroom?"

"Quite sure." Mitchell motioned with a casual gesture. "Have a look for yourself."

Elkton dropped into an armchair. "Where's the Kimble

woman? From everything I've heard, I halfway expected to find her here."

"She was," Mitchell said, seating himself on the sofa. "We had a brandy and then she went on to her room."

"So I see." Elkton studied the glasses on the coffee table. "Why didn't she finish her drink?"

"Well," Mitchell said as he fidgeted uncomfortably, "we had a slight misunderstanding, an argument."

"And she walked out on you?"

"No," Mitchell said defensively. "As a matter of fact, I asked her to leave."

"Good riddance," Elkton said in a sour tone. "I would have ordered you to break it off anyway."

"Come now," Mitchell bridled. "My personal life is my own, Stephen. I'll see her whenever I wish."

Elkton's brow furrowed. "Perhaps you'll change your mind when you hear what I have to say."

"I don't understand." Mitchell shook his head dumbly. "What possible interest could you have in Dora Kimble?"

"You ass!" Elkton said with a withering scowl. "Your infatuation with that bitch has brought us a world of grief."

"What are you talking about?"

"Tomorrow," Elkton replied angrily, "an editorial will appear in the *New Mexican*. Our old friend Max Flagg has blown the whistle on your party last night."

"Party?"

"Flagg termed it an orgy. His editorial charges that you used prostitutes and liquor to provide an evening of debauchery for the territory's leading politicians. He also names names—a complete guest list!"

"It's not true!" Mitchell protested. "I gave a party, not an orgy! Nothing improper took place. Nothing!"

Elkton fixed him with a jaundiced look. "You supplied girls and free liquor for men in public office. Whether or not they engaged in group fornication is immaterial. It has the earmarks of an orgy, and I assure you the label will stick."

"But"—Mitchell hesitated, groping for words—"I've thrown parties before, lots of parties. Why would Flagg ballyhoo this one?"

"In the past," Elkton said acidly, "you were discreet enough to include only other businessmen in the festivities. Does that answer your question?"

"You're referring to the political overtones."

"Exactly."

"How the devil did Flagg find out the names?"

Elkton arched one eyebrow and looked down his nose. "For a clever man, you're really quite naive, Warren."

"What do you mean?"

"I mean your personal life is an open book. You flaunt your mistress—the Kimble woman—in public. Then you use her to procure whores for your party."

"That's a lie!"

"No one will think so after reading Flagg's editorial. And it gets worse, much worse."

"In what way?"

"He implies that the men who attended your party are members of the ring. Then he goes on to speculate about your role." Elkton paused, and his voice rose suddenly. "He even hints that there's someone behind the scenes. Someone who directs the ring, masterminds it, using you as a front man."

"Good God!" Mitchell's face went ashen. "How did he get onto that?"

"How, indeed?" Elkton's eyes burned with intensity. "Whatever aroused his suspicions, they strike too close for comfort. I have no wish to see my name in print."

"What do you intend to do?"

"Serve notice," Elkton said with ominous calm. "I want Orville McMain killed. He was next on the list in Cimarron anyway."

"Why McMain?" Mitchell blurted. "Flagg wrote the editorial!"

"You are a fool," Elkton replied with cold hauteur. "Killing Flagg now would substantiate every charge he's made.

We'll take care of him once things have returned to normal. In the meantime, McMain's death will serve as a warning."

"I don't know, Stephen." Mitchell averted his gaze. "Won't that tend to stir up a hornest's nest? I mean, we've already killed one man in Cimarron—the minister."

Elkton gave him an evil look. "I wasn't soliciting your advice. Get hold of Donaghue and instruct him to take care of it. I want McMain dead by the end of the week."

Mitchell swallowed nervously. "If you're sure that's the best way . . ."

"Just do it!" Elkton said, rising to his feet. "Keep me informed of your progress."

Lise gently closed the bedroom door as Elkton prepared to leave. She moved swiftly to the bed and lay down with her back to the door. A few moments passed, then the door opened and Mitchell entered the bedroom. She rolled over, blinking in the glare of the light and sat up on the edge of the bed. Mitchell eyed her narrowly.

"Were you asleep?"

"Lemme tell you, honeybun." She laughed and walked past him into the parlor. "A working girl catches a snooze wherever she can. Why, did I miss something?"

"Nothing much." Mitchell was still watching her closely. "A friend with some personal problems dropped by looking for advice."

"Well, that's a relief!" She batted her china-blue eyes. "There for a minute I thought your wife had sicced the house detective on us."

"My wife!"

"You are married, aren't you?"

"I fail to see—"

"Don't worry, sweetie," she said with a vulpine smile. "I won't hold it against you. Nowadays it seems like all the good ones are married."

Mitchell took her by the shoulders. "You know I'm very fond of you, don't you?"

"Why, sure." She feigned surprise. "Why so serious?"

"A word to the wise," Mitchell said softly. "If you did overhear anything, then wipe it out of your mind. I wouldn't want anything—unpleasant to happen to you."

Her laugh was low and infectious. "Honey, where man talk's concerned, I'm deaf, dumb, and blind. You know, like the three monkeys—no see 'em, no hear 'em, no speak 'em!"

"I endorse the sentiment most heartily."

"And I'm bushed." She gave him a quick peck on the lips. "See you tomorrow night?"

"By all means."

"Sleep tight," she said with a coquettish grin. "And dream of yours truly."

Mitchell waited until the door closed. Then he walked to the sofa and flopped down. He felt reasonably certain she hadn't eavesdropped. But whether she had or not, Dora Kimble was the least of his troubles. He'd been ordered to arrange yet another man's death. And he thought it might very well be the proverbial last straw.

One murder too many.

Ten minutes later Lise stopped talking. Almost word for word, she had repeated the conversation between Mitchell and Elkton. Now, pausing to catch her breath, she awaited a reaction. Braddock seemed to look at her and past her at the same time.

"I think we'd better get you out of Santa Fe."

"Why?"

"You got lucky tonight," Braddock said quietly. "Mitchell's liable to sleep on it and change his mind."

"No chance!" Her eyes twinkled. "He's crazy about me!"

"Don't be too sure," Braddock cautioned. "You could put his head in a noose."

"That's the whole point!" She nodded vigorously. "I can testify to accessory to murder and conspiracy to murder. Put me on the witness stand and I'll hang them both!"

A stony look settled on Braddock's face. "Once before I

had a witness against a member of the ring. She was killed before she made it to the witness stand. I won't risk that with you." He stared straight at her. "Bright and early tomorrow, we'll sneak you aboard the train to Denver."

"I won't go!" she said stubbornly. "And that's final, Cole. So just save your breath."

"You'll go." Braddock's tone was harsh, roughly insistent. "You'll be on that train even if I have to hog-tie you."

"Like hell!" she flared. "I've earned the right to see this case through. And I'm staying, Cole! I mean it."

"Listen to reason," Braddock said with a stormy frown. "Your life's in danger, for Chrissake! Don't you understand that?"

"You want reason?" she replied with a charming little shrug. "All right, let's talk reason. Even with my testimony, you'd still try to drum up a corroborating witness. Am I right or wrong?"

"So?"

"So do it!" she chided him. "Find your witness and stop worrying about Mitchell. He's like putty in my hands! I'll just string him along until you're ready to move. You'll have to admit it makes sense, Cole."

"Only one trouble," Braddock said hesitantly. "All the other witnesses are in Cimarron."

"With or without me," she said in a hushed voice, "you'd still have to go back to Cimarron. You don't intend to let them kill McMain, do you?"

"I guess not," Braddock admitted grudgingly. "But I god-damn sure don't relish the notion of leaving you here by yourself."

"I'm a big girl." Her eyes sparkled with laughter. "And in a clutch, I've always got my Derringer. What could go wrong?"

"You want a list?"

"Stop fighting it, lover." She gave him a bright, theatrical smile. "You're going to let me stay and we both know it."

"Yeah, I reckon so," Braddock said uneasily. "All the same, I ought to have my head examined."

"I have a better idea."

"What's that?"

"Let's not talk any more—tonight."

Braddock smiled and took her at her word.

CHAPTER THIRTEEN

━━━◀▦▶━━━

The northbound pulled out of Santa Fe at eight o'clock the next morning. Braddock was on board, still posing as a Texas cattleman. His eyes were grim, and he watched the town fall behind with a sense of reluctance. Some dark premonition told him he'd made a mistake.

Earlier, he'd hedged his bet with Mitchell. Before leaving the hotel, he penned a note, signing it Elmer Boyd, and hired a bellboy to run it over to Mitchell's office. The note stated he'd been called back to Texas on ranch business and would return shortly. Whether or not the bogus check bounced before he returned was a moot point. He'd covered himself for the moment, providing Mitchell with a plausible excuse for his sudden departure. He doubted anyone would bother to check the story.

Lise was another matter entirely. He'd allowed himself to be persuaded by the logic of her argument. Still, he couldn't shake the feeling that he would regret the decision. He was haunted by a vision of Ellen Nesbeth. The similarity was like a nightmare repeating itself. The ring had killed one woman to stop her from testifying, and it could easily happen again.

However careful, Lise was nonetheless a tyro in outwitting sharks like Mitchell and Elkton. He thought the odds were in her favor; otherwise he would never have agreed. Yet he was far from sanguine about the outcome. There was no way to hedge the bet where she was concerned. And that preyed on his mind.

The train chugged into Raton late that afternoon. A night's layover enabled Braddock to resurrect the Reverend Titus Jacoby. When he emerged from the hotel the following morning, he wore the muttonchop sideburns and the turned-around collar of a minister. He retrieved his horse from the livery stable, where he'd rented a stall the previous week. Then he turned the swaybacked dun onto the wagon road toward Cimarron. The long day's ride allowed him to consider the knotty question of Orville McMain. He was duty bound to save McMain from the ring's assassins. Yet he was equally determined to convert one of them—preferably Florencio Donaghue—into a star witness. Only then would he have the testimony to corroborate Lise's story. And that one thought was still uppermost in his mind. Whatever the cost, her safety superseded all else.

Dusk was falling as Braddock rode into Cimarron. The plan he'd formulated was tricky and dangerous. Somewhat refined, it was a variation of the dodge he'd used to mousetrap the ring's hired guns in Cimarron Canyon. He was prepared for resistance on the part of McMain. There was every likelihood the publisher would simply refuse to go along. In the event reason failed, Braddock would then resort to some more drastic means of persuasion. He was also reconciled to the fact that he would have to deal with Buck Colter. The cooperation of McMain's bodyguard was essential, for without him the plan would never work. Braddock had him slated for a key role.

Orville McMain was again working late. Entering the newspaper office, Braddock exchanged greetings with Colter and walked on back to the publisher's desk. McMain was understandably startled by his sudden appearance. Braddock deflected his questions and launched into a quick recounting of events in Santa Fe. While he couldn't put his finger on the reason, he was still somewhat leery of telling McMain everything. So he made no mention of Lise or Stephen Elkton and thereby avoided any reference to the meeting in Mitchell's hotel suite. He related instead the contents of Max Flagg's editorial and the bombshell effect it had created in Santa Fe. Then he fabricated a story about Mitchell's reluctance to kill Flagg so soon after the editorial. He went on to explain Mitchell's ultimate decision, which involved direct orders to Florencio Donaghue. Orders to commit murder.

"You've been tagged," he concluded. "Mitchell wants an object lesson that'll get the message across, and you're it. Donaghue's hired guns will definitely try to kill you—no doubt about it."

McMain took the news with equanimity. "I suppose it was inevitable. As the leader of the coalition, I was a marked man anyway. Flagg's editorial just provoked them to take action now rather than later."

"Damn shame!" Braddock said fiercely. "I mean, it doesn't seem fair somehow. Flagg writes the editorial and you get shot at."

"One of life's inequities." McMain's smile was bleak. "I appreciate the warning, though. I'm very much in your debt."

"All part of the job." Braddock pursed his lips, considering. "What d'you aim to do?"

"Nothing," McMain said stoutly. "I won't run and I won't be intimidated. I intend to stand my ground."

"I admire your grit, Orville."

"Oh, it's not that," McMain said with false modesty. "I'm too bullheaded for my own good. I refuse to let the scoundrels dictate how I conduct my life."

"Suppose," Braddock began, scratching his jaw thoughtfully. "I'm only thinking out loud, you understand. But just suppose there was a way to beat them at their own game. Would you be interested?"

"Perhaps," McMain said slowly. "Do you have something in mind?"

"Yeah, after a fashion." Braddock leaned across the desk, his voice low and confidential. "All the way from Raton, I kept thinking how they've got us on the defensive. Then it occurred to me that it ought to be the other way round. It's high time we took it to them and attack!"

McMain nodded gravely. "The best defense is a good offense. It's one of the oldest maxims in warfare. But how do we go about it?"

"Deceit," Braddock said in a sidelong, conspiratorial glance. "What with me back in town, let's suppose a rumor pops up in the gossip mill. The word gets out that Reverend Jacoby really wasn't off riding the circuit. He was actually down in Santa Fe talking with the U.S. Marshal."

"Talking to him about what?"

"About the evidence you've got on Donaghue."

"Me!" McMain appeared bemused. "What evidence?"

"Evidence that Donaghue was behind the murder of Reverend Tolby."

"No such evidence exists!"

Braddock smiled. "You and me know that. But Donaghue couldn't take a chance. He'd have to assume it does exist, wouldn't he?"

"I imagine so," McMain said with an oddly perplexed look. "What would that accomplish, though?"

"Well, you see, that's where the second part of the rumor takes effect."

"The second part?"

"Yeah." Braddock regarded him with great calmness. "We let it slip out that the U.S. Marshal is on his way to Cimarron. It's all arranged for him to meet with you tomorrow night—here in your office—in secret. And at that time you'll personally deliver the evidence against Donaghue."

"But"—McMain frowned and shook his head—"it's all an invention. There's no evidence and no U.S. Marshal."

"True." Braddock grinned ferociously. "It's pure deceit, start to finish. Only, Donaghue won't know that."

"Good Lord!" McMain stared at him, immobile with disbelief. "It's another hoax, a trap, like the one at Cimarron Canyon. You're talking about using me as bait!"

"That's the general idea."

"And Donaghue will try to kill me!"

"You forget," Braddock reminded him, "Donaghue's already been ordered to kill you. So the attempt will be made no matter what we do."

McMain flushed and his voice went up a couple of octaves. "You left out one slight detail. I'd be sitting here like a staked-out goat. I wouldn't have a Chinaman's chance!"

"You're wrong," Braddock said flatly. "My way, we've got them on ground of our own choosing. We sucker them in and spring the trap and end up with some prisoners. In other words, we've got the edge."

"Pardon me if I take no comfort from the thought!"

"Consider the alternative." Braddock leaned forward, intensely earnest now. "You let them choose the time and place, and they've got the edge. They'll kill you sure as hell."

McMain blinked and swallowed hard. Then he very gingerly nodded his head. His voice was barely audible. "All right, we'll do it your way. I just hope you don't get too brave with my life."

Braddock sidestepped the objection. "I plan to capture whoever Donaghue sends to do the job. Then we'll offer him a deal to turn songbird and save his own neck. We ought to wind up with an open-and-shut case against Donaghue."

"And once we have Donaghue"—McMain smiled as though his teeth hurt—"we offer him a deal to testify against Mitchell. Is that it?"

"Why not?" Braddock said. "You hired me to bust the

Santa Fe Ring and Mitchell's the key. After we nail him, it's all over but the shouting."

"I'd be the first to say amen to that."

"One other thing," Braddock said almost as an after-thought. "We want the killers to think you're a sitting duck. Otherwise they're liable to play it safe and not take the bait. So we'll have to pull Colter off as your bodyguard."

"Hold on now!" McMain said, his voice clogged with apprehension. "You do that and I will be a sitting duck!"

An ironic smile tinged the corner of Braddock's mouth. "I'll be here with you, Orville. And I'm all the bodyguard you need."

"Try explaining that to Colter!"

"I intend to."

"How?"

"I've got a notion Colter and me speak the same language."

"I don't follow you."

"He will."

"God." McMain passed a hand across his eyes. "You ought to be a drummer. I think you just sold me a bill of goods."

Braddock chuckled and hitched back his chair. He walked toward the front of the office, circling around the counter. Colter stood like a gray-eyed monolith, the shotgun crooked over his arm. He nodded as Braddock halted a pace away.

"How's tricks, Reverend?"

"Not bad." Braddock kept his gaze level and cool. "You and me need to have a little talk."

"Fire away."

"I reckon you've already guessed I'm no minister."

"Now that you mention it," Colter said as he took a tug at his cookie-duster mustache, "I sort of had a sneakin' hunch along them lines."

"The reason I brought it up . . ." Braddock paused and stared at him for a long moment. "I'm in the position of having to take you into my confidence."

"That so?"

Braddock's eyes were very pale and direct. "I wouldn't take it kindly if you betrayed that confidence."

Colter's smile seemed frozen. "How would you take it?"

"Personal." Braddock underscored the word. "So personal you wouldn't like it the least little bit."

Colter barked a sharp, short laugh. "I've never been one to talk out of school. Whatever you've got to say, it stops here."

Braddock read no guile in him. "For openers, I'm a private detective."

"Figured you for a law dog of some variety or another."

"The name's Cole Braddock."

"No kiddin'?" Colter sounded impressed. "Not every day a fellow gets to meet a man with your reputation. Lots of talk about you around the bunkhouse."

"Don't believe everything you hear."

"Well, it's mostly what the boys read in the *Police Gazette*. Your name shows up pretty regular."

"Hope you took it with a pinch of salt."

"You mean it's not true?"

"Let's just say the *Gazette* tends to twist the facts."

Colter gave him a slow nod. "You still do work for the cattlemen's association?"

"Not for a while." Braddock appeared puzzled. "What makes you ask that?"

"I'm a cowhand," Colter said, grinning. "Heard you've run down some real bad hombres, rustlers and the like."

"Past history," Braddock said with a dismissive gesture. "I'm more concerned with McMain right now."

"What about him?"

"Donaghue's been ordered to punch his ticket."

"What else is new? We've been expectin' it ever since Reverend Tolby was killed."

"Suppose I told you the order came direct from Santa Fe?"

"Uh-huh!" Colter seemed to stand a bit taller. "Guess it's

time for me to get extra extra careful. Is that what you're tryin' to say?"

"Just the opposite," Braddock told him. "I want to pull you off the job."

"Leave him without a bodyguard?"

"Yeah."

"What the hell for?"

"You and me are going to do a little play-acting."

"Play-acting?" Colter said dubiously. "I wouldn't exactly call that my strong suit."

"Nothing to it," Braddock observed. "All you do is pretend you're something you're not. That ought to be second nature to you by now."

Colter stiffened. "You tryin' to tell me something?"

"You tell me," Braddock said with a hard look. "Why would a cowhand carry a double-action pistol and a fancy shotgun?"

"I carry the best I can afford. What's so peculiar about that?"

"Nothing." Braddock fixed him with an inquiring gaze. "Not by itself anyway. But when you add it to other things, it makes a man wonder."

"Other things?"

Braddock paused, staring him straight in the eye. "What was your momma—Cheyenne or Sioux?"

Colter stared back at him. "You oughtn't ask a man personal questions. It's not polite."

"Look at it this way," Braddock said casually. "I've told you who I am, and in a manner of speaking, I know who you aren't. You keep my secret and I'll keep yours."

"What makes you think I'm tryin' to hide anything?"

"Because you haven't told anyone."

"Says who?"

"It's what they don't say. A thing like that would be a pretty hot item. But nobody's put the bee in my ear, not a word. See what I mean?"

Colter wrestled with himself a moment, then shrugged.

"All right, you've got yourself a trade-off. What happens now?"

"We put on a play for the town gossips."

"How's it work?"

Braddock outlined the plan. The longer he talked, the better it sounded. Colter listened attentively and a slow grin spread over his face. He thought it entirely possible someone would get killed.

And he had a good idea who.

CHAPTER FOURTEEN

Warren Mitchell studied the note. His brow furrowed and a muscle twitched at the corner of his mouth. He dropped the slip of paper on his desk.

Yesterday he had questioned the bellboy at length. What he'd learned tended to confirm everything contained in Boyd's note. Elmer Boyd had boarded the morning northbound, ticketed through to Raton. From there, according to what Boyd had told the bellboy, he intended to travel by stagecoach to Fort Worth. Apart from that, the bellboy had nothing to offer.

Hands locked behind his head, Mitchell tilted back in his chair. His nerves were on edge and his stomach churned with gassy discomfort. He'd read the note a dozen times, perhaps more. On the surface it all sounded very reasonable, very legitimate. Yet he couldn't shake the feeling that there was something more behind Elmer Boyd's abrupt departure. It boggled the mind that a man would so casually put a three-million-dollar deal on the back burner. What sort of ranching problems could be of such magnitude that it would send

Boyd scurrying back to Texas? No ready answer presented itself.

Still, Mitchell preferred to accept the note at face value. Elmer Boyd was an odd bird, albeit a rich one, and apparently a man of impulsive nature. Then, too, he was a Texan, and as everyone knew, Texans were a strange breed. Perhaps in Boyd's mind some sudden difficulty at the ranch took precedence over all else. The fact remained that the Guadalupe County deal had been clinched, and Boyd's check for three million had been deposited. There was nothing in Boyd's departure that would materially affect what amounted to an ironclad agreement. Unless . . .

Mitchell pushed the thought aside. The possibility that the check was no good seemed wildly irrational, absurd. Of course, if the problem in Texas was financial and Boyd needed to cover the check, that would certainly explain his departure. Or if sufficient funds no longer existed, Boyd was now beyond the reach of New Mexico courts. But all that was borrowing trouble, Mitchell told himself, and at a time when he was already juggling trouble enough. Which was one of the major reasons he hadn't mentioned Boyd's departure to Stephen Elkton.

In fact, he had studiously avoided Elkton since their meeting two nights ago. The passage of time had done nothing to diminish his overriding sense of apprehension. The more he pondered it, the more convinced he became that Orville McMain's death would merely inflame an already volatile situation. He considered Elkton's order to kill the newspaperman not just imprudent; it was a senseless provocation that would serve no useful purpose. Instead, it would act as a goad on the Cimarron Coalition and unite the various factions as never before. The upshot would be even stronger opposition, perhaps some organized form of retaliation. And worse, it would bring greater public support for the coalition.

It was this latter point that troubled Mitchell most of all. By nature, he was not a violent man. In truth, just the thought of shooting someone left him a bit sick. On occasion, at Elkton's insistence he had orchestrated the death of those who posed a direct threat to the ring. Yet it was not his style, and he'd always felt somehow sullied in the aftermath. He preferred intellect to brute force. His method was to finesse an opponent, not kill him.

And his intellect warned him that the death of McMain represented a monumental hazard. For now, the Cimarron Coalition was largely isolated within Colfax County. In turn, strong opposition from the Democrats was limited principally to Santa Fe. But another killing might very well bridge the gap and bring these two very disparate groups into formal alliance. Any ground swell of public support would then tend to create a wave effect throughout the territory. Once set in motion, such a populist movement could easily prove irresistible.

The end result, in Mitchell's view, might represent a symbolic death knell for the Santa Fe Ring. On a personal note, it would mean a finish to both the power and prominence he had attained in territorial business affairs. Yet, over the years he'd learned never to second-guess Stephen Elkton. The soft-spoken lawyer was a shrewd manipulator of men and events, with an uncanny insight into the forces that shaped ordinary people's lives. He was, moreover, a man of absolute amorality, without conscience or scruples. He considered violence, even murder, nothing more than an expedient in the normal course of business.

For good reason, then, Mitchell had decided to follow orders. To do otherwise would constitute an act of betrayal in Elkton's view. And Mitchell knew that, inexorably, such an act would lead to his own execution. All the more so since he was already in hot water over Dora Kimble. The *New Mexican*'s exposé on his "orgy for politicos" had rolled off the presses yesterday. As Santa Fe's newest variety sensation, the girl's name had received prominent mention. Which was still another reason why he had avoided Elkton. Out of sight was by no means out of mind, especially with his name publicly linked to a tart who sang dirty ballads, but low visibility seemed his best option for the moment.

As for the girl herself, he suddenly felt very much the fool. His campaign to seduce her seemed, in retrospect, a rather cruel joke. Elkton's talk of murder, with the girl secreted in the bedroom, had unsettled him more than he cared to admit. Since then, he'd displayed all the virility of an aging eunuch. Solely as a matter of pride, he had appeared at the Tivoli last night and brought her back to the hotel. But it was an act of sheer bravado, and overall a little demoralizing. He doubted that even Dora Kimble, on her finest night, could make him rise to the occasion.

Still, all things considered, the girl was the least of his problems. Yesterday he'd sent a telegraph message to Donaghue in Cimarron. The wire was drafted in the form of a business communication and signed with a fictitious name. It was a prearranged code, designed for no other purpose than to summon Donaghue to Santa Fe. The order he would pass along to Donaghue was not just personally distasteful. He thought it a mistake, and the potential repercussions seemed staggering to contemplate. Yet, given the circumstances, he could only play the cards as dealt.

His hands were sweating as he folded Elmer Boyd's note and stuck it in the desk drawer.

Florencio Donaghue stepped off the southbound train late that afternoon. He walked directly from the depot to the plaza, mingling with shoppers who crowded the boardwalk. He tried very hard to look unobtrusive.

A thick-set man, Donaghue was perspiring heavily. But it was neither exertion nor the westerly afternoon sun that made him sweat. All the way from Cimarron, he'd thought of nothing but the telegraph message. Only last month he had received a similar wire summoning him to Santa Fe. Upon arriving in Mitchell's office, he had been ordered to arrange the death of Reverend John Tolby. Today, he was worried that another wire meant still another death. He wanted nothing more to do with murder.

Donaghue loitered around on the plaza until sundown. As twilight deepened, he made his way to the Mercantile National Bank. There were few passersby and he turned, unobserved, into the stairwell. He knew Mitchell's secretary would have left for the day, and he felt relatively assured that the office would be empty. Upstairs he proceeded along the corridor to the Santa Fe Land & Development Company. He entered swiftly, without knocking.

"Someone there?" Mitchell called from the inner office.

"It's me," Donaghue answered.

"Lock the door."

Donaghue complied, then crossed the outer room. He found Mitchell, who was bathed in the glow of an overhead lamp, waiting with impatience. There was no offer of a handshake and he had expected none. He took a chair before the desk.

"I got your wire."

"So I see," Mitchell said tonelessly. "I assume you took the usual precautions?"

There was a patronizing undertone to the question. Accustomed to it by now, Donaghue knew that it had nothing to do with their business relationship. He was part Irish and part Mexican, and Mitchell looked upon him as an intelligent half-breed. He understood, and he took no offense. He merely nodded, and said, "I was not followed."

Mitchell shrugged. "How are things in Cimarron?"

"Pretty much routine. Just the usual problems."

"No more trouble from the new preacher, Jacoby?"

"He's out riding the circuit. So far as I know, he hadn't come back when I left. Any special reason you ask?"

"Just curiosity. What's new with Orville McMain?"

"Same old thing. He keeps folks stirred up with his editorials. Course, he's a windbag and nobody takes any of that stuff too serious."

"I do."

Something in Mitchell's voice alerted him. Donaghue felt the sweat puddle under his armpits. "You called me down here to talk about McMain?"

"Yes," Mitchell said evenly. "I want him—eliminated."

"Do you think that's smart?"

"Are you questioning my decision?"

"Not exactly. I just don't think it's a good move right now."

Mitchell stared at him. "I wasn't asking your advice. Nor is the matter open to debate. I want it done immediately."

For years Donaghue had been the political kingfish of Colfax County. Yet he was a big fish in a very small pond. Apart from the townspeople in Cimarron, the voting rolls were dominated by homesteaders and ranchers. There was little opportunity for corruption and graft and even less reason to bribe a politician. No one got rich serving in public office.

Then, operating in absolute secrecy, Mitchell's company bought the Beaubien-Miranda land grant. Prior to the public announcement, Mitchell recruited Donaghue into the organization. Along with Donaghue, he also got control of the Colfax County political machine. In time, with the help of shady federal officials, the land grant was expanded to two million acres. Donaghue and his courthouse cronies protected the ring's interests in the legal disputes that followed. Quite literally, they'd sold their souls for a chance at the brass ring, and betrayed their friends and neighbors in the process.

Even today, Donaghue still believed Mitchell to be the head of the Santa Fe Ring. He had dealt only with Mitchell throughout their long association. Like everyone else, he knew that Mitchell was the power broker in territorial politics and a man whose influence stretched all the way to Washington. It had never occurred to him that Mitchell too might take orders, parrot the commands of some higher authority. Had he been told the truth, he would have scoffed in open derision, for he believed Mitchell to be evil incarnate, one of the Devil's own. Were he to disobey an order, he hadn't the slightest doubt that his life would be forfeit.

"Mr. Mitchell," he said now, "I was only trying to warn you. We've killed one preacher and tried to kill another. Folks just won't hold still for—"

"Spare me the lecture! We'll deal with the coalition members as the occasion demands. In the meantime, I expect you to do as you're told."

"Why not let Ortega and Johnson handle it? Hell, at least they're professionals."

Donaghue's reference was to a couple of hired guns on the ring's payroll. Their talents had been employed to great effect in the Lincoln County War. But Mitchell preferred to use them only in the most extreme circumstances. He shook his head.

"I'm offering you a chance to redeem yourself. You and your men failed me with Jacoby. Outwitted and outfought by a preacher, no less! I suggest you exercise greater ingenuity with Orville McMain."

"You're the boss," Donaghue said with a resigned look. "I just hope it doesn't blow the lid off things."

"You worry too much, Florencio."

"Maybe it's because I understand common folks, Mr. Mitchell. They try to stick by the law, but they've got their limits. You push 'em too far and they'll push back."

"Very interesting. Suppose you catch the evening northbound and get on back to Cimarron. I want this business finished quickly."

Donaghue understood he'd been dismissed. He rose with a nod and shambled out of the office. A key rattled in the lock, then the hallway door opened and closed.

Mitchell sat for a moment in the deepening silence. It occurred to him that Donaghue was a wiser man than Stephen Elkton. But, then, the wise seldom governed. In the end, might made right, and it was the strong who ruled.

The irony of it all had often amused him in the past. He wondered why he couldn't laugh tonight.

CHAPTER FIFTEEN

Shortly before noon the next day, Braddock stopped by the newspaper office. A few minutes later he emerged with Colter at his side, and they walked toward the center of town. Passersby noticed that Colter was in a foul mood, and further, that he wasn't carrying his shotgun. The preacher was talking to him in a low voice, gesturing rapidly but with no apparent success. Colter's replies were sharp and surly, increasingly loud.

Uptown, they entered a café directly across from the courthouse. The noontime crowd, most of whom worked for the county, looked around in amazement. For almost a month, Colter hadn't let Orville McMain out of his sight. Wherever the publisher went, night or day, the shotgun-toting cowhand had been his constant shadow. Now, inexplicably, Colter was seating himself at a table with Reverend Titus Jacoby. All the more mystifying, Colter's expression was that of a mad bull hooking at cobwebs. Everyone within earshot leaned closer to catch the conversation.

"I don't care what you say, parson. He's plumb off his rocker!"

"Now, now," Braddock soothed. "You mustn't take it personally. Orville is simply doing what he thinks best."

"For my money, he's actin' like the town idjit!"

A waitress appeared and the conversation momentarily ceased. Colter ordered beefsteak and Braddock settled for the blue-plate special. The waitress went away and Colter sat lost in a glowering funk. Braddock clucked sympathetically, wagging his head.

"I do believe you're being too harsh on yourself—and Orville."

"Not by half," Colter grunted. "I should've talked him out of it. He's just not thinkin' straight!"

"You can only advise, Buck. In the end the decision is his alone."

"Oh, yeah?" Colter said in an abrasive tone. "Nobody in the coalition's gonna think so. I mean, there he sits with the evidence—"

"Lower your voice," Braddock admonished him. "We're in a public place."

"Sorry, parson." Colter leaned forward and went on in a froggy rasp. "Anyway, he's got the goods on the killers and he's just gonna sit there on his duff waitin' for the U.S. Marshal. It don't make sense!"

"Why not?" Braddock said, not asking a question. "I spoke with the marshal myself. He promised he would arrive no later than tonight. You know that."

"Course I know it!" Colter snorted. "But that don't justify Orville tellin' me to take a powder. Who's gonna look after him till the marshal shows?"

"Calm yourself," Braddock temporized. "You've performed sterling duty and Orville saw no need to impose on you further. Nothing will happen to him between now and tonight."

"Hope so, parson. I shore do hope so!"

"Set your mind at rest, Buck. He's perfectly safe."

The waitress, as though on cue, returned with their meals. Colter dug into his charred steak and Braddock took a bite of meat loaf. A look passed between them, and Colter got the message. All the lines had been spoken and their one-act drama had played to a receptive audience. It was now time to lower the curtain.

Braddock was pleased with himself. There had been no mention of Reverend Tolby or Florencio Donaghue. But to those sitting nearby, the murdered preacher and Cimarron's political kingfish were part and parcel of the conversation. Before the noon hour was over, the gossip mill in the court-house would be churning at full speed. Word of McMain's meeting with the U.S. Marshal would spread, and with each retelling, the evidence would broaden in scope. By sundown Donaghue would have arrived at the only logical conclusion. Tonight was the night Orville McMain must be killed.

All in all, Braddock thought the ruse was a small gem. And he was vastly impressed by Colter's performance. Whatever his real name, there was no question about his gift for deception.

The young half-breed was a born ham.

The last step in the ruse was performed in public view.

After their noon meal, Braddock and Colter returned to the newspaper office. McMain, who was in a state of nervous agitation, questioned them at length. Braddock assured him that all had gone well at the café. The courthouse crowd had swallowed the story whole.

As Braddock turned to leave, Colter paused to collect his shotgun. McMain acted quickly, his movements momentarily obscured behind the counter. He stuffed a folded slip of paper into Colter's vest pocket, pushing it out of sight. He shook his head, forestalling questions; his eyes beseeched the younger man to say nothing. Colter hefted his shotgun and followed Braddock out the door.

From the newspaper, they walked down to the livery stable. There Colter saddled his horse, hesitating afterward on the streets for a brief handshake with Braddock. Then he mounted and rode north out of town. Everyone watching assumed his destination was Isaac Coleman's ranch, where he was employed as a cowhand. His departure was the clincher, visible proof that he'd been dismissed as McMain's bodyguard. It was, in fact, more truth than playacting. The young half-breed's offer of assistance had been refused yesterday and yet again on the noontime stroll to the café. Braddock preferred to work alone.

A mile or so outside town, Colter reined to a halt. He fished the slip of paper from his vest pocket and unfolded it. His eyes narrowed as he scanned the note. Hastily scrawled, it was a message to Isaac Coleman. It revealed Braddock's identity and the results of his undercover work to date. Then, in an apprehensive tone, it outlined the details of Braddock's plan for tonight. Fearful the plan would go awry, McMain asked Coleman and Allison to slip into town before dark. He cautioned them not to alert Braddock to their presence. Nonetheless, they were to keep a close watch on the newspaper office and await his signal. He wanted them near at hand at the first sign of trouble.

Colter tucked the note back into his vest pocket. With the reins looped around the saddle horn, he built a smoke and lit up. He sat there, his expression abstracted, mentally reviewing the situation. His immediate impulse was to ride back to town and inform Braddock. But that would compromise McMain, who had entrusted him to act in good faith. Then, too, there was the matter of his employer, Isaac Coleman. He owed a certain loyalty to the man who paid his wages.

Yet the whole thing stuck in his craw. Braddock had confided in him, enlisting his support. The detective clearly extended his trust to few people. Their handshake, in Braddock's view, represented an agreement, one man's bond to the other. In the strictest sense, delivering the message wasn't a betrayal of that trust. Colter had agreed to only one thing; not to personally divulge Braddock's true identity. It was the note that would actually let the cat out of the bag. He was nothing more than a message bearer.

Colter grunted to himself. While it wasn't betrayal, it wasn't altogether aboveboard either. But he was caught in the middle, pulled in opposite directions by McMain and Braddock. Whichever way he leaned, one or the other of them would feel he'd broken faith. So he couldn't win, for the simple reason that there was no way to satisfy everybody. Put in that light, the choice boiled down to no choice at all. His greatest loyalty was to the man who paid him top dollar to act as McMain's bodyguard. And the note was, after all, addressed to Isaac Coleman.

Gathering the reins, Colter gigged his horse into a lope. Only now, with the decision made, would he allow himself to consider what bothered him most. His uneasiness about the note centered to a large degree on Clay Allison. From all he'd seen, Allison was a loudmouthed braggart who bullied other people for the sheer sport of it. There was a mad-dog mentality about Allison, and that warped quality had resulted in the deaths of several men. Allison's only saving grace was that he'd somehow earned the respect of Isaac Coleman. Their friendship went back many years, and in certain ways they were closer than blood kin. Coleman treated him somewhat like a Dutch uncle.

A good listener, Colter had heard several variations of the same story. Allison and Coleman had first met in Texas, where they worked as cowhands for the legendary Charlie Goodnight. In 1870 they had teamed up as stock contractors, trailing a herd to New Mexico Territory. Their payment, taken in lieu of cash, was three hundred head of cattle. With breeder stock, they had then laid claim to a vast stretch of grazing land north of Cimarron. Later, after the operation had grown to a respectable size, they'd split the land and cattle down the middle. Their ranches, which abutted one another, eventually became the largest outfits in Colfax County.

Other stories, spoken of less openly, were also common bunkhouse fare. Before his Texas days, Allison was reported to have been discharged from the Confederate Army for emotional instability. The tale took on credence as his reputation

spread for getting into drunken brawls and seemingly mind-
less shooting scrapes. He was generally feared for his murderous temper, and local wisdom had it that he went a bit
loony when antagonized. Whatever the truth of the rumors,
there was no questioning his violent nature. He was known,
with ample reason, as a mankiller.

The single moderating influence in Allison's life was
Isaac Coleman. Still, in the extreme not even Coleman could
control him. And that was what worried Colter most of all.
Anyone who organized a lynching bee and later decapitated
the guest of honor was a man who warranted concern. Some
years ago, Allison had done precisely that and displayed
the severed head in a Cimarron saloon. So his crazy streak
made him dangerous, and not just to his enemies.

Colter's uneasiness ticked a notch higher. The note burned
in his vest pocket like a red-hot coal, and he silently cursed
Orville McMain. He rode north with the disquieting sense
that he was headed in the wrong direction.

The ranch compound was located on a rise overlooking a
wooded creek. The house was a sprawling adobe structure,
faintly resembling a fort. Nearby were several outbuildings,
the bunkhouse, and a large corral. The place looked deserted.

Colter checked the angle of the sun. It was going on three
o'clock and he wondered if Coleman was out working with
the other hands. Then, approaching the house, he spotted a
horse standing hip-shot at the hitch rack. His edgy feeling
took a turn for the worse. The mousy dun cow pony belonged
to Clay Allison.

Coleman's wife met him at the door. She was a plain
woman who looked older than her years. Her mouth was
perpetually down-turned, and in answer to his question, she
waved him along the hall. Walking to the end of the corridor, he paused in the doorway of Coleman's office. The ranch
owner was seated at a rolltop desk, an open ledger spread before him. Allison was slouched nearby in a leather armchair.

"Colter!" Allison's voice sounded surprised. "Where the hell'd you drop from?"

"Allison." Colter nodded. "Mr. Coleman."

Coleman motioned him forward. "C'mon in, Buck. How come you're not in Cimarron?"

"It's a long story."

Colter told it briefly. From Braddock's arrival yesterday to his own departure today, he covered the salient points. Throughout the recounting, he referred to Braddock as "Reverend Jacoby." It merely delayed the inevitable, but he felt he'd at least kept his word. He concluded by handing Coleman the note.

Coleman stiffened as he read McMain's words. He passed the note to Allison and looked around. "How long have you known about Braddock?"

"Yesterday," Colter said flatly. "He told me who he was after he'd talked to McMain. By then they'd already agreed on the plan."

"Plan!" Allison shouted. "Hell, that ain't no plan. It's goddamn suicide!"

"Hold on, Clay," Coleman interjected. "Let's take first things first. Buck, you say you only found out about Braddock yesterday?"

"That's right."

"You got any idea when McMain hired him?"

"Nope."

"Any notion at all of how he contacted Braddock?"

"Nobody said and I never asked."

Allison snorted. "Nobody has to say. It's got the smell of Frank Kirkland's work. Only a dumb-ass lawyer would waste our money on a dee-tective."

"Not exactly a waste," Colter observed. "Braddock's reputation speaks for itself. He generally gets the job done."

Allison peered at him. "You takin' sides?"

"I'm just stating a fact."

"Sounds to me like you and Braddock got real cozy."

"Allison," Colter said evenly, "how it sounds to you don't concern me. Savvy?"

Allison started out of his chair. Coleman jumped to his feet, arms outstretched. "You two pull in your horns! We haven't got time for personal arguments."

"Wouldn't take long," Allison grated. "I'd settle his hash lickety-split."

Colter just smiled. Coleman stepped between them, his expression somber. "Buck, what's your best guess? You think Braddock's scheme will sucker them into makin' a try on McMain?"

"If I was Donaghue," Colter allowed, "I'd figure it was tonight or never. Braddock laid the bait pretty slick."

"How much faith you got in Braddock? Any chance they'll get past him and kill McMain?"

"I reckon there's always a chance. But if I was a bettin' man, I'd say the odds favor Braddock."

"Why's that?"

"Just a hunch. He strikes me as the kind that don't make mistakes. In his line of work, he can't afford it."

"Yeah," Coleman mused almost to himself. "I suspect you're right."

"Wouldn't hurt to play along and find out."

"Tell you what, Buck. Joe Phelps and Jack Noonan are workin' the north fork. They're pretty handy boys when push comes to shove. Go fetch 'em for me and hotfoot it on back here."

"You mean to let Braddock make his play?"

"Why not? Like you said, it's his line of work."

After Colter was gone, Allison rose from his chair. He cocked one eye at Coleman. "I hear the wheels turnin'. What you got in mind, Isaac?"

"We'll hide and watch. See what Braddock flushes out of the weeds."

"Go on, there's more to it than that."

"Well, the worst that could happen"—Coleman paused, his mouth razored in a crafty smile—"is that poor ol' Orville will get his ass shot off. And it wouldn't bother me a whole hell of a lot if he does. Wasn't right, him not tellin' us about Braddock."

"And whatever happens, we end up a step closer to Donaghue. Is that it?"

"We might just get the goods on Donaghue. We're shore as hell due a change of luck."

"You're one sly son of a bitch, Isaac. I like it, like it a lot."

"Yeah, but there's a hair in thc butter. We don't wanna get ourselves crosswise of Braddock."

"Comes down to it, you let me handle that. I talk the kind of language he understands."

"Just keep your head, Clay. Don't go off on one of your— spells."

"Goddammit, you know better'n that, Isaac. When'd I ever cause trouble 'less it was necessary?"

Coleman thought it prudent not to answer. He slapped the other man on the shoulder and went off in search of his wife. Allison stared after him, grinning strangely. His eyes were fixed in a faraway look.

As though from a great distance, a voice spoke to him and he laughed softly to himself. Tonight seemed a long time to wait.

CHAPTER SIXTEEN

The moon went behind a cloud. For a moment the alley was cloaked in inky darkness. Then the cloud scudded past and the town was bathed in spectral moonlight. A dog barked somewhere in the distance.

On the street lampposts flickered like guttering candles. The supper hour had come and gone, and the street itself was virtually deserted. Farther uptown, the sound of a piano and laughter drifted faintly from the saloon. Then a ghostly stillness settled over Cimarron.

The front window of the *Beacon* was lit by the glow of a single lamp. The alleyway directly beside the newspaper separated it from a dry goods emporium. The newspaper had no side windows, but a door opened onto the alley. Opposite the door a narrow loading platform jutted outward from the emporium's stockroom.

Braddock stood hidden in the shadows. He was pressed back against the loading platform door, which was recessed slightly into the wall. A lamppost lit the mouth of the alley, and toward the rear of the buildings the far end was dappled with moonlight. All the more important, directly across from him was the side door of the newspaper. It was the reason he'd chosen this particular spot.

The plan had gone off smoothly. After Colter's departure, Orville McMain spent the afternoon at the newspaper and continued working into the evening. With nightfall, Braddock had left his hotel by the rear entrance and made his way to the alley. There he'd taken up a post on the loading platform, all but invisible in the shadowed doorway. He'd long ago mastered the skills essential to a stakeout or a manhunt. He stood perfectly still, loose and relaxed, avoiding any movement that might betray his position. He thought it would be a short wait.

Under normal circumstances, Braddock knew the killers would have delayed until McMain left the newspaper. Then, on his way home the publisher would have been shot down on some dark side street. Yet the circumstances tonight were anything but normal. A U.S. Marshal was expected, and the killers would have to strike before McMain had a chance to surrender the evidence. Their attempt would almost certainly be made by the side door; the risk of being spotted on the street was much too great. So, exactly as he'd planned, Braddock waited on ground of his own choosing. The killers had lost the edge.

Shortly before ten, the crunch of dirt underfoot sounded at the end of the alley. Braddock's every sense alerted, and his hand snaked inside his suit jacket. The footsteps were slow and stealthy, and his ears told him there was only one man. Several moments later a figure emerged from the shadows and halted at the side door. The light from the street lamp glinted on gun metal as he took hold of the doorknob. Braddock pulled his Colt and thumbed the hammer.

"Don't move or you're dead!"

The man froze rock-still. Braddock crossed the loading platform and stepped to the ground. He quickly disarmed the man, stuffing the pistol in his waistband. Then he rapped out a sharp command.

"Inside! The door's unlocked."

Braddock followed him through the door and slammed it shut. McMain was standing behind his desk, watching intently as they moved from the darkened pressroom into the office. Braddock nudged the man forward and shoved him down in a chair. In the light from the desk lamp, his features were angular, with the swarthy complexion of a Mexican. His mouth was down-turned beneath a droopy mustache, and his eyes were black as obsidian. His expression was stoic.

Braddock holstered the Colt. "How about it, Orville? Do you recognize him?"

"Certainly," McMain replied. "His name is Cruz Vega."

"Well, now." Braddock nodded, smiling. "We met once before, didn't we, Vega?"

"No, señor," Vega said with a guttural accent. "I believe you are mistaken."

"Cimarron Canyon," Braddock reminded him. "We swapped lead out there not too long ago."

"I know nothing of that, señor."

"Course you do," Braddock said matter-of-factly. "That's the day I killed your cousin—Manuel Cardenas."

Vega's eyes shuttled away. "I know you killed Manuel, señor. But I was not there."

"You're here tonight, though."

"Sí."

"And you were sent here to kill Mr. McMain."

"How could you prove a thing like that?"

"You had a gun in your hand."

"A very small crime, señor. Verdad?"

The front door abruptly burst open. Clay Allison and Isaac Coleman trooped into the office. The ranchers were followed by Buck Colter and two more men who had the look of cowhands. Allison and Coleman moved around the counter and stopped before the desk. Allison glared at McMain.

"You were supposed to signal us, Orville."

"I haven't had a chance."

"Well, it's a damn good thing I had somebody watchin' the window. We could've grown beards waitin' on you."

"Hold it," Braddock interrupted. "What's going on here?"

Allison chuckled and flashed a wide grin. "Orville figured you could use some help—and we're it!"

Braddock turned to McMain. "Is that true?"

"Yes." McMain gave him a hangdog look. "I wasn't convinced you could do it all by yourself. So I asked Buck to carry a message for me."

"Colter told them?"

"No," McMain amended hastily. "I wrote a note explaining the situation."

Braddock's frown deepened. "How much do they know?"

"Everything," McMain said with a weak smile. "I couldn't ask them to help and leave them in the dark. Besides, they're members of the coalition. They have a right to know."

"That wasn't part of our agreement."

"Simmer down," Allison broke in. "We're all workin' toward the same end. No need to get your nose out of joint."

"Stay out of it, Allison!" Braddock's jaw set in a hard line. "Your help's not needed and I don't want it. Take your men and vamoose—now!"

A moment elapsed while they stared at one another. Then Allison let go with a rolling laugh. "Well, I'll tell you how it's gonna be, Mr. Detective. You've got our help whether you want it or not. What d'you say to that?"

"I say clear out"—Braddock's eyes hooded—"and do it damn quick."

"By jingo!" Allison said with a mirthless smile. "You talk like the cock o' the walk when you ought to be listenin' with both ears. Whyn't you take a peek and see what Isaac's holdin' on you?"

There was a metallic whirr as Isaac Coleman eared back the hammer on his six-gun. Braddock turned his head and saw the snout of the pistol centered on his chest. Allison relieved him of the Colt and the revolver jammed in his waistband, and dropped them on the desk. Then he moved past

Braddock and halted in front of Vega. He spoke to McMain over his shoulder.

"What's the greaser told you so far?"

"Nothing," McMain said blankly. "He refused to admit anything."

"Do tell!" Allison spit on his hands and rubbed them together. "Well, I got some medicine that'll open his mouth lickety-split."

"Allison!" Braddock's voice stopped him. "Vega is my prisoner. Touch him and you'll answer to me."

"Isaac, keep our detective friend covered. I'm gonna give this greaser a taste of knuckle sandwich."

Allison laughed a wild, braying laugh. Then his fist lashed out in a blurred movement. The blow connected with a sharp crack, and Vega slammed backward in the chair. A bright fountain of blood jetted from his nose, spilling down over his mustache. Before he could recover, Allison clubbed him on the side of the jaw and his head bounced off the wall. He slumped forward and Allison caught him with a looping roundhouse that knocked him out of the chair and onto the floor. Allison took a step back and kicked him in the pit of the stomach.

Vega's mouth snapped open in a whoofing whoosh of breath. He doubled over and clutched his midsection, eyes bulging with pain. His nose was broken and a jagged cut had been opened over his right eyebrow. He grunted as Allison lifted him bodily off the floor and propped him up in the chair. His mustache glistened wetly and the whole right side of his face was covered with blood. Allison took a handful of hair and wrenched his head back against the wall. The rancher's gaze was dulled and out of focus.

"Had enough?" Allison shook him like a rag doll. "You ready to gimme some straight talk, amigo?"

Vega coughed raggedly. *"No hablo inglés."*

"Whoo-ee!" Allison cackled. "You are some tough pepper-gut! Wanna think it over, change your mind? Give us just a few words!"

"No sé."

"You'll savvy before we're done, greaser."

Allison backhanded him across the mouth. Vega brought his arms up, attempting to protect himself, but Allison grabbed him by the lapels of his coat and pinned him to the wall. Supporting him with one hand, Allison then administered a brutal beating. His right arm worked like a piston, and the blows were delivered with methodical ferocity. Vega's features dissolved into a pulped mass that looked something like a freshly butchered side of beef. A final punch broke off his front teeth at the gum line, and he sagged sideways into a chair. Allison gripped his hair, jerking him upright.

"Last chance," Allison said in a jovially menacing voice. "Talk to me or I'll beat you to death where you sit."

Vega gagged and spit out a mouthful of teeth. The stumps left a bloody gap in his gums, and his lips were like puffed mush. His left eye was swollen completely shut and the split over his right eyebrow had been widened to a raw wound. He took several deep breaths, frothing bubbles from his mouth like a goldfish. Then he slowly nodded his head.

"That's the ticket!" Allison crowed. "Just to show you there's no hard feelin's, we'll start with something simple. You remember Reverend Tolby, don't you?"

"Sí."

"And you killed him, didn't you?"

"Sí."

"Who helped you?"

"Manuel Cardenas."

"He's dead," Allison scoffed. "Who else?"

"Pancho Griego."

"Who's he?"

"Mi compañero," Vega mumbled. "A friend. He did not help kill Reverend Tolby, but he help us other times."

"He live in Cimarron?"

"No."

"Where's he from?"

"Rayado."

"That little burg south of here?"

"*Sí.*"

"All right," Allison said with a vinegary satisfaction. "You're whistlin' the tune I wanna hear. Now we'll get down to the important stuff. Who paid you to kill Reverend Tolby?"

"No one."

Allison cuffed him across the mouth. "You're not listenin', amigo. Who was it that hired you?"

"We robbed him, señor. Only the two of us; no one else. *Es verdad.*"

"The truth, hell!"

Allison drew his pistol. He placed the tip of the barrel under Vega's nose and slowly cocked the hammer. His mouth zigzagged in a cruel grimace.

"One more time," he snarled. "And if the answer don't suit me, I'm gonna blow your fuckin' head off. Who hired you?"

Vega looked petrified. His one good eye widened and beads of sweat glistened on his forehead. His lips barely moved.

"Donaghue," he sputtered. "Florencio Donaghue."

"What'd he pay you?"

"A hundred dollars."

"For all three of you?"

"*Sí.*"

"Cheap bastard," Allison said in disgust. "Why'd he want Tolby killed?"

"He did not say, señor."

"Was it because Tolby was preachin' against the Santa Fe Ring?"

"I think so."

"Bullshit!" Allison jabbed the gun muzzle into his nose. "Talk to me about the Santa Fe Ring. Who does Donaghue get his orders from?"

"Madre de Dios!" Vega shook his head wildly. "I was told nothing, señor. Nothing!"

Allison studied him with a mocking scowl. "Well, it don't surprise me. I wouldn't've told you neither." He lowered the hammer and bolstered his gun with one quick motion. "Just for the record, Donaghue sent you here tonight, didn't he?"

"Sí, señor."

"I reckon that does it." Allison turned away, his mouth set in an ugly grin. "One of you boys run fetch your lariat. We're gonna hang ourselves a greaser."

Braddock tensed, on the verge of objecting. Isaac Coleman stilled him with a warning look and a wave of his gun. While one of the cowhands went for a rope, Colter and the other man were assigned to guard Braddock. Allison collared Vega by the scruff of the neck and waltzed him outside. Coleman and McMain exchanged a glance, then fell in behind. Colter and his sidekick, with Braddock wedged between them, brought up the rear.

"Sorry," Colter said in a low voice, "I was obligated to carry McMain's message."

"Why?" Braddock demanded. "Because you work for Coleman?"

"A man pays my wages, he buys my loyalty too."

"You sell yourself awful cheap, Buck."

"I kept my word," Colter said with a wooden expression. "I didn't say nothin' about what you told me. All I did was carry a message."

"Who are you trying to convince—me or yourself?"

Colter fell silent, stung by his tone. As they halted on the boardwalk, Allison and Coleman already had Vega positioned beneath a lamppost. The cowhand trotted back from the saloon, where his horse was tied to the hitch rack. He gave Allison the lariat, and Vega stood with a look of pop-eyed terror while the loop was cinched around his neck. Then Allison tossed the coiled lariat over a crossbar on top of the lamppost.

Upstreet several men were bunched in a knot outside
the saloon. Bud Grant, the town marshal, separated from
the crowd and hurried down the boardwalk. He stopped a
couple of paces away, scanning their faces. His gaze finally
settled on McMain.

"What's the problem, Orville?"

McMain shifted uncomfortably. "Vega tried to kill me.
He also confessed to the murder of Reverend Tolby."

"Then press charges," Grant said forcefully. "Let the law
do its job."

"The law!" Allison said with a sourly amused look. "Hell,
everyone knows who runs the courthouse. You really think
Donaghue would let him swing?"

"That's up to a jury."

"We're the jury!" Allison said vindictively. "We tried him
and found him guilty—and he's gonna hang!"

"You've lynched too many men, Allison. Turn him over
to me and I'll see to it that he stands trial. Otherwise your
coalition's nothing but a gang of vigilantes."

"Yeah, and it's high time we started cleanin' house.
There's a whole goddamn list of people that need their necks
stretched."

"Start somewhere else," Grant ordered. "I won't let you
hang him in my town."

"You won't, huh?" Allison's eyes blazed. "Turn around
and walk away, Grant. 'Cause if you don't, I'll put a leak in
your ticker. That badge don't mean shit to me."

Bud Grant was no coward, yet he was a realist and readily conceded he was no match for Allison. A gunfight would
end with Cimarron looking for a new town marshal. At last
he concluded Cruz Vega wasn't worth getting himself killed
for. He turned and walked back toward the saloon.

Allison still had the loose end of the lariat in his hand.
He suddenly stepped off the boardwalk and hoisted Vega a
few inches into the air. Coleman leaped to help, and together
they hauled the thrashing Mexican to the top of the lamppost. Allison took a couple of quick hitches around the base

of the post and tied off the lariat. Then he moved back to watch the show.

Vega died hard. He dug at the lariat, gouging long welts down the front of his neck. His walnut features slowly turned purple and then black as the noose cut deeper into his throat. He kicked and danced as though searching for a foothold, and his heels drummed frantically against the lamppost. Several minutes passed, with the men watching in silence, before he choked to death. His struggles gradually weakened, then his body went slack and there was a noxious stench as his bowels voided. He dangled open-eyed at the end of the lariat.

A strained stillness fell over the group. Allison continued to stare up at the corpse with a dopey smile, but the others looked away, their expressions showing embarrassment. No one spoke, and the creak of the lariat was like a scratchy metronome in the silence. After a time, Braddock brushed Colter and the other cowhand aside. His eyes were stone cold and his hands were knotted into fists. He walked straight toward Allison.

"You'll recollect that I said you'd answer to me."

CHAPTER SEVENTEEN

⚊⚊⚋⚌⚋⚊⚊

"You're a regular rooster, aren't you?"

Allison backpedaled to the middle of the street. Braddock stepped off the boardwalk and followed him without a break in stride. Something told Allison he'd offended the wrong man. He threw up his hands as though warding off evil spirits.

"Whoa, hoss! I got no fight with you!"

"Fight or get whipped—your choice."

"No sense to it!" Allison reversed directions, circling toward the boardwalk. "I done told you we're on the same side."

"We were," Braddock said coldly. "Not anymore."

"You're gonna fight me over a stinkin' greaser?"

"Quit running and let's get to it."

"No siree bob!" Allison pulled his pistol, holding it loosely at his side. "I don't allow no man to lay hands on me."

"What's the matter?" Braddock said with wry contempt. "You acted mighty tough with Vega."

"Goddammit, he had it comin'!"

"So do you." Braddock continued advancing on him. "And it's time to pay up."

Allison cocked his pistol, leveling it. "Hold 'er right there! You take another step and I'll kill you deader'n hell."

"Allison!"

Colter's shout was like a thunderclap. Braddock stopped and saw the young half-breed move away from the other men. His pistol was extended at arm's length, pointed at Allison. He halted on the edge of the boardwalk.

"Drop your gun, Allison."

"God a'mighty!" Allison darted a quick glance over his shoulder. "What's got into you, Buck?"

"I don't hold with killin' unarmed men."

"You gonna turn Judas for him!"

"Drop it," Colter said with dungeon calm. "Or I'll drop you."

There was a stark silence. A sense of suppressed violence hung in the air, and the men seemed frozen in a stilled tableau. Colter's eyes were hard and deadly, and Allison regarded him with a look of wary hostility. At last Isaac Coleman broke the spell. He took a step toward Colter.

"Don't!" Colter warned him. "You try anything and Allison's a goner."

"Listen to me," Coleman said in a shaky voice. "You don't wanna do this, boy. The man's an outsider!"

"I just switched sides."

"For Chrissake!" Coleman took another step. "I treated you like a son, Buck. You owe me!"

"I'm not funnin', Isaac." Colter sighted along the barrel. "You or anybody else makes a move and Allison is cold meat."

"You'll double-damn regret it all your days!"

"Maybe." Colter's finger tightened on the trigger. "What d'you say, Allison? I'm through waitin'."

Allison muttered an unintelligible curse and gingerly lowered the hammer on his pistol, dropping it at his feet. A strange light came into his eyes, and he abruptly laughed. He tossed his hat on the ground, spit on his hands. Then he cocked his fists and waved Braddock forward.

"All right, you sorry son of a bitch. Come and get it!"

Braddock shuffled toward him, arms raised. He feinted with a left, then a right, and let go a stinging left hook. Allison shook off the blow and popped him on the chin. Braddock went down, losing his hat as he landed flat on his back. He was stunned by the power of the punch and was vaguely surprised to find himself on the ground. The brassy taste of blood filled his mouth and pinwheels of light flashed through his head. Allison sensed victory and moved to end the fight with a rough-and-tumble stomping. His first kick missed as Braddock rolled away, but he was uncommonly agile for a big man, and he lashed out with his other boot. Braddock took the force of the kick on his side, and for an instant he thought his rib cage was shattered. Then his head cleared and he caught his wind. He scrambled crablike to his feet.

Breathing heavily, he circled Allison with a new respect. The man was clearly a barroom brawler of some experience— and dangerous. Braddock gave ground as Allison waded in, windmilling with both arms. Bobbing and weaving, Braddock absorbed most of the blows on his arms and shoulders. But a looping overhead right got through his guard and caught him flush on the jaw. A shower of sparks rocketed before his eyes and the whole left side of his face went numb. He instinctively crouched, slipping inside the flurry of punches, and clinched Allison in a tight bear hug. The shooting stars and swirling dots slacked off a bit, and the groggy sensation passed. He allowed Allison to manhandle him and roughly shove him away. The tactic gave him a brief respite, room to maneuver.

Braddock dimly realized he wouldn't last. Allison was a punishing scrapper, and the sheer volume of blows would eventually beat him down. To win, he would have to end it fast, outfox rather than outmuscle him. He backed off, his guard lowered, acting wobbly and disoriented. Allison advanced on him, fists cocked, snarling an oath as he ambled forward. Braddock retreated a step farther, looking slow and clumsy, inviting a move. The ruse worked, and Allison went for a quick kill. His shoulder dipped, faking a straight left, then he launched a murderous haymaker. Braddock ducked under the blow and buried his fist in Allison's crotch. The big man roared like a bull elephant and doubled over, clutching himself as violent spasms knifed through his groin. Shifting slightly, Braddock grabbed the back of his head and kneed him squarely in the face.

Allison hurtled backward as if he'd been shot out of a cannon. He tripped over his own feet and sat down heavily in the dirt. His face was splattered with blood, and he retched, his mouth puckered in a pained oval. Yet he was far from whipped, and he shook his head, gulping great lungfuls of air. He rolled onto his hands and knees, struggling to maintain his balance. Then, his back to Braddock, he planted one hand on the ground and slowly levered himself upright. He stood and turned around.

Braddock was waiting. He exploded a short left hook to the jaw, followed by a chopping right cross to the temple. The splintering combination sent Allison reeling backward in a nerveless dance. He slammed into the lamppost, jarring it with the impact of his weight, and stood there as if transfixed. His eyes went blank, then his knees buckled and he settled to the ground on the seat of his pants. Overhead the corpse of Cruz Vega swayed beneath the shimmering light.

Brushing himself off, Braddock collected his hat and walked forward. His side ached, one of his molars was loose, and his ears rang with a faint buzzing sound. He glanced down at Allison and decided he wouldn't care for a repeat performance. He felt he'd been run through a gristmill.

Colter was still holding a gun on the other men. Braddock mounted the boardwalk and stopped beside him. McMain kept his gaze averted, looking somewhat shamefaced. But Isaac Coleman was having no part of humble pie. His eyes were smoky with rage.

"Don't change a thing," he said angrily. "We're gonna do what's got to be done."

A vein pulsed in Braddock's forehead. "I take it one hanging just whetted your appetite?"

"Damn tootin'!" Coleman glowered at him through slitted eyes. "Before we're done, we'll hang Griego and Donaghue, and anybody else that don't toe the line. We only just started!"

Braddock regarded him with an odd, steadfast look. "You're a fool, Coleman. A goddamn simpleton."

"Here now!" Coleman squared himself up stiffly. "You watch your mouth or I'll—"

"No, you won't." Braddock fixed him with a cold stare. "You mess with me one more time and I'll bury you. The same goes for Allison."

"That'll be the day!" Coleman hooted. "You try him with a gun and you're in for a surprise. It's you that'll get buried!"

"When he wakes up, you give him my message. Just steer clear—or else."

"Oh, I'll tell him. But you better find yourself a hole and pull it in after you. That goes for Judas Iscariot there too."

"If you're talkin' to me," Colter said, his voice flat, "you and Clay get off the street when you see me comin'. We're quits from here on out."

"You goddamn ingrate! You haven't heard the last—"

"Yeah, he has," Braddock said brusquely. "Take Allison and be on your way. I won't tell you a second time."

Coleman gave him a dirty look. There was a prolonged silence, and the rancher appeared on the verge of saying something more. Then he changed his mind and motioned the cowhands forward. They moved to the lamppost and, one on either side of him, hefted Allison off the ground. With his toes dragging in the dirt, they walked in the direction of the saloon. Coleman turned and stalked along behind them.

"You know," Braddock said, watching after them, "it occurs to me that Coleman's not the only fool around here."

Colter looked puzzled. "How's that?"

"I'm not heeled," Braddock said sardonically. "All that

big talk and my gun's still inside. Guess it's a good thing Coleman didn't call my hand."

"You had him buffaloed," Colter noted. "He wasn't gonna push too hard. Not after the way you cleaned Allison's plow."

"I hear you're pretty handy with your dukes too."

"Fair to middlin'."

"You ever tangle with Allison?"

"Nope," Colter said, smiling. "He left me alone and I returned the favor."

"Wish I'd done the same." Braddock rubbed his jaw. "Couple of times, he damn near tore my head off."

"I got the feelin' you enjoyed yourself."

Braddock laughed. "I would've enjoyed it a hell of a lot less without you to back my play. I'm obliged."

"I owed you one." Colter looked down at his boots. "Wasn't for me, they wouldn't've showed up here tonight."

"Hell, forget it." Braddock turned toward the office door. "Hold on a minute and I'll go get my gun."

Neither of them had acknowledged McMain's presence during the conversation. As Braddock entered the newspaper, McMain edged around Colter and hurried inside. Colter followed him through the door and stopped near the counter.

Braddock collected his pistol off the desk. Out of habit, he checked the loads, lowering the hammer on an empty chamber. Then he holstered the Colt and picked up Vega's gun. He glanced around as McMain approached.

"Here you go, Orville." He extended the gun. "A keepsake of your lynching bee."

"No, thanks." McMain bowed his head. "I'm not proud of tonight, Cole. It was just . . . necessary."

"How do you figure that?"

"Vega deserved to hang! After all, he murdered Reverend Tolby. We were within our rights to exact retribution."

"An eye for an eye?"

"Yes, exactly!"

"Why not let the law do it for you?"

"Don't be absurd!" McMain said with sudden vehemence. "Vega would never have gone to the gallows. Not in Colfax County."

"You could've requested a change of venue."

"To what end!" McMain asked cynically. "Every official in the courthouse is on the ring's payroll. We wouldn't have gotten an indictment, much less a conviction."

"Maybe not." Braddock dropped the gun on the desk. "Well, see you around sometime, Orville."

"Wait!" McMain appeared confused. "Where are you going?"

"I quit," Braddock said evenly. "I'm off the case."

McMain stared at him, aghast. "But you can't do that. We've already paid half your fee!"

"You got your money's worth."

"I beg to differ," McMain said promptly. "We retained you to perform an investigation. A full investigation!"

"Who're you kidding?" Braddock looked at him impassively. "You hired me to do your dirty work. I should've caught on sooner."

"I don't know what you mean."

"Yeah, you do," Braddock rebuked him. "Frank Kirkland conned me good when he showed up in Denver. Investigating the ring was strictly back burner, wasn't it?"

"No."

"C'mon, admit it!" Braddock said crossly. "What you really wanted was revenge for Reverend Tolby. You hired me to do your killing."

"You're mistaken."

"And you're lying, Orville. You sicced me on Donaghue the minute I hit town. You wanted him dead and out of the way."

"That's ridiculous!"

"Is it?" There was open scorn in Braddock's gaze. "With Donaghue dead, you and your coalition could've taken over Colfax County. You probably justified it by telling yourself he was behind Tolby's death. But it was perfect timing where your political plans were concerned. So you sent Kirkland out to hire you a killer."

"Why would I do that?" McMain waved his hand as though dusting away the accusation. "Allison and Coleman are quite capable along those lines. Tonight proved it."

"You lost control tonight," Braddock said with a short look. "You pulled the cork and then you couldn't put the demon back in the bottle. A bullet was the only thing that would've stopped Allison once he'd sniffed blood. And you don't have the guts for it, do you, Orville?"

McMain was caught up in a moment of indecision. His eyes drifted to the gun on the desk, and he studied it with a somber expression. Then he shrugged and looked up at Braddock.

"We had no way of knowing Vega would come alone tonight. I was afraid for my life, Cole. I honestly believed you needed help. That's the only reason I sent for Allison."

Braddock rocked his head from side to side. "I reckon the joke's on you, Orville. You let Allison out of the bottle and all you got for your trouble is a dead Mexican. Not much, is it?"

"I regret the whole affair."

"You'll be even sorrier before it's over. The marshal hit the nail square on the head. Before Allison's done, your coalition will be known as the Cimarron Vigilantes. I doubt that'll win you too many votes at the ballot box."

"It's not too late," McMain said hastily. "You could still complete your assignment."

"Wishful thinking," Braddock replied. "Donaghue probably skipped town before Vega was cold. He'll run even faster—and farther—with Allison on his trail. So it appears we're fresh out of witnesses."

"What about Pancho Griego, Vega's accomplice?"

"Same thought holds for him."

"Wait, Cole." McMain's voice was low and urgent. "Allison's a rancher, not a professional manhunter. Suppose you were able to capture Griego or Donaghue before he got to them? Then we'd still have a case, wouldn't we?"

"You talking about the Santa Fe Ring?"

"I am how," McMain assured him. "All you need is one witness to make a case against Warren Mitchell. And I know you could beat Allison to Donaghue. I'm certain of it!"

Braddock seemed to look through him. "You're switching horses in the middle of the stream. What you really wanted was Donaghue's scalp, and now you're hot to bust the ring. Why's that?"

McMain's lips peeled back in a weak smile. "I made a mistake and I'm willing to admit it. You've shown me the light, Cole."

"Uh-huh." Braddock nodded, digesting the thought. "You've lost control of Allison, and Donaghue's off to who knows where. So all of a sudden I'm your last-ditch chance. Wouldn't that about cover it?"

"Aren't you being a tad too skeptical?"

"I try never to stub my toe in the same place twice. I'm still waiting for an answer."

"Very well," McMain said sheepishly. "You are my last chance. The coalition won't survive if Allison gives it a black eye. You're the only one who can stop that from happening."

Braddock silently congratulated himself on his foresight. He'd been wise to make no mention of Lise or Stephen Elkton. He saw now that McMain was both slippery and ambitious, a man with political aspirations who dealt in expediency and raw pragmatism. He was not one to be trusted.

"Tell you what, Orville," he said at length. "I'll go along with you on two conditions."

"Anything you say, Cole."

"First, I'm only interested in the ring. Whether or not your coalition survives is immaterial to me. If busting the ring helps you in some way, that's fine. If not, then it's tough titty."

"And the second condition?"

"Even more personal," Braddock said with a hard grin. "You agree not to switch horses again. That includes Allison or any other cute ideas that might pop into your head. Because if you double-cross me again, I'll kill you."

"You're not serious!"

"Dead serious," Braddock said coolly. "You could've gotten me killed tonight. I won't stand for any more tricks."

"That's a rather harsh condition, isn't it?"

"Say no and I'll head on back to Denver. It's your chestnuts in the fire, not mine."

"In that event"—McMain bobbed his head—"I have no choice but to agree."

"Looks like I'm back on the case."

"Where will you start?"

"I'll let you know . . . sometime."

Braddock walked forward and circled the counter. Colter fell in beside him, and they went out the door. On the street he paused a moment, looking toward the saloon.

"Buck, why don't I buy you a drink?"

"I've got nothin' better to do."

"Let's do it, then."

Cruz Vega's dead eyes stared down as they turned upstreet.

CHAPTER EIGHTEEN

The crowd in the saloon was unusually subdued. Townsmen for the most part, they were discussing the lynching in low voices. Allison and Coleman were nowhere in sight.

Conversation abruptly stopped as Braddock and Colter walked through the door. The men ranked along the bar had witnessed the hanging and the bloody slugfest that followed. Their stares were bemused, filled with undisguised curiosity.

The man they knew as Reverend Titus Jacoby was by now a total enigma. Scarcely a fortnight past, he had killed a robber in a pitched gun battle. Tonight, employing the tactics of a seasoned brawler, he had beaten Clay Allison to a pulp. Speculation was rampant, and few of them any longer believed he was a preacher. Still, the obvious question would not be asked directly. None of them was feeling especially foolhardy.

Braddock led the way to a rear table. The barkeep hustled back, and Braddock ordered a bottle of rye with a water chaser. After they were served, he took out his handkerchief and dipped it into the water pitcher. He dabbed at his split lip and wiped the caked blood off his face. Finished, he wadded the handkerchief into a ball and dropped it in a spittoon. Then he uncorked the bottle and poured. He raised his glass, smiling at Colter.

"Happy days."

Colter sipped, watching him quietly. Braddock downed the whiskey in a single draught and slowly lowered his glass. He waited for the rye to hit bottom, then eased back in his chair. He jerked his chin toward the bar, where the townsmen were conversing in low monotones. His smile widened into a broad grin.

"I'd bet they never saw a Bible thumper take it neat."

"What the hell!" Colter chuckled softly. "You've already killed one man and whipped the daylights out of another. I reckon nothin' would surprise 'em now."

"Probably not." Braddock refilled his glass. "I might as well retire this preacher's outfit. The word's sure to get out by tomorrow anyway."

"Or sooner," Colter added. "McMain won't have no choice but to 'fess up. There'll be a regular parade of busybodies through his office."

"You got a smoke?"

Colter dug into his pocket and tossed the makings across the table. Braddock curled a paper between his fingers and spilled tobacco out of the sack. He rolled the paper with one hand, then licked it lightly and twisted one end. Colter gave him a match, which he popped on his thumbnail. He lit the cigarette and took a long drag.

"Hard habit to break." He exhaled, snuffing the match. "I'm glad it's over and done with. Acting like a preacher puts a real crimp in things."

"I can see how it would. You were mighty convincing, though. I even bought it myself—till you killed Cardenas."

"I meant to capture him." Braddock studied the fiery tip on the cigarette. "If I had, the case would've been wrapped up by now. Damned inconsiderate the way he went and broke his neck."

"Yeah, it was." Colter began building himself a cigarette. "You roll a smoke like you've had experience."

"Some," Braddock acknowledged. "I used to be in your line of work. Smoked roll-your-owns for a lot of years."

"Where was that?"

"Texas," Braddock remarked. "I started out on the Rio Grande and ended up in the Panhandle. Toward the last, I was foreman for the LX spread."

"How'd you get into the detective business?"

"Long story." Braddock flicked an ash into the spittoon. "I worked as a range detective for about seven years. Then people started offering me different types of assignments. So I finally opened my own agency."

Colter struck a match and puffed. "You ever ride for the International?"

Braddock caught something in his voice. The International Cattlemen's Association was an organization comprised of stockgrower associations throughout the western states and territories. Detectives who worked for the International were noted for their ruthlessness toward cattle rustlers and horse thieves. Summary execution, without due process of law, was standard policy.

"I turned them down," Braddock said casually. "Figured I was better off on my own. What makes you ask?"

"No reason." Colter idly blew a smoke ring. "Why'd you turn 'em down?"

"I hire my services but not my gun. That didn't fit in with their method of operation."

"Oh." Colter seemed to lose interest in the subject. "I forgot to mention it a minute ago. Clay Allison's a Texan too. His stompin' grounds was somewheres over around Fort Belknap."

Braddock played along. "Any idea why he moved his outfit to New Mexico?"

"I heard he got himself in some sort of scrape."

"Figures," Braddock said with heavy sarcasm. "He strikes me as a natural-born troublemaker."

"The worst," Colter said, smiling. "Folks say he could start a fight in an empty room."

"How long have you known him and Coleman?"

"Four months or thereabouts."

"What's your opinion?" Braddock asked. "Do you think they'll be satisfied with hanging Vega? Or will they go after Donaghue?"

"Well, first off"—Colter paused to drain his glass—"I overheard part of what you told McMain, and you're right. Donaghue wouldn't stick around town, not after tonight."

"Any idea where he'd head?"

"Your guess on that would be as good as mine."

"Which brings us back to Allison and Coleman."

"I'd bet they've already checked around town. They had plenty of time while you were talkin' with McMain. So it's likely Donaghue skipped out and they know it."

"What would they do next?"

"Go after Vega's compadre—Pancho Griego."

"Tonight?"

"Probably not," Colter said after a moment's reflection. "You whipped Allison pretty good. They'll more'n likely lay over at his place tonight and let him lick his wounds. I'd judge they won't hit the trail before mornin'."

"So you think they'll head for Rayado?"

"Vega said that's where Griego lives."

"How far south is it?"

"Fifteen miles, maybe a little less."

Braddock mulled it over a minute. "You told me Coleman's threats were all hot air. What about Allison?"

"How do you mean?"

"Let's suppose I cross paths with him again. Would he try gunplay or not?"

"Only if he got the drop on you. His bark's a lot worse'n his bite."

"I thought he'd killed a couple of men in shoot-outs?"

"Way I heard it, he took 'em by surprise. Course, there's no question he's a killer. But that don't make him a gunhand, not in my book."

"Is that why he gave you a wide path?"

"I don't follow you."

"Allison's no dimwit," Braddock commented. "He knows a dangerous man when he sees one."

"Who, me?" Colter said blandly. "What makes you think that?"

"Why were you picked to guard McMain?"

"Coleman offered me double wages."

"Yeah, but why?" Braddock pressed him. "Coleman must've had a reason. He didn't just pick your name out of a hat."

Colter's stare revealed nothing. "What're you tryin' to say?"

"You're evidently no slouch with a gun. So it sets me to wondering whether you're a cowhand—or something else."

"I'm no hired gun!" Colter declared. "Besides, what difference would it make anyway? I'm nothin' to you."

"You weren't," Braddock amended. "Not till you saved my bacon tonight."

"Why do I get the feeling you're leadin' up to something?"

A moment passed, then Braddock shrugged. "I could use some help on the case. Interested?"

Colter was visibly surprised. "What kind of help?"

"For one thing, I don't know the country too well. You'd be a big help tracking down Griego and Donaghue."

"I'm still listenin'."

"From what you said about Allison, it wouldn't hurt to have somebody watching my back. I could use an extra set of eyes."

"Extra eyes or an extra gun?"

"Whichever's needed."

Colter sipped his whiskey, peering over the rim of his glass. "I got to admit the idea interests me. Somebody should've taken Allison down a peg or two way back when."

"Only one thing."

"What's that?"

"I don't ride with a man until I know something about him. You'd have to come straight with me."

"On what?"

"For openers," Braddock said firmly, "you could start by telling me your real name."

Colter gave him a quick, guarded glance. "You got a lotta brass. What makes you think I changed my name?"

"Tell me I'm wrong and we'll let it drop."

"Why should I tell you anything?"

Braddock eyed him with a steady, uncompromising gaze. "One way or another, I'll find out who you are. A half-breed on the run isn't all that hard to identify." He paused, lending emphasis to the thought. "Why not just spill it? Whatever you say stops here."

"How do I know that?"

"I owe you," Braddock said simply. "And I always pay my debts. You might need a friend somewhere down the line."

A blanket of silence enveloped the two men. Colter stared off into the middle distance and seemed to fall asleep with his eyes open. Presently he blinked and took a couple of quick puffs on his cigarette. He looked back at Braddock.

"I got crosswise of the law last summer."

"Where?"

"No-man's-land."

"What happened?"

"I killed some men."

"How many?"

"Ten."

"Jesus Christ." Braddock looked startled. "You killed ten men by yourself?"

"It wasn't hard."

"Sounds like you declared war on somebody."

"I had reason."

"Why don't you tell me about it?"

"It started a long time ago, in Colorado."

Colter stubbed out his cigarette and began talking. His Cheyenne name was An-zah-ti, Little Raven. Like many squaws, his mother had been sold as wife to a white mountain man. After only one winter the trapper rode away, never to return, and a few months later a boy was born. At the naming ceremony, the boy was called Little Raven, for he had coal-black hair and strange gray eyes. He lived eight winters with the Cheyenne, growing strong and sturdy. Their village was on a remote backwater known as Sand Creek.

The Pony Soldiers came on a cold, blustery morning. There was no warning, no attempt to identify the village as peaceful or hostile. Another Cheyenne band had raided a white settlement, and swift retribution was demanded. That the village chief was Black Kettle, a friend to all white men, made no difference whatever. The battle cry was "Nits make lice," and the Pony Soldier leader ordered his men to kill anything that walked. What followed was a slaughter; the snow turned crimson with the blood of the Cheyenne. Little Raven saw his mother raped and then finished off with a bullet through the head. He also caught a glimpse of the Pony Soldier leader, laughing and goading the troopers on in their butchery. It was a face the boy never forgot.

Afterward, the slaughter was called the Sand Creek Massacre, and there was a great outcry from white men of conscience. The Pony Soldier leader, Colonel John Covington, was relieved of command and soon disappeared from Colorado. Little Raven, along with other captured children, was sent to a Quaker missionary school in Indian territory. There he was taught the white man's way. The Quakers prepared him well, wiping out the Cheyenne intonation from his speech and opening his mind to the customs of a world apart from his childhood. Some years later, grown to a strapping youth of eighteen, he put the reservation behind him. Though tawny-skinned, he passed himself off as white, growing a bushy mustache to complete the disguise of his pale gray eyes. Thereafter, he walked the white man's road.

A wanderer, he drifted from one ranch to another, working

his way up from horse wrangler to cowhand. He called himself Buck Colter, and he spent three years learning his new trade. Then, shortly after turning twenty-one, he saw Colonel John Covington's name in a newspaper. The leader in a movement to open public lands, Covington had been instrumental in settling no-man's-land. Colter quit his job and rode north out of Texas, bent on revenge. He hired on with a cattle outfit and spent the next three years awaiting an opportunity. Not an eye for an eye, but white man's justice. Some legal means of bringing about a final settlement of accounts.

"Three years," Braddock observed thoughtfully. "That would've been last summer."

Colter nodded. "Things didn't work out the way I'd planned. Covington was head of the Stockgrowers' Association, and he used all kinds of tricks to discourage farmers from settlin' on rangeland. But he kept his nose clean where the law was concerned."

"So you got tired of waiting?"

"Nope." Colter caught his eye for an instant, then looked quickly away. "I hooked up with a farm girl and started hearin' wedding bells. We even staked out a piece of land."

"What stopped you?"

"The association had a hard and fast rule. No cowhand was allowed to own stock while he was still ridin' for an outfit. The idea was to stop little operations from springin' up."

Braddock lit another cigarette. "And you broke the rule?"

Colter's expression became somber, then pensive. "I wanted to build a spread of my own. Whenever trail herds would pass through, I'd buy a few head. All legal and aboveboard."

"Let me guess," Braddock said, exhaling smoke. "You thumbed your nose at the association, and Covington got his bowels in an uproar. He probably had somebody rough you up or stampede your herd."

"Worse'n that," Colter said with a quick swipe at his mustache. "He bribed a cattle inspector and got me railroaded for rustlin'. I was convicted on nothin' but trumped-up evidence."

Braddock searched his eyes. "Were you a hundred percent innocent?"

"Damn right!" Colter flared. "I aimed to get married. I was walkin' the straight and narrow."

"What happened after the trial?"

"I escaped." Colter wrapped his hands around his whiskey glass. "I cornered the cattle inspector and tried to get him to change his story. He made a fight of it."

"Was he the first one you killed?"

"Yeah," Colter mumbled. "Then Covington brought in a hired gun, fellow by the name of Doc Ross. One night Ross and some of Covington's men waylaid me at the girl's house. I got away without a scratch."

"And the girl?"

Colter looked into his drink as though he might find revealed there the answer to life's mystery. "She was killed."

Braddock smoked in silence a moment. "I take it that's the night you declared war?"

"Wasn't nothin' left to lose. I rode out to Covington's place, but he wasn't there. So I walked into the bunkhouse with my shotgun and cut loose. All seven of the bastards was the same ones that'd been at the girl's house."

"Seven at a whack." Braddock slowly shook his head. "That explains why you use a lever-action shotgun."

"It gets the job done."

"Was Doc Ross in the bunkhouse?"

"No," Colter said, poker-faced. "I rode directly from there into town. Covington and Ross were in the saloon, celebratin'. They thought I was dead."

"You showing up that way must've been a real shock."

A smile touched Colter's lips. "Froze the sonsabitches in their tracks. They thought they were seein' a ghost."

"How'd you kill them?"

"I used the shotgun on Ross. Covington didn't deserve no

more chance than a mad dog. All the same, I gave him an even break with pistols. He lost."

"Were there witnesses?"

Colter's smile turned grim. "Witnesses weren't no help at that point. Killin' that many men in one night just naturally tagged me a murderer. Covington being the head of the Stockgrower's Association only made it worse."

"When you mentioned Covington, it sort of jogged my memory. I recall reading about it now."

Braddock briefly explained his rogues'-gallery file. Shortly after the killings, the International Cattlemen's Association had circulated a dodger on Colter. The reward was five thousand dollars, and he was wanted dead or alive.

"I'm curious," Braddock concluded. "Why aren't you using a phony name?"

Colter shrugged. "The International's detectives won't ever stop doggin' my tracks. I decided to lay low and only work for small outfits. That way there's less chance of being recognized. But I won't change my name—not again."

"Are you talking about the missionary school?"

"Yeah." Colter's brow puckered in a frown. "For better'n ten years, the Quakers called me Sam Raven. I picked my own name when I lit out from the reservation. It's the one I aim to stick with."

Braddock gave him a quizzical side glance. "Aren't you asking for trouble?"

"Maybe," Colter said with a fatalistic look. "I suppose the Quakers halfway turned me into a white man's Injun. But when it's all boiled down, I'm still Cheyenne. I won't turn tail just to avoid a fight."

"One man against the International makes it pretty long odds. Sooner or later their hired guns will track you down."

"The Cheyenne Dog Soldiers had the right idea. Before they went into battle, they'd say, 'Today's a good day to die.' I reckon I never got that out of my blood. It's as good a way as any to live—or die."

Braddock marked again that the young half-breed was prodded by strange devils. Yet, given the circumstances, Braddock's admiration was stirred. The code by which Colter lived was one of courage and absolute fearlessness. A quiet acceptance that death was preferable to cowardice.

"What now?" Colter said at length. "You sure you want to associate with a common murderer?"

"I never go back on my word, Buck."

"You're liable to wind up on the International's list yourself."

Braddock laughed. "Then I'll tell them what I told 'em when they offered me a job as a bounty hunter."

"What's that?"

"Stuff it where the sun don't shine!"

CHAPTER NINETEEN

The morning sky was overcast. A chill wind whipped down out of the north, and there was a touch of dampness in the air. All the signs pointed to a hard winter.

There was no road as such between Cimarron and Rayado. A washboard trail stretched south across a vast emptiness. The terrain sloped gently downward, leveling off into flatland broken occasionally by arroyos and dry creek beds. It was inhospitable country, and the few ranches south of Cimarron were scattered far apart. As they had for generations, Mexicans subsisted on what they could coax from the flinty soil.

Braddock and Colter sighted Rayado shortly before nine o'clock. Earlier, almost at the crack of dawn, Braddock had awakened the proprietor of the livery stable in Cimarron. After haggling briefly, he'd swapped the swaybacked dun and thirty dollars for a blaze-faced roan. He knew he'd been cheated, but the press of time hadn't allowed for prolonged dickering. The roan was sound of wind, and in the event his search for Pancho Griego turned into a manhunt, he needed a horse built for endurance. He was also prompted by a greater and even more pressing urgency. He had to beat Clay Allison to Rayado.

The town was little more than a wide spot in the road. There was a general store and a cantina and a small church with a bell tower. The church looked more like a fort, and had probably doubled as a defensive stronghold during the Apache wars. Clustered around the town's main buildings were a crude collection of adobe houses. Indistinguishable in appearance, the adobes resembled a handful of dice tossed randomly onto the bleak landscape. The inhabitants of Rayado were poor, if not impoverished, typical of Mexicans who lighted a candle to the Virgin and prayed for a brighter tomorrow. Their goats and runty pigs wandered at will in and among the dwellings.

On the edge of town, Braddock reined to a halt. He traded glances with Colter and neither of them appeared any too cheerful. There were four horses hitched outside the cantina.

"What do you think?" Braddock inquired. "Anybody we know?"

" 'Fraid so," Colter said dourly. "The same bunch we tangled with last night. Allison and Coleman and the two hands."

Braddock let out his breath in a sharp grunt. "Looks like Allison has more staying power than I thought. That whipping doesn't seem to have slowed him down any."

Colter nodded in agreement. "They must've been on the road long before daylight."

"Wonder why he didn't bring more men?"

"Maybe he figures we're off chasing Donaghue."

"Whatever his reason, we played into luck."

"How do you figure that?"

"Four against two." Braddock smiled, staring at the horses. "Sounds like pretty decent odds."

"What've you got in mind?"

"You take the back door and I'll take the front. We do it fast enough and nobody'll get any foolish ideas."

"And if somebody does get foolish?"

"Then I guess we'll have to explain it to the coroner."

"You fight my kind of fight, Cole."

Braddock grinned and shrugged out of his greatcoat. He was no longer wearing the turned-around collar, but he was still dressed in the funereal minister's suit. He pulled his pistol and stuffed a sixth cartridge into the empty chamber. Colter, meanwhile, slipped his shotgun from the saddle boot. A quick crank of the lever jacked a shell into the breech and cocked the hammer.

Behind the nearest adobe, they dismounted and left their horses tied to a scraggly tree. A Mexican woman appeared at the window and Braddock motioned her back inside. Then they circled around several houses and crossed the road in line with the cantina. Colter peeled off and hurried toward the rear of the building. Braddock walked to within a few feet of the door and flattened himself against the front wall. On the count of ten, he stepped away from the wall and cocked his pistol. He pushed through the door in one swift stride.

The cantina was empty. Braddock stood for a moment with a mildly bewildered look. Then a door at the rear of the room opened and a sleepy-eyed Mexican emerged with his hands overhead. Colter nudged him forward with the nuzzle of the scattergun. The Mexican saw Braddock and his eyes suddenly turned wary. Colter moved to the side and stopped.

"He's got living quarters out back. Nobody else but his woman and a litter of kids."

Braddock arched one eyebrow. "You're sure those horses belong to our friends?"

"No two ways about it."

"You talk Mexican?"

"Some."

"Ask him if he's had any visitors this morning."

Colter addressed the Mexican. *"Habia hombres aqui hoy?"*

"Sí, señor."

"Fueron americanos?"

"Sí." The Mexican nodded rapidly. *"Polícia americano."*

Colter glanced at Braddock. "They've been here, all right. Allison told him they were lawmen."

"Figures," Braddock said with a trace of irony. "Ask him where they are now."

Colter turned back to the Mexican. *"Adonde van después de salir de aqui?"*

"A casa de Pancho Griego."

"Usted le dio la direction?"

"Sí."

"Donde esta la casa de Pancho Griego?"

"Al otro lado de la calle." The Mexican pointed out the door. *"Vaya detrásde la tienda. Vive en la tercera casa."*

"Gracias."

Colter dismissed him with a wave of the shotgun. He looked from Colter to Braddock, clearly confused by the sudden invasion of Anglo *pistoleros.* Then he swallowed his curiosity and trudged on back to his sleeping quarters. Colter turned to Braddock.

"They're at Griego's house."

"Where's he live?"

"Behind the store and three houses down."

"Maybe we got here in time. If he was dead, they'd already be gone."

"One way to find out."

"Let's go."

Braddock led the way through the door. Outside they crossed the road and skirted around the store. Turning south, they were both struck by the absence of people. No one was about, including women and children. Upon closer examination of the houses, they noticed that the doors were closed and the windows shuttered. It seemed the people of Rayado had locked themselves in, or locked someone out. Then, faintly, the morning stillness was broken by a muted scream.

The cry came from the third house down. While the door was shut, the window shutters were open, and the keening moan of a man in pain sounded from within the house. Braddock and Colter increased their pace, covering the door as they approached. At the corner of the house, they wheeled sharply right and moved toward a side window. Colter waited while Braddock removed his hat and eased his head past the windowsill. The scene inside was much what he'd expected.

A woman and two wide-eyed children were huddled against the far wall. The two cowhands were guarding them, and Isaac Coleman was positioned near the door. In the center of the room, Allison kneeled astride a man on the floor. The man's features were a mask of blood, and his head lolled from side to side. He groaned as Allison swatted him with a stinging backhand.

"C'mon, Griego! Wake up and gimme some answers!"

Griego's eyes fluttered open. *"Por favor, señor."*

Allison cocked his fist. "Quit beggin', you goddamn greaser. Where's Donaghue?"

"No sé."

"Who you think you're shittin'? You understand English plenty good, so speak it!"

"Please, señor," Griego said with a thick accent. "I cannot tell you what I do not know."

"You know Cruz Vega, don't you?"

"Sí."

"He says you helped him kill Reverend Tolby."

"Dios mio! I killed no one!"

"He says you and him and Manuel Cardenas rode out to Cimarron Canyon. You ambushed the preacher there and rigged it to look like robbery—*bandidos.*"

"I swear on my mother's head! I would not kill a man of God. Never!"

Allison popped him in the mouth. "You lyin' son of a bitch! Vega spilled the whole story. He told us everything."

"Where is Vega, señor?"

"What's that to you?"

"Take me to him," Griego implored. "You will see then that I speak only the truth."

"How would that prove anything?"

"He will not lie to my face. He would not dare!"

"Vega's in jail," Allison said with a crafty smile. "We don't have time to haul you back to Cimarron."

"But I am innocent, señor! You must believe—"

Allison slugged him twice in rapid succession. Griego's nose flattened and his head bounced off the dirt floor in a puff of dust. Blood streamed down his face as Allison grabbed him by the shirtfront.

"Cut the crap! I wanna hear about Donaghue—pronto!"

Griego moaned, caught his breath. "I know nothing— *nada*."

"Horseshit!" Allison cuffed his head back and forth with hard slaps. "Vega says Donaghue hired the three of you to kill the preacher. He says you know where Donaghue's hidin' out."

"Lies," Griego said weakly. "All lies."

Allison cursed and resumed the savage beating. Outside the window, Braddock felt a tug on his sleeve and moved back a step. Colter looked worried.

"We better stop it," he whispered. "Allison's liable to beat him to death."

"I don't think so," Braddock said in a low voice. "Without Griego, he's got nowhere to turn. He's smart enough to realize that."

"You're runnin' an awful risk."

"Maybe," Braddock allowed. "But we couldn't do any better. Unless Griego talks, we'll never get a line on Donaghue. We might as well let Allison do the job."

Colter wasn't convinced. "I think you're makin' a mistake."

"We'll wait and see," Braddock said crisply. "I wouldn't want to bust in there anyway. Griego's wife and kids are over against the far wall. Any shooting starts and they'd get caught in the crossfire."

A loud oath from inside attracted Braddock's attention. He peeked through the window and saw Allison climb to his feet. Griego lay sprawled on the floor, out cold. His wife's eyes were filled with terror, and the children clutched at her skirts, wailing at the top of their lungs. Allison shouted them down, and the woman quickly hugged them to her legs. Glaring at her, Allison crossed the room and snatched up a bucket of water. Then he walked back and threw the water in Griego's face. He dropped the bucket as Griego rolled onto his side, moaning softly.

Coleman shifted away from the door. "What're you fixin' to do, Clay?"

"Hang the sorry bastard!"

"He can't talk if you stretch his neck."

"Don't worry." Allison's tone was clipped and stiff. "I'll hang him a little bit at a time. Strangle it out of him!"

"You ever stop to consider he might be tellin' the truth? Hell, maybe he don't know nothin' about Donaghue."

"Hope you're wrong, Isaac. He's all we got."

Allison motioned to the cowhands. They moved to Griego and lifted him off the floor. He sagged between them, conscious but still wobbly from the beating. Coleman opened the door and stepped aside. Allison strode purposefully across the room.

"Let's go find ourselves a tree."

Outside, Allison stopped and looked around. The cowhands appeared next, supporting Griego under the arms. Coleman followed them out and closed the door. There was a moment's silence as Allison searched the skyline for a suitable tree. Then, from inside, the grief-stricken cries of the woman and her children shattered the stillness.

"Don't anybody move!"

Braddock and Colter materialized around the corner of the house. Braddock's pistol was cocked, extended at arm's length. Colter held the shotgun at waist level, the butt snugged tight against his side. The range was less than three yards, and the bore of the shotgun looked like a mine shaft. Allison and the other men took Braddock's command in deadly earnest. No one moved.

"Listen close, Allison." Braddock gave him a dark look.

"I want a word with Griego. You just stand still and keep your mouth shut."

"Go to hell!" Allison's chin jutted out defiantly. "He's ours and it stays that way."

"How'd you like me to shoot your kneecap off?"

"You don't scare me, Braddock."

"Then keep talking." Braddock drew a bead on his right knee. "One more word and folks will start calling you Pegleg."

Allison's mouth clicked shut. Braddock watched him a moment with a bitter grin. Then, lowering the pistol, he turned his attention to Griego. There was steel underlying his voice.

"These men lied to you, Griego."

"I do not understand, señor."

"Last night they hung Cruz Vega."

"Muerto!" Griego choked out the word. "Vega is dead?"

Braddock nodded, his face expressionless. "These men will hang you too, and I won't stop them unless you accept my offer."

"Offer?"

"Tell me about Donaghue. If you do that, I'll escort you to jail and personally guarantee your safety. Otherwise, I will stand aside and let these men hang you."

Griego blanched. His eyes glazed and his Adam's apple bobbed. "How do I know you will honor your words, señor?"

"What choice do you have?"

Griego glanced at Allison out of the corner of his eye. His features went taut, and his gaze quickly returned to Braddock. "I have never met Donaghue, señor. I know only what Cruz Vega told me."

"And what was that?"

"We were talking one day, and he mentioned that Donaghue owns a saloon in Raton. He said it was a secret, that another man operates the saloon for Donaghue. He thought it a strange thing."

"What's the man's name?"

"He did not say."

"And the name of the saloon?"

"Something about *el toro*. I do not recall the exact—"

The door opened and Griego's wife started outside. He took a step toward her, arms flung wide to stop her. One of the cowhands seized on the momentary distraction. As Griego moved past him, the cowhand pulled his pistol and shifted aside for a clear shot. Colter triggered the shotgun and a load of buckshot sizzled across the yard. The blast caught the cowhand high in the chest, shredding him with a widespread pattern of lead. He stumbled backward, dropping his gun, and pitched to the ground. A stray ball struck Griego directly behind the ear. The back of his skull exploded in a cloud of blood and brain matter. He slumped forward and fell face-down in the dirt.

Isaac Coleman reacted out of blind panic. As the shotgun roared, his hand streaked toward his holster. Braddock shot him the instant his pistol cleared leather. The slug drilled through Coleman's breastbone and impacted on his heart. He stood there a moment, dead on his feet, then slowly toppled over like a felled tree. The pistol slipped from his grasp and his left leg jerked in afterdeath. All in the same split second, Colter cranked another shell into the scattergun and covered the remaining cowhand. Braddock's arm moved in a slight arc as he thumbed the hammer. His pistol was pointed directly at Allison.

A deadened silence settled over the yard. The woman's hand was clamped to her mouth in a look of stifled horror. Allison and the other man stood stock-still, scarcely breathing. What seemed an interminable length of time slipped past without sound or movement. Then Braddock motioned with his pistol.

"Drop your gun belts."

Allison and the cowhand hastily obeyed. Braddock jerked his chin toward the outskirts of town to the south. "Take off walking and don't look back."

"Holy shit!" Allison bawled. "There's nothin' out there for fifty miles! What about our horses?"

"I'll drop them off at the livery in Cimarron."

"You can't leave a white man stranded out here! It ain't—civilized."

Braddock fired and a spurt of dust kicked up at Allison's feet. "Don't talk anymore. Just move."

Allison turned away with a look of baffled fury. The cowhand fell in beside him and they walked off. Braddock stared after them until they passed the last adobe and headed into open country. Finally, he holstered his pistol and glanced around at Colter. His expression was tightlipped and grim.

"Wish it'd been him instead of Coleman."

"You might still get your chance."

"Not while you're backing me up with that shotgun. Allison plainly didn't care for the odds."

Colter appeared somewhat downcast. "There's times when a scattergun does more'n you intend. I'm real sorry about Griego. Wasn't no way to avoid it."

"Don't blame yourself," Braddock said quickly. "Griego just happened to be in the wrong place at the wrong time. He would've gone to the gallows eventually anyway."

"Yeah, but he'd have talked some more before he took the drop."

"Way it worked out, he told me everything I wanted to hear."

"About Donaghue?"

"None other."

"So what's next?"

Braddock smiled. "Raton."

CHAPTER TWENTY

The telegram staggered Mitchell.

For a moment the words blurred before his eyes. Unnerved, he sat down at his desk, trying to calm himself. He took a couple of deep breaths and read through the message a second time. His expression was one of astonished disbelief, and he stared blankly at the signature. The telegram was from Sheriff Floyd Mather.

A long while passed before Mitchell was able to collect his wits. He rose from the desk, aware that the decision he'd made was not altogether rational. Stuffing the telegram in his coat pocket, he strode through the outer office. His secretary glanced up with a look of surprise, but he went past her without a word. He hurried through the door.

Early morning was the busiest of times on the plaza. Mitchell pushed through the crowds, remembering now that he'd forgotten his hat. Several passersby greeted him, turning to stare strangely as he rushed along without acknowledgment. He rounded the corner onto a side street and walked directly to Stephen Elkton's office. Inside, he barged past the secretary, waving her off as he moved to the private office at the rear. He closed the door behind him.

Elkton appeared startled. "What's the meaning—?"

"Here." Mitchell handed him the telegram. "Read this."

Mitchell dropped into a chair. Elkton unfolded the slip of paper and quickly scanned the message. His mouth tightened and he was silent for a time. He finally placed the telegram on his desk top.

"You appear to have lost your nerve, Warren."

"What's that?" Mitchell snapped.

"Half the people in town must have seen you storm in here. I would imagine the other half will know it before noontime."

"Good God! Didn't you read—?"

"Please don't change the subject. We were discussing your lapse of sound judgment. Why didn't you follow our usual arrangement?"

"I couldn't wait till tonight to contact you. Don't you understand that?"

"I ask for a reason and you offer me an excuse."

"The reason is right in front of you."

Elkton frowned, wagged his head like a schoolmaster confronted with a backward pupil. He leaned forward and studied the telegram a moment. "Who is Cruz Vega?"

"Donaghue's hired killer—an assassin."

"And apparently rather inept at his job. From this, I take it he was paid to kill McMain."

"Yes."

"But he failed and got himself hung in the process."

"So it appears."

"Mmm." Elkton traced a line in the message with his finger. "I gather he talked before he was hanged. Otherwise why would Donaghue have gone into hiding?"

"That's how I interpret it."

"A messy situation, indeed. What we have is a botched murder and Donaghue on the run. To compound matters, he's being pursued by two different factions. Is that correct?"

Mitchell seemed to recover a measure of his composure. He sat straighter and nodded. "Allison and Coleman are the largest ranchers in Colfax County. Along with McMain, they were the original organizers of the coalition."

"Which brings us to the Reverend Jacoby." Elkton tapped the telegram. "According to this, he's not a minister after all. How does the sheriff phrase it—'a lawman of some sort operating in disguise.'"

"Yes, but that's rather vague. Is he a Deputy U.S. Marshal or what?"

"Good question. We can only surmise that the coalition somehow got him involved. Of course, after last night he would seem to represent a disruptive influence."

"How do you mean?"

"Well, quite obviously he's at odds with these ranchers. And I suspect that might very well create problems for McMain. So long as they're fighting each other, we gain a little breathing room."

"You seem to have forgotten that both sides are chasing Donaghue."

Elkton appeared distracted. He slowly shook his head, his gaze fixed on the telegram. "Extraordinary. You'd think a sheriff would know better than to put all this in a wire."

"He had to advise me somehow."

"Then he should have come here, done it in person. This represents a very incriminating document."

"Not really. Everything there will be reported in today's newspapers. It's public information."

"You fool! It's a direct link to you, quite clearly a report. Suppose the newspapers got wind of it? Wouldn't that make a story!"

"I hadn't stopped to consider that. I was only thinking of what it said."

"No, Warren, you weren't thinking at all. You simply reacted."

Elkton was suddenly weary. He saw himself surrounded by incompetents and dullards, men lacking either initiative or foresight. All the years of scheming and planning had ended in yet another crisis. He felt weighted by command, sorely burdened. His grand design seemed to him a cross that he alone bore.

A Missourian, Elkton had come west in 1864. After settling in Santa Fe, he had established a lucrative law practice, specializing in civil litigation. Later, using Mitchell as a front, he had set in motion a far-reaching conspiracy. To exert political leverage on a broad scale, he put together an organization of businessmen, financiers, and influential Republicans. It was a diverse group, united by a common interest in the exploitation of New Mexico's resources. Out of the conspiracy emerged the Santa Fe Ring.

The land-grant scheme was intended as Elkton's boldest masterwork. Yet from the very outset resistance in Colfax County posed a major obstacle. At bottom, the conflict with the Cimarron Coalition was one of ideology. The homesteaders and ranchers held that frontier lands were public domain, open to settlement. Elkton saw it in Old World terms, with himself as the *patrón* and therefore master of a realm. He was willing to enforce that view with whatever measures the situation demanded.

Watching Mitchell now, it occurred to him that his confidence had been sadly misplaced. But today, as so many times in the past, the situation demanded hard decisions. The most immediate decision involved Florencio Donaghue, and clearly there was no one to make it but himself. He stared across the desk.

"How reliable is Donaghue? Would he talk if he was caught?"

"Not likely," Mitchell said hesitantly. "He wouldn't risk implicating himself in murder."

"Perhaps. But, then, that's a risk we can't afford either. Your men—what are their names?"

"Johnson and Ortega."

"How quickly could they reach Cimarron?"

"Possibly tonight. No later than tomorrow."

"Order them to find Donaghue."

"And then what?"

"Silence him."

"You mean kill him."

"Exactly. While they're about it, have them kill our bogus holy man, Jacoby. No unturned stones, hmmm?"

Mitchell passed a hand across his eyes. "Where will it end, Stephen?"

"I beg your pardon?"

"The killing! We can't go on murdering people ad infinitum."

"There would be no need"—Elkton paused for emphasis—"if you had handled it properly to start with."

"No, that's not true. I'm not responsible for what's happened. All I do is transmit orders!"

"How nicely you dodge reality."

"What do you mean by that?"

"Come now, Warren. You can't divorce yourself from the act by saying 'All I do is transmit orders.' You're no less culpable than the thug who pulls the trigger."

"I regret to say you're correct. I'd probably sleep better if I pulled the trigger myself."

"Then I fail to take your point."

"I meant I'm not responsible for what's happened in Cimarron. After all, you're the one who ordered McMain killed."

"And?"

"And now it's no longer a matter of legal actions or the courts. We've convinced the coalition that murder is the most practical way to settle disputes. So they've turned into vigilantes—hangmen."

"To our great benefit, I might add. Vigilantes represent indiscriminate violence, and that frightens people. I suspect the coalition will be roundly condemned for taking the law into its own hands."

"You're wrong, Stephen. If anything, they've won even more public support. God help us if they ever form an alliance with the Democrats."

"Well, that's a philosophical discussion for another day, isn't it? At the moment we're faced with more mundane matters."

"Donaghue?"

"His name certainly heads the list. I suggest you attend to it immediately."

"I suppose you're right. We'd all swing if he ever talked."

"And none quicker than you, Warren. Everything he's done would be laid at your doorstep."

"Very well. I'll talk to Johnson and Ortega within the hour."

"Don't forget to mention the good reverend."

"I think you should reconsider on Jacoby. It would be a great mistake to kill a lawman."

"It would be a greater mistake to let him live. He's much too close to the truth to risk leaving him alive. So just do as I ask."

"Of course, I always do."

"And, Warren."

"Yes?"

"Impress on your men that they mustn't fail. You see, in the end you are responsible—to me."

The threat needed no elaboration. Mitchell bobbed his head and rose hastily to his feet. As he turned toward the door, Elkton's voice stopped him.

"One last thing."

"Yes?"

"Never again are you to come here during office hours. Never!"

"I understand."

The door opened and closed and Elkton was alone. He steepled his hands, slowly tapping his forefingers together. For a moment he considered the possibility that Johnson and Ortega would fail. By extension, he was forced then to assess the direct link to his own doorstep.

All of which led him to a personal consideration of the logistics of murder. The most efficient means by which to silence Warren Mitchell.

It was an interesting problem.

Mitchell stared blankly at his desk top. His thoughts were turned inward and he seemed lost in dark introspection.

A knock sounded at the door. His secretary ushered Slim Johnson and Pedro Ortega into the office. Ortega, unlike his rawboned partner, was short and stout, with a handlebar mustache. The men removed their hats as the door closed behind them.

"I have a job for you," Mitchell informed them.

Johnson and Ortega alerted at the tone of his voice. Like all predators, they were attuned to mood and telltale behavior. They somehow sensed that Mitchell was repelled by violence, unnerved by death. They enjoyed his discomfort.

Johnson grinned. "Anybody we know, boss?"

"Yes," Mitchell said quietly. "Our man in Cimarron . . . Donaghue."

"You want him roughed up"—Johnson let the thought dangle a moment—"or buried?"

"Don't play games with me, Slim. You know what I want."

"Why, sure thing, boss. You just go ahead and X him off your list. He's good as dead."

Ortega chuckled jovially. "Slim wouldn't lie to you, *patrón*. We never miss, him and me."

"How reassuring," Mitchell said in an aloof voice. "If you will allow me to finish, there's more. Another one."

"Well, God a'mighty!" Johnson cackled. "You mean to say you want somebody else killed too?"

"Exactly," Mitchell said with no great enthusiasm. "His name is the Reverend Titus Jacoby. Also of Cimarron."

"*Caramba!*" Ortega boomed. "Another son-of-a-bitch preacher!"

"Lower your voice, you fool! They'll hear you on the street."

"Sorry," Ortega apologized. "I meant no harm, *patrón*."

"Just pay attention," Mitchell went on dully. "There's reason to believe that Jacoby is a lawman of some sort. Probably a Deputy U.S. Marshal."

Johnson and Ortega exchanged a look. Mitchell rapped his desk to get their attention. "I want you to proceed cautiously. Once you get to Cimarron, take your time and look the situation over carefully. We can't afford mistakes, not with a peace officer involved. Understood?"

"Don't worry, boss," Johnson replied. "We won't let you down."

Ortega bobbed his head. "Is the truth, *patrón*. Slim and me take care of it for you *muy pronto*."

"*Muy pronto*," Mitchell repeated, "but with care. Great care. No mistakes."

"*Si, patrón.*"

"It's in the bag, boss. Good as done."

Nodding and grinning, Johnson led the way out. Ortega flashed a wide smile as he went through the door. Watching them, Mitchell passed a hand across his forehead. He suddenly felt feverish, and slightly ill.

CHAPTER TWENTY-ONE

Soon after dark that evening, they halted on the outskirts of Raton. The mountains were a dark silhouette against a starswept sky, and the night was bitter cold. Their horses snorted frosty clouds of vapor.

Braddock was once more in the guise of a Texas cattleman. Earlier that day they had dropped Allison's horses off at the livery stable in Cimarron. To avoid delay, they had steered clear of Orville McMain. Colter waited while Braddock collected his carpetbag from the hotel. Some miles north of town, they stopped and Braddock had discarded his preacher's outfit. From his carpetbag, he'd donned the clothing and fake mustache that transformed him into Elmer Boyd.

Their plan was loosely formulated. Braddock would enter Raton and conduct the search for Donaghue. Colter, who was known to Donaghue, would wait outside town. Based on the description provided by Colter, the man they sought wouldn't be all that difficult to recognize. In the event Braddock located Donaghue, he would then determine their next move. The overriding imperative was to effect the capture

quietly and without gunplay. Donaghue was of value only if
he was taken alive. He represented the one direct link to
Warren Mitchell and the Santa Fe Ring.

The main street of Raton was brightly lit by corner
lampposts. On either side of the street, the boardwalks were
jammed with men out for an evening's entertainment.
Braddock held his horse to a walk and rode slowly through
town. He was looking for a saloon with the word "bull" in its
name. Even if Donaghue had skipped Raton, it was the place
to begin the search. Yet, while his eyes scanned the street,
his thoughts were on Lise. By now word of the blowup in
Cimarron would have reached Santa Fe. Mitchell and Elkins
were doubtless aware of the danger to themselves, especially
if Donaghue was made to talk. Their normal caution would
now be multiplied manyfold, which further jeopardized Lise's
position. One slip, no matter how inconsequential, would
very likely serve as her death warrant. Time was running
out, and Braddock was driven by a growing sense of urgency.
He had to find Donaghue tonight or call it quits and return
to Santa Fe. He saw no alternative.

The Bull's Head Saloon was a block past the town's central intersection. Braddock hitched his horse out front, and
followed a crowd of teamsters through the door. He found a
spot at the bar, ordered rye, and subjected the place to a casual examination. Gambling layouts were ranged along the
wall opposite the bar, with several tables toward the rear of
the room. There was a single door behind the tables, and the
absence of stairs indicated there was no upper floor. After a
few drinks, he engaged one of the barkeeps in conversation.
He learned that the dealer at the faro layout was also the
owner of the Bull's Head. His name was Blacky O'Neal.

An hour or so later Braddock decided hanging around the
saloon was a waste of time. He'd seen nothing of anyone who
faintly resembled Donaghue's description. The only thing to
arouse his interest was the door at the rear of the room. Apparently O'Neal possessed the lone key. He had stopped the

faro game at one point and unlocked the door, waiting while a bartender fetched a case of whiskey. Braddock thought it entirely possible that O'Neal didn't trust the barkeeps with the stockroom key. He also wondered whether there was an office or some sort of living quarters behind the door. For the moment there was no way to tell.

Around nine o'clock, Braddock rode back to where Colter waited. He explained what he'd found and voiced the opinion that there was little chance of Colter being spotted. Neither of them had eaten supper, and they proceeded to a café near the railroad depot. After a meal of beefsteak and fried potatoes, they lingered over several cups of coffee. Then they walked their horses uptown and located a saloon catty-corner to the Bull's Head. Inside, they took a position at the bar that afforded a view through the front window. For the balance of the night, they nursed their drinks and kept one eye on the street. No one entering or departing the Bull's Head bore any resemblance to Donaghue.

Shortly after three in the morning, Braddock led the way outside. The saloons were closing for the night, and he wanted a better vantage spot. Halfway down the block was a pharmacist's shop, and they took up posts in the darkened doorway. Within the hour, the Bull's Head emptied of customers and a short while later the lights inside were extinguished. Blacky O'Neal emerged, locking the door behind him, and walked off down the street. Braddock left Colter to watch the Bull's Head, and trailed O'Neal by a discreet distance. The saloonkeeper led him to a modest frame dwelling on the south side of town.

A parlor lamp was the only light burning in the house. Braddock watched through a side window while O'Neal lit a lamp in the bedroom, then returned and lowered the wick on the parlor lamp. When O'Neal went back to the bedroom Braddock moved along the side of the house and stopped outside the window. He saw a woman asleep in the bed, and he noted that O'Neal was at some pains not to wake her.

Undressing, O'Neal draped his clothes over a chair and
slipped into a nightshirt. He crossed to a bed and sat down,
reaching for the lamp. The room went dark.

Braddock walked back uptown. He somehow doubted
that Donaghue was being hidden out in O'Neal's house. The
saloonkeeper's actions were too routine; his manner betrayed
none of the signs of someone harboring a wanted man. That
left only the Bull's Head and the locked storeroom. It was a
long shot, but nonetheless worth a look. Braddock fully expected to find nothing more than a room stacked with beer
barrels and cases of whiskey. Yet that in itself would elimi-
nate one more possibility. And tomorrow was time enough
to have a talk with Blacky O'Neal.

The business district was deserted. Braddock found Colter still waiting in the pharmacy doorway. They crossed the
street and walked halfway down the block to an alley. Turning in, they moved to the back door of the Bull's Head. While
Colter held a match, Braddock took out his pocketknife and
began working on the lock. Less than a minute passed before
the tumbler clicked over. To Braddock's surprise, there was
no crossbeam barring the door from the inside. He wondered
at the oversight, then put it from his mind. Whatever the reason, it simplified the job of gaining entry. A twist of the knob
opened the door, and they stepped into a room dark as pitch.
Then, somewhere very close, they heard a man snoring.

Colter struck another match. In the flare of light, they saw
a room filled with crates and cases. Squat barrels were
stacked along the back wall, and on their left, toward the
front of the room, was an open door. Braddock pulled his
pistol, and Colter held the match high, lighting the way. They
cat-footed to the door and stepped into a small office. A floor
safe was wedged into one corner, and nearby was a desk and
chair. Beside the desk was a metal cot with wire springs
and a padded mattress. A man was sprawled on the cot, his
mouth agape, snoring loudly. He was heavily built, with a
square, thick-jowled face, and he wore only long johns. His
clothes were neatly hung on the chair.

"Donaghue."

Colter whispered the name as he snuffed the match. While Braddock kept his gun trained on the cot, Colter moved silently to the desk. He flicked a match on his thumbnail and quickly lighted a lamp. When he turned up the wick, the office was bathed in a bright amber glow. The man on the cot stirred, pulling the blanket down as he rolled onto his side. The snoring stopped and he lay there a moment without moving. Then, still half asleep, he put his hand up, trying to block out the light. His eyes slowly fluttered open.

"Wake up and join the party, Donaghue."

Braddock's voice brought him upright in the cot. His eyes widened and his gaze shuttled from Braddock to Colter. His jaw dropped open and his features contorted in a look of thunderstruck amazement. Colter grinned and leaned back against the wall. Braddock seated himself on the edge of the desk. He aimed the pistol at a spot between Donaghue's eyes.

"You remember Colter, don't you?"

Donaghue tried to collect his wits. "Who are you?"

"Take a closer look." Braddock permitted himself a grim smile. "You probably saw me around Cimarron. Or maybe your boys told you about me. Reverend Titus Jacoby."

"I—" Donaghue regarded him with profound shock. "What do you want with me?"

"I guess you heard how Allison and his crowd hung Vega?"

"So what?"

Braddock looked at him without expression. "Yesterday, Pancho Griego told us where to find you. Then Colter shot and killed him."

Donaghue's face went chalky. "Who's Pancho Griego?"

"One of the men you hired to kill Reverend Tolby. Vega and Griego both confessed before they died. And by law, a deathbed confession is admissible in court. Their word alone would convict you of murder."

"You'll never make it stick."

"I wouldn't even try," Braddock said, suddenly tight-lipped.

"What I would do is turn you over to Allison and his crowd. By sundown, you'd be decorating a tree somewhere. How's that idea strike you?"

Donaghue shook his head as though a fly had buzzed in his ear. "I don't get it. Are you offering me a choice of some kind?"

"I'll only say it once." Braddock's eyes took on a cold tinsel glitter. "I want the goods on Warren Mitchell. You cooperate and I'll guarantee immunity from prosecution. Otherwise I'll hand you over to Allison."

"Some choice!" Donaghue studied him with the sideways suspicion of a kicked dog. "Why should I trust you to keep your word?"

"Figure it out," Braddock said in a measured tone. "I want you alive and talkative. You're no good to me dead."

"How do I know you're not bluffing about Allison?"

Braddock's gaze bored into him. "The other side of the coin speaks for itself. You're no good to me alive—unless you talk."

There was no immediate response. Donaghue's eyes dulled as he turned thoughtful. The silence stretched out as he debated something within himself. Finally, with a great shrug of resignation, he nodded. His voice was strained.

"What do you want to know?"

"Who ordered you to kill Reverend Tolby?"

"Warren Mitchell."

"Who ordered you to kill Orville McMain?"

"Mitchell."

"How were the orders delivered?"

"By him or one of his men."

"What do you mean, one of his men?"

"He keeps a couple of hardcases on his payroll. They work out of Santa Fe."

"What're their names?"

"Pedro Ortega and Slim Johnson."

"Were all your orders delivered by them?"

"No." A nervous flicker crossed Donaghue's lips. "I met

with Mitchell once a month in Santa Fe. All the routine stuff was handled then."

"Are you talking about political business?"

"Yeah."

"Mitchell told you what he wanted done, and you passed along his orders to the courthouse crowd. Is that how it worked?"

"Generally."

Braddock watched him intently. "Was there ever any personal contact between Mitchell and the courthouse crowd?"

"Never," Donaghue said with a blank stare. "All the orders came through me."

"But they knew he was the boss?" Braddock insisted. "The head of the Santa Fe Ring?"

"Oh, nobody had any doubts about that."

"What was their payoff in the deal?"

"Mitchell let them run the county to suit themselves. Any graft or bribes went into their pockets. It was like having a patent on a money tree."

"And what were they expected to do in return?"

"Whatever they were told." Donaghue smiled vacantly. "Their main job was to enforce Mitchell's demands on the farmers and ranchers."

"In other words, force everyone to pay for land they'd already settled, or else get evicted. Is that it?"

"Pretty much."

"What was your job?"

"I picked the candidates and rigged the elections. Anyone who wouldn't play along never got nominated, much less elected."

"A political kingfish usually gets a hefty slice of the graft and bribes. How about you?"

"Mitchell insisted that all under-the-table money go to the officeholders. He wanted to keep them fat and happy."

"So where was your payoff?"

"I was in for a share of everything we collected on land sales."

"How big a share?"

"Three percent."

"Not bad, considering it involved millions of dollars. You would've been a rich man."

"Someday."

"One last thing," Braddock said with a casual gesture. "Sit down here at the desk and write it all out in your own words. Just the way you told it to me."

"I don't think so," Donaghue said slowly. "You wouldn't need me if you had a signed confession."

"Strictly a precaution, nothing more."

"In case something happens to me?"

"That's right."

"Then you'd better not let anything happen. I'll testify to names, dates, and places. But I won't put it in writing."

Braddock stood and motioned with the gun. "Get dressed."

"Where are we going?"

"Cimarron."

All the blood leached out of Donaghue's face. "You said you wouldn't turn me over to Allison. You gave me your word!"

"Quit squawking. With Buck and me along, Allison won't come anywhere near you. Isn't that right, Buck?"

Colter smiled. "Not unless he's tired of livin'."

Late that evening, Braddock sat talking quietly with Bud Grant. The marshal's expression was somber and worried. He kept glancing at the door.

Braddock no longer wore the mustache. Apart from his dyed hair, his appearance was his own. He seemed calm and controlled, perfectly at ease. He'd weighed the risk of returning to Cimarron, and on balance he thought it the wisest choice. Here, at least, he knew who his enemies were.

A few minutes before nine the door opened. Colter stepped inside and waved Floyd Mather into the office. The sheriff marched straight to the desk, nodding at Grant. Then he turned his head just far enough to rivet Braddock with a look. He stared down at him with a bulldog scowl.

"What happened to the good Reverend Jacoby?"

Braddock grinned. "I put him out to pasture."

"Who the hell are you anyway?"

"Nobody you want to know, Sheriff."

"Then why'd you send Colter after me?"

"Law business." Braddock gestured toward the rear of the jail. "I've got Donaghue back there in a cell."

"Donaghue!" Mather repeated, thoroughly dumbfounded. "What's the charge?"

"One count of murder. Three counts of conspiracy to commit murder."

Mather looked surprised, then suddenly irritated. "In that case, he belongs in my custody. I'll just take him over to the county jail."

"No, you won't." Braddock shook his head firmly. "Donaghue stays here while he's in Cimarron. He'll be guarded by nobody but Colter or myself. We've already worked out the arrangements with Marshal Grant."

"It won't wash," Mather said churlishly. "Not in my jurisdiction."

"Here's the deal," Braddock went on in a pleasant voice. "You'll inform the county judge that he's to set up a preliminary hearing for tomorrow morning. I want Donaghue bound over on a charge of murder."

"Who the hell you think you're talkin' to?"

Braddock ignored the outburst. "You'll also inform the county prosecutor that he's to convene a grand jury no later than day after tomorrow. The juror list is to be made up solely of ranchers and farmers."

"What d'you think that'll accomplish?"

"Three counts of conspiracy to commit murder."

"Against who?"

"Donaghue and certain parties in Santa Fe."

There was a moment of stunned silence. Mather's face paled and little knots bunched tight at the back of his jaws.

"You talk like I'm gonna follow orders like a toy soldier. Why's that?"

"A couple of reasons," Braddock announced. "For one thing, I don't believe you or your cronies were involved in the murder conspiracy. So you're off the hook on the capital offense."

"What's the other reason?"

"I'm the only thing holding Clay Allison in check. Either you go along with me or I'll turn him loose."

"You're threatenin' a sworn officer of the law!"

"I told you once before there's a difference between a threat and a prophecy. If I turn Allison loose, I predict he'll hang you and most of your pals at the courthouse. Would you care to put it to the test?"

Mather studied him for a long while before answering. "I take it Donaghue's gonna turn state's evidence?"

A wintry smile lighted Braddock's eyes. "You'll find out tomorrow. Tell the judge I want court convened at nine sharp."

Several moments elapsed while the two men stared at one another. Then Mather turned about abruptly and strode from the office. Braddock and Colter exchanged an amused look. Bud Grant let out his breath as the door slammed shut.

"You think he'll do it?"

"Wouldn't you?" Braddock lit a cigarette. "I doubt that anybody over at the courthouse wants a midnight visit from Allison."

"Were you really serious about that?"

"Never more serious in my life."

"God! You play for all the marbles, don't you?"

Braddock smiled and blew a perfect smoke ring toward the ceiling.

CHAPTER TWENTY-TWO

The morning was crisp and bright. On the horizon, the sun rose like an orange ball of fire. Scattered clouds capped the mountaintops and the slopes were tinged with vermilion. High overhead a V of ducks winged southward.

Braddock stood at the window. The street outside the jail bustled with early morning activity. Stores and shops were opening for business, and housewives were already about their daily errands. Somewhere in the distance a school bell tolled, and a gang of tardy children hurried along the boardwalk. Cimarron prepared to meet another uneventful day.

Watching from the window, Braddock knew it wouldn't last for long. The grapevine in any small town worked with lightning speed. While it was barely past eight, the word would spread along the street within a matter of minutes. People thrived on gossip, and the self-appointed gadflies were quick to make their rounds. By nine, all of Cimarron would know that Florencio Donaghue was slated for a court appearance. That the charge was murder would merely stoke the fires of their curiosity. Braddock knew the uneventful day was about to take on the trappings of a three-ring circus. He pondered on the best way to get Donaghue from the jail to the courthouse.

Overnight Braddock and Colter had taken turns standing guard. Bud Grant had spent the night on a bunk in one of the empty cells. Shortly after sunrise, the marshal had walked up to the café and ordered breakfast trays brought down. Then, one at a time, they had shaved with a straight razor Grant kept in his desk drawer. Following the meal, there had been a lull while the town slowly stirred to life. Colter and Grant swigged coffee, and Braddock waited by the window. There seemed no need for conversation.

Upstreet, Braddock saw Orville McMain hurrying toward the jail. He checked his pocket watch, noting it was a few minutes shy of eight-thirty. Much as he'd expected, the grapevine was working overtime. McMain barged into the office with a look of towering indignation.

"I just now heard you were in town."

"Good news travels fast, Orville."

"But you arrived last night!" McMain said in a waspish tone. "Why didn't you contact me?"

"No need." Braddock gestured toward Colter and the marshal. "We've got things under control."

"Is it true? Do you have Donaghue in custody?"

"Safe and sound, not a scratch on him."

"You captured him in Raton, then?"

Braddock cocked an eyebrow. "How'd you know that?"

"Clay Allison," McMain said quickly. "He stopped by the office late yesterday afternoon. Did you really leave him stranded in Rayado?"

"I figured the walk would cool him down."

"Quite the contrary," McMain remarked. "He says you murdered Coleman and one of his hands. He's threatening to bring charges against you and Colter."

"Allison's all wind and no whistle. I wouldn't lose any sleep over it, Orville."

"But you did kill Coleman, didn't you?"

"When somebody pulls a gun on me, I generally do my damnedest to stop his clock. Coleman wasn't any exception."

McMain looked upset. "You've put me in a difficult position. Allison's telling everyone I'm responsible for Coleman's death. He says you were acting on my orders."

"I imagine most people take what Allison says with a grain of salt."

"Not enough!" McMain declared. "I may have trouble holding the coalition together."

"Tell you what," Braddock said with thinly disguised sarcasm. "You worry about the coalition and I'll worry about Donaghue. Sound fair?"

"Yes, of course." McMain seemed to regain his composure. "I'm sorry I got sidetracked. How do you think it will go with Donaghue?"

Braddock briefed him on last night's conversation with the sheriff. McMain was by turns amazed and perplexed. He appeared somewhat skeptical.

"Have you talked with Mather this morning?"

"What's there to talk about?"

"I don't know," McMain said uneasily. "But it's not like Mather to give in so quickly. He's a very devious man."

"Devious maybe, but not dumb. I've got him and his buddies over a barrel. They'll sacrifice Donaghue to save themselves."

"Perhaps," McMain said without conviction. "I'd still caution you to watch your step. They're all scoundrels, to the last man!"

"I'll keep my eyes open, Orville."

Braddock walked him to the door. McMain went reluctantly, aware he was being dismissed. Finally, with yet another warning, he stepped outside and turned uptown. Braddock closed the door and quickly checked the time.

"Quarter of nine," he said, moving back into the office. "Let's get Donaghue ready to go."

Bud Grant rose from behind his desk. "How're we gonna handle it?"

"You've got manacles, don't you?"

"Sure do."

"First things first," Braddock said briskly. "We'll bring him out of the lockup and get him fitted with bracelets."

"What then?"

"Then Buck and me will escort him to the courthouse."

"Hold on a goldurned minute! I didn't hear my name mentioned."

"You're staying here, Bud."

"Would you mind tellin' me why?"

"I've already put you out on a limb. I'm not about to saw it off after you."

"What d'you mean by that?"

"We're operating outside the law," Braddock informed him. "You've exceeded your authority just by holding Dona-ghue here overnight. I'm beholden to you for that, but let's not make it any worse."

"I got my toes wet." Grant chuckled. "I might as well take the plunge."

"Lots of things could go wrong. For all we know, some-body might try to bust Donaghue loose. You'd be in a hell of a fix if that happened."

"How so?"

"Technically, he's not in legal custody. Would you want to get involved in a shootout under those circumstances?"

"I'm not partial to a shootout under any circumstances."

"All the more reason to stay behind."

"Well, it's your show," Grant said with a shrug. "But you're liable to wish you had a badge along for the ride. It'd damn sure look legal, even if it's not."

"I'm only trying to save you trouble."

"Lemme put it this way." Grant looked him straight in the eye. "I'd sooner go than stay behind."

"I reckon that settles it."

"So what's your plan?" Grant persisted. "How do you aim to get from here to there?"

Braddock considered a moment. "Suppose you lead the

way and clear a path on the boardwalk. I'll follow directly behind with Donaghue, and Buck can bring up the rear. That ought to pretty well cover it."

"Sounds good." Colter set down his coffee mug and stood. "I'm ready whenever you are."

"Let's get to it, then."

Braddock followed Grant through the door to the lockup. The marshal unlocked Donaghue's cell and waved him outside. Somewhat the worse for wear, Donaghue's clothes were rumpled and his jaw was covered with whiskery stubble. He joined them in the corridor, and they walked him back to the office.

Grant moved to his desk and dug a pair of manacles out of the bottom drawer. The wristbands were constructed of sturdy iron and attached together by a short length of chain. He unlocked each of the bands with a stubby key and tossed it back in the drawer. Then he crossed the room, motioning for Donaghue to hold out his hands. He snapped the manacles around Donaghue's wrists and pressed until the locks clicked. He glanced at Braddock.

"How's that?"

"Just what the doctor ordered."

"What's the matter?" Donaghue laughed, staring down at the manacles. "Afraid I'll make a break for it?"

"You better not." Colter cranked a shell into his shotgun. "I'm gonna be right behind you all the way."

Grant studied the shotgun a moment, then turned to Braddock. "What about me? You think I ought to carry a scattergun?"

"Take a rifle," Braddock replied. "Too much artillery might give folks the wrong idea. We're not hunting trouble."

Grant took a Winchester carbine from the gun rack. He worked the lever and jacked a Cartridge into the chamber. Then he lowered the hammer and cradled the Winchester over the crook of his arm. He looked back at Braddock.

"All set?"

"Lead the way, Marshal."

Outside, they formed a tight column. With Braddock and
Donaghue in the middle, they marched off at a rapid pace.
Passersby stopped to stare, and early morning street traffic
came to a standstill, clogging the intersection with wagons
and buggies. Ahead of them stores emptied as shopkeepers
and townspeople crowded the doorways for a better look.
Grant bulled a path through the throngs on the boardwalk,
ordering them aside in a rough voice. At first there was total
silence as the four men proceeded uptown. Then a buzz of
excitement swelled in their wake, steadily growing louder.
All of Cimarron turned out to gawk.

Nearing the hotel, Grant wheeled right and led the way
across the street. Braddock kept a tight grip on Donaghue's
arm as they passed between vehicles halted at curbside. A
pace behind, Colter's eyes were in constant motion, sweeping the street in both directions. On the opposite curb, Grant
veered around a wagon and headed toward a short walkway
leading to the courthouse steps. Spectators mobbed the por-
tico outside the entrance and every window was jammed
with onlookers. No one moved as the men proceeded up the
walkway.

Then, suddenly, an upstairs window in the hotel erupted
with gunfire. The curtains jumped from the muzzle blast of
two rifles and an earsplitting crack echoed along the street.
Donaghue grunted, lurching forward, as a slug drilled through
his backbone and exited high on his chest. His shirtfront exploded outward in a crimson bloodburst, and he dropped like
a stone. Braddock involuntarily flinched as a second bullet
droned past his ear. Directly in front of him, Grant took the
slug in the base of the neck, shattering his spine. The carbine
slipped from his grasp and a massive jerk of nerves knocked
him off his feet. He hit the walkway on his face, arms
splayed wide.

Braddock and Colter reacted in what seemed one fluid
motion. Colter whirled around as Braddock bent low and
scooped up the carbine. The hotel window belched a sheet

of flame and rifle slugs whizzed past them with an angry snarl. Colter let loose with his shotgun, triggering three quick blasts in a roaring blaze. The buckshot whistled across the street, spreading in a fanlike pattern, and peppered the upper wall of the hotel with lead. Only a beat behind, Braddock shouldered the carbine and levered two rounds through the window. Gunfire from the hotel abruptly ceased and the snouts of the rifles vanished from view. A deafening silence settled over the street.

"Behind the hotel!" Braddock shouted. "You take the left side."

Colter nodded and took off at a lope. The drivers of buggies and wagons were fighting to control their teams, and stunned onlookers were huddled in doorways along the boardwalk. Braddock sprinted across the street, dodging a rearing horse as he neared the curb. He swerved around the right side of the hotel and ran toward the rear of the building. A few feet from the corner he skidded to a halt and jacked a fresh round into the chamber. Edging closer, he saw two saddle horses tied to a tree in the backlot. The rear door of the hotel suddenly burst open, and two men carrying rifles rushed outside. They made a headlong dash for the horses.

"Hold it!"

Braddock's command caught them in midstride. The men skittered awkwardly to a stop and spun around in unison. Their eyes fixed on Braddock, who was standing with the butt of the carbine tucked into his shoulder. For a split second they stared at him as though weighing the odds. Then one moved, and the other followed suit, and their rifles leveled in his direction. Braddock sighted quickly and touched off the trigger. His slug struck the man on the right slightly below the sternum and killed him instantly.

Colter stepped around the opposite corner of the building. He squinted down the barrel of the shotgun and fired. The man on the left was punched backward by the impact, bright red dots spurting across the width of his chest. He lost his footing and somersaulted head over heels, landing flat on his back. His bladder voided in death.

Braddock and Colter walked forward. They halted before the corpses and inspected them with icy detachment. One man was tall and lanky, a limp bundle of knobs and joints. The other man was Mexican, with fleshy features and a sweeping mustache. After a time, Colter nudged the Mexican with the toe of his boot.

"You reckon his name was Ortega?"

"I'd bet on it," Braddock muttered. "And that other jaybird was Slim Johnson."

"Mitchell's gunhands," Colter added. "The ones Donaghue told us worked out of Santa Fe."

"It all fits." Braddock hawked and spat, his eyes rimmed with disgust. "Mitchell probably sent them up here sometime yesterday. He couldn't afford to let Donaghue be taken alive and start talking. I should've figured it."

"Not unless you had a crystal ball."

"The signs were there," Braddock said glumly. "Hell, even Orville McMain suspected something. He tried to warn me this morning."

"You mean his hunch about the sheriff?"

Braddock nodded. "That's why Mather caved in so quick last night. He knew these two were in town, and he let me serve Donaghue up on a platter. I walked into it like a blind man."

Colter was silent a moment. "You gonna call Mather out?"

"No." Braddock's mouth curled at the corner. "I'll let Allison have him. He'll look good on a lamppost."

"Since you're turnin' Allison loose"—Colter paused, his eyes inquisitive—"I take it you're gonna say adios and good-bye to Cimarron."

"With Donaghue dead, I've played out my string here."

"Where to now?"

"I've got some unfinished business in Santa Fe."

"Mitchell?"

"He's first on the list."

"I'd give a nickel to see him get it."

"You're welcome to come along."

"I guess not." Colter uttered a low chuckle. "I try to steer clear of big towns. Hard to keep lookin' over your shoulder with all them people around."

"You could ride with me as far as Raton . . . I'm gonna take the train to Santa Fe from there."

"Wrong direction," Colter observed. "The last couple of days are gonna make a splash in the newspapers. I calculate my name'll get mentioned somewheres along the way."

"You figure that might put the International on your trail?"

"I'm thinkin' it'd be smart not to hang around and find out."

"Where will you head?"

"West." Colter turned slightly, staring at the Sangre de Cristos. "I've been wonderin' what's on the other side of them mountains. I suppose it's time to go have a look-see."

There was a marked silence. Braddock followed his gaze, and for a moment there was a wordless bond between them. Neither of them could have articulated it, but they both understood its origin. It was the kinship of strong men who each saw something of himself in the other. A kinship immune to time and distance.

Braddock finally broke the silence. "You won't outrun the International. Not even on the other side of those mountains."

"Never figured I would."

"One of these days you're liable to find yourself in a tight fix."

"Yeah, that's possible."

"You've got my marker when it happens."

"You don't owe me nothin', Cole."

"Let's say I do and shake on it."

Colter took his hand and gave it a hard pump. "You know, you would've made a hell of a Cheyenne."

Braddock grinned. "I think maybe you're right."

"No maybe about it! It's puredee fact."

Their laughter seemed to linger behind them as they turned and walked toward the street.

CHAPTER TWENTY-THREE

The evening train was almost six hours late. Braddock's nerves felt raw and gritty as he lit another cigarette. He stared out the window, silently cursing what seemed a sudden run of bad luck. Santa Fe was still some ten miles downtrack.

The entire day had proved to be one delay after another. Following the courthouse shootout, Braddock and Colter had walked directly to the newspaper. There a heated argument had ensued, with McMain insisting that they both remain in town until a coroner's inquest could be arranged. His sole interest was in exposing the courthouse conspiracy, and he'd stressed the importance of their testimony. But Braddock, intent on reaching Santa Fe, had flatly refused. Colter, for reasons of his own, wanted to put Cimarron far behind him. McMain had dogged their heels from the newspaper office to the livery stable, protesting all the way. Braddock finally agreed to a compromise, promising to forward a sworn deposition. Then, with Colter at his side, he'd ridden out of town.

A mile or so up the road, Colter had reined to a halt. His way was west, over the mountains, and he had accompanied Braddock this far only to lay a false trail. Their parting words were brief, for they'd both said all that needed saying. With a final handshake, Colter struck out across country, on a beeline for the Sangre de Cristos. Braddock, watching after him a moment, had then turned his horse toward Raton. There was an afternoon train for Santa Fe, and he had several things to accomplish before departure time. While he hadn't mentioned it to McMain, he'd decided there was nothing more to be gained by operating in disguise. His name was now known, and his various cover stories had fallen before events of the past few days. He figured the best bet was to forget guile and rely instead on the unexpected. He would revert to himself.

In Raton, Braddock had discovered the train was running an hour late. He'd been tempted to pay a call on Blacky O'Neal, Donaghue's partner in the Bull's Head Saloon. On second thought, however, he had concluded it would merely complicate matters. To brace the man might very well cause a ruckus, even end in gunplay. Then, too, it seemed unlikely that O'Neal would know anything damaging about the ring. For the moment, Braddock's principal concern was to reach Santa Fe as quickly as possible. So he'd stuck to his original plan.

Uptown, he had purchased a complete change of clothing. The only thing he kept was the boots he'd worn while posing as a Texas cattleman. His next stop was a public bathhouse, where several rinsings in a steamy tub removed all the dye from his hair. After a shave, the image he saw in a mirror seemed curiously unreal. He'd been operating undercover so long it was almost as though he were impersonating himself. Upon leaving the bathhouse, he had gone straight to the depot. The train finally departed an hour and ten minutes behind schedule.

Braddock hadn't been too alarmed by the delay. But around nightfall he'd begun cursing the railroad with considerable anger. A rockslide at Glorieta Pass had blocked the tracks with a small mountain of rubble. Some four hours were then consumed while passengers and crew pitched in to clear the roadbed. Once under way, Braddock had questioned the conductor and got some disturbing news. There was little likelihood of the train's arriving in Santa Fe before midnight. The conductor estimated it would be closer to one in the morning.

The added delay forced Braddock to revamp his plan. His original assessment had been based on certain assumptions about Warren Mitchell. He knew Sheriff Mather would have wired Mitchell earlier that morning. Though the sheriff still had no idea as to Braddock's actual identity, the wire itself would have been reassuring. Donaghue's death effectively severed the only direct link to Mitchell; the death of the two gunhands further eliminated any connection with the Santa Fe Ring. Mitchell would reasonably assume he was now in the clear. Apart from a phantom investigator, whose last witness was dead, he had nothing to fear from the Cimarron blowup. He would have reported as much to Stephen Elkton.

For all practical purposes, Braddock saw it in much the same light. His investigation was stymied, and he'd lost any chance of grand jury indictments. Still, upon riding out of Cimarron, his frame of mind had turned from practical to pragmatic. He told himself that the end justified the means where assassins were concerned. While it was an extreme action, he had resolved to take Warren Mitchell prisoner. The tactics he employed afterward would depend to a large extent on Mitchell. He disliked extracting a confession by violent methods and he seldom resorted to brute force, yet by hook or crook, he intended to make Mitchell talk. All other options had been foreclosed.

Braddock had thought to effect the capture immediately upon arriving in Santa Fe. His plan was to take Mitchell unawares, either on the street or in the land-company office. But a rockslide had foreclosed that option as well. By the time he reached Santa Fe, Mitchell would have settled in at the Tivoli Theater. To make matters worse, it was entirely possible Lise would be seated at Mitchell's table. The risk of taking Mitchell under those circumstances forced Braddock to alter his approach. He had no choice but to determine

Lise's whereabouts and then insure her safety. Only afterward would he turn his attention to Mitchell. The six-hour delay had changed both his plan and his priorities. Lise was now his chief concern.

Apart from the delay, Braddock was still confident he held the edge. Mitchell knew him only as Elmer Boyd, the high-roller Texan. Further, someone in Cimarron had doubtless supplied a description of the Reverend Titus Jacoby. It was safe to assume that Mitchell was now aware that one man had played both roles. Moreover, Stephen Elkton would realize he'd betrayed himself as the leader of the Santa Fe Ring. Yet neither of them would believe they were in any immediate danger of being exposed. Everyone who might have testified against them was now dead.

Their overconfidence merely enhanced Braddock's edge. Quite logically, they would anticipate his return to Santa Fe. But they would expect him to appear in some new guise, operating undercover. It would never occur to them that he might return as himself, openly and with no attempt at deception. Nor was he worried about being recognized from photos in the *Police Gazette* and other periodicals. By virtue of doing the unexpected when it was least expected, the element of surprise was in his favor. He meant to strike before anyone realized he was in town.

The train slowed on the outskirts of Santa Fe. Braddock checked his pocket watch as the engineer throttled down and set the brakes. The time was 12:43, and he recalled that Lise's act was the finale for the midnight show. He was cutting it close, perhaps too close. But if he hurried, he could still catch her before she joined Mitchell at his table. The locomotive rolled past the depot and ground to a halt, belching steam and smoke. The moment the conductor opened the coach door, Braddock stepped onto the platform. He walked quickly toward the plaza.

Lise took a final curtain call. Her naughty ballads were still the hit of Santa Fe, and the audience tonight gave her a wild ovation. She threw them kisses with both hands as the curtain rang down.

Backstage, she avoided several chorus girls who were standing around smoking. She normally paused to chat, swapping tidbits of gossip and listening to their gripes. Showgirls were constantly bitching about something, and she'd become a sort of mother confessor. But tonight she brushed them off with a smile and went directly to her dressing room. The instant she was alone her expression changed.

She was worried and upset, her nerves frayed. Almost a week had passed since Braddock had left Santa Fe. From news dispatches she was aware of his movements and his involvement in the deadly affairs of Colfax County. Local papers continued to identify him as the Reverend Titus Jacoby, and he'd been dubbed "The Fighting Parson." One story had related the lynching of Cruz Vega and the ensuing street brawl between Reverend Jacoby and Clay Allison. The following day another story recounted details of a bloody gunfight in some remote *pueblo* called Rayado. The newspapers speculated that Reverend Jacoby was too handy with his fists, and a gun, for a mere preacher. There were intimations that he was something more than he appeared.

Earlier today, Lise had heard a rumor about the courthouse shoot-out in Cimarron. Since there were no afternoon papers, she was forced to await the morning edition for confirmation. But she'd already learned sufficient details to know Reverend Jacoby had survived yet another gunfight. All of which simply added to her general state of uncertainty. She believed Braddock had failed in his mission to capture a corroborating witness. That being true, then his concern for her safety would have multiplied severalfold. Her intuition told her that he was even now on his way back to Santa Fe. And the thought left her mired in a quandary. She wondered what to do about Warren Mitchell.

Slipping out of her stage gown, she hung it on a metal costume rack. She stood there a moment, debating whether she should change into her street clothes. Then, still gripped

by uncertainty, she shrugged into a loose-fitting kimono and
seated herself before the dressing table. She was thankful
she'd badgered Ned Ingram into giving her a private dressing room. Tonight she desperately needed that privacy,
and time to think. The courthouse gun battle in Cimarron
had put an entirely new complexion on things. So far as she
knew, she was the only remaining witness against Mitchell
and Elkton. She tried to reason out her next move and found
herself confronted by hard questions. Should she play it safe,
perhaps feign an illness, and await Braddock's return alone?
Or should she put on a happy face and continue the charade
with Mitchell?

Until today there would have been no reason to pose the
question. She'd brought her considerable charms to bear, and
Mitchell was all but bewitched. In defiance of Elkton's
orders, he still paid her court every night, seemingly glued
to his chair at the front-row table. After the last show he escorted her back to his suite at the hotel, and their nightcap
had by now become something of a ritual. Apart from a
few halfhearted wrestling matches, she had managed to fend
off his advances. By scolding and cajoling, she'd thus far
kept him in line. Then, too, his lust had waned in direct pro-
portion to the news out of Cimarron. With each report in the
papers, his nerves appeared to unravel yet another strand.
The last couple of nights he'd acted like a eunuch, scarcely
touching her. His mind was clearly occupied with weightier
matters.

Tonight, however, was an altogether different story. From
the rumors she'd heard, the news out of Cimarron sounded
favorable to him, and he was certain to be in a buoyant mood.
Once in the hotel suite, that same jubilation would rekindle
his randier instincts. There was every likelihood that he
would no longer settle for promises or accept her excuses.
She might easily find herself in an untenable position, faced
with the demand that she come across or else. While the idea
itself was revolting, she was disturbed by an even more troublesome thought. She got a vivid image of Braddock arriv-

ing late sometime during the night. She saw him kicking down the door of Mitchell's suite and charging to her rescue. She shuddered as the picture formed in her mind's eye. She considered it unlikely that Mitchell would survive the encounter. And with him would die their case.

A light knock broke her spell. Then the door opened and half of the nightmare she'd just envisioned became a reality. Warren Mitchell stepped into the dressing room.

"Dora!" he said with ebullient good humor. "What's keeping you, my dear? You're not even dressed."

Lise composed herself and swiftly concocted a lie. "I sent a waiter with a message. Didn't he find you?"

"Obviously not." Mitchell crossed to the dressing table. "What message?"

"I don't feel well." Lise put her head in her hands, elbows on the table. "I think it's something I ate."

"Poor girl," Mitchell said in a solicitous tone. "You just put yourself in my hands. I have some really miraculous stomach powders at the hotel. We'll have you feeling better in no time."

Lise covered her mouth and burped softly. "I appreciate the thought, Warren. But, honestly, I wouldn't be very good company tonight."

"Nonsense!" Mitchell laughed off the objection. "I was particularly looking forward to your company tonight. Now, do hurry and get dressed. I insist."

"I'm really in no shape—"

Lise started, her eyes suddenly fastened on the dressing table mirror. She saw reflected there the other half of what she'd envisioned only minutes ago. The door opened and closed, and Braddock took a step into the room. The sound caused Mitchell to turn, and a strangely bemused expression crossed his features. He looked like a man having trouble placing a familiar face.

"Who the devil are you?"

Braddock smiled. "I go by many names. The last time we met I was Elmer Boyd."

"Boyd!" Mitchell parroted. "I don't believe you."

"I dyed my hair dark brown. I wore a fake mustache." Braddock's smile widened to a grin. "And I gave you a bogus check for three million dollars."

"Good God!"

Mitchell appeared to stagger. His imagination put a mustache in place, and turned the chestnut hair dark brown. The visage jolted him into a rude awakening. He saw the man before him transformed into Elmer Boyd.

"Don't pass out," Braddock said dryly. "I've got another little piece of information for you."

"Oh?" Mitchell paused, struggling to collect himself. "What sort of information?"

"The name I mostly go by is Cole Braddock."

Mitchell's face turned red as ox blood. His eyes froze to tiny points of darkness and his breathing quickened. His words spilled out in a choked rasp.

"You're the detective. You killed Judge Hough last year in Lincoln County."

"Glad you remember," Braddock said without inflection. "Since you do, there's no need for us to dance around. We can get straight down to business."

Mitchell recovered slightly. "I have no business with you."

"Wanna bet?" Braddock motioned toward the dressing table. "I'd like you to meet my partner, alias Dora Kimble. Her real name's not important."

Mitchell's features colored, then went dead white. A pulse throbbed in his neck and he stood numb with shock. He stared at Lise like a man gazing blindly at the moon.

"Sorry, Warren." Lise nodded, then smiled a little. "All in the line of duty."

"Y-You bitch," Mitchell stammered. "You deceived me. You lied to me!"

"She did more than that," Braddock told him. "She eavesdropped on your conversation with Elkton. You'll recollect that was the night you were ordered to kill Orville McMain."

"I remember no such conversation."

"Yeah, you do. It was the same night you implicated yourself in the murder of Reverend Tolby. She'll testify to that when you're brought to trial."

"And what if she does?" Mitchell sneered. "It's her word against mine and that of Stephen Elkton. The word of a saloon tart who sings dirty songs! She'll be laughed out of court."

"No, she won't." A broad grin spread across Braddock's face. "We've got corroborating evidence to back up her testimony."

"I don't believe you."

"What if I told you Donaghue spilled his guts?"

"I still wouldn't believe you."

"How about Donaghue's own words?"

"Don't be absurd," Mitchell countered. "I happen to know that Donaghue was killed in Cimarron. Do you propose to raise the dead, Mr. Braddock?"

"After a fashion," Braddock replied. "You see, a dead man's words are still admissible in court. Leastways, they are if it's in the form of a signed deposition."

"Deposition!" Mitchell looked as though he hadn't heard correctly. "Donaghue made a deposition?"

"A real doozy," Braddock lied, grinning wider. "He wrote it all down the night before your boys killed him. When he got around to naming names, yours was right at the top of the list. Damn shame he stopped there."

"What are you talking about?"

"Well, he never made any mention of Elkton. Hell, how could he? So far as he knew, you were the head of the ring. All his orders came straight from you."

"That's ridiculous," Mitchell snapped. "No one will believe a word of it."

"A jury will." Braddock's mouth tightened. "You'll be tried and convicted, and you'll hang for murder. Course, I reckon Elkton will have the last laugh."

"Elkton?"

"Why, sure," Braddock said soberly. "He wasn't named

in the deposition, and Dora's testimony alone won't convict him. He'll walk free and leave you to swing by yourself. Hell of a note, but I guess there's no way around it."

"You're bluffing!" Mitchell raged. "You're just trying to trick me into implicating Elkton. There's no deposition!"

"You'll see it for yourself in a couple of days."

"Why not now?"

"I mailed it to Dora before I left Cimarron. Sent it to her in care of the hotel. Figured if anything happened to me, she'd see to it you took the drop. So either way, you're a cooked goose."

Mitchell struck without warning. His left hand darted out and grabbed Lise by the hair. He yanked her to her feet and pulled her tight against his chest. His arm snaked around her throat.

Braddock was halfway across the room when he abruptly stopped. Mitchell's right hand dipped inside his coat and reappeared with a bulldog pistol. He pressed the muzzle to Lise's forehead and slowly cocked the hammer.

"Stand away from the door!"

CHAPTER TWENTY-FOUR

———◦◦◦———

Braddock saw it was futile to act. He didn't dare draw his gun, and any attempt to jump Mitchell was out of the question. He moved aside.

Mitchell kept an armlock on Lise and backed across the room. He fumbled the door open with his gun hand, then put the muzzle to her head and stepped outside. One of the chorus girls standing nearby shrieked and ran off through the wings. The others remained perfectly still, their mouths round with silent terror. Mitchell ignored them, tightening his chokehold around Lise's throat. He backed toward the stage door.

Braddock walked from the dressing room. He appraised the situation at a glance and muttered an inaudible curse. Outside the stage door was a dark alleyway. In one direction it led to the street and in the other it continued on past the Tivoli. Once outside, it was almost certain that Mitchell would turn toward the inky darkness behind the theater. There was also a strong possibility he would murder Lise and escape into the night. If he was to be stopped, then Braddock had no choice but to stop him now. He walked forward.

"Hold on, Mitchell."

"Stay back!" Mitchell shouted. "Take one more step and I'll kill her!"

"No, you won't," Braddock warned with cold menace. "Because if you do, you're a dead man. I'll shoot you down on the spot."

Mitchell edged toward the stage door. "I have nothing to lose, Braddock. You'd kill me anyway! So just stay where you are."

"Here's my last word." Braddock advanced another step. "Let her go and you can walk out that door unharmed. It's the only way you'll leave here alive."

Mitchell hesitated. "Will you come after me?"

"I'll give you a five-minute head start."

"Not enough!" Mitchell yelled. "I want at least—"

The door beside the orchestra pit banged open and Ned Ingram rushed backstage. Mitchell instinctively looked toward the theater owner, and Lise reacted with remarkable presence of mind. She wrenched free of the chokehold and threw herself sideways to the floor. Mitchell's reflexes were quick, and he tried desperately to recover. His pistol swung downward even as she fell.

Braddock seemed to move not at all. The Colt appeared in his hand and spat a streak of flame. He worked the hammer and triggered another shot within the space of a heartbeat. The slugs stitched a pair of bright red dots on Mitchell's shirtfront and he slammed backward into the stage door. He hung there a moment, as though impaled by some invisible force, then his knees buckled and he slumped to the floor, his eyes fixed on infinity.

A chorus girl screamed and fainted. Ned Ingram stared at the body a moment, then turned and bolted back through the orchestra-pit door. Braddock moved forward, holstering the Colt, and knelt beside Lise. Her kimono was pulled down over one shoulder and her hair had come undone. She smiled an upside-down smile.

"You had me worried, lover."

"Yeah?"

"Yeah," she replied with a sudden sad grin. "You weren't going to let him out of here, were you?"

"Not till he turned you loose."

"And if he hadn't?" she asked in a small voice. "What would you have done then?"

"I would've killed him."

"What about me?"

"Here or outside"—Braddock shrugged—"you were a goner unless I got him first."

"You mean he would have killed me either way?"

"What do you think?"

She slowly shook her head. "I think show business beats the hell outa the detective business."

"No argument there."

"I also think"—she gently touched his face—"I wouldn't trade you for all the tea in China."

Braddock grinned. "I'll second the motion."

"You damn sure better!" She took his arm and let him assist her to her feet. "So what's next, chief? Where do we go from here?"

"The hotel."

"Hotel?" She looked confused. "What about Elkton?"

"I want to get you under lock and key. Then I'll tend to Elkton."

"Are you worried he'll send someone after me?"

"Better safe than sorry," Braddock said solemnly. "Once he hears about Mitchell, he'll know you've been working undercover. I'd prefer to have you tucked away somewhere just in case."

"Well, lover," she said as she straightened her kimono and dusted herself off, "you won't believe your ears, but I agree. One gun at my head is enough for tonight. Let's go lock me up."

"That's him! The one there with Dora!"

Ned Ingram appeared in the doorway. His finger was leveled at Braddock, and behind him were two deputy town

marshals. The lawmen squeezed past Ingram, their guns
drawn, and approached cautiously. Braddock cut his eyes at
Lise, and his face congealed into a frown. He carefully raised
his hands.

"Looks like we're both gonna get locked up."

The interrogation lasted most of the night. Town Marshal
Harold Croy was understandably zealous. He viewed the
death of Warren Mitchell as a once-in-a-lifetime opportunity.
A case that would establish his name in the pantheon of
western lawmen.

There were several aspects of the shooting that lent it an
aura of sensationalism. The deceased was both a prominent
businessman and a powerful figure in territorial politics. He
was also widely acknowledged as the front man, perhaps
the leader, of the Santa Fe Ring. As for the man who had done
the killing, he was, by his own admission, none other than
Cole Braddock. His reputation as a manhunter automatically
guaranteed front-page coverage throughout the West. And
Santa Fe's marshal envisioned his own name emblazoned in
those same headlines.

No political neophyte, Harold Croy was a staunch, dyed-
in-the-wool Democrat. Aside from personal publicity, he
also perceived a chance to deal the Republicans a mortal
blow. The list of those rumored to be involved with the Santa
Fe Ring formed a virtual roll call of the Republican elite.
His interrogation was therefore politically motivated and, as
a result, all the more tenacious. Yet he quickly discovered
himself matched against an opponent who was versed in the
finer points of law. Braddock was by turn reticent, taciturn,
and downright uncooperative. He admitted nothing beyond
the bare bones of the shooting. He claimed self-defense on
behalf of himself and Dora Kimble.

Croy resorted to every trick in the interrogator's hand-
book. He questioned Braddock and the girl separately and
in exhaustive detail. Afterward, he compared their stories
and found himself holding two peas from the same pod.

They both claimed a lovers' triangle, ending with Mitchell's threat to kill the girl. The marshal next grilled them together, attempting to trip one on some statement made by the other. Neither of them stumbled, and he came away with the impression that they had rehearsed their stories somewhere between the theater and his office. However many times he made them repeat it, the result was always the same. They professed complete innocence, grounded in the right of self-defense.

To Croy's great disgust, their story was borne out by eyewitnesses. The chorus girls, as well as Ned Ingram, all admitted that Mitchell had indeed held a gun to Dora Kimble's head. Further, it was established that Braddock had fired only as a last resort, to save the girl. She was purportedly Mitchell's mistress, and that too tended to substantiate the story. But the marshal nonetheless thought it a fairy tale, pure invention. He was convinced Cole Braddock had not traveled to Santa Fe merely to settle a lovers' quarrel. He believed, instead, that the manhunter and the singer were working together on a case. He felt reasonably certain the case somehow involved the Santa Fe Ring.

Still, there was no evidence to support Croy's theory. Braddock and the girl adamantly stuck to their version of Mitchell's death, and the facts supported them in every particular. The upshot was that neither of them could be charged with anything. Croy advised them that there would be a coroner's inquest, but it was a hollow threat for he knew the jury would return a verdict of justifiable homicide. Then, albeit reluctantly, he released them from custody. Braddock walked out with the girl on his arm and a smile like a cat with cream on its whiskers. The marshal stood at the window, watching them cross the plaza as the first blush of daylight tinged the sky. He knew he'd been made to look the fool, and yet, despite himself, he felt a grudging sense of admiration. The first tenet for a private detective was that the details of an assignment, as well as the client's name, would never be revealed. Braddock had kept the faith.

Ten minutes later, Frank Kirkland walked through the door. An early riser, the lawyer had stopped for breakfast at a nearby cafe. There he'd heard the news of Mitchell's death and Braddock's arrest. Apparently he had run all the way, for he appeared out of breath when he entered the marshal's office. All the more suspicious were his agitated manner and his questions about the shooting, which seemed motivated by anything but simple curiosity. To Croy's inquiries, he turned evasive, offering no explanation for his interest in the affair. Upon being informed that Braddock had been released, he rushed out of the office and hurried toward the hotel. He acted like a man desperate to hear the truth about some earth-shattering event.

Harold Croy was no mathematician, but he could add two and two without counting on his fingers. He knew Frank Kirkland was the lawyer for the Cimarron Coalition and an avowed enemy of the Santa Fe Ring. He also recalled the news items about a mysterious preacher who had taken up the coalition's banner in Colfax County. Moreover, he was aware that Braddock operated undercover, generally in disguise. The sudden appearance of Frank Kirkland was the last factor in the equation. However it was figured, the marshal told himself, the answer was plain as a diamond in a goat's ass. Cole Braddock was working for the Cimarron Coalition. His assignment was to break the Santa Fe Ring.

Ergo the death of Warren Mitchell ceased to be a riddle.

Marshal Croy called a news conference at nine sharp. The reporters scribbled furiously as Croy recounted the events surrounding last night's shooting. Their mouths dropped as he added a dash of conjecture about the Santa Fe Ring and a dab of speculation about the Cimarron Coalition. Then he stirred into the broth the name of Cole Braddock and let the news hounds draw their own conclusions. He gave them everything but proof, which seemed highly irrelevant under the circumstances. Sensationalism, as he'd learned in past dealings with the press, demands no hard facts.

The story went out over the telegraph wires late that

morning. Harold Croy, chief law enforcement officer of Santa Fe, was given prominent mention.

Braddock and Lise walked directly from the marshal's office to the hotel. He saw her to her room and waited while she checked the loads in her Derringer. His orders were to stay put and shoot to kill in the event anyone attempted forcible entry. He delayed in the hallway until he heard her lock the door. Then he went in search of Stephen Elkton.

Leaving the hotel, Braddock spotted Frank Kirkland entering the marshal's office. He cursed, all too aware that the lawyer had somehow got wind of the shooting. He'd been rather pleased with the way he had misled the marshal, avoiding any hint of his mission in Santa Fe. Now, simply by showing up and asking questions, Kirkland was certain to let the cat out of the bag. But, then, in the overall scheme of things, it probably made little difference. Stephen Elkton would have long since gotten the word.

Hindsight, Braddock reminded himself, was a thing of wondrous clarity. Last night he'd figured he had the situation under control. While it surprised him to find Mitchell in Lise's dressing room, he had capitalized on the moment and turned it to advantage. He would have sworn he had Mitchell on the verge of confessing. Then, to his astonishment the cornered rat turned and fought. Somehow he hadn't credited Mitchell with the stomach for personal violence. Those who hired killers generally found the act itself repugnant. And that lapse in judgment last night had very likely cost him the case. He'd silenced the wrong man for all the wrong reasons.

Across town Braddock stopped outside Elkton's law office. He rattled the doorknob and peered in the window, and finally concluded the place was empty. Considering the early morning hour, he hadn't really expected to find anyone there. But a hunt had to begin somewhere, and apart from Elkton's law practice, he knew nothing about the man. Farther downstreet, he noticed a corner café already open for the breakfast trade. He had a cup of coffee and managed to buttonhole the owner while paying his check. His questions were framed in a casual manner, and the owner was happy to oblige. He walked out with Stephen Elkton's address.

Some while later he approached a house several blocks north of the plaza. He had no set plan in mind, but he'd already decided how it would end if Elkton was at home. After pounding on the door, he saw a frump of a woman pad down the hallway in a flannel bathrobe. She identified herself as the housekeeper and informed him in no uncertain terms that Elkton wasn't home. When he persisted, her gossipy nature won out. She told of a knock late the previous night and a whispered conversation at the door. Afterward, Elkton had hastily packed a suitcase and vanished into the night. Further probing revealed that Elkton had no wife, no children, and no family known to the housekeeper. She had no idea where he'd gone or by what means he had traveled. Nor would she venture an opinion as to when he might return. The latter comment was unsolicited, an answer to a question Braddock saw no reason to ask. He'd known the answer the moment she opened the door.

Stephen Elkton would never return to Santa Fe.

A few minutes before nine Braddock entered Frank Kirkland's office. The lawyer grinned, rising from his chair with an outstretched hand. Braddock ignored the handshake.

"You lied to me, Kirkland."

"What?"

Braddock fixed him with a baleful look. "When you hired me, you said my assignment was to bust the Santa Fe Ring. What you really wanted was somebody to do your killing."

"That's not true!"

"The hell it's not," Braddock said, jaw clenched. "I accused Orville McMain of the same thing, and he all but admitted it. He damn sure didn't deny it."

Kirkland sat down heavily. "If that's so, then he lied by omission—to both of us."

"Cut the double-talk," Braddock said sharply. "Just give me a straight answer."

"Before I came to Denver," Kirkland asserted, "I met with McMain. We agreed the ring took priority over all else. There was no discussion of recruiting a hired killer. None!"

"You're saying McMain conned you?"

"I'm saying I *did not* retain you under false pretenses."

Their eyes locked. Braddock's expression was cold and searching, and he stared at the lawyer for several moments. Finally, convinced he'd heard the straight goods, he inclined his head in a faint nod.

"I'll take your word," he said gruffly. "I broke the ring as of this morning, and I'm still owed five thousand. Write me out a check."

"This morning?" Kirkland said, baffled. "I went by the hotel, and the desk clerk said you'd gone out. Where were you?"

"Stephen Elkton's house."

Kirkland appeared even more perplexed. "What does Elkton have to do with it?"

"Mitchell and Elkton"—Braddock held out two joined fingers—"were just like that. Only Elkton called the shots and gave all the orders. He masterminded the whole operation."

"Incredible!" Kirkland was visibly astounded. "The last man I would have suspected was Stephen Elkton. He was so unsociable, almost scholarly."

"A scholar of murder," Braddock grunted. "By rough count, nine men got snuffed out because of Elkton. He missed being number ten by the skin of his teeth."

"What happened?"

"I've just come from the depot," Braddock explained.

"He hopped a late night freight bound for Denver. Bribed the stationmaster to sneak him aboard the caboose."

"Why Denver?" Kirkland asked. "Wouldn't he know that's your home base?"

"I'd judge it's a stopover to somewhere else. He'll run a

long way before he stops. Or maybe he won't ever stop, not if he's smart."

"I don't understand. You've broken the ring and driven him out of Santa Fe. Your assignment's completed."

"The assignment might be completed, but the book's not closed. Not yet."

"What book?"

"The book on Elkton."

"That sounds vaguely personal."

"Nothing vague about it. Elkton owes me and I aim to collect."

"Owes you what?"

"A life."

Kirkland began a question, then stopped. Something in Braddock's eyes told him to pursue the matter no further. He wrote out a check for five thousand dollars, and Braddock stuck it in his pocket. Then, without any great ceremony they shook hands and Braddock walked from the office. Kirkland was still staring at the door when it closed.

He wondered how far Stephen Elkton had run. He considered a moment and decided it would never be far enough. Not while Braddock was owed a life.

CHAPTER TWENTY-FIVE

Lise was like an exuberant child. The case had been long and grueling, and Braddock figured she'd earned a holiday. When he asked where she wanted to go, there was no hesitation. She squealed and clapped her hands.

"New Orleans! Ooo, please, Cole. New Orleans!"

The trip consumed the better part of a week. By rail, they traveled from Santa Fe to Denver, and then on to St. Louis. There they boarded a riverboat for a pleasant interlude down the Mississippi. On a warm autumn day, their boat steamed around a bend and slowly reduced speed. The sun was at their backs, and before them the mighty sweep of the river was like molten fire. Arm in arm, they stood in silent wonder.

New Orleans was considered the most spectacular port on the globe. For sheer size and the density of ships lying at berth, it was unrivaled by any anchorage on the world's great oceans. The wharves, which curved with the river, were lined with steam packets and windjammers flying the colors of a dozen nations. Along the levee, which extended downriver for some five miles, were row upon row of flatboats and keelboats and twin-stacked paddle-wheelers. The waterfront teemed with sailors and stevedores, and everywhere on the wharves bales of cotton were stacked in massive blocks. The sight was far grander than anything Lise and Braddock might have imagined.

Their boat docked at the Canal Street landing. Once the gangplank was lowered, a porter carried their luggage ashore and arranged for a hansom cab. Their hotel was located in the heart of the Vieux Carré, the famed French Quarter. With its many theaters and restaurants, the Vieux Carré was home to the city's Creole community. Descendants of French and Spanish émigrés who had intermarried, the Creoles seldom set foot across Canal Street, where the Anglo district of New Orleans began. Their language was French, their culture was Parisian, and their world centered on the Vieux Carré. It remained a continental outpost of grace and sophistication.

For the next four days, Braddock and Lise surrendered themselves to the languorous pace of the French Quarter. They slept late and ate breakfast in bed and made love as though there were no tomorrow. Their afternoons were spent sightseeing, from the waterfront to Jackson Square to the elite Creole residential district beyond Esplanade Avenue. One entire afternoon was devoted to exploring the area around Jackson Square, which was dominated by the Cabildo and the Presbytère and a three-spired cathedral. Their nights were an unending succession of epicurean restaurants and stage plays and after-hours suppers in intimate cafes. They gorged themselves on seafood and gumbo and a variety of exotic Creole specialties. Then they went back to the hotel and ravaged one another until exhaustion overtook them with sleep. Quite literally, they gave themselves over to the pleasures of the Vieux Carré.

On the fourth night they dined at Antoine's. The restaurant was renowned for its cuisine and catered almost exclusively to the Creole trade. The men were immaculately attired in formal evening wear and their ladies were gowned in the latest Paris fashion. The maître d', who viewed Braddock and Lise as foreigners, treated them with polite civility. They were shown to a window table, which looked out on the street and kept them somewhat removed from the regular clientele. Yet the service was impeccable and the meal was worth the slight affront. They dined on crawfish bisque, followed by *court-bouillon* and *boeuf* Robespierre. The highlight was a specialty of the house called *café brûlot*. Brandy and sugar were mixed with cloves, orange peel, and cinnamon sticks. Then the ingredients were set afire. Coffee was next poured into the bowl, and while the concoction blazed, a waiter deftly ladled it into cups. The end result was a heady brew unlike anything they'd ever tasted.

Over coffee, Braddock steered the conversation around to Buck Colter. He had told her sometime previously of the young half-breed's role in the Cimarron investigation. But he'd never talked about Colter the man, about his personal side. Lise sensed there was more to the story than he had revealed initially. For Braddock to extend his trust at all—something he'd rarely done—indicated that Colter was very unusual indeed. Yet she'd wisely just listened, asking few questions. She knew he had to tell it in his own way, in his own time. Tonight, for whatever reason, he apparently felt some need to talk about the events surrounding Colter's life. He told her everything.

"How terrible," she said when he finished. "And it's so unfair! He lost his girl and any chance he had for a decent life. I've never heard anything so sad."

"Funny about that," Braddock remarked. "He doesn't feel the least bit sorry for himself. I guess maybe it's his Cheyenne blood. He's just too proud to wallow in self-pity."

She took a sip of coffee. "You admire him, don't you, Cole?"

"Yeah, I do," Braddock admitted. "He got a rough break and he took it in stride. Not many men would show that much grit."

"I think you might envy him too."

"Envy?"

"Yes." Her voice had a teasing lilt. "He's like a wild thing. No ties, no responsibilities. He's free to pick up and go whenever he chooses. I think you miss that."

A smile tugged at Braddock's mouth. "I've got no regrets. Not yet anyway."

"Aren't you gallant!" Her eyes sparkled with suppressed mirth. "Now stop being diplomatic and tell me the truth about something."

"What's that?"

"I caught it in your voice. You were intrigued by the idea of being the hunted rather than the hunter. I got the feeling you wouldn't mind trading places with Colter."

Braddock rocked back in his chair with a belly laugh. "I wasn't intrigued by it very long. Hell, with the International on his trail, it's a good thing Colter's part Indian. He'll need a whole bag of tricks just to stay one jump ahead."

"Won't the International ever stop hounding him?"

"Not till he's dead." Braddock studied his nails, thoughtful. "Nobody kills the head of a cattlemen's association and walks away. I suppose you might call it the cardinal sin, the one unpardonable offense. Colter's a marked man the rest of his life."

"You have influence," she said softly. "Isn't there some way you could make an appeal and get him a new hearing?"

"Wouldn't work." Braddock sighed heavily. "The International's a law unto itself. There's no appeal—ever."

"So Colter will be hunted down and eventually killed?"

"Tell you a secret," Braddock said, smiling. "I damn sure wouldn't want the job. He's just about the toughest thing I've ever run across."

"Oh, my God!"

"What's wrong?"

"There!" She pointed past him. "The man crossing the street!"

Braddock twisted around and looked out the window. He saw a man step onto the curb and pass beneath a lamppost.

In the glare of the light, the face was distinct and familiar. It was Stephen Elkton.

"Here." Braddock pulled a wad of cash from his pocket. "Pay the check and have the doorman flag a cab. I'll meet you back at the hotel."

"Cole?" Her voice was a low, intense whisper. "What are you going to do?"

"Don't ask."

Braddock hurried to the cloakroom. He reclaimed his hat and walked from the restaurant. At the corner he turned onto a side street and saw the stocky figure less than a half block ahead. Braddock's stride lengthened, and he closed the gap some yards short of the next corner. His hand was inside his jacket, gripping the Colt.

"Hello, Elkton."

Elkton jumped at the sound of his name. He swiveled around and his face momentarily drained of color. He remembered the voice, and he'd seen Braddock's photograph in recent newspaper articles. A look of recognition was stamped on his features.

"How did you find me?"

"Outhouse luck," Braddock said truthfully. "Course, some people might call it divine intervention. What made you pick New Orleans?"

"Why should I tell you anything?"

"Why not?" Braddock replied. "You're through running."

Elkton was silent a moment, then shrugged. "I booked passage for South America. The ship is scheduled to leave tomorrow."

"Looks like you're gonna miss the boat."

"Would you be open to an offer?"

"Try me."

"I managed to get most of my money out of Santa Fe. I could make you a rich man."

"How rich is rich?"

"A hundred thousand—perhaps more."

"I'll think about it while we walk."

"Where are we going?"

"The waterfront."

"See here now—"

Braddock showed him the gun. "Walk."

Some minutes later they passed a warehouse and emerged onto a darkened wharf. Upshore, there were lights and laughter from a row of waterfront grog shops. Before them, the black sheen of the river stretched endlessly into the night. They halted at the edge of the wharf and turned to face one another. Braddock slipped the Colt from its holster.

"I decided to pass on your offer."

Elkton cleared his throat. "Killing me won't accomplish anything."

"Do you remember a man named Bud Grant?"

"I've never heard of him."

"He was the marshal of Cimarron."

"I don't understand." Elkton shook his head. "What was Grant to you?"

"Nothing," Braddock said quietly. "Leastways, he wasn't till he took a bullet meant for me."

"Are you talking about that affair at the courthouse?"

Braddock nodded. "Those two gunhands were supposed to get me and Donaghue. One of them missed and got Grant instead."

"They were Mitchell's men, not mine!"

"You gave the orders."

"I still deserve a trial," Elkton protested. "You have no right to appoint yourself judge and executioner."

"Bud Grant wouldn't agree."

Elkton's forehead beaded with sweat. "Don't I get any kind of chance?"

"Are you heeled?"

"No," Elkton declared. "I never carry a gun."

"Let's give it a try and see."

Braddock dug a coin from his pocket. He balanced it on his left thumb and forefinger and motioned upward. "You can make your move anytime before it hits the dock."

"I told you," Elkton pleaded hoarsely. "I'm not armed!"

"Here goes."

Braddock flipped the coin. Elkton's gaze followed it upward for a mere instant. Then he jerked his eyes down and his hand darted inside his coat. Braddock shot him.

A surprised look came over Elkton's face. He stood perfectly still, a great splotch of red covering his vest. His hand opened and a pistol dropped from beneath his coat, clattering to the dock. He took a shuffling step back and his heel caught the edge of the wharf. He tumbled headlong into the water.

There was a loud splash, then silence. Braddock stood looking down at the river for several moments. He saw the body bob to the surface and drift away in the swirling current. At last he holstered his Colt and turned from the wharf.

He walked back toward the Vieux Carré.

"Are you all right?"

"Never better."

Braddock moved through the door. Lise closed it behind him, watching as he pegged his hat on a hat tree. He crossed the room and took a seat on the sofa.

"God!" Lise said on an indrawn breath. "I was scared stiff!"

"You know better than to worry."

"You're absolutely, positively all right?"

"Fit as a fiddle."

"Was it really Elkton?"

"If it wasn't, I made a hell of a mistake."

"What happened?"

Braddock smiled. "The Santa Fe file is closed."

Lise understood there would be no further explanation. His statement was purposely vague, for he never spoke of the men he killed. Yet, in his own cryptic manner, he'd told her Stephen Elkton was dead. To her that was enough; the details were unimportant. A man had died tonight simply because justice would have otherwise gone begging. She knew he'd killed only as a last resort.

"You know something, lover?"

"What's that?"

"I think we ought to celebrate!"

"You name it," Braddock said agreeably. "We've barely scratched the French Quarter's nightlife."

"No." A slow smile warmed her face. "I won't settle for anything less than the best show in town."

Braddock chuckled. "And where do we go for that?"

"Nowhere!"

She joined him on the sofa. Her eyes were heavy-lidded and smoky, and she snuggled close in his arms. Her kiss was soft and lingering, and acted like an aphrodisiac on him. His hand caressed her curving buttocks and drifted higher to the round swell of her breasts. Her hips moved and her mouth opened in a long exhalation. A low cry drifted from deep within her throat.

"Oooh, Cole. Take me to bed—now!"

Braddock took her.

Deathwalk

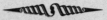

Bring on the Law . . .

Harris raised the shotgun, earing back both hammers, and brought it to his shoulder. Thompson leveled his Colt, staring over the sights, and fired. Harris staggered, a starburst of blood dotting his shirt front, and tried to right the scattergun. His eyes were crazed.

Thompson fired two shots in quick succession. The slugs struck Harris just over the sternum, not a handspan apart. He reeled sideways in a nerveless dance, dropping the shotgun, and slammed into the bar.

A sudden pall of silence fell over the room. The crowd waited in a stilled tableau, all eyes locked on Thompson. He moved just inside the doorway, placing his back to the wall. His gaze swept the startled faces, the Colt at his side. He looked at Simms.

"Go get the sheriff," he said. "Tell him to come right along."

DEATHWALK

MATT BRAUN

St. Martin's Paperbacks

This is a work of fiction. All of the characters, organizations, and events portrayed in this novel are either products of the author's imagination or are used fictitiously.

SHADOW KILLERS / DEATHWALK

Shadow Killers copyright © 1985 by Matt Braun.
Deathwalk copyright © 2000 by Winchester Productions, Ltd.

For information address St. Martin's Press, 175 Fifth Avenue, New York, NY 10010.

ISBN: 978-1-250-30854-2

Our books may be purchased in bulk for promotional, educational, or business use. Please contact your local bookseller or the Macmillan Corporate and Premium Sales Department at 1-800-221-7945, ext. 5442, or by e-mail at MacmillanSpecialMarkets@macmillan.com.

Printed in the United States of America

Shadow Killers St. Martin's Paperbacks edition / February 2000
Deathwalk St. Martin's Paperbacks edition / September 2000

St. Martin's Paperbacks are published by St. Martin's Press, 175 Fifth Avenue, New York, NY 10010.

10   9   8   7   6   5   4   3   2

AUTHOR'S NOTE

Deathwalk is based on a true story.

Ben Thompson was the foremost shootist of his time. A gambler by profession, he plied his trade from the border of Old Mexico to Denver and Dodge City and countless other boomtowns. His personal code of honor allowed neither insult nor physical threat from another man. History records that those who provoked his anger were soon bound for the graveyard. He never lost a gunfight.

Bat Masterson, who was himself a noted gunfighter, stated that Thompson was without equal. In 1907, Masterson was engaged by *Human Life* to write a series of articles on famous shootists of the Old West. At the time, Masterson was a sportswriter for the *Morning Telegraph* in New York City. Yet his reputation as a frontier lawman was still the stuff of legend, and he had personally known all of the Western gunfighters. He selected for his first article none other than Ben Thompson.

Masterson wrote: "Ben Thompson was remarkable . . . it is very doubtful if in his time there was another man living who equaled him with a pistol in a life and death struggle. He was absolutely without fear and his nerves were those of the finest steel. He had during his career more deadly encounters with the pistol than any man living and won out in every single instance. The very name of Ben Thompson was enough to cause the general run of mankillers to seek safety in instant flight."

Deathwalk deals with a specific time in Ben Thompson's larger-than-life exploits. The article by Bat Masterson was, in part, responsible for the genesis of this novel. Masterson also wrote in his article: "Thompson possessed a much higher order of intelligence than the average gunfighter or mankiller of his time. He was more resourceful than any of that great army of desperate men who flourished on our frontier." These attributes, intelligence and resourcefulness, led Thompson to the most fateful decision of his life. His personal code of honor further secured his place in the mythology of the American West.

Deathwalk is the story of a man who dared against all odds . . . the story of Ben Thompson.

ONE

"Kings bet twenty."

Thompson studied the dealer's hand. On the table were an eight, a king, a ten and a king. He figured it for two pair, probably kings and eights. Homer Watts, the dealer, was a tombstone peddler who fancied himself a poker player. The other men in the game had dropped out of the hand.

Watts stared across the table with an eager smile. The game was five-card stud, and Thompson's hand revealed a jack, a three, a jack and a king. In the hole he had another jack, but it was the king that impressed him most. With three on the board, the dealer would have to hold the case king to win. The odds dictated otherwise.

"Your twenty—" Thompson shoved chips into the center of the table—"and raise fifty."

"You're bluffin', Ben."

"One way to find out."

"Call your raise," Watts cackled, "and bump it another fifty."

All afternoon the two men had butted heads. The other players were largely spectators, seldom winning a hand. Ben Thompson was the owner of the establishment, the Iron Front Gaming Parlor & Saloon. A gambler of some repute, he invariably drew players to his game. Today was no exception.

"Let's make it interesting," Thompson said casually. "How much in front of you?"

Watts quickly counted his chips. "Hundred and thirty."

"I'll tap you, then. The raise is a hundred and thirty."

"You're tryin' to buy yourself a pot. No way you've got three jacks."

"You'll have to pay to see, Homer."

The other players watched with amused looks. Watts fidgeted a moment, then pushed his chips into the pot. "You're called," he said. "What's your hole card?"

Thompson turned over the third jack. Watts glowered at the cards with an expression of dumb disbelief. "*Gawddamn* the luck!" he howled. "I would've sworn you was bluffin'."

"Another day, another time, Homer. Your luck's bound to change."

"Hold my chair!" Watts announced, jumping to his feet. "I ain't outta the game yet."

The deal passed with each hand. One of the men began collecting the cards. "We're fixin' to play poker here, Homer. You gonna be gone long?"

"Won't take a minute," Watts called, rushing toward the door. "Just gotta go to my wagon."

Thompson shook his head, chuckling to himself, and raked in the pot. He was a blocky man, not quite six feet tall, with square, broad shoulders and rugged features. His gray eyes were alert and penetrating, and even with a full mustache, he looked younger than his thirty-nine years. Over his vest, he wore a spring-clip shoulder holster, the leather molded to the frame of a Colt pistol. The lustrous blue of steel was set off by yellowed ivory grips.

The Iron Front was located just off the corner of Mulberry and Colorado. The establishment got its name from a heavy metal sign that extended the width of the building. A lifelong resident of Austin, the capital of Texas, Thompson had bought the gaming parlor two years ago. In that time, he had transformed it into one of the premier gambling clubs of the city, frequented by lawmakers and influential businessmen. The state capitol building was only two blocks away.

Homer Watts rushed back through the door. A granite tombstone, weighing at least a hundred pounds, was cradled in his arms. In the afternoon lull, there were few men at the long mahogany bar, and fewer still at the faro and twenty-one layouts along the opposite wall. Yet they paused, bemused by the sight, as he staggered toward the poker tables at the rear of the room. He lowered the tombstone to the floor with a thump.

"There you are," he said, grinning at Thompson. "Solid granite and smooth as a baby's butt. Carve anything you want on it."

Thompson nodded appreciatively. "That's a fine looking headstone, Homer. What does it have to do with poker?"

"Well, it's worth a couple of hundred, easy. You credit me with a hundred and I'm back in the game. You got yourself a bargain."

"What the devil would I do with a headstone?"

Watts gave him a crafty look. "Everybody needs one sooner or later. C'mon, Ben, be a sport. What's a hundred?"

Thompson glanced at the men seated around the table. "How about it, gents? Think it's worth a hundred?"

None of them thought Ben Thompson had any immediate need of a headstone. He was the most renowned shootist of the day, reported to have killed eight men in gunfights. The *Police Gazette*, ever in search of a sensational headline, ranked him more deadly than Doc Holliday, or the infamous John Wesley Hardin, now confined to the state penitentiary. His name on a headstone seemed as remote as the stars.

"All right, Homer," Thompson said amiably, tossing chips across the table. "Have a seat and let's get on with the game. You just made a sale."

"Five-card draw," the dealer said, shuffling the cards. "Everybody ante up."

Homer Watts found luck to be as elusive as ever. He opened with a pair of queens and failed to improve his hand on the draw. Yet he rode it to the end, confident he couldn't be beat.

A pair of aces left him poorer, if not wiser.

The game ended shortly before six o'clock. The players cashed in their chips and drifted to the bar. There, over whiskey, they commiserated with one another on the turn of the cards. Few of them had won more than the price of a drink.

Thompson walked to his office at the rear of the room. He was a family man, and unlike most gamblers, he made it a point to have supper with his wife and son. Then, around eight in the evening, he would return to the Iron Front for a night of poker. He usually played until two or three o'clock in the morning.

A dandy of sorts, Thompson was an impeccable dresser. His normal attire was a Prince Albert suit, with a somber vest and striped trousers, and a diamond stickpin in his tie. He topped it off with a silk stovepipe hat, and the result was a man who looked the very picture of sartorial fashion. As he slipped into his coat, tugging the lapel snug over his shoulder holster, the door opened. Joe Richter, who managed the club, stepped into the office.

"You're a corker, boss," he said with a toothy grin. "Everybody in town will have a good laugh over that game."

Thompson shrugged. "Homer had his mind set on playing. How could I turn him down?"

"Damn fool ought to stick to sellin' headstones. Poker's not his game."

"Joe, the same might be said about most of our customers. Sometimes it gets discouraging."

Thompson was known and respected on the Western gamblers' circuit. Over the past decade he had played poker from the Mexican border to the Dakotas. In the Kansas cowtowns, during trailing season, he'd never failed to find a high stakes game with wealthy Texas cattlemen. His name alone brought high rollers to the table.

Austin was a different kettle of fish. On occasion he would host a high stakes game with legislators from the state capitol and local ranchers. But for the most part, the Iron Front catered to a clientele who viewed gambling as a pastime. Faro and roulette, and other games of chance, made the enterprise immensely profitable, even for low stakes. Still, it was a world apart from the action he'd known on the gamblers' circuit. Some days were more boring than others.

Joe Richter saved him from the drudgery of daily operations. A slender stalk of a man, Richter was a veteran of the gaming life and a highly competent manager. His responsibility included everything from hiring and firing dealers to overseeing the bartenders. He was trustworthy and capable, and his expertise with gaming tables was reflected in the monthly balance sheet. His attention to detail relieved Thompson of the tedium associated with running a business, albeit one of a sporting nature. He was, for all practical purposes, the backbone of the Iron Front.

"Before you go," he said now. "What should I do with the tombstone? We have to get it off the floor."

"Donate it to one of the churches," Thompson replied. "Preachers are always burying somebody."

"And if they ask how we got it?"

"Tell them Homer Watts took it out in trade."

Thompson moved to the door, his stovepipe hat tilted at a rakish angle. He went through the club and emerged onto the street, struck by the cloying warmth of day's end. Austin was sometimes brutally hot in the summer, and July had proved to be a scorcher. He turned toward Congress Avenue, where the streetcar line bisected the city.

A short distance ahead, three cowhands were congregated at the corner of Mulberry and Colorado. Thompson saw that they were reasonably sober, and wondered why they had strayed into the uptown area. The cattle trade usually kept to the red light district, which was some blocks south, nearer the river. As he approached, the men inspected his fashionable attire with wiseacre grins. One of them stepped into his path.

"Well, looky here," the cowhand gibed. "We got ourselves a regular swell. Where you from, pilgrim?"

Thompson realized he'd been mistaken for an Easterner. The idea amused him, and he decided to play along. "Why, I came West for my health. I have a lung condition."

"Ain't too healthy for Yankees around these parts."

"On the contrary, I've found it quite pleasant."

"Yeah?" The cowhand reached out and swatted his top hat into the gutter. "What d'you think now?"

Thompson retrieved his hat. "I think your ma never taught you any manners. You give cattlemen a bad name."

"Listen to the sorry shit-heel talk! Maybe I'll just teach *you* some manners."

"Fun's fun and you've had yours, cowboy. Let it drop."

"Hell I will!"

The cowhand drew back a doubled fist. Thompson had survived a lifetime of random violence on sharp reflexes and flawless instincts. The odds were three to one, and he wasn't about to engage in a street brawl. He popped the Colt out of his shoulder holster.

"Holy shit!" one of the men yelled. "He's got a gun!"

The cowhands took off running in different directions. All along the street, passersby scattered and ducked for cover. Then, in an act of bravado, the cowboy who had started the trouble skidded to a halt and pulled his pistol. He darted behind the awning post of a barbershop and winged a shot at Thompson. The slug exploded through the window of a store across the street.

Thompson extended his Colt to arm's length. The cowhand was concealed by the awning post, but the right side of his head and his wide-brimmed hat were partially visible. Drawing a fine bead, Thomson sighted carefully and feathered the trigger. The man's ear lobe vanished in a spray of blood.

A wild, gibbering screech followed upon the Colt's report. The cowhand dodged past the opposite awning post, momentarily obscured from view, and broke into a headlong sprint. Thompson kept him fixed in the sights, silently urging him not to turn and fight. He disappeared around the far corner at the end of the block.

Some thirty minutes later City Marshal Ed Creary appeared at the scene of the shooting. Thompson was waiting with a policeman who had responded to the sound of gunfire. A crowd stood watching, spilling out into the intersection, buzzing excitedly about the latest escapade of Austin's resident gunman. Creary elbowed his way through the onlookers.

"What's the trouble here?" he demanded. "Who'd you shoot now, Thompson?"

"I didn't take the time to get his name."

"Did you kill him?"

"Not likely," Thompson said in a wry tone. "Last time I saw him, he was still going hell-for-leather."

Creary was a beefy man with pugnacious features and a dark scowl that gave him a satanic look. He considered Thompson a smudge on the reputation of Austin, and the sense of dislike was mutual. For his part, Thompson thought the town's chief law enforcement officer was a politician hiding behind a badge. He'd never known Creary to take hand in a shooting involving the police. The marshal invariably appeared after the fact.

"Who started it, anyway?" Creary persisted. "Did you fire the first shot?"

"I defended myself," Thompson said. "He let loose and I returned fire. You won't have any problem recognizing him."

"How's that?"

"Look for a cowhand missing his right ear lobe."

"And you're gonna tell me you shot off his ear on purpose?"

"I generally hit just exactly what I aim at."

Creary grunted. "I'll have to charge you with the discharge of firearms. You know the law."

"Do whatever you've got to do. I'll pay the fine in the morning."

"I ought to arrest you."

"Don't even think about it, Ed." Thompson smiled at him with a level stare. "I wouldn't take kindly to being rousted for no reason."

There was a moment of leaden silence. Creary was aware of the crowd watching him, and his face flushed with anger. But he was even more aware of Thompson's stare, pinning him in place like a butterfly on a board. He knew better than to push too far.

"I'm late for supper," Thompson said when the silence held. "Send somebody around if you find that cowhand. The goofy bastard tried to murder me."

Creary ground his teeth. "You just make sure you're in court tomorrow."

"I always obey the law, Marshal. It's one of my finer virtues."

Thompson walked off toward the center of town. He thought it unlikely the cowhand would be found, and curiously unjust that he was the one who would be fined. Yet there was a bright side to any fracas.

He wasn't the one who'd lost an ear lobe.

TWO

A short walk brought Thompson to Congress Avenue. The broad thoroughfare sloped gently from the state capitol grounds to the Colorado River, which bordered the southern edge of the city. A mule-drawn streetcar clanged back and forth from the river to a residential district north of the capitol.

Thompson hopped aboard the streetcar when it stopped at the corner. He took a seat at the rear, tipping his hat to a lady with a folded parasol nestled in her lap. Directly ahead, a fiery sunset bronzed the dome of the capitol and boiled the blue out of the sky. A lamplighter walking along the avenue ignited gas vents that illuminated round globes in the quickening dusk.

The streetcar bell clanged and Thompson settled back in his seat. Outwardly calm, he was still seething from his encounter with Marshal Ed Creary. He considered himself a businessman, and many of Austin's most prominent civic leaders accorded him their respect. Yet lawmen, not to mention the press, labeled him a shootist and mankiller. He sometimes wondered if he would ever outdistance his reputation.

A native of England, Thompson's family had immigrated to the United States in 1851. He was nine years old, and along with his parents and his younger brother, the family landed at Galveston and settled in Austin shortly afterward. He was educated in a private school, but he was a hot-tempered youth, and constantly in trouble. His name first made newspaper headlines when he was fifteen, and challenged a schoolmate to a duel. They fought at forty paces, with shotguns, and both were severely wounded.

Some three years later, when he was eighteen, he became embroiled in an argument over the attentions of a girl. The affair turned deadly, and after an exchange of gunshots, Thompson was tried and acquitted on a charge of manslaughter. During the Civil War, while serving under the Confederate flag, he killed two men in gambling disputes, and was exonerated in each instance. On the gamblers' circuit, in the years that followed, he sent five more men to their graves in what were ruled justifiable homicides. By then, his reputation was known across the breadth of the West.

Two years ago, in league with Bat Masterson, Thompson took part in what was widely publicized as the Royal Gorge War. A group of gunmen were recruited in Dodge City by the Atchison, Topeka & Santa Fe Railroad. They proceeded to Colorado and fought several pitched battles with mercenaries of the Denver & Rio Grande Railroad over the right-of-way through Raton Pass. Afterward, with the five thousand dollars earned in the railroad war, Thompson returned to Austin and bought the Iron Front. Today was the first time he'd fired a gun in anger since departing Colorado.

But now, in the summer of 1881, little or nothing seemed to have changed. The *Police Gazette* still wrote articles about him, and the law jumped to the conclusion that he'd fired the first round in today's shootout. Thompson stared off into space as the streetcar trundled along, feeling oddly haunted by his own reputation. He'd killed men for what he considered sound reasons, and for the past two years he had been a model citizen and businessman. Yet he was still the most notorious figure in Austin.

The streetcar tracks circled around the state house grounds. A last ray of sunlight glinted off the capitol dome, and Thompson seemed to awaken from his ruminations. His gaze was drawn to the dome, and then downward over the immense three-story structure. He tried to recall when it was completed, and vaguely recollected the last block of limestone being laid the summer he was sixteen. A year later the Governor's Mansion had been erected catty-corner from the capitol grounds, between Colorado and Lavaca streets. He had grown to manhood watching the city double and redouble in size.

The original town site, situated along the banks of the river, had been named for Stephen Austin, the founder of Texas. The year was 1839, shortly after the war for independence with Mexico, and six years later Texas was admitted to the Union as a state. Austin spread northward from the river, and like ancient Rome, the town was built upon seven hills. The setting was pastoral, surrounded by rolling prairie and limestone mountains, and attracted immigrants by the thousands. A city began to take shape.

The decade following the Civil War brought explosive growth. In 1871, with the arrival of the Houston & Texas Central and the International & Great Northern, Austin became the railroad hub of central Texas. By 1874 gaslighting illuminated Congress Avenue, and shortly afterward waterworks and sewage systems were installed to serve the burgeoning city. The population swelled to more than ten thousand, and two of the largest banks in Texas established headquarters opposite the Capitol Square. The frontier town grown to a city led the state into an era of commerce and prosperity.

Thompson was seldom given to introspection. Yet today, reflecting inwardly, he thought his life was somehow intricately bound to the place of his boyhood. His parents had passed on some years before, and his younger brother, Billy, was a gypsy without family or roots. Over the years, that same wanderlust had taken him to cowtowns and mining camps dotting the West, always chasing the rainbow. But wherever he roamed, he was drawn, inexorably, back to the banks of the Colorado, and Austin. His inner compass seemed forever fixed on the city of his youth.

Dusk darkened the land as he stepped off the streetcar. His home was seven blocks north of the capitol, on University Avenue, with a spacious lot. The house itself was a classic Victorian, white with green trim, with a pitched roof, square towers, and arched windows. Directly across the street was College Hill, campus for the University of Texas, which now had four hundred students. The proximity to the university, in one of the city's more affluent neighborhoods, was the principal reason he'd bought the house. He wanted his son raised among decent people, well-born and educated.

Catherine was waiting in the parlor. She was a svelte woman, pleasantly attractive with lively green eyes and a mass of auburn hair piled atop her head. Five years younger than Thompson, she still had her figure, full breasts accentuated by a stemlike waist. She walked into the hallway as he entered the door.

"Home is the stranger," she said with a dimpled smile, kissing him on the cheek. "I thought maybe the streetcar had gone out of service."

"No, nothing like that," Thompson said, hooking his hat on a coatrack. "I got waylaid downtown."

"I kept your supper in the warmer oven. Tell me about it while you eat."

"Where's Bobby?"

"In his room, working on his model ship. I sometimes wonder he hasn't run off to sea."

She led the way through the parlor. The furniture was French Victorian, with slender cabriole legs and balloon-shaped cushions. Thompson took a seat in the dining room, at a glistening rosewood table with a carved rose motif bordering the edge and along the legs. She returned from the kitchen with his plate.

"Well, now," he said, studying rare cuts of roast beef surrounded by potatoes and vegetables. "I'm glad I made it home for supper."

"I just hope it's not overdone from sitting in the oven."

Catherine made several trips to the kitchen. She brought fluffy dinner rolls, fresh water, and finally a pot of coffee, all carried one at a time. Thompson had long since learned that an offer to help would be quietly refused. She insisted on doing everything herself, even though it was a chore at times with one hand. The left sleeve of her dress was folded double and pinned beneath her upper arm.

Some years ago, the summer of 1871, Thompson had

taken the family on holiday to Kansas City. He'd rented a buggy for sightseeing, and the second day there, when their horse bolted, the buggy overturned. Bobby, who was four at the time, was thrown clear, and Thompson's leg was broken. Catherine was pinned underneath the frame of the buggy, her left arm crushed beyond repair. A surgeon at the city hospital performed an amputation just above the elbow. Undaunted, never once expecting pity, she emerged from the ordeal with her spirit intact.

Thompson had long ago grown accustomed to her shortened arm. Over the years, in some way he couldn't define, he'd come to admire her even more than before. Her indomitable will, her refusal to withdraw in the face of adversity, was to him the measure of the woman. They had been married in 1863, while he was on furlough during the Civil War, and eighteen years had done nothing to diminish what he felt for her. Nor had the loss of her arm affected the physical bond between them. Her appetite matched his own, and she was still the most sensual woman he'd ever known. He never got enough of her.

"Well—" She paused, pouring him another cup of coffee. "I'm dying of curiosity. Aren't you going to tell me how you got—what was it—waylaid?"

Thompson rarely kept any secrets from her. All the more so when he knew she would read about it in the morning paper. He speared a chunk of beef with his fork, waved it with an idle motion. His expression was one of feigned innocence.

"Some fool cowboy braced me," he said, popping the beef into his mouth. "Knocked my hat off, and tried to take a swing at me. So, naturally, I had to defend myself."

"Oh, no!" she exclaimed, her eyes wide. "You drew your gun?"

"Now keep in mind, he fired first. Not that there's a cowboy alive any good with a gun. I just winged him a little bit. Nothing serious."

"How serious is 'nothing serious'?"

"Took a little piece of his ear."

"You intentionally shot him in the ear?"

"Katie, I don't mind saying I'm surprised at you. Have you ever known me to miss?"

Catherine had no trouble at all imagining the scene. Her husband lived by a code that was immutable as day and night. He would not be insulted, and he would not tolerate being manhandled, or struck a blow. Any man who violated the code was at risk.

"I'm so sorry, Ben," she said in a soft voice. "I know you've tried your best to avoid problems. It's been what—two years?"

"Two years, three months," Thompson observed, chewing thoughtfully. "Guess it was too good to last."

"Were the police involved?"

"Ed Creary tried to play the big lawdog. I'll have to pay a fine in city court."

"But that's not fair!" she said in a sudden temper. "Why should you be fined when the cowboy fired first?"

"I haven't got the least notion," Thompson said. "Especially when he's the one that started it. Anybody that dumb deserves to get shot."

"You shot somebody, Pa?"

The voice brought them around. Bobby, addressed as Robert only when being scolded, was standing in the parlor doorway. He was tall for his age, barely fourteen, with the promise of his father's sturdy build. His eyes bright with excitement, he advanced into the dining room.

"You've turned Injun on me, son," Thompson said. "How'd you sneak downstairs so quiet?"

"I dunno," Bobby said, refusing to be sidetracked. "Who'd you shoot, Pa?"

Catherine motioned him to a chair. "Have a seat and let your father eat in peace. No more questions."

"Cripe's sake, Ma, all I asked was who he shot. What's wrong with that?"

"Listen to your mother," Thompson admonished him. "Let's not have any back talk, buddy boy. Understand?"

Bobby pulled a face. "I never get to hear anything. It's not fair."

Thompson playfully tousled his hair. "Some things are better left to grown-ups. Maybe we'll talk about it when you're older."

"All the guys will be talkin' about how you shot somebody. What am I gonna say when they ask me, Pa? I'll look like a stupe."

"You heard your father," Catherine said sternly. "We'll not have any more discussion on this subject. That's final!"

Thompson nodded agreement. The boy was overly fascinated with his father's reputation as a gunman, often badgering him for details. He remembered that he was hardly older than Bobby when he'd engaged in his first shootout, and it was an unsettling thought. There was nothing particularly heroic about the life he'd led; he didn't want the boy following in his footsteps. He intended an altogether different life for his son, something respectable and proper. A doctor, or perhaps a lawyer. Anything but a gambler.

"How's the model ship?" he asked, diverting the boy onto safer ground. "Have you about got it finished?"

"Well, just about," Bobby said in a sulky voice. "I've got the masts and everything pretty much finished. Still needs sails."

"What was it you called it—a brigantine?"

"No, Pa, that's a pirate ship. This's gonna be a schooner, a big one. Like for the China trade."

"Your mother worries you're liable to run off to sea someday. Think you'd like to be a sailor?"

"Maybe," Bobby allowed. "I dunno yet."

"You've got plenty of time to decide. No rush."

Thompson took a last swig of coffee. He fished a thin cheroot from his inside coat pocket and struck a match, puffing wads of blue smoke. There was no real concern that Bobby would run off to sea and follow the China trade. The boy was bright, one of the better students at school, and got top marks. One day, he would attend the university, and from there . . . anything was possible.

A little later, Thompson allowed himself to be led upstairs for a look at the model ship. Catherine began clearing dishes from the table, carrying them to the kitchen sink. Yet her mind was on the men in her family, and how impressionable young boys were at fourteen. She saw so much of her husband in her son.

Not that there was anything wrong with that. Her husband was faithful and loving, generally even-tempered, and a good father. All a wife could ask for in a man.

She just wished he weren't so quick with a gun.

THREE

Thompson was seated at the desk in his office. His eyes glazed as he stared at rows of figures in an accounting ledger. The numbers seemed to blur.

Twice a month, on the first and the fifteenth, he went over the books. Today was July 15, and he'd been dreading the chore since awakening that morning. He was not a bookkeeper, and reconciling daily operating expenditures with gross revenues seemed to him an exercise in boredom. The task invariably put him in a foul mood.

Joe Richter was meticulous with the books. His penmanship was flawless, and he accounted for every dime as though he owned a part of the Iron Front. Still, Thompson thought it only appropriate that he fulfill his duties as proprietor, and however tedious, perform the role of a businessman. The one saving grace was the impressive financial balance shown in the ledger. Every month added to his already sizeable net worth.

The door rattled under a hammering fist. He turned from the desk, a scowl on his face, and started out of his chair. Halfway to his feet, the door flew open and his expression abruptly turned to one of amazement. His brother Billy strode into the office.

"Goddamn, I knew it!" Billy howled. "Got you chained to a desk!"

"Where the hell'd you drop from?"

"Here, there, and yon. Never let the dust settle under your feet. That's my motto."

"You no-account rascal!"

Thompson smothered him in an affectionate bear hug. Billy was three years younger, lithe and muscular, with a sweeping mustache. The family resemblance was striking; even in a crowd, they would have stood out as brothers. Their features were all but a mirror image.

"Never thought I'd live to see it," Billy chided. "You slaving over the books like some blue-nosed banker. I'll bet you're rich as Midas."

"I eat regular," Thompson said expansively. "How about you?"

"Livin' high on the hog, big brother. Things couldn't get no better."

Their closeness was born not just of blood. They genuinely liked one another, and each considered the other his staunchest friend. Hardly more than boys, they had joined the Second Texas Cavalry Regiment and fought under the Confederate flag for four long, bloody years. Their wartime service included engagements in Texas, New Mexico, Louisiana, and finally, skirmishes along the Mexican border. They emerged from the conflict as veterans of the killing ground, having killed their share. Neither of them ever flinched in the heat of battle.

Following the Civil War, thousands of Rebels could

not come to terms with the Yankee occupation of their homeland. The Thompson brothers, like many Confederates, crossed the border and joined the army of Emperor Maximilian. Under the patronage of France's Louis Napoleon, Maximilian was then waging war on the forces of Benito Juarez, a Mexican revolutionary. In 1867, when Maximilian was captured and executed, the imperial army scattered to the winds. Thompson, by then the captain of a cavalry troop, escaped with Billy and returned to Austin.

A year later, Billy killed a Union army sergeant during a drunken argument in a brothel. Thompson, working quietly and quickly, engineered his brother's escape to the sanctuary of Indian Territory. But the incident pushed Billy into the wild life, and he began a wayward pilgrimage that had yet to end. He never married, and like so many drifters in the West, he was forever in search of the next El Dorado. He became a vagabond gambler, occasionally joining Thompson in a cowtown or mining camp, only to disappear with news of the latest bonanza. Over a year had passed since his last visit to Austin.

"Where have you been?" Thompson asked. "Wouldn't hurt you to write a letter now and then."

Billy waved it off. "I never was one for letters. By the time you answered, I would've been somewheres else, anyhow."

"So where's somewheres else?"

"Tombstone."

"Arizona?"

"Last time I checked," Billy said with a crooked smile. "Lots of the old Dodge City crowd out there, too. Damnedest silver strike this side of kingdom come."

Thompson nodded. "I heard Wyatt Earp and his brothers were there. Who else?"

"Doc Holliday showed up right after Wyatt. Those two always were thicker'n fleas on a dog."

"How's Doc's health these days?"

"Still coughin' his lungs up a piece at a time. Most days, he looks like death warmed over."

"Billy, he'll probably outlive us both."

"Speak for yourself," Billy said, rolling his eyes. "I aim to live till hell freezes over."

"Sure you do," Thompson said dryly. "The Devil himself will be there to crack the ice."

"You interested in hearin' about Tombstone or not?"

"What's there to tell besides Wyatt and Doc?"

"Bat Masterson."

"Now that I hadn't heard."

"And Luke Short."

"I'll be damned."

"Told you it was the whole crowd."

Thompson counted all of the men as longtime friends. He'd first met Earp and Masterson in Wichita, and later renewed the acquaintance when the cattle trade moved to Dodge City. Through them, he had been introduced to Holliday and Short, two of the more widely known names on the gamblers' circuit. But he was particularly close to Masterson, whom he admired as both a man and a lawman. He considered Masterson a cut above the others.

"What's Bat doing in Tombstone?"

"Dealin' faro," Billy said, wagging his head. "Him and Luke Short are workin' for Wyatt. Don't that take the cake!"

"Sure as hell does," Thompson agreed. "Are you saying Wyatt owns a gaming club?"

"Well, he's partners in a place called the Oriental Saloon. Fanciest dive in Tombstone."

"And Bat's just a dealer—that's all?"

"Yeah, that's it," Billy said. "'Course, I guess he wore a badge too long. He still tries to play the peacekeeper."

"Peacekeeper?" Thompson repeated. "How so?"

"That dust-up between Short and Charlie Storms. Bat tried to talk 'em out of it."

"Who's Charlie Storms?"

"Don't they print the news in Austin anymore? I thought everybody knew about that."

"I haven't read anything."

"Then you missed a humdinger. I was there that night, playin' poker. Saw the whole thing."

Billy quickly related the details. Charlie Storms, who was playing faro at Short's table, questioned the deal. An argument ensued, and the two men were on the verge of drawing guns. Masterson intervened, talking fast, and persuaded them to call a truce. Storms stalked out the door, only to return later in the day, with gun in hand. Short rose from behind his faro layout and calmly fired three shots. The first broke Storms's neck and the other two slugs struck him in the heart. He fell dead with the cocked gun still in hand.

"Never got off a shot," Billy concluded. "Damnedest thing you ever saw."

"Sounds like Luke hasn't lost his touch."

"Went back to dealin' faro—cool as you please."

Thompson, unwittingly, was reminded of another shooting, long ago. The summer of 1873, he and Billy were running faro games in Ellsworth, a Kansas cowtown. They got into an altercation with a couple of gamblers, one of whom owed Thompson money. The local sheriff attempted to defuse the situation, only to be caught in the middle. Billy, who was drunk at the time, accidentally discharged a shotgun, and the sheriff was killed. In the confusion, Thompson spirited his brother out of town and put him on a horse for Texas. Murder charges were promptly brought against Billy.

Four years passed, with Billy on the dodge and Thompson working to have the charges dismissed. Then, in 1877, Texas Rangers finally captured Billy, and he was extradited to Kansas. Thompson hired a battery of lawyers, who mounted an aggressive defense when Billy was brought to trial. The lawyers managed to obfuscate the facts, and witnesses to the shooting, fearful of offending Thompson, suffered a lapse of memory. The jury rendered an acquittal verdict, and Billy was once again a free man. The legal bills, and four years in hiding, came at a stiff price. Thompson ultimately shelled out more than ten thousand dollars.

"So anyway," Billy went on, "Virgil Earp practically walked Luke through the coroner's inquest. Took about ten minutes to get a ruling of self-defense."

Thompson appeared surprised. "Virgil's a lawyer now?"

"That'll be the day! Virgil's the city marshal of Tombstone. Still wearin' a badge."

"What about Wyatt?"

"Wyatt's got his hand in lots of things," Billy said. "I told you about the gaming dive, and he's bought some mining claims. 'Course, everybody knows he's got his eye on the sheriff's job."

Thompson chuckled. "Wyatt always was the ambitious one in the family."

"Hell, you don't know the half of it. Him and Virgil mean to take over the law and run the whole show. They'll wind up ownin' Tombstone."

"That's a little too ambitious—even for Wyatt."

"Ben, I'm tellin' you, he's got brass balls."

Billy recounted the story with some gusto. Wyatt Earp intended to make his fortune in Tombstone, where the silver mines were turning out millions in ore. His brothers, Virgil and Morgan, were part of the grand design, one the city marshal and the other a deputy. Wyatt, meanwhile, was campaigning to discredit the sheriff, a man named Behan. The campaign was directed at the Clanton gang, a band of robbers operating under Behan's protection, and a connection that could bring about his downfall. The accusations by Wyatt were the talk of Tombstone.

"These Clantons are a hard bunch," Billy finally said. "Wyatt's liable to get more than he bargained for."

"But if he gets in as sheriff," Thompson remarked, "he'll control the county. He can write his own ticket."

"Yeah, he could wind up a goddamn millionaire. Or get himself bushwhacked some dark night."

"Is Bat in with the Earps on the deal?"

"Funny thing about Bat," Billy said in a musing voice. "Way he talks, he's plumb done wearin' a badge. Guess he got a bellyful back in Dodge City."

"Politics is a rough game," Thompson noted. "Even so, I'm still surprised to hear that Bat's turned faro dealer. He was a damn fine peace officer."

"Not everybody's like you and Wyatt," Billy joshed. "Some men weren't cut out to be business tycoons. There's more to life than money."

"Spoken like a man who sleeps wherever he hangs his hat. I offered to go partners with you years ago. What would you say if I asked you now?"

"Well, you know me, Ben. A rolling stone gathers no moss. I like to keep movin'."

Thompson couldn't argue the point. All their lives, he'd been the one determined to make his mark in the world. Perhaps being the older brother was the driving force, but his reach had always exceeded his grasp. Billy, on the other hand, was happy-go-lucky and irresponsible, and not the least bit ashamed of his shiftless attitude. He was a nomad who wandered wherever the impulse took him. Tomorrow was his vision of the future.

"You're a case, little brother," Thompson said ruefully. "I suppose you're just passing through to somewhere else. Am I right?"

Billy laughed. "I need a change of scenery every now and then. Never was one to get stuck in a rut."

"So how long can you stay?"

"I reckon I could spend the night. Wouldn't want to wear out my welcome."

"One night!" Thompson barked. "Haven't seen you in a year and all you can spare is one night? What's your rush?"

"No rush a-tall," Billy said, spreading his hands. "We'll be talked out long before mornin' anyhow. One night ought to do it."

"Katie's gonna raise the roof. You're her only brother-in-law, and believe it or not, she likes you. She'll be damned upset."

"I'll sweet-talk her out of it, don't you worry. How's she been?"

"She's been just fine, thank you. Too bad you never found somebody like her."

"No weddin' bells for me," Billy said, amused by the thought. "I never was much for strings and things. How's little Bobby?"

"Not so little anymore," Thompson said. "You might recollect, he's going on fifteen."

"Fifteen."

Billy spoke the word in a subdued voice. He stared off into the middle distance, as though looking backward through a cobweb of years. He was silent for a long moment, then he blinked, the reverie broken. His mouth curled in the old devil-may-care grin.

"Time flies when you're havin' fun, don't it, Ben?"

Thompson felt a lump in his throat. He thought he'd never seen a lonelier man than the one across from him, his brother. The insouciant manner and the easygoing charm were all pretense, a veneer to mask what was inside. He debated whether to insist—demand—that a single night in a year was not nearly enough. But then, knowing his brother all too well, he discarded the notion. Some men were not meant for strings and things.

"So tell me, Mr. Fiddlefoot," he said, forcing a jocular tone. "Where're you headed like your pants are on fire?"

"Brownsville," Billy said with his loopy grin. "Figured I'd sashay on down to the border."

"What the hell's in Brownsville?"

"I hear the Rio Grande's the last holdout for riverboats. I always fancied myself a riverboat gambler."

"You know something—" Thompson studied him a moment, "I think you might have found your calling. By God, a riverboat gambler!"

Billy looked pleased. "Got a good ring to it, don't it?"

Thompson nodded, smiling, as though he agreed. But in the back of his mind, he was wondering how long it would last. The answer came to him almost immediately.

Not long.

FOUR

The men began arriving at the Iron Front shortly before eight o'clock. The evening of July 20 was sultry, with roiling clouds and the smell of rain in the air. Off to the west, beyond the mountains, jagged streaks of lightning split the sky.

Thompson hosted a private game every Tuesday night. The players were drawn from a list of businessmen and politicians, and the game was by invitation only. Those attending tonight's session were shown to a back room, opposite Thompson's office. The walls were paneled in dark hardwood, with plush maroon carpeting on the floor, and a walnut sideboard stocked with liquor. The baize top of the poker table was bathed in the cider glow of an overhead lamp.

The men represented a cross-section of Austin's civic leaders. Among those present tonight were Mayor Tom

Wheeler; James Shipe, president of the Mercantile National Bank; and Will Cullen, the largest liquor wholesaler in Central Texas. Luther Edwards and Jack Walton, partners in a law firm, were noted litigators and Thompson's personal attorneys. They all enjoyed a friendly game of poker, even though they played by cutthroat rules. The stakes were ten-dollar limit, with three raises, check and raise permitted. No one thought to make his fortune at the Iron Front.

The mood of the game was genial, a once-a-week rivalry with cards. Thompson was by far the most seasoned player, and he often folded decent hands rather than win too heavily. Yet the men relished testing themselves against a professional, particularly one whose name commanded respect within the gambling fraternity. There was, as well, the fact that he was considered the most deadly shootist of the day. Only a week ago, according to the newspapers, he'd shot off a cowboy's ear! A sense of danger added spice to the game.

The mayor won the first hand for a modest pot. The deal passed from man to man, with agreement that only standard draw and stud were allowed. Jim Shipe, the banker, dealt five-card draw, and raised the opener upon discovering he'd dealt himself three fours. Thompson, who was nursing a pair of kings and easily read Shipe's gloating expression, folded after the draw. Everyone else stayed in, contributing to the pot, as Shipe and Cullen, the liquor wholesaler, took it to thrce raises. Shipe, certain he'd won, proudly spread his three fours on the table. Cullen turned over three sixes.

"Well now," he said, raking in the pot. "You boys better be on your toes. Tonight looks to be my night."

"Talk about luck of the draw," Shipe countered. "I

deal myself three of a kind and you stumble onto another six. What, may I ask, are the odds on that? Any idea, Ben?"

Thompson chuckled. "I'd take your hand anytime. Like you said, Jim—luck of the draw."

The deal passed to Walton. As he shuffled, his law partner, Luther Edwards, glanced at the mayor. "Did you read the editorial in the *Statesman* this morning? John Cardwell certainly minced no words about the sporting district."

"John likes to play the moralist," Wheeler said indignantly. "Guy Town is one of our city's oldest institutions. Not that I'm defending prostitution, you understand."

"If you don't I will," Cullen said with ribald humor. "Where would City Hall be without the fines on whores? Our property taxes would go sky high."

"Excellent point," Edwards added with a sly smile. "Not to mention that some of our best friends expend all their carnal lust downtown. Who knows how many marriages the floozies have saved?"

Walton, in the midst of dealing the cards, snorted laughter. "Now *that* would make an editorial!"

The newspapers adopted a moral tone when lambasting the world's oldest profession. Yet, along with righteous indignation, there was frequently a tongue-in-cheek twist that lent a note of levity. The *Statesman* editorial that morning had hinted at the name of a prominent legislator seen in the company of a *"fille de joie,"* and demanded that the prostitutes be subjected to higher fines. No one objected to stiffer fines; but apart from clergymen, few people favored reform. Somewhat like their mayor, the citizens of Austin looked upon the sporting district as a landmark. A holdover from frontier days.

The immediate area north of the railroad depot was known locally as Guy Town. Located between the river and Cedar Street, it was the heart of the sporting district, occupying several square blocks. The streets were lined with saloons, gaming dives, dance halls, and whorehouses, devoted solely to vice and separating working men from their wages. Over the years, as Austin doubled and doubled again in size, the district had grown to encompass the entire southwestern part of the city. People called it Guy Town because it was the haunt of men out for a night's fun. The bordellos, with sin for sale, catered to their most exotic tastes.

Austin itself had been transformed from a riverside outpost into a thriving center of commerce. With the advent of the railroads, business and industry had replaced cattle and ranching as the mainstay of the economy. Yet there was an odd mix of the old and the new, with spurred cowhands still jostling among the sidewalks among laborers, railroad men, and factory workers. The town itself might have changed, but some aspects of life were seemingly immutable to the upheaval of the modern era. A generation of men had frolicked to the pulse of the sporting district, and they remarked on only one change. Guy Town had simply grown larger.

Austin, like many cities in the West, was still reasonably broad-minded about vice. Though it was the county seat of Travis County, and the state capital, the community itself was largely controlled by local politicians. The city government imposed so-called occupation taxes on saloons, gaming dives, and bordellos. Further revenues were generated through periodic raids on the brothels, with court fines levied against madams and prostitutes. The city treasury was kept afloat, and a truce was maintained with the sporting crowd. So long as immorality was confined to Guy Town, the law was tolerant.

Uptown, where the better class of people conducted their business, nothing unseemly was tolerated. There were gambling clubs, saloons, and variety theaters, but none of the depravity to be found in the sporting district. As though the town fathers had drawn a line of demarcation, everything north of Guy Town was held to a different standard. There the streets were free of violence and whores, and clubs such as the Iron Front operated under the benevolence of City Hall. Everyone, saint and sinner alike, benefited by the arrangement.

"Speaking of whores," Cullen said, as another hand was dealt, "I was in Guy Town yesterday afternoon. Even on a Monday, business was really quite brisk. Amazing."

Edwards looked at him with a satiric smile. "Getting your ashes hauled, were you, Will? What would the little woman say?"

"Nothing of the sort!" Cullen protested. "We move carloads of liquor in Guy Town, and I sometimes go out on calls with my salesmen. A man has to keep his eye on business."

"And maybe a little monkey business on the side? Sounds very suspicious to me, Will."

"Leave it to a lawyer to think the worst. Although, I have to admit I did something damned foolish."

"Uh-*huh*!" Edwards crowed. "Now the story comes out."

Cullen glanced at Thompson. "Do you know Al Loraine? He has the faro concession at the Tivoli Saloon."

"I know the name," Thompson said. "I've never had any dealing with him. Why do you ask?"

"We had some time to kill before our next call. I thought I'd amuse myself with a few hands of faro . . ."

"And he took you to the cleaners."

Cullen nodded soberly. "I've never seen such a run of cards. Do you think he's honest?"

"I'll ask around," Thompson replied. "What if he's a sharper? Do you want to press charges?"

"No, no," Cullen said hastily. "I wouldn't want it made public I'd been duped. My wife would never let me hear the end of it."

"Well, I'll check it out, anyway. Never hurts to know who's straight and who isn't."

"Don't put yourself to any trouble. I was really just curious."

"No trouble at all, Will."

Their attention was drawn to their cards as the mayor opened for ten dollars. The conversation about Al Loraine seemed casual enough, but Thompson considered it a serious matter. Gambling, more so than most professions, was susceptible to adverse public opinion. A cardsharp, even in Guy Town, was bad for business.

His mind elsewhere, he idly called the mayor's bet.

The Tivoli Saloon was located on the corner of Cypress and Congress Avenue. A knot of revelers burst from one of the nearby dance halls, lurching drunkenly along the sidewalk. Their raucous laughter mingled with the strains of a rinky-dink piano.

Thompson stepped off the streetcar at the corner. The game had ended shortly after midnight, and nothing more had been said about the faro dealer at the Tivoli. After the mayor and the others were gone, he'd caught the streetcar down to Guy Town. He decided to check it out for himself.

The inside of the saloon was thick with smoke. The bar was lined with men, mostly railyard workers fresh off the late shift. Thompson was known here, as he was anywhere in Austin, and the bartender greeted him with a nod. He seldom ventured into Guy Town, and his frock coat and top hat gave the impression that he was slumming. He ordered a whiskey.

Al Loraine was operating a faro game directly opposite the bar. Thompson knew him on sight, though he couldn't recall ever having spoken to the man. He was hesitant to take a seat at the faro layout, for no one would risk offending him by dealing crooked cards. Instead, as though he'd just stopped by for a nightcap, he watched the game with mild interest. He noted that Loraine was slick, a man with nimble hands.

Faro, even more than poker, was governed by the luck of the draw. An old and highly structured game, it had originated a century before in France. The name was derived from the king of hearts, which bore the image of an Egyptian pharaoh on the back of the card. All betting was against the house, with the odds weighted in favor of the dealer. In Western parlance, it was known as "bucking the tiger."

A cloth layout on the table depicted every card from deuce through ace. After being shuffled, the cards were placed in a dealing box, and then drawn in pairs, displayed face-up. Before the turn of each pair, players placed bets on one or more cards of their choice. The first card out of the box was a losing bet, and the second was a winner. All bets were canceled if there were no wagers on either card.

To one side of the table was an abacuslike device known as the casekeeper. The casekeeper indicated the cards already dealt and allowed a player to figure percentages on cards remaining in the deck. Players could bet win or lose on the layout, and a losing wager was "coppered" by placing a copper token on the chips. A daring player would often bet win and lose on the same turn of the cards.

Thompson caught the gaff within a few minutes. A crooked dealer rigged a faro game in advance with a small rectangular device known as a card trimmer. The metal device was flat on top, with a gauge to position and measure cards, and what resembled a hinged cleaver on one side. By turning a knob on the left side, a thin plate moved the card a millimeter to the right, the edge held firmly in place. The cleaver was then snapped downward in a slicing motion.

The razor-sharp blade cleanly trimmed a millimeter off the side of the card. The trim was discernible only to an educated finger, and left the edge smooth and undetectable to anything but a magnifying glass. A deck of cards put through a trimmer allowed a skilled dealer to "read" individual cards simply by touch. By watching the wagers on the layout, a dealer could hold back certain cards and deal "seconds" to put losing cards into play. The result was akin to shooting fish in a barrel.

Halfway through the deck, Thompson walked to the table. Loraine paused, about to deal a card, and looked at him with a strange expression. The players turned, confused by the halt in the game, uncertain as to what Thompson was about. He nodded to Loraine.

"You're slick," he said with a hard smile. "But I never could abide a goddamned tinhorn. You're running a crooked game."

Loraine blanched. "I've got no quarrel with you, Mr. Thompson. What's going on here?"

"Yesterday you clipped a friend of mine. Trash like you give gamblers a bad name."

"I've never dealt crooked in my life. Your friend is mistaken."

"Save your breath," Thompson told him. "Those cards are trimmed and you're dealing seconds. I know it when I see it."

"That's one man's opinion," Loraine said reasonably. "You'll never prove it."

"Here's your proof."

Thompson snapped the Colt out of his shoulder holster. He thumbed the hammer and brought the pistol to bear as the players dove for cover. Hardly a heartbeat apart, he fired two shots and the dealer's box exploded in splinters of wood and cards shredded into pasteboard. He leveled the Colt on Loraine.

"You care to argue the point?"

Loraine sat frozen in his chair. "No . . . no argument."

"Thompson!"

Sol Simon, owner of the Tivoli, pushed through the crowd. Thompson lowered the hammer on his Colt, shoved it into the holster, and turned away from the table. Simon skidded to a halt.

"What the hell you mean shootin' up my place?"

"You ought to be more careful, Sol. You've got a cardsharp running your faro concession."

Simon went beet red. "You accusing me of operating fixed games?"

"What size shoe do you wear?" Thompson glanced down at the dive owner's feet. "Well, what d'you know about that, Sol? Looks like it fits."

"I'm gonna call Creary and his whole damn police force. I'll put you in jail!"

"Don't lay odds on it."

Thompson walked to the door. As he went out, the northbound streetcar stopped at the corner. He stepped aboard, handing the driver the nickel fare. His mouth creased in a slow smile.

He thought he'd done a good night's work.

FIVE

‹‹‹‹‹‹ ❦ ›››››

Thompson awoke around nine the next morning. The thunderstorm had passed overnight, and brilliant shafts of sunlight flooded through the bedroom windows. He rarely lingered in bed, for when he awoke he was instantly and fully awake. A wide, jaw-cracking yawn usually got him off to a quick start.

In his nightshirt, he padded barefoot into the bathroom. He first relieved himself in the commode, an invention he still considered the marvel of the age. Then he set about his morning ritual, scrubbing his teeth, bathing and shaving, and trimming his mustache. Upon emerging from the bathroom, his checks glowed from a splash of bay rum.

A tall armoire occupied one wall of the bedroom. His array of suits were somber in color, each one hand-tailored, cut from the finest fabrics. His shirts, imported from New Orleans, and his underclothing were neatly arranged in separate drawers. For casual wear, his garments were store-bought and somewhat less sedate in tone. He selected twill trousers and a cotton shirt, and shrugged into his shoulder holster. A lightweight corduroy jacket completed his outfit.

Downstairs, he found Catherine in the kitchen. Her hair was upswept and she was wearing a brightly patterned calico dress. Today was the day she baked bread, and her forehead was dotted with beads of perspiration from the heat of the stove. She removed a golden loaf from the oven, gingerly holding the pan with a folded towel, and set it on a rack to cool. He wrapped his arms around her from behind, and placed his hands over her breasts. She laughed a low, throaty laugh.

"Your timing is terrible," she murmured, blowing a damp wisp of hair off her forehead. "Why didn't you think of that last night?"

"I got in late," Thompson said, teasing her nipples with his fingertips. "And besides, you were asleep."

"That has never stopped you before."

"Maybe I'll surprise you tonight."

"Promises, promises."

"Where's Bobby?"

"Off playing somewhere. And don't let that give you any bright ideas."

She slipped out of his embrace. Turning, she gave him a quick kiss, tugging playfully at his mustache, and moved away. He took a chair at the kitchen table, watching as she arranged strips of bacon in an iron skillet and collected a bowl of eggs. His eye fell on the morning *Statesman* which was positioned by his silverware. A headline leaped off the front page.

THOMPSON TERRORIZES GUY TOWN

"I'll be damned," he said blankly. "How'd they get it in the morning edition?"

"Sweetheart, I just imagine they stopped the presses. After all, you are the hottest news in town."

Catherine placed a steaming mug of coffee on the table. She walked back to the stove while he read the account of his raid on the Tivoli Saloon. When he looked up, he found her watching him with a curious expression. He smiled sheepishly and took a swig of coffee. She waited him out.

"Anything for a headline," he said, rapping the newspaper with his finger. "They make too much of it, way too much. I shot the dealer's box, not the dealer."

"Oh, that makes all the difference." She removed bacon from the frying pan and cracked an egg. "The paper says you accused the dealer of being a cheat. Why would you care?"

"Will Cullen was in the game last night. He told me he'd been taken by this dealer at the Tivoli. I promised I'd look into it."

"So you did it for a friend?"

"Well, partly," Thompson allowed. "Guess I did it for myself, too. Tinhorns give all gamblers a bad name."

"Why not let the police handle it?"

She brought his plate to the table. He tore off a chunk of warm fresh bread and dipped it in egg yolk. As he chewed, he smeared butter and jam on the slice of bread, and then took a bite of bacon. She waited for him to answer her question.

"The police would have botched it," Thompson finally said. "First off, they would've never spotted the gaff. Takes a good eye to catch a man dealing seconds."

"And?" she pressed. "There's something else, isn't there?"

"Word's around that Ed Creary is on the take. The dives in Guy Town pay him off to look the other way. Not much chance of a crooked dealer getting arrested."

"Have you told Mayor Wheeler?"

"Didn't have to," Thompson said, loading his fork with hunks of egg. "So I hear on the grapevine, the mayor wants Creary off the ticket in the next election. Trouble is, there's nobody who could beat him at the polls."

She was thoughtful a moment. "Is that the reason you've never liked Creary? Because he takes payoffs?"

"I suppose that's part of it. But mainly it's because he's a pitiful excuse for a lawman. He's just another jackleg politician."

A knock sounded at the front door. Catherine left him to finish breakfast and hurried through the parlor. As he drained his coffee mug, she returned to the kitchen. She looked upset.

"There's a policeman at the door. Are they going to arrest you?"

"Don't get yourself worried."

Thompson walked through the parlor into the hallway. Lon Dennville, a sergeant on the police force, stood on the porch. He was a tough, no-nonsense officer and one of the few men on the force that Thompson respected. He nodded with an apologetic smile.

"Ben, I'm sorry to bother you at home. So far as I'm concerned, it could have waited till you got to the Iron Front. Marshal Creary ordered me to come here."

"Orders are orders," Thompson said evenly. "What can I do for you, Lon?"

"That incident last night—" Dennville offered him

a lame shrug. "You'll have to pay the fine for discharge of firearms, and Creary wants you in court at one o'clock. Otherwise, he'll swear out a warrant for your arrest."

"And he'd probably make you serve it. I doubt he's got the brass to try it himself."

Dennville tactfully held his silence. After a moment, Thompson gestured aimlessly. "Tell Creary he's lucky to have a man of your caliber on the force. I'll be there and pay the fine."

"You've taken a big load off my mind, Ben. I'd hate to be the one to serve that warrant."

"Let's consider it water under the bridge. I'll see you in court."

Dennville looked relieved. Thompson watched as he went down the porch stairs and turned toward the street-car stop at the corner. He felt no animosity for the sergeant, but he was boiling mad at being confronted in his home. Ed Creary was, plain and simple, a son-of-a-bitch.

He told himself there were ways to settle the score.

Bobby always accompanied his father to Waller Creek. For a gambler, a gun was a tool of the trade, and Thompson considered routine practice all part of the profession. He spent every Wednesday morning in pistol drills.

The creek was a mile east of the house. Bobby was awed by his father's skill, and these outings were his favorite time of the week. Thompson was nonetheless ambivalent, and Catherine shared his mixed feelings. He believed that every boy should be taught the proper use of a gun, and respect for a deadly weapon. Yet he was wary of his son following in his footsteps, either as a gambler or a gunman. On their trips to the creek, he generally spoke more of college than of firearms. The message he instilled was clear, and simply stated.

A man with an education was the odds-on favorite in life. A gun, on the other hand, was merely a tool. One should never be confused with the other.

Whatever his plans for his son, Thompson was pragmatic about himself and the life he led. Over the years, he had been involved in far more gunfights then he cared to remember, and witnessed countless others. Experience, and personal reflection in the aftermath of shootings, led to the conclusion that the victor was not necessarily the faster man. Speed was fine, but in his view, accuracy was final.

Thompson operated by a cardinal rule. The shot that killed an opponent, rather than the first shot, was what counted. More often than not, the man who hurried his first shot, the victim of his own nerves, was soon bound for the graveyard. So in his weekly drills, he practiced on a speedy draw, yet his focus was on placing every shot dead center. He was quick, but deliberate.

Bobby positioned himself upstream. He carried a gunnysack filled with empty whiskey bottles collected from the Iron Front. The bottles were corked and airtight, guaranteed to float, and made targets that required deadly accuracy. The boy tossed a bottle into the creek, and then lobbed four more in rapid succession. The bottles bobbed to the surface and floated downstream.

Thompson's hand snaked beneath his jacket. His arm leveled, time fragmented into split seconds, and the pistol roared. The first bottle erupted in a geyser of water and glass, and he locked onto the second. His eyes sighted along the barrel, bottles exploding in quick order, until the last one burst as the current swept it past his position. Less than five seconds had elapsed from the moment he pulled the gun.

Timing himself, Thompson shucked the empty shells and reloaded. On the count of ten, he holstered the Colt, looked upstream at Bobby, and nodded. The drill was repeated, five shots at a time, until thirty bottles had gone to the bottom. Finally, he reloaded, lowering the hammer on an empty chamber, and wedged the Colt into his shoulder holster. He was satisfied that his reflexes were still sharp.

"Goldurn!" Bobby shouted, scampering along the creekbank. "You never miss, Pa!"

"That's the whole idea," Thompson said genially. "I'd hate to lose my touch."

"When you gonna teach me to shoot, Pa? I just bet I'd be good, too."

"We'll get around to it, son. You're a little young yet."

"You always say that," Bobby sulked. "How old do I hav'ta be?"

Thompson tousled his hair. "I'd judge sixteen's a good age. No need to rush things."

"Holy Hannah, that's almost two years off! C'mon, Pa, have a heart—*pleeeze*."

"Keep your grades up and maybe we'll work something out. Your schooling's more important than popping away at bottles."

"School don't start till September. What about between now and then?"

"We'll wait to see your first report card."

Bobby groaned and pulled a face. Thompson understood his disappointment, for a boy's first gun was thought to be a rite of passage into manhood. But he wanted something more for his son, something better. A life where knowledge, not force of arms, made the difference.

His legacy to the youngster would never be a gun.

City Hall was located at the corner of Mesquite and San Jacinto. The offices of city officials were on the ground floor of the two-story structure, and the jail was in the basement. The city court was on the second floor.

Judge Horace Warren presided over the court. His authority extended to misdemeanor offenses committed within the city limits. For the most part, he dealt with drunk and disorderly, breach of peace, and family disputes. Graver crimes, such as robbery and murder, were tried at the county courthouse.

Thompson walked into the courtroom on the stroke of one o'clock. Marshal Creary, who was standing near the bench, gave him a sour look. The marshal's job, since there was no prosecutor for misdemeanors, was to present the case to the judge. His expression upon spotting Thompson was somehow disgruntled. He clearly would have preferred to request an arrest warrant.

Judge Warren was on the sundown side of fifty. He was squat and pudgy, with rheumy eyes, and noted for dispensing evenhanded justice. He motioned Thompson forward, and waited until he stopped before the bench. Then he nodded to Creary.

"All right, Marshal, let's hear the particulars."

Creary laboriously outlined the case. He dwelled on the fact that Thompson had discharged a firearm in a public establishment, at great risk of bodily injury, perhaps even death, to the patrons. The incident was unprovoked and a clear violation of the city ordinance.

"Your Honor, it's just not tolerable," he concluded. "This is the second time in less than two weeks he's appeared in court for the same offense. I'd hope you'd see fit to give him some jail time."

"Well, Mr. Thompson?" Judge Warren peered down from the bench. "Two times in two weeks is twice too often. What do you have to say for yourself?"

Thompson looked unrepentant. "Judge, for openers, nobody was in any danger. You know yourself, I've never missed in my life." He paused, shook his head. "I hit the mark dead center."

"I grant you are a marksman of the first order. But that doesn't make it any less a violation of the municipal code."

"Maybe not, but I had good cause. That dealer, Al Loraine, he's crooked as they come. I caught him dealing seconds."

"Did you now?" Judge Warren sounded personally offended. "Dealing seconds violates the code to hell and gone. There's no place for a cardsharp in Austin."

"Those are my sentiments exactly, Judge. A man has a right to expect a square deal."

"Your Honor!" Creary interjected loudly. "This isn't about a crooked dealer. It's about firing a gun in public."

The judge squinted at him. "Perhaps you ought to devote more time to cleaning up Guy Town, Marshal Creary. Tinhorn card cheats are a blight on our city's fair name."

"But that's not the point here! We're faced with—"

"Hundred dollar fine," Judge Warren interrupted, banging his gavel. "Pay the bailiff, Mr. Thompson. Case dismissed."

Thompson peeled a hundred off his roll. He grinned

at Creary and let the bill flutter onto the bailiff's desk. Judge Horace Warren rose from the bench, quickly smothering a laugh, and walked toward his chambers. He called back over his shoulder in what he hoped was a stern voice.

"Let's not see you in my courtroom again, Mr. Thompson."

SIX

On the first Friday in August, business was brisk. There was a cattlemen's convention in town, and many of the larger ranchers were inveterate high rollers. By late evening, several of them would gravitate to the tables at the Iron Front.

Thompson nonetheless went home for supper. A table stakes poker game, which attracted the high rollers, wouldn't get under way before eight or so. Until then, he was content to leave the club in the capable hands of Joe Richter. The house odds virtually guaranteed a profit no matter who was on the floor.

Around seven, Thompson hopped aboard the streetcar across from College Hill. He was stuffed with Catherine's meatloaf, savoring the aroma of a half-smoked cheroot. The sky blazed with stars, and a pale sickle moon hung lopsided on the horizon. As the streetcar pulled away, he took a long draw on the cheroot, his gaze fixed on distant, blinking stars. He felt all was right in his world.

For no particular reason, he was in a jolly good mood. Perhaps it was Catherine's meatloaf, or perhaps it was the promise of a high-stakes poker game. Or perhaps, as he reflected on it further, it was the pleasant memory of having bested Ed Creary in court. Some two weeks had passed, but rarely a day went by that it didn't pop into his mind, and he still relished the moment. He'd left Creary with egg on his face!

Not that he had done it without friends. Judge Horace Warren, along with the mayor, shared his distaste for Ed Creary. Granted, the customary fine for discharge of firearms was fifty dollars, and the judge had doubled it to a hundred. But Creary had pressed for jail time, doubtless reveling in the thought of Thompson confined to the dungeon beneath City Hall. The fine, however stiff, had amounted to little more than a slap on the wrist.

Yet the crowning moment was Judge Warren's sharp rebuke of Creary. In blunt terms the judge had admonished him to police Guy Town, and put an end to card cheats. Though unstated, there was the implicit charge that Creary was taking payoffs from the gaming dives. The look on Creary's face still gave Thompson a chuckle, and even greater appreciation of Judge Warren. Good friends, particularly in a courtroom, were a blessing.

Downtown, Thompson walked from Congress Avenue to the Iron Front. With the supper hour over, the bar was already crowded, and men were starting to congregate around the gaming tables. He moved to the end of the bar, where Richter stood watching the action. One of the barkeeps brought him a brandy, which was the only drink he would have until the place closed for the night. He lit a fresh cheroot, nodding to Richter.

"Looks to be a good night," he said, exhaling smoke. "I expect some of the cowmen to drift in later."

"They throw quite a shindig," Richter said. "Word's out they rented the ballroom at the Austin Hotel for their final banquet."

"Joe, money's no object when they hold a convention. They're all trying to impress one another with how rich they are."

"Somebody told me Shanghai Pierce is in town. Think he'll join your game?"

"I sincerely hope so. He's my kind of poker player—a happy loser."

Abel Pierce was one of the largest ranchers in Texas. His Rancho Grande cattle spread in Wharton County covered a quarter-million acres, and ran a herd of thirty thousand longhorns. A sailor in his youth, he'd been dubbed "Shanghai" for bragging about his seafaring adventures. His vast holdings made him one of the wealthiest men in the state.

Thompson knew him from Dodge City. A heavy drinker, Pierce was six-foot-four, loud and boisterous, and overly impressed with himself as a poker player. Some years ago, after he'd trailed a herd to railhead in Kansas, Thompson had relieved him of several thousand dollars in a marathon poker game. Despite his size, and a rowdy manner fueled by alcohol, he had proved to be a congenial loser. He was, in many respects, still something of a drunk sailor.

"Maybe he'll drop by," Richter said. "Everybody says he's got more money than God."

Thompson smiled. "God doesn't play poker. I'll take Shanghai Pierce any day."

Luther Edwards slammed through the door. His features were the color of oxblood, and his eyes were dark with anger. Thompson thought he'd never seen the lawyer in such an agitated state, and wondered what might have happened. He motioned Edwards to the rear of the bar.

"Luther, you're a sight," he said. "Somebody light your fuse?"

"Whiskey!" Edwards pounded on the bar. "I've never been so insulted in my life. Dirty bastards!"

"Who?"

"The goddamn cattlemen. They threw me out!"

"Threw you out of what?"

The bartender placed a shot glass on the counter. Edwards downed the whiskey neat, shuddering as it struck bottom. He waved a hand in wild outrage. "Threw me out of their banquet. That's what! Goddamn them."

Thompson appeared confused. "Why would you go to their banquet? You're not in the cow business."

"Captain Lee Hall is their keynote speaker. I wanted to hear his speech."

"I didn't know you were an admirer of Captain Hall's."

"Christ, Ben, who wouldn't want to hear him? He's only the greatest Ranger of our time."

There was no arguing the point. Captain Lee Hall, though scarcely in his thirties, was already a legend among Texas Rangers. Under his command, a troop of Rangers had all but ended the infamous Sutton-Taylor feud, arresting over four hundred men in the process. Some three years ago, he was with the Rangers in

Round Rock, the day they killed Sam Bass, a daring young robber who was now the subject of ballads. No one doubted that ballads would one day be sung about Lee Hall.

"So what happened?" Thompson asked. "How'd you come to be thrown out?"

Edwards quaffed another shot of whiskey. "I walked in, polite as you please, and took a seat at the rear of the room. One of the ranchers, the tallest son-of-a-bitch you've ever seen—"

"Sounds like Shanghai Pierce."

"Yes, that's what the others called him, Shanghai. They told him, and I quote, 'boot his ass out the door.' "

"Because you're not a cattleman?"

"Well, I tried to explain. But I hardly got a word out of my mouth when he grabbed me by the neck and waltzed me to the door. Ben, he picked me up and actually *threw* me out."

"Got yourself manhandled," Thompson said thoughtfully. "Not a hospitable bunch, are they?"

"Hospitable?" Edwards hooted. "The bastards aren't even civil! They laughed to beat the band."

"All a big joke . . . at your expense."

"I was ridiculed, Ben. Ridiculed!"

Thompson was silent a moment. Over the years, Edwards had proved to be a good and loyal friend, and indispensable in legal matters. But he was a thinker, not a physical man, and incapable of defending himself. A valued friend, Thompson told himself, deserved loyalty in return. He started toward the door.

"Let's go."

"Go?" Edwards said. "Go where?"

"To the hotel."

* * *

The Texas Livestock Association held a convention every year. The membership roll included the largest and most influential cattlemen in the state. Their combined herds numbered in the hundreds of thousands.

Shanghai Pierce sat at the head table. Seated beside him was Captain Lee Hall, and ranged along the table were such notable cowmen as Richard King, Alonzo Millett, and Seth Mabrey. They listened as the president of the association, Ellsbery Lane, droned on about issues vital to their industry. Issues that would determine the future of the cow business in Texas.

Lane was anything but a fiery speaker. Yet the message he delivered was a summation of two days of intense, and often rancorous, debate. There was now a consensus among the members that a policy of open range led to increased cattle rustling and sometimes violent disputes about land boundaries. A resolution would be presented to the state legislature requesting laws that would require the fencing of all rangeland, from the smallest spread to the largest. Open range, a tradition in Texas for generations, was about to become a thing of the past.

Richard King, the largest landholder in the state, was a staunch advocate of the proposal. His Santa Gertrudis Ranch was located near the lower Rio Grande, a sprawling empire founded in 1853 with the purchase of an old Spanish land grant. The original grant was for fifteen thousand acres, and over the years, King had transformed it into a virtual fiefdom encompassing one-and-a-quarter million acres. He saw barbed-wire as a means to protect his range.

Another rancher, conspicuous by his absence, was the second largest landholder in Texas. Charlie Goodnight, fabled for having blazed the Goodnight Trail to

Colorado, ruled his own fiefdom in the Texas Panhandle. His JA spread was located along Palo Duro Canyon, encompassing a million acres and a hundred thousand head of cattle. A year ago, he had formed the Panhandle Stockgrowers Association, and he remained an advocate of open range. He dissuaded rustlers by the simple expedience of hanging them.

Pierce and King swapped a glance as Ellsbery Lane plodded on with his speech. There were twenty ranchers seated at the banquet tables, and all of them were bored with Lane's recital of the agreement hammered out over the past two days. They were eager to hear a rousing oration from their keynote speaker, Captain Lee Hall. They fully expected to be regaled with tales of the Sutton-Taylor feud, and who actually fired the shot that killed Sam Bass. To a man, they wanted the business to end and the fun to begin. Their eyes glazed as Lane went on and on . . . and on.

The ballroom was stuffy from the lingering warmth of an August evening. To stir the air, the windows directly behind the head table had been opened earlier. Pierce was momentarily distracted by sounds from the street, and heaved a heavy sigh, wondering if Lane would ever finish. He leaned sideways in his chair, looking around at Richard King. He spoke in a low, disgruntled rumble.

"You reckon Ellsbery's ever gonna quit?"

"The man's a talker," King murmured softly. "You'd think he was running for political office."

"Hell's bells, we already elected him president."

"Maybe that was our first mistake."

"Shanghai Pierce!"

The booming shout froze everyone in the room. They turned and saw Thompson standing in the door-

way, Luther Edwards at his side. Thompson moved forward, the Colt Peacemaker in his hand, covering the
men seated at the tables. His gaze drilled into Abel
Pierce.

"You recognize this man?" he demanded, jerking
a thumb over his shoulder at Edwards. "You tossed
him out of here on his butt. Time to pay the piper,
Shanghai!"

Thompson started toward, the speakers' table. Ellsbery Lane ducked beneath the podium, and the other
cattlemen dropped to the floor. Shanghai Pierce bolted,
his nerves deserting him, overturning his chair as he
spun around. He dove headlong through an open window and landed in the alleyway beside the hotel. He
sprinted off into the night.

Captain Lee Hall hadn't moved until now. He knew
Thompson on sight, though they had never met. Careful of sudden moves, he rose from his chair and walked
around the end of the table. He kept his hands at his
sides.

A tomblike silence settled over the room. The cattlemen eased from beneath the tables, and watched bug-
eyed as Hall moved forward at a measured pace. He
was a man of square features, with steely blue eyes and
a thatch of red hair. His expression was composed, almost phlegmatic, betraying nothing. He halted in front
of Thompson.

"I'm Lee Hall," he said levelly. "I don't believe we've
met, Mr. Thompson."

"No, we haven't," Thompson acknowledged. "The
pleasure's all mine, Captain."

"Sorry I can't say the same. I'll thank you to hand
over that gun."

Thompson smoothly snapped the Colt into his

shoulder holster. "I've never surrendered my gun to any man, Captain. Tonight's no different."

"Don't push me," Hall said in a flat voice. "I mean to disarm you."

"Well, I suppose you could try, if you've got your mind set. I wouldn't recommend it."

Their eyes locked in a staring contest. After a prolonged moment, the tense look went out of Hall's features. He cocked his head with an inquisitive frown. "You've scared the living hell out of these men, Mr. Thompson. What's your purpose here?"

"I'd like you to meet a friend," Thompson said. "This is Luther Edwards, one of Austin's finest attorneys."

Edwards stuck out his hand. "Captain Hall, I consider it a personal honor. I've admired you for many years."

"I'm obliged," Hall said, accepting his handshake. "I apologize for the rough treatment you got earlier. Pierce had you out the door before I could stop him."

"That's why I'm here," Thompson injected. "Luther just wanted to hear your speech, and he meant no harm. Shanghai had no right to manhandle him."

Hall allowed himself a tight smile. "I just imagine we've seen the last of Shanghai Pierce. He's probably halfway back to Wharton County."

"Good riddance," Thompson' said. "Maybe he's learned his lesson."

"Did you intend to use that gun?"

"Captain, I thought to teach the rascal some manners. I won't tolerate an insult to a friend."

"I'll take you at your word, Mr. Thompson." Hall motioned them toward the tables. "Why don't you gents have a seat and make yourselves comfortable? I was just about to give a speech."

Luther Edwards grinned like a frog. As Hall turned toward the speakers' dais, Thompson led his friend to the nearest table and got him seated. The cattlemen slowly filed into their chairs, not quite sure what they'd witnessed. Their attention was drawn to the square-jawed Ranger at the podium.

Captain Lee Hall told them who really shot Sam Bass.

SEVEN

—◁▦▦▦▷—

Macbeth was playing a limited engagement. Everyone who was anyone in Austin was attending the opening performance, and a line of carriages blocked the street outside the opera house. Opening night was sold out.

Drivers hopped down to assist their passengers from the carriages. For the gala occasion, the men were dressed in white tie and tails and tall top hats. The women wore fashionable gowns and were adorned with their finest jewelry. One carriage after another disgorged a gathering of the town's elite. They slowly made their way into the opera house.

Thompson stepped from the coach of a brougham. The elegant carriage was drawn by a team of blood-red bays, rented for the evening from Purdy's Livery. As he assisted Catherine from the coach, her features bathed in the lights from the marquee, he thought she had never looked lovelier. She wore a pale rose gown of gossamer silk and a matching cape, her hair arranged in the latest chignon style, with an exquisite pearl choker at her throat. She was a vision, somehow regal.

A breeze off the river cooled the late August evening. As carriages pulled away, the crowd filed into the opera house with a buzz of excitement. Opening night was a major social event, and the lobby was packed with people who paused to exchange greetings. Thompson checked his hat at the cloak room, and turned back to Catherine, wending a path through the throng. Up ahead, near the theater entrance, he saw James Shipe, whose wife dripped with diamonds. The banker was talking with Mayor Tom Wheeler, also accompanied by his wife.

"Good evening," Thompson said cordially. "A pleasure to see you all again. Looks to be quite an affair."

"Indeed it does," Wheeler agreed. "Nothing like a little culture to bring out the best in folks."

After a round of handshakes, the ladies quickly engaged in animated conversation. Thompson counted it a source of pride that he and Catherine were accepted in the better circles of Austin. A gambler, particularly one with his reputation for gunplay, was more often than not excluded from polite company. He was especially gratified that the women were fond of Catherine. She enjoyed mixing with cultivated people.

"Just think of it," Shipe marveled, as the women chattered away. "Edwin Booth on the stage in Austin. We have reason to celebrate."

"We are the envy of Texas," Wheeler added. "Imagine that he bypassed Dallas in favor of Austin! I'm drunk with the thought of it."

Edwin Booth was the foremost Shakespearean actor of the day. His renown as a tragedian was unsurpassed, and even in England, the home of Shakespeare, he was considered a master of the art. In 1865, his younger brother, John Wilkes Booth, an actor of lesser fame, had assassinated Abraham Lincoln at the Ford Theater in Washington. Yet the public adoration of Edwin Booth went undiminished, and he remained an icon of the stage. His current tour would take him to twenty cities throughout America.

"There's the governor," Shipe said, pointing off into the crowd. "I understand he held a reception for Booth at the state house this afternoon. He must be quite an admirer."

The men watched as Governor Oran Roberts and his entourage moved through the theater doors. Wheeler shook his head with a rueful smile. "One of his aides called on me last week," he said, glancing at Thompson. "The governor's no admirer of yours, Ben."

"What's he got against me?" Thompson asked, somewhat taken aback. "I've never even met the man."

"Apparently he got a sizzler of a letter from the cattlemen's association. They filed a protest about your disrupting their banquet."

"I'd lay odds the protest came from Shanghai Pierce. Last time I saw him, he was still running."

Shipe chuckled with some humor. "Is it true that Pierce jumped out a window? That's what I read in the paper."

Articles had appeared in both the *Statesman* and the *Republican*. For several days following the incident, Thompson's encounter with Captain Lee Hall had been the talk of the town. The papers had treated the affair with satirical wit, chastising the cattlemen more than Thompson. The public, in turn, thought the matter somewhat laughable.

"So what's the governor's problem?" Thompson said. "All I did was take up for Luther Edwards."

"Oh, it's politics as usual," Wheeler said dismissively. "The cattlemen's association contributed to the governor's war chest in the last election. He felt obligated to complain that you hadn't been arrested."

"Well, it wasn't exactly a matter for the Rangers. Captain Hall was there, and he didn't arrest me."

"Didn't or couldn't?" Shipe joked. "The papers say he tried to disarm you. What happened?"

Thompson smiled. "Captain Hall's a reasonable man. We came to an understanding."

"Yes, I'm sure you did, Ben. I'm sure you did."

Wheeler snorted laughter. "I'd like to have been a fly on the wall."

Their conversation was cut short when curtain time was announced. Thompson nodded genially to the men, collected Catherine, and moved toward the doors. An usher escorted them to the best seats in the house, fifth row center in the orchestra. A vaulted ceiling rose majestically in the theater, with intricately carved woodwork bordering a spacious mural of robed figures and fleeting nymphs. The proscenium stage was crowned by an elaborate arch, bounded on the front by an orchestra pit, empty of musicians for tonight's performance. A few moments after they were seated, the house lights dimmed. The audience quieted.

Edwin Booth entered from stage left in Act One, Scene One. He was playing the lead role, Macbeth, a Scottish general of the King's army in ancient times. His costume revealed a fine figure of a man, lithe and tall, strikingly handsome, with a stage presence that dominated the play. His voice was a rich baritone, commanding and resonant, ringing out over the footlights into the farthest corner of the theater. His opening scene was with a fellow general, Banquo, and three haggish creatures revealed to be witches. From his first line, he held the audience enthralled.

Thompson was no stranger to Shakespeare. His schooling as a boy had given him a taste for the Bard, and he'd carried it with him into manhood. On occasion, in idle moments, he still perused favored passages in a well-thumbed volume of the poet's complete works. Tonight, watching Edwin Booth move about the stage, he soon found himself caught up in the lyrical rhythm of the verse. He was not as familiar with *Macbeth* as he was *Hamlet* and *Julius Caesar*, and he strained to follow every nuance of the story. He was quickly engrossed in Booth's performance.

The play opened when Duncan the Meek reigned as King of Scotland. Macbeth and Banquo, victorious generals returning from a great battle, were stopped in a desolate place by three unearthly creatures. The witches prophesied that Macbeth would become king of Scotland, a prophecy that amazed him since Duncan had legitimate heirs, two sons. Then, no less astounding, the witches foretold that though Banquo would never wear the crown, his sons would rule Scotland. Macbeth and Banquo were left to ponder the meaning of their strange encounter.

By the end of Act One, it became apparent to Thompson that something foul was afoot in Scotland. Upon returning to his castle, Macbeth related the incident with the witches to his wife. Lady Macbeth, a woman of cunning and evil, saw opportunity in the prophecy. By playing on his ambition, she convinced Macbeth that murder was an acceptable means to the crown. A visit to their castle by King Duncan and his sons, Malcolm and Donalbain, set the plan in motion. The sovereign would be killed in his sleep.

Catherine gripped Thompson's arm as the death scene unfolded. Edwin Booth masterfully portrayed a Macbeth who turned squeamish at the last moment. But Lady Macbeth was resolute, far more ruthless than her husband, and she goaded him to murder. Macbeth, armed with a dagger, entered the king's bedchamber and killed him in a bloody attack. The following morning, with discovery of the murder, the king's sons, and the rightful heirs to the throne, feared for their own lives. Malcolm, the eldest, fled to England, and Donalbain escaped to Ireland.

Macbeth, with no one to dispute his claim, was crowned King of Scotland. Yet Lady Macbeth could not forget the witches' prophecy that Banquo's children would one day claim the throne. She and Macbeth again plotted murder, and their henchmen, in the dark of the night, waylaid and killed Banquo. Scottish noblemen were repulsed by still another murder, and they joined Malcolm, the late king's heir, in England. An army was raised, with the purpose of restoring Malcolm to the throne, and marched on Scotland. Lady Macbeth, suddenly overcome by guilt and perhaps fearful of reprisals, was unable to face the consequences. She took her life by her own hand.

Edwin Booth, thoroughly immersed in the role of Macbeth, appeared devastated when informed of the queen's death. He moved downstage, his anguished features almost ghastly in the footlights, and stared out over the audience. His voice resonated with sorrow.

Tomorrow, and tomorrow, and tomorrow,
Creeps in this petty pace from day to day,

To the last syllable of recorded time;
And all our yesterdays have lighted fools
The way to dusty death. Out, out, brief candle!
Life's but a walking shadow; a poor player,
That struts and frets his hour upon the stage,
And then is heard no more: it is a tale
Told by an idiot, full of sound and fury
Signifying nothing.

Thompson was electrified by the words. His eyes were riveted on the stage, but the words resounded in his head. He was struck by the eerie sensation that something within him was no longer the same. Still, even as his mouth went dry and his scalp tingled, he was unable to formulate the change into thought. He stared, uncomprehending, at the actors.

The play moved to swift conclusion. Macbeth and his forces engaged the army besieging his castle. In the ensuing battle, he clashed in mortal combat with Macduff, one of the Scottish noblemen aligned with Malcolm. The fight ended with Macbeth defeated, his head chopped off (gruesomely depicted through stage magic), and the grisly trophy displayed on the tip of a sword. Malcolm, the rightful heir, then ascended the throne, at last victorious. The noblemen, one and all acclaimed their new monarch. *Hail, King of Scotland!*

The audience broke out in cheers as the curtain fell. Then, as the applause swelled to a crescendo, the curtain parted and the actors stepped forward to take their bows. Edwin Booth, the star of the show, was the last to appear onstage, his head magically restored. The theater reverberated with applause, and the crowd rose to give him a standing ovation. He took four curtain calls, bathed in a spotlight, glorying in the adulation. Finally, his arms raised in triumph, he backed away as the curtains swished closed for the last time. The house lights came up full.

"Oh, Ben," Catherine said, her eyes misty. "Wasn't he just magnificent!"

Thompson nodded. "Nobody will top that."

"I've never seen anything so tragic in my life. I simply loathed Macbeth—but then, somehow . . . I felt sorry for him."

"Shakespeare knew how to pull all the strings."

Thompson eased into the aisle, taking her arm. They joined the crush, moving toward the doors, aware of excited exclamations all around them. Everyone in the theater was talking about the remarkable performance delivered by Edwin Booth. A common thread, expressed in one fashion or another, ran through their comments. None of them would ever forget tonight.

Outside the opera house, Thompson waited with Catherine for their carriage to be brought around. Mayor Wheeler and James Shipe appeared with their wives, and the conversation centered as much on Edwin Booth as on the power of the play. The women were taken with the actor, and the men were perhaps more impressed with the story of a good man gone wrong. All of them agreed that it was tragedy at its best.

On the way home, Thompson lapsed into a brooding silence. As the carriage turned north, he stared out into the night, remembering the moment that had so electrified him during the play. The sensation washed over him again, and he heard the words, not altogether in order, but with ringing clarity. *Life is a tale told by an idiot, full of sound and fury—signifying nothing.*

The words seemed to hammer at him. A realist, seldom at odds with himself or his world, he was not given to moments of philosophical deliberation. But now his thoughts turned inward, sparked by some greater wisdom penned to paper by Shakespeare. He weighed in the balance all he'd done with his life, from the vast sums of money he had won at gaming tables to the men he had killed in the name of honor. Oddly, in a way he didn't quite understand, he suddenly found it wanting.

A tale signifying nothing.

"You're awfully quiet." Catherine snuggled against his shoulder. "Thinking about the play?"

"After a fashion," Thompson said, mentally switching gears. "I was wondering what the moral was. What Shakespeare meant."

"Does there have to be a moral?"

"I just suspect that's what he intended."

She looked at him. "And what was the moral you got from the play?"

"I'm not sure," Thompson said absently. "Maybe a man ought not to listen to witches. Macbeth damn sure got steered the wrong way."

"Honestly, aren't you the big tease! I thought you were serious."

"Nope, just having a little fun. I'll leave the serious stuff to Shakespeare."

Thompson knew he'd fobbed her off with nonsense. For again, as his gaze was drawn to the starlit sky, he heard the words, a different stanza. Words that stuck like a spear in his mind.

Life is but a walking shadow. A player struts his hour upon the stage, and then is heard no more.

He wondered what he'd done with his life, all those years. His hour upon the stage . . .

EIGHT

"Deuces bet twenty."

"Too rich for my blood."

"I'll fold."

"I'm right behind you."

The man with the deuces was Roger Tucker. A stock-broker, and by his very nature a gambler, his passion was poker. He generally wandered into the Iron Front every Friday afternoon in search of a game. Today, the first Friday in September, was no exception.

There were five men at the table. Tucker, a notions drummer, a railroad superintendent, an insurance sales-man, and Thompson. The game was five-card stud, and Thompson was the last man in the hand. He was hold-ing two pair, but something told him that Tucker had a third deuce in the hole. He felt obliged to find out.

"I'll just call," he said, tossing chips into the pot. "Have to keep you honest, Roger."

Tucker turned over the third deuce. "Read 'em and weep," he said with a wide grin. "Got you that time, Ben."

"No question about it, Roger. You won yourself a pot."

Thompson folded his hand. Tucker and the other men were mediocre players, several notches below the competition he'd faced on the gamblers' circuit. They lacked insight into percentages and odds, often betting on the come, hoping to improve a poor hand. Even on a good hand, they seldom played it with finesse.

The proper play for Tucker would have been to check his deuces. The drummer, with queens on the board, would likely have bet the limit. One or more of the other players might have called, and Thompson would have probably tested the waters with a raise. If Tucker was able to read players as well as he read cards, he would then have raised the limit. A little finesse would have allowed him to drag down a large pot.

Over the years, Thompson had developed his own technique for winning at cutthroat poker. There was no pattern to his betting and raising; his erratic play made him unpredictable, and he won on what appeared to be weak hands. He would bluff on a bad hand as often as he folded, and he seldom folded. More often than not his bluff went undetected. The secret was to keep them guessing.

On good hands, he would sometimes raise the limit, allowing the money to speak for itself. At other times, when he held good cards, he would lay back and sucker his opponents into heedless raises. On occasion, merely calling all bets and raises, he let the other players build the pot only to turn up the winning hand. No one was ever sure of what he held.

Tucker, still grinning, raked in the pot. The deal passed to Thompson and he called five-card draw. In some Eastern casinos the traditional rules of poker had been revised to include straights, flushes, and the most elusive of all combinations, the straight flush. The highest hand back East was now a royal flush, ten through ace in the same suit. By all accounts, the revised rules lent the game a whole new element.

Poker in the West was still played by the original rules observed in earlier times on riverboats. There were no straights, no flushes, and no straight flushes, royal or otherwise. There were two unbeatable hands west of the Mississippi. The first was four aces, drawn by most players only once or twice in a lifetime. The other cinch hand was four kings with an ace kicker.

Four kings, in combination with one of the aces, surmounted almost incalculable odds. The ace kicker precluded anyone from holding what amounted to the granddaddy of all hands, four aces. Seasoned players looked upon it as a minor miracle, or the work of a skilled cardsharp. Men spoke of it in mystical terms.

A waning afternoon sun filtered through the front windows. Thompson was bored with the game, even though he was ahead almost two hundred dollars. Sometimes he felt mired in quicksand, slowly being dragged under, and all the more so since the performance of *Macbeth*. A fortnight had passed, but he was still troubled by thoughts that his life was a circle within a circle, slogging ever deeper into the mire. One day was like any other.

The man on his right cut the cards after he'd shuffled. He dealt around the table, than placed the deck beside his chips. A cheroot jutted from the corner of his mouth, and he puffed a cloud of smoke as he spread his cards. He managed a deadpan expression, though he was suddenly no longer bored with the game. He had three sevens.

Tucker, who was on his left, checked. The drummer, a pudgy man named Willis Orcutt, bet twenty. The next two players folded, and Thompson, exhaling a streamer of smoke, airily raised twenty. Tucker reluctantly folded, and Orcutt bumped it another twenty. Thompson took the last raise.

On the draw, Orcutt held four and drew one. Thompson kept the three sevens and dealt himself two. When Orcutt squeezed his cards apart, the corners of his mouth lifted in a fleeting telltale smile. He checked.

Thompson caught the smile. He figured Orcutt had filled on two pair and was trying to sandbag him. He fanned his cards, inwardly amazed that he'd drawn the case seven. He hesitated, as though weighing his options, and bet twenty. Orcutt beamed.

"Your twenty," he said smugly—"and twenty more."

Thompson feigned surprise, pausing a moment, and raised. Orcutt took the last raise, waiting for Thompson to call, and barked a short laugh. He spread his cards.

"Full house! Jacks over nines."

"Very pretty," Thompson said, turning his cards. "Unfortunately, I filled out too, Mr. Orcutt. Four sevens."

Orcutt stared at the cards. "You dealt yourself the case seven."

"Appears to be my lucky day."

"Anybody else, I'd raise the roof. Good thing you run a straight game."

"I'll take that as a compliment, Mr. Orcutt."

"Tried to sandbag you and sandbagged myself. Helluva note!"

"Well, like they say, that's poker."

The game ended shortly before five o'clock. Thompson treated everyone to a drink on the house, then walked to his office. As he shrugged into his suit coat, there was a knock on the door and he turned to find Jim Burditt. A fellow gambler and an old friend, Burditt generally plied his trade in clubs other than the Iron Front. There was common agreement among professionals that friendship and cards were a poor mix.

"Hello there, Jim," Thompson said, pleased to see him. "How's tricks these days?"

Burditt closed the door. "Not worth a damn, and that's a fact. Guess you heard about last night?"

Everyone in the sporting crowd had heard the story. Last night, celebrating a big win at the faro tables, Burditt had gotten drunk and attended a show at the Capital Variety Theater. Overly rambunctious, he'd disrupted the performance and then turned belligerent when confronted by the owner, Mark Wilson. A tough Irishman, with a hair-trigger temper, Wilson had bodily thrown him out of the theater. The word was out that Wilson had threatened harsher treatment if he ever came back.

"I've come to ask your help," Burditt said solemnly. "I think Wilson will try gunplay the next time I walk in there."

"That's simple enough," Thompson said. "Stay out of the place."

"Would you let him scare you off?"

"We're not talking about me."

"I won't have people say I'm yellow. I'm going back in there tonight and I'm asking your help. How about it, Ben?"

Thompson frowned. "I've been in two shooting scrapes the last month or so. Another one and Judge Warren will nail my hide to the wall."

"Nobody's gonna get shot," Burditt protested. "I just need you to watch my back. Wilson likes the odds stacked in his favor."

"What if things go haywire? What if I have to plug somebody to keep them off your back?"

"Things won't come to that. This here's strictly between me and Wilson. You being there will make him think twice about loading the dice. He wouldn't mess with you."

"And if somebody goes stupid and still deals me a hand? What then?"

"For chrissakes, Ben!" Burditt flung out his arms. "You took on Lee Hall and the cattlemen's association for your lawyer friend. Are you telling me I don't rate that high anymore?"

Thompson looked offended. Yet he was unable to muster a reasonable argument. Some years ago, when the Rangers were chasing his brother, Burditt had volunteered to assist in Billy's escape. On any number of occasions, particularly in the Kansas cowtowns, Burditt had proved to be a steadfast friend. A friend in need, Thompson told himself, should never go begging. A debt was a debt.

"All right," he said at length. "What's your play?"

Burditt explained what he had in mind.

The Capital Variety Theater was located on Brazos Street, a block east of Congress Avenue. A number of vaudeville acts were presented every night, with the usual array of chorus girls, jugglers, and magicians. The clientele was largely composed of workingmen and their women, and the sporting crowd. Few of the so-called respectable element ever set foot in a variety theater.

A large barroom occupied the front of the building. The bar extended the length of the room, with tables and chairs along the opposite wall. At the rear of the bar, there was a spacious theater, with seating for a hundred patrons, and a raised stage. There were three shows a night and people were already filing in for the early performance. Friday nights always drew a sellout crowd.

Thompson and Burditt arrived a few minutes before eight. As they walked through the barroom, they saw Mark Wilson, the proprietor, stationed at the entrance to the theater. He was a beefy man, thick through the shoulders, with florid features and quick eyes. He looked around, surveying the crowd, and his gaze suddenly stopped when he spotted them. His expression went flat and cold.

A moment elapsed, then Wilson darted a glance at the bar. Thompson followed his gaze and saw Charlie Mathews, one of the bartenders, slowly nod his head. Mathews was a local toughnut, handy with his fists and a gun, and also served as the house bouncer. The look that passed between Wilson and Mathews was clearly a signal, and Thompson sensed there was some sort of prearranged plan of action. Mathews would cover his boss in the event of trouble.

Burditt strolled past Wilson as though he hadn't a care in the world. He took a seat at the rear of the theater, turning slightly in his chair, so that he could keep one eye on the barroom. As they had agreed beforehand, Thompson casually moved to the end of the bar and placed his back to the wall. From there, he could watch Burditt and Wilson, and ensure, no matter what happened, that his friend got a fair shake. One of the bartenders drifted over and he ordered a whiskey, which he left untouched. He noted that Mathews was positioned farther along the bar.

Halfway through the show, a magician produced a dove from beneath a silk scarf. A group of rowdies seated in the front row were obviously waiting for the moment. One of them, the practical joker in the bunch, tossed a lighted string of firecrackers onto the stage. The dove took wing at the first explosion, and the magician backpedaled furiously as the firecrackers popped and danced at his feet. The crowd roared with laughter, hurling jeers and catcalls at the magician. They thought it was the best part of his act.

A city policeman rushed through the street door. Thompson recognized him as Carl Allen, and wondered that an officer was so conveniently handy when the commotion started. Then, all in an instant, he realized that it was a setup, the rowdies and the firecrackers orchestrated by Wilson. Jim Burditt was about to be blamed, at the very least arrested, perhaps killed if he tried to resist arrest. His appearance at the theater had set the plan in motion.

Thompson moved away from the wall. Wilson, just as he'd suspected, was blaming the incident on Burditt, and demanding his arrest. Carl Allen, gesturing wildly with his nightstick, grabbed Burditt by the collar and hustled him toward the door. Thompson got ahead of them, by now convinced that Burditt would never make it to the street alive. Wilson and Mathews were too alert, swapping hurried glances, as though awaiting some sign of resistance. Thompson stepped in to Allen's path.

"Let him go," he said sternly. "Jim didn't set off those firecrackers. I saw the whole thing."

Allen waved his nightstick. "Stand aside and don't interfere. I'm taking him to jail."

"Why put yourself to the trouble? Let me be responsible for him and I'll have him in court first thing in the morning. We'll get to the bottom of things then."

Wilson pushed forward. "You're out of line, Thompson. I want him arrested."

"Nobody's arresting him," Thompson said roughly. "You know damn well he wasn't involved. You rigged the whole game yourself."

"You're a lying son-of-a-bitch—"

Thompson backhanded him in the mouth. Wilson lurched sideways, blood spurting from a split lip. Allen moved to separate them, and Thompson pulled Burditt to his side. He looked directly into the policeman's eyes.

"I'm taking Jim out of here. Any objections?"

"No, go on," Allen said lamely. "Maybe it's for the best."

Thompson backed away a few steps. Then he turned, Burditt still at his side, and started toward the door. Wilson, his features twisted with rage, motioned frantically to his bouncer, Charlie Mathews. Ducking down, Mathews brought a sawed-off shotgun from beneath the counter and handed it across the bar. Wilson eared back the hammers.

"Watch out!" someone screamed. "He's got a gun!"

Officer Allen whirled around, losing his balance. His shoulder collided with the shotgun, which was centered on Thompson's back, jostling the barrels upward. Wilson tripped the trigger and the crowd scattered as a load of buckshot punched a hole in the ceiling. Thompson spun, drawing his Colt, and fired three shots in a staccato roar. The slugs stitched bright red dots up Wilson's shirtfront.

Arms flailing, the shotgun spinning away, Wilson went down like a felled tree. As he struck the floor,

Mathews came up with a pistol from beneath the bar. He fired a hurried snap-shot that plucked at the sleeve of Thompson's coat and ripped through the flesh of his left arm. Thompson staggered, quickly righting himself, and leveled the Colt, caught the sights. He feathered the trigger.

The slug drilled into Mathews's throat. His head arched upward and the back of his neck blew out in a gout of blood and bone matter. He stood there an instant, dead on his feet, then his legs buckled and he collapsed behind the bar. A pall of gunsmoke hung over the barroom, and for a long moment, no one moved. Finally, levering himself off the floor, Officer Allen got to his feet. He took a tentative step toward Thompson.

"Jesus Christ A'mighty," he said in a piping voice. "Just put your gun away and don't kill nobody else. I'll let you surrender to Marshal Creary."

"Not tonight," Thompson said, his features hard as stone. "I'll turn myself in to the sheriff. Anybody wants me, that's where I'll be."

"The marshal's not gonna like that."

"Tell him I said to stuff it."

Thompson backed out of the barroom. Droplets of blood leaked from his sleeve, but he kept the Colt trained on Allen. Burditt fell in beside him and they went through the door onto the street. Thompson turned in the direction of Congress Avenue.

Burditt looked ashen. "Goddamn, I'm sorry as hell, Ben. I never meant for it to come to that."

"Then you shouldn't have asked," Thompson said gruffly. "Next time, do your own killing."

"Are you hurt bad?"

"I'll live."

They trudged off toward the courthouse.

NINE

⟞⟝

Sheriff Frank Horner took Thompson and Burditt into custody. Until he could complete his investigation, the question of bail was a moot point. The prisoners were locked in a cell on the top floor of the courthouse.

Thompson was permitted to contact his attorneys. A deputy was also dispatched to advise Catherine that her husband was under arrest. Within the hour, Luther Edwards and Jack Walton arrived at the county jail. They were allowed to meet privately with their client in a holding room normally reserved for court trials. An armed deputy stood guard outside.

Walton, who was the more experienced criminal attorney, took charge. He reminded Thompson that anything said fell under the attorney–client privilege, and could never be divulged. After a bit of coaxing, Thompson related the incidents of the day, from the time Burditt had walked into his office at the Iron Front. Walton and Edwards listened intently, and made copious notes. Walton finally shook his head.

"Your friends will be the death of you, Ben."

"And that includes me," Edwards hastily confessed. "I got you involved in that scrap with the cattlemen's association. Small wonder it didn't end as badly as tonight."

"You've got it all wrong," Thompson informed them. "A man has to stick by his friends when there's trouble. Otherwise, he's a poor excuse of a man."

"Let's leave that for now," Walton said. "I want to go back to what Burditt told you this afternoon. He was convinced that Wilson meant to kill him. Correct?"

"That's right."

"And you agreed to accompany him to the theater. To cover his back?"

"Yeah, that was the general idea."

"Even though Wilson had kicked him out of the theater last night. And with just cause."

"You're missing the point. Jim had to go back in there and face Wilson. If he didn't, everybody would think he was yellow."

"In other words, you went there knowing the situation could turn violent. You were prepared to kill to protect a friend. Is that a fair statement?"

"Fair enough."

"And that is exactly what happened. You killed two men."

"Not before they tried to kill me."

Thompson's left arm was cradled in a sling. Before the lawyers arrived, a doctor had been summoned to the jail. Upon examination, he proved to be suffering from a flesh wound, painful but easily treated. The doctor had pronounced him a lucky man.

Walton looked at him. "Do you understand what I'm driving at, Ben? A case could be made that you and Burditt went there to provoke a fight."

"That'll never hold water."

"On the contrary, the state will contend that it was calculated. Nothing less than premeditated murder. A hanging offense."

"What about all the witnesses?" Thompson countered. "They'll testify it was self-defense."

"I hope you're right," Walton said. "But you've put yourself in an extremely precarious position. The county attorney will almost certainly charge you with murder."

"How do we get around that?"

"We present *our* version of the truth. Hard as it sounds, we're fortunate you killed both Wilson and Mathews. Their version will never be heard in court."

"Sorry state of affairs," Thompson grumped. "You defend yourself and you wind up charged with murder. Things used to be different."

Walton nodded soberly. "I'm afraid we've entered the modern age. The old days are long gone."

"Don't worry, Ben," Edwards quickly added. "We'll get you off somehow."

A rap of knuckles sounded on the door. Sheriff Horner entered the room, closing the door behind him. "Thought you'd want to know I've turned Burditt loose. Everybody at the variety theater says he wasn't part of the shooting."

"What about Ben?" Walton asked. "Didn't they tell you it was self-defense?"

"Well, it's not quite that simple. We'll have to have a coroner's inquest and that'll tell us what's what. Until then, Ben stays in jail."

"How soon can a jury be impaneled?"

"Tomorrow," Horner said. "I stopped by Judge Tegener's house on the way back here. He ordered me to move things right along."

Judge Fritz Tegener was presiding justice over the Third District Court. Though irregular, he was empowered to order a coroner's inquest on a Saturday. "The sooner the better," Walton remarked. "But I have to say I'm curious. Why so expeditious?"

"Mark Wilson was a popular man with the sporting crowd. There's bound to be hard feelings, and the judge wants to put a lid on things. Either Ben's cleared, or he'll get bound over for preliminary hearing."

"Frank, I'm in the clear," Thompson said earnestly. "I was on my way out the door and Wilson tried to backshoot me. I was just defending myself."

Horner was a lawman of the old school. He subscribed to the theory that a backshooter, a coward by definition, deserved to be shot. Added to that was the fact that he considered Thompson a man of honor, and a passable friend. His brow wrinkled in a troubled frown.

"Ben, I hope to hell you beat it. But it's out of my hands now. We'll just have to wait and see."

The door opened and Catherine walked into the room. Horner and the two attorneys made their excuses, and quickly moved into the hallway. When the door closed, Catherine stepped into Thompson's free arm and they stood locked in silent embrace. He finally found his voice.

"Where's Bobby?"

"I left him with the neighbors."

"Does he know I'm in jail?"

"Not yet." She stepped back, tears welling up in her

eyes, inspecting his sling. "I thought my heart would stop when the deputy told me you'd been wounded. How bad is it?"

"Just a little nick," Thompson said lightly. "Doc Phelps told me he'd seen worse bee stings."

"I wish that's all it were. Are they going to let you out of here?"

"There's a coroner's inquest set for tomorrow. I just expect they'll turn me loose."

"Is it truc——" she hesitated, searching his eyes— "two men?"

Thompson grimaced. "Katie, the way it worked out, I didn't have any choice. Things went to hell in a hurry."

She sometimes hoped he would change, finally hang up his gun. But then in reflective moments, she chided herself for wishful thinking. He was a prideful man when she married him, and he'd grown more so with age. She knew he would rather die than surrender his honor.

"Well, you're safe and that's all that counts. I'm sure the charges will be dropped."

Thompson touched her face. "I'm glad you came, even if I am in jail. I didn't want you worrying."

"Oh, Ben, you're such a fool sometimes."

She threw her arm around his neck and hugged him tightly.

Third District Court convened on Thursday, September 16. The spectator benches were packed, with people standing at the rear of the courtroom. The uptown sporting crowd, particularly the gamblers, were drawn to what promised to be a sensational hearing. One of their own was charged with murder.

For nearly two weeks, the newspapers had carried

the story on the front page. The coroner's jury had returned a finding of homicide, and Thompson had been bound over for preliminary hearing. Bail was set at $5,000, which was posted the same day, and he'd gone about business as usual while awaiting a court date. The oddsmakers were laying 5–3 on dismissal.

Catherine was seated in the front row. With her was Billy Thompson, who had traveled from Brownsville upon hearing of the shooting. He had arrived a week ago, full of confidence and good cheer, regaling them with stories of his adventures as a riverboat gambler. He expressed no concern whatever that his brother would beat the charges and walk out of court a free man. His conviction was based on the fact that he himself had done the same, several times.

Thompson was seated at the defendant's table, with his attorneys. Jack Walton radiated confidence, and Luther Edwards looked as if the result were all but a foregone conclusion. On the opposite side of the courtroom, George Upshaw, the county attorney, was seated with his assistant at the prosecutor's table. A vain man, Upshaw was short and slight of build, with sleek hair, muddy eyes, and a pencil-thin mustache. He had been quoted in the *Statesman* as saying Thompson would stand trial for first-degree murder. He looked like a fighting cock ready to be pitted.

"All rise!"

The bailiff's ringing voice brought everyone to their feet. Judge Fritz Tegener emerged from his chambers and walked briskly to the bench. He was a rotund German, the son of immigrants, noted for his pungent humor and his sometimes bizarre interpretation of the law. Every lawyer in Austin had at one time or another been dusted by his acerbic wit, and left to ponder the vagaries of the judicial system. He plopped down in his chair and nodded benignly to the spectators. His gaze settled on the advocates.

"Are we ready to proceed, gentlemen?"

Upshaw snapped to attention. "The state is ready, Your Honor."

Walton was only a beat behind. "We're prepared as well, Judge."

"Let's get on with it then."

Upshaw's first witness was the county coroner. His testimony dealt with the nature of the wounds suffered by Wilson and Mathews. On cross-examination, Walton asked if men who had sustained mortal wounds would still be capable of firing their weapons. Over Upshaw's strong objection the witness was allowed to answer the question. He thought it unlikely that the deceased had fired their guns after being wounded.

The next witness was Sheriff Frank Horner. His investigation, he testified, indicated that an altercation between Thompson and Wilson was the direct cause of the shooting. A waiter from the Capital Variety Theater was then called to the stand. He related that the incident began with a string of firecrackers being thrown on the stage. His recollection was that James Burditt was seated among the men who had thrown the firecrackers. Walton grilled him mercilessly on cross-examination, and the waiter finally reversed himself. He wasn't certain where Burditt had been seated.

Policeman Carl Allen was the next witness for the prosecution. He testified that Wilson had asked him to stay close to the theater on the evening of the shooting. Wilson expected trouble, he said, because Burditt had been ejected the night before. He went on to state that Burditt, following the incident with the firecrackers, had resisted arrest. Thompson, he recounted, had interfered with the arrest, and then, without provocation, struck Wilson when the theater owner tried to intervene. His recollection of who had fired the opening shot was vague; he had been knocked aside, and everything had happened too fast. His impression was that Thompson had been the first to draw a gun.

Thompson, watching from the defense table, was barely able to restrain himself. Walton reassured him with a pat on the shoulder, then proceeded to savage Officer Allen under cross-examination. He got Allen to admit that Thompson had *requested* Burditt's release, and promised to have him in court the following morning. Then, rattling Allen with a flurry of questions, he forced the admission that the blow struck by Thompson was the result of something said by Wilson. Allen pleaded a faulty memory as to the exact words; but conceded it might have been an insult. He refused to budge as to his vague recollection of who fired the first shot.

Jim Burditt was then called to the stand. Upshaw bullied and badgered, alleging that Burditt and Thompson had conspired to create a violent situation. His contention was that Burditt, through Thompson, planned to take revenge for having been roughly ejected from the theater. He attempted to extract a confession that Wilson's death was nothing short of premeditated murder. Burditt held his own in the verbal sparring match, flatly denying any thought of conspiracy, or intent to commit violence. On cross-examination, Walton subtly planted the seed that Burditt, far from seeking revenge, had actually feared for his own life. He had merely asked Thompson to guard his back.

George Upshaw informed the court that he had no further witnesses. Walton promptly called to the stand three theater customers, who were present at the time of the killings. Their testimony established that Wilson had fired first, while attempting to shoot Thompson in the back. The cross-examination by Upshaw was testy but futile; the men refused to alter their stories. Thompson was the last witness for the defense, and took the oath with his hand on a Bible. Walton approached the stand.

"Mr. Thompson, did you kill Mark Wilson and Charles Mathews?"

"Yessir, I regret to say I did."

"Would you tell the court why?"

Thompson squared his shoulders. "They did their level best to kill me. I fired in defense of my life."

"Mark Wilson fired on you first?"

"Yes."

"Charles Mathews fired on you first?"

"Yes."

"And only then did you return their fire?"

"That's how it happened."

Walton paused, playing for effect. "Tell me, Mr. Thompson," he said. "Why did you strike Wilson with your hand?"

"You'll pardon the language," Thompson said, glancing at the judge, who nodded. "Wilson called me a 'lying son-of-a-bitch'!"

"What prompted him to curse you?"

"I'd just told him what was clear to everybody in the theater. Namely, that he'd rigged it to have Jim Burditt arrested."

"And what did you do next?"

"Carl Allen got between us and I headed for the door. That's when Wilson turned loose with a shotgun."

"With your back to him?"

"Yes, with my back to him."

"On your oath, Mr. Thompson—" Walton struck a dramatic pose. "Did you conspire with James Burditt to commit murder? Did you go to the Capital Variety Theater with the intent of killing the deceased, Mark Wilson?"

"No, I did not."

"And did you fire on Mathews only after he had wounded you?"

Thompson's arm was still in a sling. Though the arm was healed, Walton thought the sling made an effective courtroom prop. As if on cue, Thompson gave the answer they had rehearsed.

"I've got the scar to prove he fired first."

"No further questions."

The cross-examination by Upshaw was wasted effort. Thompson calmly rebutted the questions, and Upshaw went back to his chair with a look of defeat. Judge Fritz Tegener announced that he saw no reason for lengthy review of the evidence. He would render an immediate decision.

"The court rules that the deaths of both Mark A. Wilson and Charles N. Mathews were justifiable homicide. Mr. Thompson, you are forthwith discharged. Bail will be remanded."

The courtroom erupted in cheers. Thompson shook hands with his attorneys, and pulled Catherine into a warm embrace. Billy slapped him on the back, whooping loudly, grinning like a jack-o'-lantern. As they made their way up the aisle, the spectators crowded around, offering congratulations. There was a mood of celebration in the air.

Outside the courthouse, reporters from the *Statesman* and the *Republican* waited on the steps. "Mr.

Thompson!" one of them shouted. "Do you feel vindicated?"

"Boys, I'll tell you, fresh air never smelled so good."

"What will you do now?"

Thompson smiled. "I think I'll stay out of variety theaters."

The spectators thronged around broke out laughing. Catherine clutched his arm, and Billy cleared a path through the crowd. As they walked off along the street, Thompson's smile quickly faded. His eyes took on a somber cast.

He wondered what he'd won, and the answer seemed all too clear. Nothing.

TEN

—⁓⁓—

Thompson was seated in the parlor. Billy was standing in the dining room doorway, talking with Catherine. She was bustling around the kitchen, preparing a celebration dinner. The aroma of a roasting hen filled the house.

Through the window, Thompson saw Bobby out in the front yard. The boy was playing with a couple of his neighborhood pals, and the game they played was disturbing to watch. They were reenacting the variety theater shooting, and the other two boys were cast in the roles of Wilson and Mathews. Bobby was playing his father.

The game was a juvenile fantasy of a gunfight. Bobby would face off against the other boys, who pretended to draw pistols holstered at their sides. When they made their move, he would draw from what was clearly an imaginary shoulder holster. Their forefingers were extended, thumbs cocked like the hammer of a pistol, and shouts of "BANG! BANG!" drifted through the window. Bobby always won.

Thompson watched with a growing sense of concern. He thought the game was probably based on neighborhood gossip about the shootout. Yet to the boys it was just that—a game—played out with imaginary guns. They didn't understand that dead men, in real life, never got up to play the game again. The thing that troubled him most was that Bobby was cast in the role of hero, and there was nothing heroic about killing two men. He was sorely reminded of the old saying: like father, like son.

Earlier that afternoon, upon returning home, Bobby had greeted him with something akin to hero worship. Catherine and Billy were elated by the outcome of the court hearing, and their enthusiasm had spilled over onto the boy. Bobby had stayed with neighbors during the hearing, and he was aware that an adverse ruling could send his father back to jail. On being told the news, he'd flung himself on Thompson, wild with joy, overcome with relief. Anyone watching would never doubt that the boy idolized his father.

But now, looking out the window, Thompson was deeply concerned. Any father wanted the admiration of his son, relished the idea of being thought a hero. The difference was that few fathers killed men in gunfights and got their names in newspaper headlines. Or worried at the sight of their sons playing make-believe, and acting out what was too close to the truth. Notoriety, and killing men, was not the stuff of games.

Thompson leaned out the window. "Bobby, come on in now! Time to get washed up for supper."

"Be right there, Pa!" Bobby hurried toward the

porch, motioning to his friends. "See you guys later. Gotta go."

A moment later the boy burst through the door. His features were flushed with youthful exuberance. "Did you see us, Pa? I got 'em ever' time."

Thompson returned to his chair. "Yes, son, I saw you."

"Was that the way you got Wilson and Mathews? Was it?"

"Where'd you hear those names?"

"Aren't those the ones you shot, Pa? All the guys are talkin' about it. They're jealous as all get-out!"

"Jealous of what?"

Bobby beamed. "Their dads haven't killed nobody. They'd swap places with me in a minute."

Billy ambled in from the dining room. Thompson exchanged a glance with him, then looked back at the boy. "I want you to listen to me, son."

"Yeah, Pa, sure."

"There's no honor in killing a man. Nothing to be proud of or brag about. You understand me?"

"I dunno." Bobby appeared confused. "I mean, what's so wrong with it? You did it."

"Well . . ." Thompson rubbed his jawline, searching for words. "Sometimes another man comes after you with a gun, and you've got no choice. You have to defend yourself." He paused, underscoring the point. "But it's still nothing to be proud of."

"All the same, I'm proud of you, Pa. I'll bet Mom is, too."

"Son, I'm trying to tell you it's not an honorable thing. I don't want you bragging to your friends about me."

"I guess I see what you mean."

"We'll talk about it later," Thompson said gently. "You get yourself ready for supper. Comb your hair."

Bobby started toward the hallway. At the door, he turned and looked back at his uncle. "You ever killed anybody, Uncle Billy? The way Pa has?"

"Not just exactly, squirt." Billy managed to keep a straight face. "'Course, there's not many the equal of your Pa. He's strictly one of a kind."

"Boy, don't I know it! You oughta see him shoot bottles."

Bobby took the stairs two at a time. Thompson slowly wagged his head. "How do you tell him it's not right to kill people? He thinks I rode in on a white horse."

"You worry too much," Billy said. "Hell, he's just a kid, Ben. He'll grow out of it."

"Did we?"

"Did we what?"

"Grow out of it," Thompson said sternly. "I'm pushing forty and I've just put two men in their graves. I haven't learned a helluva lot along the way."

Billy laughed. "You're still kickin', aren't you? Better them than you."

"Maybe so, but I still feel like some Bible-thumpin' hypocrite. I hear myself telling Bobby 'do what I say, not what I do!'"

"I never saw a man so hard on himself. You got sprung today, big brother. Cheer up."

"Why don't you go help Kate? I'm not in a mood to talk."

"Guess I know a hint when I hear one."

Billy walked off through the dining room. Thompson slumped back in his chair, his eyes fixed on the ceiling.

All afternoon, since they'd left the courtroom, he had been wrestling with a problem. Watching Bobby and his pals playfully kill each other had only aggravated a sore spot. He was worn out with killing.

The root of the problem was Carl Allen. During the hearing, the policeman had lied under oath about the theater shooting. His testimony, when read between the lines, confirmed that he'd been in league with Mark Wilson. Yet Wilson was dead, and that left the question of why Allen would perjure himself for a corpse. Why would he still try to put a noose around Thompson's neck?

The answer, Thompson told himself, was Ed Creary. The city marshal had a score to settle, and he'd found the solution in a man with no backbone. Logic dictated that Creary had persuaded Allen—somehow intimidated him—into swearing false on the witness stand. Allen had no score of his own to settle, and perjury without purpose made no sense. The purpose was to get Thompson bound over on a charge of murder.

All of which raised a more troubling problem. Thompson had just told his son that there was nothing honorable in killing. Yet he asked himself now if he was too proud to overlook perjury and insult, a veiled threat. Or was it possible to follow his own advice?

He didn't want to kill Ed Creary.

Supper was not the celebration Catherine had planned. Thompson was quiet and thoughtful, almost withdrawn. His mind was elsewhere, and he scarcely joined in the conversation. He picked at his food with no great interest.

Billy tried to revive the spirit of the occasion. He joshed with Bobby and lavished praise on Catherine about her roast hen. Halfway through the meal, he launched into a rollicking story involving a one-eyed riverboat gambler on the Rio Grande. Catherine and Bobby dutifully laughed when the gambler was thrown overboard for dealing marked cards. Thompson merely nodded with a distracted smile.

By the time Catherine served angel food cake, there was little levity at the table. Thompson's mood seemed to have dampened the humor of everyone else, and they hurried through dessert in subdued silence. Bobby kept darting glances at his father, fearful that their earlier conversation had somehow spoiled the party. He finally asked to be excused, on the pretext that he'd just started building a new model ship. Billy, expressing great interest in the project, went along for a look.

Catherine hurried off to the kitchen. She returned in a moment with the coffeepot, and filled Thompson's cup. He spooned sugar into the cup, idly stirring as she took the chair closest to him. She noted his cake was only half eaten, and shook her head. She tried to keep her tone light.

"I never thought I'd see the day your sweet tooth failed you. You've hardly touched your cake."

"Best cake you ever baked," Thompson said mechanically. "I'm just off my feed tonight."

"Is your stomach bothering you?"

"No, my stomach's fine."

"Something else then?"

Thompson shrugged. "Sorry I rained on the parade. I wasn't in much mood to celebrate."

"Yes, I noticed," she said softly. "Do you want to talk about it?"

"You won't like it."

"Why not let me be the judge of that?"

A moment of brittle silence slipped past. Thompson stopped stirring his coffee, finally looked up at her. "Katie, I have to get out of town awhile."

"Why?" she said, openly surprised. "What brought that on?"

"I've decided I don't want to kill Ed Creary. If I stay, I likely will."

"Ben, I know you've never liked Creary. But why would you want to . . . harm him?"

"Creary tried to get me hung," Thompson said, his eyes suddenly cold. "You heard Carl Allen lie through his teeth in court today. That was Creary's work."

"Honey, I'm not following you," she said, startled by the anger in his voice. "What does Creary have to do with anything?"

"Why, that's simple enough. He saw a chance to settle my hash. He got Allen to perjure himself."

"Do you really believe he hates you that much?"

"No doubt about it," Thompson told her. "I've shamed him in public too many times to count. He meant to put me in a coffin."

"Perhaps it was all Carl Allen's doing. You said yourself he was part of Wilson's scheme."

"Allen's just a stooge. He wouldn't lie about me unless somebody held his feet to the fire. Creary's behind it."

"How can you be so sure?"

"I keep hearing a little voice in my ear. Call it a gut hunch or gambler's instinct, or whatever you want. I just know, that's all."

"I see," she said on an indrawn breath. "And you couldn't overlook it . . . this one time?"

"Time's what I need," Thompson said simply. "If I

stay here, I'd feel obliged to force Creary into a fight. I have to get away."

"Do you think that will change anything?"

"Maybe I'll learn to turn the other cheek. Time and distance might do the trick."

"Where will you go?"

"I've been thinking of Dodge City. I hear it's still a good stop for a gambling man."

She saw now that he'd thought it through. His mind was made up and nothing she could say would dissuade him. "How long will you be gone?"

"All depends," Thompson said, not sure himself. "However long it takes to get my mind straight. A month, maybe longer."

"What will happen to the club?"

"Joe Richter will look after things. I trust him, and he's sharp as a tack. I'll talk to him tonight."

She suddenly looked wistful. "When will you leave?"

"The sooner the better." Thompson reached out, took her hand. "I'll catch the morning train to Dallas and go on from there." He squeezed her hand. "You understand, don't you, Katie?"

"Yes, I understand. But I want you home early tonight. We have to say good-bye properly."

"Sounds like you've got something wicked in mind."

"Let's just say you won't get much sleep."

She rose from her chair and kissed him full on the mouth. Then, as though nothing unusual had happened, she began clearing the table. Thompson walked from the dining room to the parlor, and saw the glow of a cigar through the window. He moved into the hallway, opening the door, and stepped out onto the porch. Billy was seated in a rocker.

"You ought to have a word with Bobby," he said, puffing a cloud of smoke. "You weren't exactly the life of the party, and he thinks it was his fault. He needs to hear otherwise."

"I was too hard on him earlier," Thompson admitted. "I'll talk with him and make it right."

"What got you so down in the mouth?"

"You wouldn't understand if I told you. I'm catching the train for Dodge City tomorrow. How'd you like to come along?"

Billy straightened in the rocker. "You're a sackful of surprises. What's in Dodge City?"

"One way to find out," Thompson said. "Unless you're still set on being a riverboat gambler. Want to think it over?"

"Hell, I'm game for anything. But it's all sort of sudden, isn't it? I thought you'd took permanent root in Austin."

"Nothing here that won't keep for a while. I've got an itch to travel."

"How's Katie feel about that?"

"You ask too many questions."

"Well, you know, I am her brother-in-law. I have to look after her welfare."

"Just to set your mind at rest, I've got the home fires covered."

Billy gave him a lopsided grin. "By God, it'll be like old times again. You and me and Dodge City!"

"Wonder if the Comique and the Lady Gay, and all those other joints are still there. Things change in two years."

"I'll give you odds there's nothin' changed. They're probably shootin' up the South Side just like always."

Thompson grunted. "I sincerely hope not."

"Why do you say it like that?"

"I get all the gunplay I want here in Austin."

"Careful, Ben," Billy chided. "You're startin' to sound like you just got religion."

" 'All our yesterdays have lighted fools the way to dusty death.' "

"You quotin' scripture?"

"After a fashion," Thompson said. "It's a line from *Macbeth*."

"Who the hell's Macbeth?"

"I'll tell you about it on the way to Dodge."

ELEVEN

Dodge City billed itself as "Queen of the Cowtowns." The Santa Fe railroad tracks bisected the town east to west, and to the south a wooden bridge spanned the Arkansas River. The business district was spread along a broad plaza north of the tracks.

Thompson and Billy stepped off the train shortly before eleven on the morning of September 24. The Western Trail, which had replaced the old Chisholm Trail for cattle drives, spiraled north from Texas to the bridge over the river. But there was no direct train route from Texas, and the trip required traveling to Kansas City and then doubling back to Dodge City. Their journey had consumed the better part of a week.

Fort Dodge, the nearest army post, was situated five miles east along the Arkansas. Until 1872, with the arrival of the railroad, Dodge City had been a windswept collection of log structures devoted to the buffalo trade. But then, hammered together with bustling industry, it had sprung, virtually overnight, into the rawest boomtown on the Western Plains. A sprawling hodgepodge of buildings, the town was neatly divided by the railroad tracks.

The dusty plaza along Front Street was clearly the center of commerce and trade. Down at one end were the Dodge House Hotel, Zimmerman's Mercantile, and several smaller establishments. Up the other way were shops and the newspaper, bordered by cafes and various business places, including the Long Branch Saloon. Farther north, beyond the plaza, was the residential district of town.

Thompson rented them lodging at the Dodge House. A bellman lugged their bags upstairs, and got them quartered in an airy room overlooking the plaza. They unpacked and took turns at the wash basin, scrubbing off the accumulated grime and soot from their long train trip. Then, anxious to revisit old haunts, Thompson led the way out of the hotel. They walked back toward the railroad depot.

The sporting district, known simply as the South Side, was directly across the tracks. There, during trailing season, saloons, whorehouses and gambling dives pandered to the rowdy nature of cowhands. But at the railroad tracks, dubbed the Deadline, all rowdiness ceased. The lawmen of Dodge City, with a no-nonsense attitude toward troublemakers, rigidly enforced the ordinance. Anyone who attempted to hurrah the respectable part of town was treated to a night in jail.

Thompson thought it a sensible arrangement. The wages of sin on one side of the tracks and the fruits of commerce on the other. The neutral ribbon of steel in between served as a visible, and clearly effective, dividing line. The rule containing the wild-and-woolly cowhands to the sporting district seemed to work uncommonly well for all concerned. On the north side of the Deadline, the townspeople went about their business in relative peace.

The Lady Gay was one of the more popular watering holes. A combination saloon and gaming den, it was located across from the depot, on the corner of Second Avenue. As Thompson and Billy approached the boardwalk, a man dressed in whipcord trousers and a dark wool jacket crossed the street. He was lean and muscular, with a soup-strainer mustache, the bulge of a holstered pistol apparent beneath his jacket. He seemed lost in deep thought.

"I'll be damned!" Thompson said. "There's Jim Masterson."

"Jim!" Billy called out. "Hullo there, Jim. Wait up!"

Masterson turned at the sound of his name. His expression changed from quizzical to one of gladdened recognition. "Ben! Billy!" He rushed forward with his hand outstretched. "What the deuce are you doing in Dodge?"

"Long time, no see," Thompson said, returning his handshake. "We got lonesome for our old stamping grounds. Thought we'd pay a visit."

"You're a sight for sore eyes," Billy added. "We wondered who'd be here from the old crowd."

"Well, you got more than you bargained for," Masterson said. "Bat's comin' in on the noon eastbound. All the way from Tombstone."

"I was there!" Billy crowed. "Not more'n two months ago. He was dealin' faro for Wyatt Earp."

"Guess it's our lucky day," Thompson said jovially. "What brings Bat back to Dodge?"

Masterson frowned. "Boys, it's a long story and nothin' sweet about it. Let me buy you a drink."

They followed him into the Lady Gay. Though it was not yet noon, Thompson felt he couldn't refuse the offer of a whiskey. Over drinks, Masterson briefly explained why he'd summoned his brother from Arizona. After serving a term as town marshal, he and a man named Alonso Peacock had gone partners and bought the Lady Gay. Peacock, acting on his own, had hired a bartender named Updegraff, who was noted throughout the South Side for rough treatment of customers. Masterson promptly fired him.

The next day Peacock and Updegraff stormed into the saloon. An argument ensued, and within moments, all three men pulled their guns. As happened in so many cases, nerves undercut accuracy, and none of the shots took effect. But Masterson drove them into the street, and they beat a hasty retreat across the railroad tracks. For nearly two weeks, Peacock had avoided the Lady Gay, even though he was a full partner. Still, he and Updegraff were bent on revenge, and word of their threats had spread through town. Masterson had wired Bat in Tombstone.

"I see them around," he concluded. "But so far, they've kept their distance, and I send Peacock's cut of the receipts over to his house. I think they're waiting to catch me on a dark night."

"Sorry bastards!" Billy huffed. "So what happens when Bat gets here? You aim to force a fight?"

"Don't see any way around it," Masterson said. "Looks to me like it's fight or get bushwhacked. I told Bat as much in the telegraph I sent him."

"Count on me and Ben, too," Billy volunteered. "You've got our marker for that Nebraska business. Don't they, Ben?"

"Damn right," Thompson agreed. "Friends stick together."

A year ago, the summer of 1880, Billy was in Ogallala, Nebraska. He killed a man in a gunfight, and was himself seriously wounded. After a doctor treated him, he was confined to his bed in the local hotel, attended by a male nurse. The killing was ruled justifiable, but the dead man's friends were of another mind. Scornful of the law, they planned a lynching party in Billy's honor, once he was able to walk. They wanted him fit for his own hanging.

Billy, through his male nurse, managed to wire Thompson. Speed was essential, and Thompson wired Bat Masterson, who was living in Denver at the time. Without hesitation, Bat hopped a train to Ogallala, and arrived in the dead of night. He enlisted the aid of the male nurse and spirited Billy out of town aboard the midnight train. Had they been caught, his own life was at risk, but he refused all thanks. He told Billy it was the least a friend could do.

Today, reflecting on it, Thompson was struck by the irony of the situation. He'd left Austin to avoid more killing, and now, his first day in Dodge City, he was involved in yet another dispute. Still, putting irony aside, he thought it only fitting that he and Billy volunteer their services. Bat Masterson had done as much in Ogallala, and there was no greater debt than one owed a friend. Then, too, there was the matter of personal esteem, and respect. He admired the Masterson brothers.

For nearly a decade, in various Kansas cowtowns, he'd developed a lasting friendship with the Mastersons. Bat, a former buffalo hunter, had been elected sheriff of Ford County and earned a reputation as a tough lawman. Ed, the oldest brother, had served as marshal of Dodge City, only to be killed three years ago in a gunfight with Texas cowhands. A year later, Jim was appointed city marshal, and served with distinction until he quit to pursue business interests. Law and order in Dodge City was, to no small degree, the handiwork of the Mastersons.

"Who's sheriff now?" Thompson asked at length. "Anyone we have to worry about?"

"His name is Fred Singer," Masterson said derisively. "Fred's always a day late and a dollar short when it comes to law enforcement. His game is politics."

"Jim, it's no different in Austin. We've got a city marshal who's a disgrace to the badge."

"I often wonder—"

A train whistle cut him off. Masterson walked to a window on the north side of the saloon. The noon eastbound rocked to a halt before the depot, and a man stepped down from the lead passenger coach. Masterson laughed out loud.

"There's Bat!" he said. "Just got off the train."

Thompson and Billy joined him at the window. Masterson suddenly stiffened, pointing at two men crossing from the South Side to the business district. His features were taut with anger.

"That's Peacock and Updegraff," he muttered furiously. "What the hell are they doing there?"

Thompson peered closer. "Did they know Bat was on the train?"

"I don't see how. But Bat damn sure knows them. C'mon, we'd better get out—"

His voice trailed off. Through the window, they saw Bat turn toward the South Side and stop abruptly as he spotted Peacock and Updegraff. He shouted something at them, and in the next moment, all three men went for their guns. Bystanders scattered in every direction as shots rang out across the street. Bat dove headlong behind the rail embankment, and Peacock and Updegraff took cover behind a building just south of the tracks. They traded shots in a flurry of gunfire.

Masterson hurled a chair through the window. He drew his pistol, standing shoulder to shoulder with Thompson and Billy in the open maw of the window-frame. From the Lady Gay, they had an oblique field of fire on the building south of the railroad tracks. Peacock and Updegraff ducked as slugs thunked into the frame of the building around their heads. Caught in a cross-fire, Peacock continued to exchange shots with Bat. Updegraff turned to engage the assault from the Lady Gay.

The men in the window fired in unison. None of them would ever know whose shot took effect, but at least one slug found the mark. Updegraff dropped his gun, clutching at his chest, and slammed backward into the building. As he slumped to the ground, Peacock's nerves deserted him, and he sprinted west across Second Avenue. Bat, still firing from the rail embankment, emptied his pistol in a rattling volley. Peacock disappeared into an alley halfway down the block.

Masterson hurried toward the door. Thompson and Billy followed along, and as they emerged from the Lady Gay, they saw him grab Bat in a back-pounding bear hug. Bat looked at them with a dumbfounded expression.

"Jesus Christ!" he said blankly. "Wherc'd you two come from?"

"Texas," Thompson replied, shaking his hand. "We got here just in time for the fireworks."

"Well, you boys damn sure saved my bacon. I was pinned down with nowhere to go."

Billy pumped his arm. "What was it you yelled at them?"

"Hell, my mouth got ahead of my brain. Told 'em I knew they were heeled and let's get the fight on. Guess they took me serious."

A crowd began gathering on the boardwalks. Bat's suit was covered in dust from the rail bed, and a dent marred the crown of his derby hat. He was chunkier than his brother, solidly built, with pale eyes and a brushy mustache. He glanced around as a man with a star on his jacket approached them.

"Ford County's gone to hell," he said, eyeing the badge. "How'd you ever get elected, Fred?"

Sheriff Singer bobbed his head. "Bat, I'll swear, you're a regular lightnin' rod. I'm gonna have to arrest somebody for shootin' Updegraff."

"You're not arresting anybody, Fred. The son-of-a-bitch pulled a gun on me the minute I stepped off that train. Tell the coroner to rule it suicide."

"I got witnesses that'll say otherwise."

"Here's what I say," Bat informed him in an icy voice. "Before dark, Al Peacock will sell out to my brother. I guarantee it." He thumped the badge with his forefinger. "You cause Jim any trouble and you'll answer to me. Got it straight?"

Singer swallowed hard. "No need to threaten people thataway, Bat. You was a lawman yourself."

"I had to come a thousand miles to do your job for you. Peacock and Updegraff should've been arrested a couple of weeks ago, when they pulled guns on Jim. Why weren't they?"

"There wasn't any call to arrest them. Nobody was hurt."

"You're full of it," Bat said, pushing past him. "Just remember what I told you about Updegraff. He committed suicide."

Thompson and the others followed Bat into the Lady Gay. The bartender brought glasses and poured drinks all around. Bat hoisted his glass in a toast and tossed off the whiskey. His mustache lifted in a tight grin.

"Dodge City's gone to hell in a handbasket. Not like the old days."

"You haven't changed," Thompson said with a chuckle. "You're still up for a scrap."

"Look who's talking," Bat joked. "You and Billy jumped right in when the guns went off. Guess we're birds of a feather."

Jim Masterson laughed. "Damn good thing, too. We owe you boys one."

"Hell you do!" Billy said. "Bat pulled my fat out of the fire in Ogallala. We just returned the favor."

"Well, anyway," Bat observed. "We gave the good folks of Dodge something to talk about. The newspapers will have a field day."

"So what's next?" Thompson asked. "You heading back to Tombstone?"

"Ben, I think I've had my fill of dealin' faro. I believe I'll test the waters in Denver."

"Denver's nice this time of year. Never cared for it when the snow flies."

"Why don't you and Billy join me?"

"Not a bad idea," Thompson remarked. "After today,

we've likely worn out our welcome in Dodge. How's it sound to you, Billy?"

"Lead the way," Billy said agreeably. "Here today, gone tomorrow, that's my motto."

Thompson smiled. "Looks like we're along for the ride, Bat. When do we leave?"

"Why, hell, anytime suits me. But I just suspect Billy's got the fix on things—gone tomorrow."

They drank a toast to Denver.

TWELVE

Dusk was settling over the land. Off to the west, the snowy spires of the Rockies rose majestically against a backdrop of fading light. The mountains towered skyward like an unbroken column of sentinels.

Denver was a center of finance and commerce. Originally a mining camp, the raw boomtown reproduced itself a hundredfold, until finally a glittering metropolis stood along the banks of Cherry Creek and the South Platte. By 1881, it was a cosmopolitan beehive, with a stock exchange, three railroads, and a population of thirty thousand. The city was unrivaled by anything on the Western plains.

Bat Masterson stepped out of the Brown Palace Hotel. He was accompanied by Thompson and Billy, dressed for an evening on the town. They had arrived early that afternoon, and there was a brisk scent of oncoming winter in the air. Thompson marked the date as October 1, a Saturday, and thought it might be a short stay. He had visited Denver on several occasions, once during the middle of a blizzard. He wasn't anxious to repeat the experience.

From the hotel, they turned downtown. Billy was a newcomer to Denver, and Masterson appointed himself as tour guide. For reasons lost to time, he explained, the sporting district was known as the Tenderloin. There, within a few square blocks of Blake Street, every vice known to man was available for a price. Saloons and gaming dives catered to the sporting crowd, and variety theaters featured headline acts from the vaudeville circuit. The nightlife attracted high rollers from all across the West.

One block over, on Holladay Street, was Denver's infamous red-light district. Billy, who hadn't had his ashes hauled in a while, was a rapt listener. Masterson observed that it was known locally as the Row. A lusty fleshpot of dollar cribs, girls posed in the windows, soliciting customers, available by the trick or by the hour. Hook shops dominated the Row, and newspapers wryly referred to the girls as "Brides of the Multitude." Yet there was no scarcity of high-class whores.

The parlor houses offered younger girls and a greater variety, all at steeper prices. Masterson, not unlike a civic booster of the risqué, noted that something over a thousand soiled doves plied their trade on Holladay Street. The expensive bordellos were the domain of the more exotic tarts, and Thompson was reminded of Guy Town in Austin. The ladies of the evening, though barred under the municipal code, were nonetheless a steady source of revenue. Their license fees were a large part of the city's budget.

Masterson next took them on a brief tour of Hop

Alley. A narrow passageway running between Larimer and Holladay, it was Denver's version of Lotus Land. Chinese fan-tan parlors vied with the faint, sweet odor of opium dens, and those addicted to the Orient's heady delights beat a path to a backstreet world of pipe dreams. There was no taste too bizarre, and to a select clientele, China dolls were available day or night. Hop Alley managed to blend the exotic with the erotic.

Their tour ended at the Progressive Club. Masterson noted that the gaming den was owned by Ed Chase, and frequented by the top professionals. Chase was considered the czar of the Tenderloin, as well as Denver's underworld element. He enforced his authority through a gang of hooligans who collected weekly payoffs from every dive in the sporting district. Vice was an organized business.

The rackets, Masterson commented, operated under the protection of Denver's political machine. On the first of every month one of Chase's thugs, carrying a black bag, made the rounds at city hall. From the mayor on down, every elected official in Denver shared in the spoils. The payoffs were the grease of politics, a partnership of sorts with the sporting crowd. The Tenderloin operated without interference of any sort.

For all that, Masterson was quick to extol the virtues of Ed Chase. The Progressive Club, he remarked, was known for honest cards and a square deal. Thompson thought the comment revealed more about Masterson than it did Denver's vice czar. Despite his reputation as a lawman, Masterson apparently had no qualms about associating with a rackets boss. A square deal was now more important than the law. The badge was history.

Thompson was impressed by the gaming club. A large diamond-dust mirror was centered behind a mahogany bar that dominated the front of the room. Opposite the bar were dice and roulette tables, faro layouts, and other games of chance. The walls were adorned with paintings of brazen women, and crystal chandeliers, blazing with light, were suspended overhead. A section at the rear was reserved for a grouping of six poker tables.

Masterson was clearly something of a celebrity. The bartenders greeted him by name, and several of the dealers waved from their tables. Ed Chase hurried forward from the rear of the bar, his features warmed by a smile. He was slim and angular, with iron-gray hair, impeccably attired in a charcoal gray suit and an elegant silk cravat. He extended his hand.

"Always a pleasure, Bat," he said cordially. "The last I heard, you were in Tombstone."

Masterson shook his hand. "A mining camp's no place for a civilized man. I decided Denver's the place for me."

"Well, whatever the reason, it's good to have you back."

"Ed, I'd like you to meet a couple of old friends. Ben Thompson and his brother, Billy."

"Gentlemen," Chase said, exchanging handshakes. "Welcome to Denver."

"They're from Texas," Masterson went on. "You and Ben have something in common. He owns a club in Austin."

Case nodded amiably. "I'm familiar with your name, Mr. Thompson. As is anyone who reads the *Police Gazette*."

"Don't believe everything you read," Thompson said with a casual gesture. "I'd rather be known as a club owner."

"You're too modest, sir. Why, just last week, I read how you single-handedly took on two men. I admire grit."

Billy laughed. "Ben's got grit, awright. A bushel full!"

"And you, Mr. Thompson?" Chase said, glancing at Billy. "Are you a club owner as well?"

"Not for all the tea in China. I'm just another gamblin' man."

"That's why we came by," Masterson interjected. "Figured some high rollers might drift in later. We're interested in a game."

"Bat, there's always a game at the Progressive Club."

"Then you won't mind holding three chairs. We'll be back about nine or so."

"Why not stick around?" Chase said. "We could probably find you a game before nine."

Masterson grinned. "I've got a special treat in store for the boys. Thought I'd take them to see Lola Montana."

"No better way to start the night," Chase said agreeably. "Just between us, I prefer Lola Montana to poker myself."

"I'm damn glad to hear it," Billy said, with a broad smile. "Way Bat talks, she's hotter'n a three-dollar pistol. I was startin' to wonder."

"Take my word for it, she's the toast of Denver. You won't be disappointed."

Thompson watched the byplay with interest. He was struck by Chase's urbane manner, and thought it unusual for a man who ruled Denver's vice district with an iron fist. But even more, he suspected Ed Chase was prone to shade the truth.

Lola Montana couldn't be better than a game of poker. No one was that good.

Some while later Masterson led them through the doors of the Alcazar Variety Theater. The owner greeted Masterson with an effusive handshake, and personally escorted them to a table down front. A waiter materialized when he snapped his fingers, and he ordered a bottle of champagne. The bubbly, he told them, was on the house.

"Enjoy the show, Mr. Masterson," he said, rusɪ off. "Nice to have you back in Denver."

A man seated alone at a nearby table turned in hi: chair. "Masterson?" he called out in a loud voice. "Would that be *the* Bat Masterson?"

Masterson looked around. "Luke!" He grinned, moving forward with an outstretched hand. "I should've known you'd be here."

"I never miss a show. Why don't you and your friends join me?"

Thompson judged the man to be in his early thirties. He was tall, lithely built, with smoky blue eyes and light chestnut hair. A pistol in a crossdraw holster rode at belt level beneath his suit coat. Masterson quickly performed the introductions.

"Ben Thompson. Billy Thompson." He motioned them over to the table. "I'd like you to meet another old friend. This is Luke Starbuck."

"A pleasure," Thompson said, exchanging a handshake. "Your name is well known in Texas."

Starbuck smiled. "Yours is well known everywhere. I'm afraid we're grist for the mill with the *Police Gazette*."

"Well, you can't blame 'em," Billy said with a laugh. "You and Ben sell a lot of newspapers."

"Not by choice," Thompson remarked. "I wish they'd forget how to spell my name."

Starbuck nodded. "Amen to that."

Three private detectives in the West were widely recognized by the public. Charlie Siringo worked for the Pinkertons, and Harry Morse was headquartered in San Francisco. But Luke Starbuck, operating out of Denver, was regarded as the foremost manhunter of the day. He was reputed to have killed a dozen men.

The *Police Gazette* considered Starbuck front-page news. Among others, he'd been involved in the downfall of such noted badmen as Dutch Henry Horn and Billy the Kid. His fame as an investigator had spread throughout the country, and the attendant publicity had destroyed his anonymity forever. These days he operated undercover.

The house lights dimmed. A hush fell over the crowd as the curtains parted onstage. Lola Montana stood bathed in the cider glow of a spotlight. Her exquisite features were tilted in a woeful expression, and her clear alto voice filled the theater. She sang a heartrending ballad of unrequited love, her eyes misty.

The performance was flawless. Lola's voice was at once sultry and virginal, and she held the audience captivated to the last note. A moment slipped past, then the theater vibrated to wild cheers and thunderous applause. She took a bow, then another and another, and still the house rocked with ovation. She signaled the maestro.

The orchestra segued into a rousing dance number. A line of chorus girls exploded out of the wings and went highstepping across the stage. Lola raised her skirts, revealing a shapely leg, and joined them in a prancing cakewalk. The girls squealed and Lola flashed her underdrawers and the tempo of the music quickened. The audience went mad.

Thompson found his toe tapping in time to the music. There was a wanton exuberance to the routine, with Lola and the girls cavorting around the stage. Then the orchestra thumped into the finale with a blare of trumpets and a clash of cymbals. The chorus line, in a swirl of upraised skirts and jiggling breasts, went romping into the wings. The spotlight centered on the star of the show.

Lola Montana waved to the crowd. Then, bending over the footlights, she blew a kiss to Starbuck. She winked a bawdy wink, wig-wagging her behind, and strutted offstage. The audience roared with delight.

Starbuck looked embarrassed. When the curtain rang down, Masterson was still laughing. "I forgot to tell you boys," he said, glancing around the table. "Lola's the toast of the town, but she's Luke's woman. Doesn't say much for her taste in men."

"Look who's talking," Starbuck joshed him. "You'd give your eye-teeth to be in my place."

"Hell, I'd give my right arm!"

Billy poured a round of champagne. They toasted Lola Montana and congratulated Starbuck. Thompson nodded over the rim of his glass.

"You're a fortunate man," he said. "She's quite a lady. A real beauty."

Starbuck chuckled. "All I have to do is keep from getting shot. Lola doesn't much care for my line of work."

"How'd you get into the detective business?"

"I started out as a stock detective. One thing led to

another, and I quit chasing rustled cows. Got to where I just chase men."

"Well, you're good at it," Thompson said. "You must find it worthwhile."

"Yeah, I do," Starbuck admitted. "Not that it's the same as wearing a badge, you understand. But I reckon it takes all kinds."

"Don't let him kid you," Masterson interrupted. "Luke takes on the cases that most lawmen wouldn't touch. He just doesn't like to toot his own horn."

"You make too much of it, Bat."

"What about those payroll robbers? The ones you tracked to Hole-in-the-Wall? How many lawmen tagged along?"

Thompson was familiar with the case. Hole-in-the-Wall was an outlaw sanctuary in the wilds of Wyoming. Starbuck had gone in alone and come out alive, which said it all. No peace officer had ever ventured into the hideout.

"I got lucky," Starbuck said, uncomfortable with the conversation. "Lots of men could have pulled that off."

"Name one," Masterson countered. "I don't know anybody who would even try it. Go ahead, tell me I'm wrong."

Starbuck was saved by Lola Montana. She appeared from backstage, dressed in a low-cut gown, and walked to the table. The men jumped to their feet, offering her a chair, and poured her a glass of champagne. She immediately became the center of conversation.

Thompson thought she was even prettier in person. Her face was a perfect oval, her features expressive and animated, and her laughter was infectious. Yet her vivacity was largely lost on him, and he sat like an eavesdropper gone deaf. He was thinking of Hole-in-the-Wall.

Or more to the point, he was thinking about how men conduct their lives. He had met Luke Starbuck scarcely an hour ago; but the impression he got was distinct. Here was a man who challenged life, routinely went where others dared not go. A man not content with the ordinary.

The line from *Macbeth* popped into his mind. The line that had troubled him for over a month now, and wouldn't go away. A *tale told by an idiot, full of sound and fury, signifying nothing.* Or perhaps it was simply too little. Less than he was willing to accept.

Thompson told himself that his life was far from ordinary. Yet compared to the manhunter seated across the table, his existence bordered on the humdrum. Perhaps that was what had eluded him over the past month, the sense of challenge. The certainty . . .

The thought suddenly crystallized into words. The certainty that there was more to life than a fast gun and a deck of cards. A reason to believe that a tale signifying nothing was just a line in a stage play. Not a prophecy.

Nor was it an epitaph.

The answer was there all the time, and he wondered how he'd missed it. Distance sometimes cleared a man's perspective, opened his eyes. He saw it now.

He had to get back to Austin.

THIRTEEN

—◆◆◆—

The engineer set the brakes with a racketing squeal. A moment later, belching clouds of steam, the train ground to a halt before the stationhouse. High in a cloudless sky, a warm noonday sun stood at its zenith. Passengers began debarking the train.

Thompson gathered his valise from the overhead luggage rack. Followed by Billy, he moved to the end of the coach and went down the steps onto the platform. Autumn was slowly settling across the land, and the trees along the river were tinged with color. He was reminded that he'd been away not quite a month. The date was October 11.

Before departing Colorado, he had wired Catherine their schedule. The train route had taken them through Raton Pass and into New Mexico, with connections eastward for Texas. All the way from Denver, Billy had badgered him for the reason behind their sudden departure. But he'd put Billy off with excuses, artfully skirting the truth. He first wanted to discuss it with Catherine.

There were carriages for hire outside the depot. On the way uptown, Thompson was more aware of the city than ever before, as though seeing it from a new perspective. By now Billy was disgruntled with asking questions, and sat wrapped in silence. The ride took them past the state capitol, and Thompson again warned himself that politics was a dirty game. He thought he would need help.

Upon arriving home, Catherine met them at the door. Her eyes were bright with excitement, and she kissed Thompson soundly on the mouth. Billy accepted a peck on the cheek, and she closed the door as they dropped their bags in the hallway. She looked them over with a happy smile.

"I'm so glad you're back," she said gaily. "You'd better prepare yourselves when Bobby gets home from school. He's wild to hear about your adventures."

"Don't know as I'd call it that," Billy said grumpily. "Your husband's not a man to light long in one spot. We spent most of our time on trains."

Thompson waved him off. "Billy took a shine to Denver. He wanted to stay longer."

"Longer!" Billy croaked. "We was only there one night."

"One night?" Catherine repeated with surprise. "Why did you leave so quickly?"

Billy cocked an eyebrow. "You'll have to ask your husband that. He's kept it a big, dark secret."

"Goodness, that sounds mysterious."

"Ben's a mystery, all right. Maybe you can get him to talk."

Catherine laughed. "I've never had any problem before."

"Lemme know when you hear the lowdown. Think I'll get myself cleaned up and presentable. What I'm wearin' could stand up all by itself."

Billy hefted his bag, walking to the stairs. Thompson hooked his hat on a coatrack, took Catherine's arm, and steered her into the parlor. He waited until he heard Billy moving around upstairs, then lowered himself into a chair. Catherine gave him a curious look.

"What is it?" she said. "I've never known you to keep secrets from Billy."

Thompson motioned her to the sofa. "Billy can wait. I wanted to talk to you about it first."

"I'm on needles and pins. What's so important?"

"Katie, I've decided to run for city marshal. I figured you ought to hear it before anyone else."

Catherine sat perfectly still. Her mouth ovaled in a tiny gasp, and her eyes were round with shock. "Are you serious?" she finally managed. "I thought you detested politics."

"I do," Thompson affirmed. "It's the dirtiest game around."

"Then why would you get involved? What on earth gave you the idea?"

"Well, it's hard to explain. I've been troubled by things for a couple of months now. Not satisfied with the way things are."

"What things?" she asked. "Are you talking about Ed Creary and the police force?"

"No, I'm talking about me," Thompson said. "I'm trying to tell you I'm not satisfied with myself. I want my life to count for something."

"I don't understand, sweetheart. You have a family

and a successful business. You're respected by the people who matter. Doesn't all that count?"

"'Course it does. But when you boil it all down, I'm still just a gambler. I want to be known for more than that."

She looked dazed. "How does being a peace officer accomplish anything?"

"Folks remember the good ones," Thompson said with conviction. "Not that I'll ever be a Lee Hall, or any of the other Ranger captains. But I'll make a good city marshal."

"You want to be remembered, is that it?"

"Katie, I'm not looking to have people build statues of me. I just want my life to count."

Catherine suddenly saw it. He wasn't talking about what others thought of him. Nor was he concerned with immortality, statues erected in his honor. He was talking about what he thought of himself.

A moment passed while she came to grips with the idea. All in a rush, she realized that he considered his accomplishments inadequate, shy of some personal benchmark. He wanted to do something singular with his life.

"You know something?" she said, reaching out to touch his hand. "I think you'll make the best marshal Austin ever had."

Thompson squeezed her hand. "With you backing me, how can I miss? I'll give this town some real law and order."

"You haven't much time, and Ed Creary is a smooth politician. The elections are less than a month off."

"You're right on both counts. I've got to get busy."

The city charter mandated a general election every year. The race for mayor, as well as for aldermen and the marshal's post, would be decided on the first Monday in November. Thompson had three weeks to win an election.

Something he hadn't told Catherine was in the back of his mind as well. On the way home from Colorado, he'd decided that Creary's attempt to get him hanged deserved a special form of retribution. Instead of killing Creary, he would humiliate him in public, by defeating him in the political arena. The sweetest revenge was in disgrace, not death.

"Where will you start?" Catherine said. "There's so much to do."

"The mayor hates Creary worse than the Devil hates holy water. That's the place to start."

"Do you think he'll drop Creary from the ticket?"

Thompson grinned. "I'm damn sure gonna find out."

She thought he'd never looked more confident of anything.

"Jesus H. Christmas!"

"I figured that's how you'd feel."

"You want to be a *lawdog?* You're off your rocker."

"There's worse things."

"Name me one!"

Billy paced to the edge of the porch. Thompson had brought him outside to break the news. He knew it would cause fireworks, and he meant to have it resolved before Bobby came home from school. Catherine, wisely, had retreated to the kitchen.

"Listen to yourself," Thompson said. "Bat Masterson was a lawman, and you never had a better friend. Am I right or not?"

"That was Kansas," Billy sulked. "This is home ground, Ben. Texas!"

"So what?"

"So it's a whole different ball of wax. Lawmen in Texas get their heads twisted on crooked. They think a badge makes them God."

"Well hell, Billy, it's not contagious. Don't you think I can keep my head on straight?"

"You lay down with dogs, you get up with fleas. That's the moral of that story."

Thompson understood his brother's bitterness. Billy was thirty-six years old, and he'd been running from the law half of his life. The Rangers had chased him from the Rio Grande to the Red, and treated him none too gently whenever he was caught. He had never been convicted of a crime, but that was the result of Thompson's bankroll and the clever attorneys hired in his defense. He held all Texas lawmen in contempt.

"Hear me out," Thompson said. "A badge won't change me one iota, even if I wore it the rest of my life. You ought to know me better than that."

"Kee-rist," Billy moaned. "Don't you see, it's just the thought of it. A lawdog in the family."

"You'd better get used to the idea. I'm going to run and I intend to win."

"You made up your mind before we left Denver, didn't you? Why'd you wait till now to tell me?"

"We both know you've never kept a secret in your life. You would've spilled the beans the minute we walked in the house. I figured Katie deserved to hear it first—from me."

"What'd she say about you wearin' a badge?"

"She's behind me a hundred percent. Which is a damn-sight more than I can say for you."

Billy stalked to the end of the porch. He stared out at College Hill, absently watching students cross the campus. A prolonged moment slipped past, and finally he turned back to Thompson. He lifted his shoulders in an elaborate shrug.

"What the hell," he said with a dismal smile. "Katie's got more sense than both of us put together. I'll tag along."

"Glad you came around," Thompson said, relieved. "Family has to stick together, especially brothers. I'll be needing your help."

"What kind of help?"

"A city marshal can't operate a gaming parlor. The voters would consider it a conflict of interest."

"Yeah?" Billy said, his expression guarded. "And . . . ?"

"I want you to run the Iron Front," Thompson said with a grand gesture. "We'll go partners, just like I always talked about. Split it down the middle."

"Nice try, but no sale. I never was one to be tied down, and nothing's changed. You'll have to find somebody else."

"I'd rather keep it in the family. Besides, it's high time you settled down. You're not getting any younger."

Billy grinned. "You might as well save your breath. I'm headed back to the Rio Grande and the riverboats. I like it on the border."

"Billy, you disappoint me."

"Just think of me as the black sheep in the family. You always said I was shiftless and no-account."

"I'll be damned if I ever said any such thing!"

"You won't hurt my feelings . . . it's true."

"Pa!"

The shout brought them around. They saw Bobby racing across the street, a load of school books under his arm. He scampered up the steps, dropping the books, and threw himself at his father. His eyes were like saucers.

"You're back!" he yelled. "I missed you somethin' awful, Pa."

"Well, I'm home now, son."

"For keeps?"

Thompson smiled. "For keeps."

Late that evening Thompson stepped off the streetcar. He waved to Billy, who was on the scout for *filles de joie,* and headed for a parlor house in Guy Town. The streetcar trundled off down the tracks.

Thompson crossed the intersection at Congress Avenue. He was reconciled to the fact that Billy had rebuffed his offer with casual indifference. His brother preferred the gypsy life, and he'd never held out any great faith that a partnership was in the cards. He proceeded along Mulberry Street.

The alternative, he told himself, was probably the best bet anyway. He'd worked out a contingency plan on the train from Denver, all too aware that Billy was a wayward spirit. He had been truthful when he'd said he would rather keep it in the family. But on the other hand, business was business.

The Iron Front was crowded for a Monday night. After nearly a month's absence, Thompson was greeted with more than customary good cheer. The dealers and bartenders gave him the high sign, and the club's patrons eagerly ganged around to shake his hand, He was flattered by all the attention.

Joe Richter hurried forward. "Good to see you, boss," he said with genuine warmth. "When'd you get back?"

"Just this afternoon," Thompson replied, accepting his handshake. "How'd things go while I was away?"

"I don't like to brag—"

"Go ahead, brag."

"—But you'll like what you see when you check the books. We're up six percent over normal."

"Joe, that's damn good work," Thompson said, openly pleased. "You do better when I'm gone."

"No way, boss." Richter tried for a modest tone. "We just hit a streak, that's all."

"Let's go back to the office. You won't be missed for a minute. I've got some news for you."

"Why sure, whatever you say."

In the office, Thompson took a seat behind the desk. He waved Richter to the only other chair in the room, and proceeded to outline his plans. Richter suddenly got attentive when he spoke of declaring his candidacy for city marshal. He finished with a reference to the conflict of interest issue.

"So it's a problem," he said. "Nobody would stand for the marshal operating a gaming parlor. I'd get roasted by the newspapers."

"Boss, I'm damn near speechless," Richter said in a serious voice. "You're not thinking of selling the Iron Front, are you? I'd hate to find myself out of a job."

"I was thinking the other way 'round, Joe. How'd you like to be a partner?"

"Are you joking?"

"I never joke about money."

"Well, I like that idea a whole lot. What d'you have in mind?"

"Here's the deal," Thompson told him. "You run the Iron Front and I'll run the town. Your partnership gets you ten percent of the net."

Richter held his gaze. "Fifteen percent sounds more like it."

"Don't get greedy, Joe."

"I'm worth it."

"Tell you what I'll do," Thompson said, poker-faced, "Twelve percent and that's my last word on it. Deal?"

"Done," Richter said with a pearly grin. "You won't regret it, boss."

They shook hands on it. Thompson started toward the door, then stopped. "One last thing."

"What's that?"

"Don't call me 'boss' anymore. That handshake just made us partners. From now on, it's Ben."

"Whatever you say—Ben."

Thompson led the way through the door. A poker game was in progress at the rear of the club, and he briefly considered taking a chair. Then, just as quickly, he discarded the notion. He needed a good night's sleep.

Tomorrow he planned to start the bandwagon rolling.

FOURTEEN

Early the next morning Thompson walked into City Hall. He was attired in a dark suit, with a sedate cravat, the stovepipe hat fixed squarely on his head. He looked the very picture of an affluent businessman.

Sueann Mabry, the mayor's secretary, looked up from her desk. A spinster, she had plain dumpling features and her hair was pulled severely behind her head in a tight chignon. She greeted him with prune-faced civility.

"May I help you, Mr. Thompson?"

"Good morning, Sueann," Thompson said, doffing his hat. "I'm here to see the mayor."

"Oh?" Her voice was tinged with mild reproach. "Do you have an appointment?"

The anteroom was empty. Thompson had purposely arrived early, before the day's schedule became too hectic. He smiled, shook his head. "Ask the mayor if he can spare a moment. Tell him I'm the bearer of good tidings."

Sueann Mabry gave a rabbity sniff. She disapproved of anyone involved with the sporting crowd, even an uptown club owner. Yet she knew the mayor often played poker with Thompson, and counted him a friend. She rose from behind her desk.

"Please wait here."

She moved to the door of an inner office. She knocked lightly, then stepped inside and closed the door. A moment later she reappeared, her features neutral. She nodded crisply. "Mayor Wheeler will see you."

"Thank you, Sueann," Thompson said pleasantly. "By the way, I was admiring your dress. You ought to wear that color more often. Very nice."

She blushed, batting her eyes. She stepped aside, waiting until he entered the office, and closed the door. Tom Wheeler stood behind his desk, wagging his head with amusement. He motioned Thompson to a chair.

"You should be ashamed of yourself. Sueann will think you're flirting with her."

"No harm in paying a lady a compliment. I doubt she ever gets one from you."

"Touché," Wheeler said, chuckling. "I hadn't heard you'd returned to town. Have a good trip?"

Thompson lit a cheroot. "I spent some time in Dodge City and Denver. Enjoyed it, but I'm glad to get home."

"Well, I'm glad to see you back. Our weekly poker games aren't the same without you."

"I missed them myself. But I didn't drop by to talk poker. I'm here on another matter."

"Oh?" Wheeler said curiously. "Something official?"

"Yeah, after a fashion," Thompson acknowledged. "I plan to run for city marshal in the November elections. I'm here to ask for your support."

Wheeler's mouth dropped open. "Marshal?" he stammered. "You're pulling my leg."

"Never more serious in my life. How's the idea strike you?"

"Why would you run for marshal? I never heard you express any great love for lawmen."

"Tom, I have to level with you. I've decided I want to do more with my life than shuffle cards. I think I'll make a damn good peace officer."

"I've no doubt you would."

Thompson puffed on his cheroot. "You've said yourself you'd like to dump Creary. Here's your chance."

"Ed Creary's no problem," Wheeler observed. "So far the party hasn't endorsed anyone. We're letting him sweat it out."

The politics of Austin was ruled principally by Democrats. The Republican Party, for more than a decade, had been shunned by Texas voters. During the Reconstruction Era, following the Civil War, the scalawags and carpetbaggers had left a bitter legacy. These days, though the Republicans fielded a slate of candidates, it was virtually a lost cause. Few of them ever got elected to office.

"You *are* the party," Thompson remarked. "When you say frog, everybody squats. So if Creary's not the problem, what is?"

Wheeler looked uncomfortable. "You have a certain reputation, Ben."

"That's true, and I plan to turn it to my advantage in the election. Who better to police the town than a man

who won't take guff off anybody? I'll give troublemakers a real dose of law and order."

"Yes, I'm confident you would. But that doesn't
offset the other problem."

"What other problem?"

"In politics, perception is everything. You are
perceived—rightly or wrongly—as one of the sporting
crowd."

Thompson grinned around the cheroot. He took it
from his mouth and exhaled a perfect smoke ring. "As
of last night," he said, "I became the silent partner in
the Iron Front. No one will be able to accuse me of conflict of interest."

"What does that mean," Wheeler asked—"silent
partner?"

"I'm not a gambler anymore. I won't be playing poker
at the Iron Front, or anywhere else. Joe Richter will run
the club from now on."

"You've given up poker . . . for good?"

"Tom, I've cut the cord with the sporting crowd.
You're looking at a new man."

"I'm frankly amazed," Wheeler said, stunned. "I find
it hard to believe."

"Believe it," Thompson said earnestly. "I'm a re-
formed gamblin' man."

"You must want the job of marshal pretty bad."

"Once I make up my mind, that's it. I mean to win
this election."

Wheeler nodded soberly. "The question is, will it be
good for the ticket? There's a lot at stake."

"You're talking about getting yourself reelected."

"I am indeed! Nothing is a given in this town."

The city founders believed that long terms of office

fostered corruption and unscrupulous political alliances. To avoid shady dealings, they drafted a municipal charter that mandated a one-year term for the mayor, the aldermen, and the city marshal. The result was a frequent change in the roster of those who governed the city, and a constant shifting of loyalties. There were no political dynasties in Austin.

There were ten wards, with an alderman elected from each ward. The city council was composed of the mayor and the aldermen, with the mayor positioned to break a tie vote. The list of aldermen might include contractors, grocers, lawyers, real estate agents, liverymen, and usually one saloonkeeper from Guy Town, the Third Ward. The diversity tended to keep everyone halfway honest, and made for contentious bedfellows. Wheeler, who governed the factions through diplomacy, was seeking a third term.

"Look at it this way," Thompson said. "Everyone in town knows Creary is taking payoffs from the dives. I'll campaign on a pledge to make the sporting crowd toe the line. Wouldn't you rather endorse an *honest* marshal?"

Wheeler was silent a moment. "Let's not kid ourselves," he finally said. "Creary will still run, and he has supporters. He'll just turn Republican."

"I don't care if he changes his name to Santa Claus. I'm telling you I'll win, Tom. You can take it to the bank."

"By God, I believe you will. I really do."

"You'll support me then?"

"Here's my hand on it."

"You're shaking hands with Austin's next marshal."

"Is that what you saw in your crystal ball?"

Thompson grinned. "Just call me a prophet."

* * *

The balance of the morning was spent calling on potential supporters. Thompson's first stop was the Mercantile National Bank, where he spoke with the president, James Shipe. His next stop was the county courthouse.

By noon, he had secured the endorsement of Shipe as well as Sheriff Frank Horner. The banker, who was impressed by Thompson's sincerity, readily climbed aboard the bandwagon. The sheriff required considerably more persuasion, but he finally came around. He agreed that an honest city marshal would be a welcome change.

Thompson was encouraged by their support. Shipe was one of Austin's most prominent bankers, and an influential voice within the business community. Horner was the county's chief law enforcement officer, known for his integrity and his unbending attitude toward criminals. Their backing, along with that of the mayor, would rapidly broaden the base of support. All that remained was the newspapers.

The *Statesman* was located near the corner of Congress Avenue and Beach Street. Shortly after the noon hour, Thompson walked into the office of John Cardwell. A lifelong resident of Austin, Cardwell was the editor and publisher, widely respected for his objective reporting of civic affairs. He was a man of distinguished bearing, with gray hair and the eyes of a sage. He knew where the skeletons were buried in Travis County.

Thompson presented his case in a forceful manner. Apart from the need for impartial law enforcement, he underscored the support he'd garnered by the mayor, the sheriff, and James Shipe. He planned to announce his candidacy in tomorrow's paper, and he made no pretext about the purpose of his visit. He wanted the endorsement of the *Statesman*.

Cardwell listened with an impassive expression. He never once interrupted, staring across the desk, his fingers steepled, until Thompson finished talking. His features were inscrutable.

"You make a persuasive argument," he said. "Certainly no one questions your honesty."

"I appreciate the sentiment, Mr. Cardwell."

"Did you ever meet Wild Bill Hickok?"

"Yes," Thompson said carefully. "We met in the Kansas cowtowns."

"Unfortunate thing," Cardwell mused. "How he was assassinated, I mean. But in any event, he was considered to be an honest lawman. Wouldn't you agree?"

"That's what I always heard."

"Even so, he enforced the law with his guns. Summary justice without the benefit of the courts. Would that be a fair statement?"

"Fair enough."

"So here's my question to you, Mr. Thompson. Would you turn out to be Austin's Wild Bill Hickok?"

Thompson held his gaze. "I believe a gun is the last resort, Mr. Cardwell. All the more so when it involves a peace officer." He paused for emphasis. "I advocate law and order, not summary justice."

"Excellent answer," Cardwell said approvingly. "You're certain to be asked that question during the campaign. I think you'll do quite well."

"Does that mean you'll endorse me?"

"Oh, you can definitely count on the support of the *Statesman*. I agree, it's time to send Ed Creary packing. Long past time!"

Across town, Thompson's message was received

with less enthusiasm. George Harris, editor and publisher of the *Republican*, gave him a chilly reception. The masthead of the newspaper had nothing to do with the Republican party, but Harris was nonetheless vitriolic in his opposition to Mayor Wheeler. A reformer by nature, he supported the clergy's efforts to abolish Guy Town and drive the sporting crowd from Austin. He wanted nothing to do with the mayor's candidate for city marshal.

Thompson figured one out of two wasn't all that bad. The *Statesman* was the older paper, with larger circulation, and its editorial policy reflected the popular views of the public. He would have preferred the *Republican* in his corner as well, but he wasn't displeased with the outcome. He'd started the morning a candidate without affiliation or support, and he now had the backing of key players in Austin's political arena. All in all he thought it had been a pretty good day.

Early that afternoon, when he arrived home, he was in a splendid mood. As he came through the door, he saw Billy's valise on the floor in the hallway. He found Catherine and Billy in the parlor, and his mood evaporated on the instant. Billy was ready to travel.

"What's this?" Thompson said. "Leaving without saying good-bye?"

Billy shrugged. "We were never much on good-byes. Figured I'd be gone by the time you got home."

"You might have told me this morning."

"Guess it slipped my mind. I was still half asleep when you left."

Thompson let it pass. "You headed back to Brownsville?"

"Yeah, it's the riverboats for me," Billy said lightly. "I'm catching the three o'clock train."

"Why not stay on a few days? What's the rush?"

"A rolling stone gathers no moss. Gotta keep movin'."

Billy kissed Catherine on the cheek. Then he turned, wringing Thompson's hand with a crooked grin, and moved into the hallway. A moment later the front door closed, and they watched from the window as he walked toward the corner. His stride was brisk, almost a swagger, the valise swinging from his hand. He looked like a man in a hurry to get somewhere.

Catherine sighed. "I always hate to see him go. He's such a loveable scamp."

"That's Billy," Thompson agreed. "Blink your eyes and he's off again."

"Well, anyway," she said softly, linking her arm in his. "How did things go downtown?"

"Katie, I think you'd better get used to a lawman in the family."

"You've announced your candidacy?"

"Wait till you see tomorrow's paper."

The announcement appeared the following morning in the *Statesman*. The print was big and bold, spread over a half page, and went directly to the point. There was no mistaking the message.

To the Good People of Austin:

A number of our leading citizens have convinced me to become a candidate for the office of City Marshal. I can truthfully say that the difficulties of the independent life I have led were the result of an impulse to protect the weak from the aggressions of the strong. I am thoroughly acquainted with the character of Austin and her citizens, and I propose to restore honest law enforcement to our streets. If honored with election

to this important post, my whole time and atten-
tion shall be devoted to official duties, and no law
abiding member of our community shall regret
the choice. Upon these terms I invoke the support
of all my fellow citizens.

Your obedient servant
Ben Thompson

FIFTEEN

———◆———

The announcement created a furor. By the next day Austin was divided into two camps. One faction applauded Thompson's candidacy for city marshal. The other roundly condemned him as an opportunist.

The clergy was particularly vocal. The Austin Ministers Association was an organization composed of preachers and priests from every church in the city. On Wednesday morning, the association convened an emergency session and issued a statement to the newspapers. The pastors denounced Thompson as unfit for public office.

Opposition from a sector of the business community was no less strident. Alexander Wooldridge, president of the Austin National Bank, quickly formed a coalition of prominent businessmen. A civic leader and philanthropist, Wooldridge had been instrumental in founding a public school system, and was generally credited with bringing the University of Texas to Austin. His opposition served to buttress the outrage of the clergy.

The furor was offset to some extent by statements of support issued by Mayor Wheeler and Sheriff Horner. James Shipe, reacting to Wooldridge's outcry, rapidly formed a coalition of his own. By late Wednesday morning the business community was split down the center, with the town's leading bankers spearheading the factions. John Cardwell, true to his word, came out in staunch support of Thompson. His editorial in the *Statesman* went to the heart of the issue.

> Mr. Ben Thompson announced himself a candidate for City Marshal in yesterday's issue. He is well and favorably known to everyone in the city, and is in every way worthy of the confidence and support of the people. Mr. Thompson is a formidable competitor for the office, and if elected will serve the people faithfully. This paper endorses his candidacy with every certainty that he will bring a new sense of law and order to the streets of Austin.

The *Republican* fired a broadside of its own. George Harris proved to be a man of his word as well. His editorial was scathing, and personal.

> The decent people of Austin reel under the shock of Ben Thompson's candidacy for public office. Thompson is a notorious shootist and mankiller, long aligned with the tawdry element of Guy Town. The mere thought of Thompson empowered with a badge is repugnant to this editor and to all people who respect the law. We urge good-minded

voters to cast their ballot for City Marshal Ed
Creary, who was betrayed by the Democrats and
will now run on the Republican ticket. Elect a
God-fearing man, not a mankiller.

The editorial enraged Thompson. His normal reaction
to such insults would have been to call Harris out, force
a fight or an apology. Yet mudslinging was common
to politics, and any rash act on his part would add credence to the slurs. All morning, he'd stalked through
the house, muttering to himself, stumped for a proper
response. When Catherine called him for the noon
meal, he came to the table with no great appetite. His
mind was on matters other than food.

"Dammit anyway!" he grumbled, cutting into a slab
of beefsteak. "I'd like to box his ears till he's bloody.
That's the least he deserves."

Catherine seemed unperturbed. "You knew politics
was a shabby business. You have to play the game
by their rules."

"That doesn't make it any easier to swallow. Where's
the man get off saying I'm aligned with Guy Town?
That's just a flat-out lie."

"Perhaps you should arrange an interview with the
Statesman. You're entitled to tell your side of the story."

"Yeah, maybe so." Thompson chewed thoughtfully
on a hunk of steak. "But how the deuce do I take on
the churches? No one wins fighting with preachers."

"I'm afraid that's a lost cause," she said with a teasing smile. "Particularly since you haven't set foot in a
church since we were married. You'd be very much like
a fish out of water."

"I suppose I'll leave the churches to Ed Creary. What

was it the *Republican* called him, a 'God-fearing man'? Wonder if they know he takes payoffs from the parlor houses."

"Well, at least Governor Roberts has taken a neutral position. The *Statesman* said he declined to comment on local affairs."

"Guess I got lucky there," Thompson conceded. "You'll recall he wanted me arrested over that dust-up with the cattlemen's association. Maybe the mayor put a bee in his ear."

She took a sip of coffee. "You really should count your blessings, sweetheart. Some of the most influential men in town have taken your side."

"I need more than 'some.' I need a majority."

"You've only just begun. I'm sure you'll win them over. Give it a little time."

"Katie, time's in short supply. I've got nineteen days till election."

Thompson paused, a bite of steak speared on his fork. His gaze became abstracted, and he stared off into the middle distance. A ghost of a smile touched the corner of his mouth.

"What is it?" she asked. "You look very . . . devious."

"I'm thinking, nothing ventured, nothing gained."

"You're talking riddles. Ventured how?"

"What was it you said, I have to win them over?"

"Yes, that's right. And . . . ?"

Thompson smiled. "Time to beard the lion in his den."

The Austin National Bank was located on the corner of Colorado and Mesquite. Directly across the street was the State House grounds, and the capitol building. The legislature was in session, and the broad plaza swarmed with activity. The lawmakers were returning from a leisurely noon meal.

Alexander Wooldridge watched the activity from his desk. His office fronted the bank building, with a large window looking out onto the capitol grounds. The office was lavishly appointed, furnished with wing-back chairs and a sofa crafted in lush morocco leather. The walls were lined with oil paintings, and the massive desk appeared carved from a solid piece of walnut. The room seemed somehow appropriate to the man.

The banker was in his late forties. Tall and slim, his bearing was ramrod straight, a posture of worldly self-assurance. He wore a frock coat with dark trousers, and a dull gray cravat discreetly pegged with an onyx stickpin. The watch chain across his vest was woven in intricate strands of gold. He was a commanding figure of a man, his salt-and-pepper hair offset by eyes the color of slate. He gave the impression he could see through walls.

Wooldridge was one of the movers-and-shakers in Austin. Apart from the bank, and his personal wealth, he was on a first-name basis with the governor and a great number of the legislators. A year ago, his prestige in the community had persuaded voters to tax themselves in a referendum to support the local school system. His lobbying efforts, along with a large philanthropic endowment, had resulted in legislation directed at higher education. Governor Oran Roberts had praised his role in the creation of the University of Texas.

Today, staring out the window, Wooldridge was absorbed by the sight of the legislators. He planned an even more aggressive lobbying campaign to secure funds for expansion of the university. A light knock interrupted his reverie, and he turned from the window. His secretary, Myrtle Peppard, waited just inside the door.

"Mr. Wooldridge," she said nervously, "that Ben Thompson is outside. He insists on seeing you."

"Did you tell him I was busy?"

"Yessir, but he won't listen. He demanded that I give you the message."

"Demanded, did he! Very well, Myrtle, show him in."

Wooldridge thought it typical of a man he considered a ruffian. He respected James Shipe, who was his sole rival in business affairs and civic matters. But he could only speculate as to why a fellow banker would endorse an infamous gunman for public office. He wondered as well as to the purpose of this unannounced visit.

Thompson walked through the door like he'd foreclosed on the bank. "Mr. Wooldridge," he said with open charm, "I appreciate you seeing me. It's most kind of you."

"Not at all." Wooldridge accepted his handshake, motioned him to a chair. "What can I do for you, Mr. Thompson?"

"I won't waste your time fencing around. I've come to ask how I can win your support in the election for City Marshal. Anyone who knows me will tell you I'm the best man for the job."

"You certainly don't suffer from lack of confidence."

"That's never been one of my faults. You're a man of some confidence yourself, Mr. Wooldridge. There ought to be a way we can find common ground."

Wooldridge assessed him with icy calm. "You no doubt read the editorial in today's *Republican*. I share those sentiments, Mr. Thompson." He paused, his features sphinx-like. "You are who you are."

"And no apologies for it." Thompson rocked his hand, fingers splayed. "I've killed a few men in my time. But I never fired on a man who hadn't fired on me first. Wouldn't you say that's an enviable quality for a peace officer?"

"I won't be drawn into debate. You are a professional gambler and a member of the so-called sporting crowd. Your interests are not in the best interests of Austin."

"How do you arrive at that conclusion?"

"Let me pose a question," Wooldridge said. "We have a cancer in our community known as Guy Town. I propose the eradication of evil and vice in every form. As our city marshal, would you work to that end?"

Thompson returned his stare. "Except for the churches, most folks find no harm in Guy Town. Until they do, I'll enforce the law and keep a lid on things. I'm not in the business of policing people's morals."

"Then we are at an impasse, Mr. Thompson. I cannot support a man who condones vice. Anything else?"

"No, that pretty well covers it. Thanks for your time, Mr. Wooldridge."

Thompson rose from his chair. He walked to the door, not altogether sure he'd been right about nothing ventured, nothing gained. The truncated conversation had merely rubbed salt into a festering sore. Alexander Wooldridge was a cleric without the collar. A reformer.

He thought he'd better move fast. Damn fast.

Sueann Mabry started when he came through the door. Thompson waved her down, moving past her desk with a breezy smile. He proceeded on to the inner office, rapping once with his knuckles, and stepped inside. He found the mayor hunched over a stack of correspondence.

"Afternoon," he said with cheery vigor. "How goes the paperwork?"

"Don't ask," Wheeler grumped. "You seem in high spirits for a man who got roasted by every preacher in town. Not to mention the *Republican*."

"God loves saints and sinners alike. But since you brought it up, that's why I'm here. I just met with Alexander Wooldridge."

"You what—?"

"Thought you'd be interested," Thompson said, dropping into a chair. "I had some notion of winning him over to the cause. You might say he was too polite to laugh."

"That's Wooldridge," Wheeler said quickly. "One oar in the water with the legislature and the other with the churches. He's a regular diplomat."

"No, Tom, he's a reformer. He wanted to know if I would back a movement to close down Guy Town."

"What did you say?"

"I told him it's not the city marshal's job to police people's morals. I figured it would be a waste of breath to ask him what he thinks of Ed Creary."

"You figured right," Wheeler commented. "He'll oppose you to get at me. He knows Guy Town will never be closed down while I'm in office. I'd rather keep vice under control than have it go underground."

"You took the words out of my mouth," Thompson said. "All the same, I'm glad I called on Wooldridge. He gave me a real eye-opener."

"How so?"

"We're up against some solid citizens. Wooldridge

and his business cronies are in thick with the churches. We've got to fight fire with fire."

Wheeler eyed him dubiously. "I'm not sure I like the sound of that. What's on your mind?"

"A rally," Thompson said, gesturing wildly. "Torches, lots of speeches, a band and a big crowd. Our own evangelical meeting—spread the gospel."

"And what sort of gospel are we preaching?"

"Law and order. No more special treatment for the sporting crowd, and no more payoffs. Honest law enforcement."

Wheeler considered a moment. "That could reflect badly on me. As mayor, I could be held accountable for Creary's payoff scheme."

"You saw the light!" Thompson said zealously. "You caught on to his crooked dealings and you dumped him. You'll look like the hero."

"By God, you've got a point. I did dump him!"

"And you damn well deserve the credit."

"Not a bad angle," Wheeler said, toying with the idea. "Of course, our opposition could turn the tables on you. All that stuff about being too quick with a gun. They'll have stooges planted in the crowd."

"I'll handle it," Thompson said with conviction. "I'm the man for the job because *nobody* in the sporting crowd wants trouble with me. Austin will have the safest streets in Texas. That's my new campaign slogan."

Wheeler laughed. "Ben, you're starting to think like a politician."

"I have Alexander Wooldridge to thank for that. He taught me a lesson about the rules of politics."

"I wasn't aware there were any rules."

"Offhand, I'd say there's two."

"Which are?"

"Anything goes . . ."

"And?"

"No holds barred."

Mayor Tom Wheeler thought that summed it up perfectly. He thought as well that Ben Thompson was a quick learner. Politics could be reduced to a fundamental truth.

No holds barred was the name of the game.

SIXTEEN

The rally was held on Saturday, October 16. Shortly before seven that evening, the Austin Fire Brigade Band marched from the firehouse to the capitol. A large crowd was already gathered on the state house lawn.

Mayor Tom Wheeler had pulled out all stops. For the past three days, full-page advertisements for the rally had appeared in the *Statesman*. Flyers promoting the event had been plastered on lampposts and buildings from the railroad depot to the uptown business district. Aldermen from nine wards had spread the word, and turned out their constituency in force. The only dissenter was the alderman from the Third Ward, Guy Town.

By seven o'clock fully a thousand people were congregated on the state house lawn. Thompson stood with the mayor and the aldermen at the intersection of Congress Avenue and Mesquite. They were joined by James Shipe and Sheriff Frank Horner, who were on the roster of speakers for the evening. Policemen were posted on street corners around the plaza, and several sheriff's deputies were in attendance. Conspicuous by his absence was City Marshal Ed Creary, newly endorsed by the Republican Party.

Catherine and Bobby, along with the mayor's wife, were in the vanguard of the crowd. The evening was chilly, and Catherine wore a fashionable Eton jacket, with the left sleeve pinned to the coat. Bobby was all eyes, barely able to contain himself, caught up in the excitement of the buzzing throng. As dark settled over the plaza, torches were lighted, and a flickering blaze reflected off the capitol. Colorful placards, mounted on short poles, bobbed over the heads of the crowd. The theme of the signs, in bold letters, was LAW AND ORDER.

On signal from the mayor, the bandleader raised his staff. Trumpets blared and the band broke out in a thumping rendition of John Philip Sousa's *The Washington Post March*. The stirring air filled the plaza, and the band, resplendent in brass-buttoned uniforms, quick-stepped onto the street. Formed in ranks of four, Wheeler and Thompson, along with Shipe and Horner and the aldermen, strode off behind the band. The assembled townspeople massed in a long column to the rear.

The torchlit parade circled the state house grounds. Onlookers ganged the sidewalks, and as the band marched past, hundreds more rushed to join the column. On the south edge of the plaza, having looped the capitol, the band wheeled left on Mesquite. Still more people tagged along, and by the time the parade approached City Hall, the crowd had swelled to almost two thousand people. The bandleader, walking backward, pumped his staff and the band segued into *Dixie*. The column jammed into the intersection of San Jacinto.

A tall platform stood raised before City Hall. The wooden structure was festively decorated with red, white and blue bunting, and the seal of the City of Austin was painted on the front of the speakers' podium. Wheeler and Thompson, followed by the other dignitaries, mounted a flight of stairs at one side of the platform. Streetlamps paled in the blaze of torches as the crowd pressed closer and the men arrayed themselves on line behind the mayor. He walked directly to the podium, and the band thumped to a halt. The crowd fell silent.

"People of Austin!" he boomed, his arms outstretched. "We come here tonight to celebrate our city's march toward a progressive new era. An era of law and order—for all!"

Wheeler went on to review the positive measures undertaken during his administration. He dwelled at length on the improved waterworks, the construction of a new grade school, and a reduction in property taxes. Then he turned to the subject of law and order, the reason for tonight's rally. He acknowledged official corruption in Guy Town—readily confessed his inability to police the police—and laid out a plan for the abolishment of unscrupulous graft. His voice ringing, he extolled the virtues of the man who would bring honor to the badge—Ben Thompson. A marshal for the new era!

The crush of spectators roared approval. Wheeler postured a moment, then brought James Shipe to the podium. The banker spoke of his long association with the candidate, a friendship founded on honesty and moral values. He noted that all of Austin's aldermen—with the exception of the one who represented the sporting crowd—were present to welcome Thompson aboard the Democrat bandwagon. After another burst of applause, he was followed to the podium by Sheriff Frank Horner. The lawman was succinct and blunt, relating problems caused for the county by poor law enforcement in Guy Town. He heartily endorsed Thompson as a man equal to the job—and worthy of the badge.

Mayor Wheeler then performed a resounding introduction of the candidate. The crowd gave Thompson a wild and boisterous ovation as he walked to the podium. He stood staring out over the throng with a broad grin, his arms raised in the universal sign of victory. The applause gradually faded, and as the onlookers quieted, his features took on a somber cast. His voice was strong and forceful, confident.

"I pledge to you that as your next city marshal I will bring law and order to our streets. And in particular, I will enforce the law without favoritism in the gaming parlors, saloons and *other* establishments in Guy Town!"

The crowd understood that "other establishments" was a delicate reference to whorehouses and prostitution. There were snickers among the men, and imperceptible nods of approval among the women. Thompson then went to the heart of the accusations leveled by his opposition, what he termed "character assassination." As marshal, he declared, he would never resort to "gun law" unless confronted by armed and deadly criminals. His so-called reputation, he asserted, would work to the benefit of Austin. The rougher element would be deterred from violence.

A murmur of agreement rippled through the onlookers. Thompson next tackled accusations charging him with conflict of interest. "Any man who knows me," he announced, "knows that my word is my bond. All personal ties to gambling will be severed for however long I wear a badge. You have my oath on it." With wry amusement, he then broached allegations that he was a member of the sporting crowd. "I will not be tarred with that brush," he said forcefully. "I have no obligation to anyone—man or woman—among the sporting class. Guy Town will declare a day of mourning the day I am elected marshal."

"What're you gonna do?" someone yelled contentiously. "Shoot 'em if they don't walk the straight and narrow? You're a gunman, not a lawman!"

Thompson expected hecklers. He was surprised the rally hadn't been interrupted before now. Yet he was determined to handle agitators with humor. He looked down at the man with an indulgent smile.

"I won't have time to shoot anybody," he said amiably. "I'll be too busy marching tinhorns and grifters off to jail. You might be my first customer."

The spectators hooted with laughter. Thompson quickly launched into a ringing denunciation of the current marshal, Ed Creary. He remarked that crime was at an all-time high, citing figures for the last year. Nine murders, with four as yet unsolved. Assault and robbery and burglary at record levels. But not one arrest in an entire year for disorderly houses and bunco games. Streetwalkers and crooked gamblers, he thundered, enjoyed immunity from the law. A free ride for those who greased the palm of the city marshal.

"Let's call a spade a spade," he went on. "Graft and payoffs are an open secret in Guy Town. Ed Creary's a crook with a badge."

Thompson paused, one arm thrust overhead. "Elect

me marshal and Austin will have the safest streets in Texas. I promise you honest law enforcement!"

The crowd erupted in cheers. The band thumped to life and people shouted themselves hoarse. A sea of LAW AND ORDER placards danced and jiggled in the light of the torches. Mayor Wheeler joined Thompson at the podium, their arms raised in victory, laughing and waving to their supporters. Flash-pans popped as newspaper photographers caught the image in a frozen moment.

The excitement of the rally gradually faded. Within a matter of minutes, as Wheeler and Thompson shook hands with the dignitaries, the band marched off under the cadence of flutes and drums. The majority of the crowd straggled along, still carrying their torches and placards, talking quietly among themselves. Only a few supporters remained behind for a handshake with the candidates.

The newshounds were waiting as Thompson descended the steps from the platform. A reporter for the *Republican* pushed forward. "Mr. Thompson, you've brought serious allegations against Marshal Creary. Do you have any proof?"

"The court of public opinion," Thompson responded. "Lots of people in Guy Town will tell you anything you want to know about payoffs. All you have to do is ask."

"I asked if you have proof."

"And I told you where to find it."

"Hardly the same thing," the reporter countered. "Abraham Lincoln once said: Deception is the distinguishing characteristic of snake-oil peddlers and politicians. You're starting to sound like a politician, Mr. Thompson."

Thompson forced a laugh. "Whatever else I am, I don't accept bribes. That'll be a welcome relief from Ed Creary."

"Mr. Thompson," the reporter for the *Statesman* broke in. "You pledged to make the streets of Austin the safest in Texas. What are your plans for that?"

"A good peace officer is johnny-on-the-spot. He stops trouble before it has a chance to get started. That's how our police department will operate in the future."

"Are you satisfied the officers on the force will be able to handle the job?"

"I'm satisfied they will when I become marshal."

Thompson ended it on a positive note. He waved the reporters off, and moved to where Catherine waited with Bobby. The youngster stared up at him with something approaching awe, for once reduced to silence. The mayor was hosting drinks for the aldermen at the Austin Hotel bar, and Thompson was expected to attend. He first wanted to see Catherine and the boy safely on the streetcar. They walked toward Congress Avenue.

"I thought it went splendidly," Catherine said, taking his arm. "You're quite the speaker, Mr. Thompson."

Thompson chuckled. "Tom Wheeler's been coaching me for two days. I felt like a ventriloquist's dummy."

"Fiddlesticks! Those were your words, not his, and the crowd loved it. You were very . . . genuine."

"In politics, sincerity counts for more than substance. I'm liable to end up a cynic yet."

"You will not," she protested. "That's why you've received such favorable support. People know you would never engage in trickery."

"That's my finest attribute," Thompson said, gently mocking her. "A square deal, even in politics."

Bobby tugged at his sleeve. "Pa, what'd that reporter fellow mean? The one talkin' about Abe Lincoln?"

"You know what a snake-oil peddler is, don't you, son?"

"Why sure, Pa, that's one of them medicine shows. Where they sell stuff for whatever ails you."

"Do you believe their cures work?"

"Mom says it's all hokum."

"Well, according to the reporter, Abe Lincoln said the same thing about politicians. They lie to people."

"Yeah . . . ?" Bobby looked perplexed. "How come they called him Honest Abe then? A president's a politician, isn't he?"

Thompson ruffed his hair. "There's an exception to every rule, and Lincoln proves the point. Even if he was a Yankee."

"So that means you're like Honest Abe, doesn't it? You don't tell lies."

"Son, just between us, I'm pretending to be a politician. I wouldn't be one for a million dollars."

"I figgered that's what it was, Pa."

Bobby ran ahead to the corner. Thompson shook his head, and Catherine squeezed his arm. "You're terrible," she said, trying not to laugh. "He'll never trust a politician again."

"Then I've taught him a good lesson, Katie. Anybody who makes public speeches shouldn't be taken at his word—except for me and Honest Abe."

"You really are a prankster."

"Yes, that too."

Thompson put them on the streetcar. He waved as

the driver clanged the bell and the mule plodded off
along the tracks. Then he turned back downstreet, and
walked toward the Austin Hotel. As he approached the
corner, he saw Ed Creary and policeman Carl Allen
standing in the aureole of light beneath a lamppost. His
mustache lifted in a tight smile.

"Good evening, Ed," he said without a trace of humor. "You missed the rally."

"I heard about it," Creary said, jerking his chin at
Allen. "Carl told me you were on your high horse. Like
you were preachin' the Sermon on the Mount."

"Well, we know Carl's a liar, don't we? Perjured
himself after taking an oath on the Bible. Didn't you,
Carl?"

Allen blanched. "That wasn't the—"

"Button your lip," Creary snapped. "Let's get down to
cases, Thompson. You're spreadin' hogwash about me."

Thompson stared at him. "What hogwash is that?"

"All this stuff about Guy Town and payoffs. I want
it stopped."

"And if it's not?"

"I'll tend to you," Creary said roughly. "One way or
another, you'll get yours."

"Are you threatening me, Ed?"

"You take it any way you want."

Thompson's eyes went hard. "I'd hate to kill my only
opponent for public office. The voters might think I
acted in haste."

"Goddamn you!" Creary bridled. "You don't
scare me."

"Walk away or pull your gun. I'm through talking."

The men stood enveloped in a cone of silence. Creary
seemed to be debating the odds, whether two against
one would take the play. Then, as though dissuaded

of the notion, he turned on his heel. Allen hurried after him.

Thompson watched until they rounded the corner. He realized that he'd almost broken his promise to himself. A shaky promise, but nonetheless well meant.

He still didn't want to kill Ed Creary.

SEVENTEEN

Thompson lathered his face from a soap mug. The steel of his straight razor glinted as he stropped it back and forth on a leather strap hanging from the wall. He tested the edge on his thumb and began shaving.

A shaft of sunlight flooded the bathroom window. He studied himself in the mirror and thought it was a fine day for an election. The date was Monday, November 1, and the polls would open in less than an hour. Gingerly, careful not to nick himself, he worked the razor across his jawline. He wanted to look his best.

Some minutes later, reeking of bay rum, he walked back to the bedroom. He moved to the armoire, opened the double doors, and surveyed his suits. After a moment, he selected a dark jacket with a matching vest and gray trousers. A white shirt, hand-stitched from Egyptian cotton, and a striped cravat completed his outfit. He began dressing.

The past two weeks seemed lost in a blur of activity. Since the night of the rally, he had campaigned relentlessly, gladhanding voters all over town. He had appeared as guest speaker at various fraternal orders and the weekly luncheons of several business organizations. A major appearance had been the monthly meeting of the Confederate Veterans Society, where his record during the war assured a warm reception. He'd hammered away on the issue of law and order wherever he spoke.

No less determined, his opposition had continued its smear campaign. Ed Creary and the Republican Party had lambasted him at every opportunity. Their attacks were personal and vitriolic, and centered on his notoriety as a mankiller. The gunfight two months ago at the Capital Variety Theater had been bandied about endlessly; their argument stressed the folly of licensing a shootist with a lawman's badge. Yet Creary kept his distance, and avoided any chance of a confrontation like the one he'd provoked the night of the rally. He seemed content to vindicate himself at the ballot box.

Finished dressing, Thompson paused before the full-length mirror on the armoire. He subjected himself to critical inspection, noting that the holstered Colt was concealed by the drape of his jacket. The pistol was an unwitting reminder that a personal showdown with Ed Creary was as remote as the stars. Creary might back-shoot him, or arrange his murder, but even that seemed improbable. A lifetime of assessing men and tight situations left him with no real concern. He thought Creary was all wind and no whistle.

A final tug of his jacket satisfied him that he would pass muster. Turning away from the mirror, he went out of the bedroom and moved along the hallway. Bobby had darted in earlier, wishing him luck with the election, and hurried off to school. The boy was jumping with excitement, loudly confident that by the end of the day his father would be the new city marshal of Austin. Thompson privately agreed, for he thought the youngster was on the money. He planned to win it going away.

Downstairs, he found Catherine in the kitchen. She was radiant, brimming with enthusiasm, her vitality all but infectious. Over the past three weeks she had become his most ardent supporter, obsessed with the idea of him wearing a badge, She alluded to it only in an oblique manner, and yet there was never any doubt that she shared his vision. A means to a new life, something more than a gambler, the honor of public office. She desperately wanted him to win.

"Don't you look elegant!" she said, kissing him on the cheek. "You'll be the best-dressed candidate in town."

"I figured I ought to look the part."

"And never with better reason. It's your big day."

Thompson took a seat at the table. She brought a platter with beefsteak and eggs, and a basket of fluffy buttermilk biscuits. As he began loading his plate, she poured him a steaming mug of coffee. He broke the yolk on an egg.

"That's some breakfast," he said, nodding at the platter. "You'd think I was a lumberjack."

"A man needs to fortify himself on election day. You probably won't get another bite until the polls close."

"I just suspect you're right. Tom Wheeler says it's important to be out and about shaking hands. He calls it 'pressing the flesh.' "

"You're certainly my choice," she said brightly. "I wish I could vote for you."

Thompson slathered butter on a biscuit. "One of these days women will have the vote. I'd say it's just a matter of time."

"Well, the important thing is to get you elected. I can't wait to see your new badge!"

"Careful now, let's not get overconfident. I haven't won it yet."

"You will," she said with conviction. "And don't play Mr. Modest with me. You know very well you're the front-runner."

"I don't know any such thing." Thompson took a bite of steak, waved his fork. "Any gambler's superstitious by nature, and that includes me. Never count the pot till you've seen the last card."

"Yes, but you're forgetting something, sugar. As of tonight, you won't be a gambler anymore. You'll be a marshal."

"Katie, I hope to hell you're right. I want it so bad it makes my teeth ache."

"Then eat your breakfast and stop worrying. You already have it won."

"What makes you so sure?"

She smiled an enigmatic smile. "I've seen the last card."

The polls were located in the Knights of Pythias Building. A fraternal order devoted to charitable causes, the organization donated space each year for the city elections. It was considered neutral ground.

The weather was crisp and clear. A bright morning sun edged higher in the sky as Thompson approached the building. Tom Wheeler was talking with several of his cronies on the front steps. He hurried forward with a hearty smile.

"There you are, Ben!" He pumped Thompson's arm with vigor. "I started to wonder if you'd forgotten it's election day."

"I thought the polls didn't open till eight."

"A politician is always johnny-come-early. You want to be the last face the voters see before they cast their ballot."

"Press the flesh," Thompson said genially. "Wasn't that how you put it?"

"Absolutely," Wheeler replied. "We'll make a politician of you yet."

"I'd rather be marshal."

"A rose is a rose by any other name. Even a marshal has to cultivate the political garden."

Thompson nodded. "How are things looking?"

"Tiptop," Wheeler said cheerily. "I have every confidence it'll be a clean sweep. We'll skunk the Republicans again."

Wheeler was rabid on the subject of the Republican Party. Like all Texans, he had suffered the injustices committed by Yankee occupation forces during the Reconstruction Era. With Republican puppets in the state house, Texas hadn't been readmitted to the Union until 1870. His political career in large part stemmed from dark memories.

The past few weeks had done nothing to alter old animosities. The *Statesman* and the *Republican*, like battleships under full sail, had exchanged daily broadsides. Yet the *Republican* editorials had been charged with acrimony and malice, vilifying Democrats in slanderous terms. Wheeler had been singled out for having thrown his support to Thompson in the marshal's race. He was still steaming from the rough treatment.

A large crowd was gathered outside when the doors opened at eight o'clock. Thompson and Wheeler and the Democratic candidates for aldermen waited on the steps, shaking hands and offering a last word of encouragement. The polling station was located in a cavernous room on the ground floor, with monitors from both parties to supervise the election. A steady stream of voters began filing into the building to cast their ballots.

The Republican candidates were working the crowd as well. They kept to the other side of the steps, ganged in a loose phalanx, wringing hands like drowning men. Ernest Cramer, the mayoral contender, was a chunky man with a waxish grin and heavy jowls. His manner was agitated, somehow jittery, and he shifted nervously from foot to foot. Not unlike his cohorts, he seemed to be playing a role, and doing it badly. He looked like a loser.

Ed Creary was the last to make an appearance. His features were gaunt, with dark circles under his eyes, as though he'd awakened late for the party. He wore his marshal's badge on his suit jacket, and he waded into the flurry of handshaking with a bogus smile. His one hope was that Democrats would forego partisan politics and vote for an experienced lawman. His problem was that everyone in town now believed he was a crook. He seemed like a man waiting for bad news.

Alexander Wooldridge arrived with a group of clergymen. He studiously ignored the Democrats, and greeted Creary with a warm handshake. The preachers flocked around, careful to ignore the Republicans for fear of offending their Democratic parishioners. Yet they offered their good wishes to Creary, bestowing a public blessing despite his unsavory links to Guy Town. They were impervious to the irony of the situation, or perhaps simply unmindful. A crook, in their view, was the lesser of two evils. There was no redemption for a shootist.

A moment later James Shipe came up the steps. He exchanged a barbed glance with Wooldridge, and shook his head with a satiric look. Then he walked directly to Wheeler and Thompson, greeting them with jaunty good humor. "Mr. Mayor. Ben," he said, extending his hand. "Let me be the first to congratulate you."

"Jim, you're a little premature," Wheeler said. "They've just now opened the doors."

"Now or later, it's all the same. You'll come away with the keys to City Hall."

Thompson chuckled. "What did your tea leaves say about a badge for me?"

"I'm no swami, you understand. But I'm a prognosticator of impeccable credentials. You are our next city marshal, Ben."

"Tell me that when the polls close."

"Speaking of the polls," Wheeler said, "why don't we cast our own votes? No time like the present."

Shipe cocked his head. "Who do you plan to vote for?"

"The process of the ballot is secret. But I think it's safe to say I'll vote for myself—and Ben."

"And will you vote for yourself, Ben?"

Thompson laughed. "I sure as hell won't vote for Ed Creary."

"The question is, who will?"

They sauntered unhurriedly into the Knights of Pythias Building.

* * *

The lights burned bright in City Hall. Thompson was seated in the mayor's office, staring out the window into the darkening night. Wheeler's gaze was fixed on a wall clock, which ticked inexorably toward nine. Neither of them had spoken in the last half hour.

All day they had worked the election crowds. When the polls finally closed at seven o'clock, they stopped by a café for a quick supper. Then, walking back to City Hall, they made small talk while awaiting a count of the ballots. Their vigil was now into the second hour.

"Nearly nine," Thompson said, breaking the silence. "How long's it usually take?"

"Depends on whether there's a recount—"

The door burst open. Buddy Hubbart, the mayor's brother-in-law and the city tax assessor, walked in with a horsey smile. "Won it by a landslide!" he crowed. "You carried every ward, Tom."

Wheeler beamed. "How about Ben?"

"Creary only took the Third Ward," Hubbart said, nodding to Thompson. "You just got yourself elected marshal."

"I'll be damned." Thompson looked relieved. "Who cares about Guy Town anyway? They knew I wouldn't take payoffs."

"Congratulations, Ben." Wheeler offered him a firm handshake. "You're going to make a fine lawman."

"I couldn't have done it without you. I'm obliged for your support."

"Keep the sporting crowd in line and we'll be even. You've got a free hand to do whatever you want in Guy Town."

"Don't give it another thought," Thompson assured him. "Cardsharps and grifters are at the top of my list."

"That's the ticket." Wheeler turned back to his brother-in-law. "How'd we do with aldermen?"

"Nine out of ten," Hubbart said. "Lost the Third Ward to a Republican. All this law and order talk scared off the sporting crowd."

"Damned ingrates!" Wheeler cursed. "After all I've done to put the quietus on the reformers. Ben, I want you to teach them a lesson. Understood?"

Thompson nodded, "I'll figure out a way to rap their knuckles."

"Well, enough of that for now. We're the big winners tonight and *that* calls for a celebration. Let's find the rest of the boys."

The election eve party was held in the bar at the Austin Hotel. Wheeler was surrounded by the aldermen, his City Hall cronies, and a large contingent of Democratic supporters. Everyone was quick to congratulate Thompson, praising his victory, and there was a round robin of toasts to the winners. The party got progressively louder and more drunken.

Thompson ducked out shortly before midnight. He caught the last streetcar of the evening, with just himself and the driver aboard. The ride to College Hill cleared his head of whiskey fumes, and gave him time to reflect on his new position. By now the initial rush of elation had turned to a sense of deep satisfaction. He'd carried the vote, and with it, the trust of the people of Austin. He quietly resolved to bring honor to the badge.

Catherine was waiting when he came through the door. He saw by the expression on her face that she'd already heard the news. She put her arm around his neck, hugging him fiercely, and kissed him full on the mouth. Her voice was husky with emotion.

"Welcome home . . . Marshal."

"Marshal," Thompson repeated with a chipper grin. "Got a good ring to it, doesn't it? How's it feel to be the wife of a lawman?"

She looked into his eyes. "I've never been more proud in my life."

"Katie, I'm not the least bit tired. You up to a celebration?"

"I'm up to anything tonight."

"You're liable to get more than you bargained for."

"Braggart."

She slipped into his embrace with a musical laugh.

EIGHTEEN

A week later Thompson was sworn in as city marshal. The ceremony took place in the mayor's office, early on Monday morning. Horace Warren, the city court judge, administered the oath.

By law, new office-holders were sworn in a week after their election. Mayor Wheeler and his secretary, Sueann Mabry, were witnesses to the ceremony. Judge Warren had Thompson raise his right hand and place his left hand on a Bible while repeating the oath. He was charged to uphold the laws of the City of Austin and the State of Texas.

Traditionally, the city marshal wore civilian clothes. But Thompson was attired in a uniform he'd designed himself and had tailored over the past week. The color was navy blue, with brass buttons on the jacket and a five-pointed star for a badge. The cap was round and flat, with a leather brim and gold braid, and a laurel-wreathed CITY MARSHAL affixed on the front. He looked the part of a modern police officer.

"Congratulations," Judge Warren said upon completing the oath. "I wish you every success in your new position."

"Thank you," Thompson replied with a broad smile. "You won't see me in your court anymore—except in an official capacity."

"You are welcome in my court anytime, Marshal. Allow me to compliment you on your uniform."

"Seemed only right, since the men are required to wear uniforms. Why should the marshal be the exception?"

"Indeed," Warren said, nodding approval. "You'll set a fine example."

Sueann Mabry shyly offered her congratulations. When she and Judge Warren went out, Wheeler closed the door. He looked around at Thompson. "I wanted to wish you my personal best, Ben. What's your first order of business?"

"I'll meet with the men and officially take charge. How do I go about relieving Ed Creary?"

"I'm happy to say he saved you the trouble. He sent word he'd vacated office as of last night. I suspect he wanted no part in the changing of the guard."

"Good riddance," Thompson said. "Just so you know, I plan to fire Carl Allen. I won't have a perjurer on the police force."

Wheeler appeared dubious. "That's certain to draw criticism. People will think you're settling a personal score."

"I've been criticized before. He lied under oath in a court of law. He's not fit to be a police officer."

"Why not wait a week or so? Your first day on the job makes it look like sour grapes."

"No, it won't wait," Thompson informed him. "I campaigned on a promise of *honest* law enforcement. I expect you to back my play."

"Don't concern yourself about that," Wheeler said hastily. "You're the marshal and you call the shots. Do whatever you have to do."

"Tom, I appreciate the vote of confidence. Let me get to work."

"Keep me advised on things."

"You can depend on it."

Thompson walked down the hall. The police department was located at the rear of the building, near a back door. Outside, a recessed stairway led to the city jail, a holding pen and six cells which occupied the basement. Locally, it was referred to as "The Tomb."

The graveyard shift was going off duty as Thompson entered the squad room. There were twelve men on the force, rotating shifts on a weekly basis. Six men worked the night shift from four in the afternoon to midnight, when Guy Town was at its most troublesome. Four men were assigned to days, and two usually sufficed for late night patrols. Half the force was present for the morning change of shifts.

The men snapped to attention on a barked command from Sergeant Lon Dennville. As the highest-ranking officer on the force, he ran the office and was on call, night or day, in case of an emergency. He welcomed Thompson to the department, and formally introduced him to the six officers present. One of them, just off the graveyard shift, was Carl Allen.

"While the men are here," Dennville asked, "would you like to say anything, Marshal?"

"I'll keep it short," Thompson said, looking from man to man. "You're experienced law officers and you know what's expected of you. Do your job and we'll get along just fine. Come see me if you have any problems."

The men wore blue uniforms and black helmets, and went armed with revolvers as well as billy clubs. All of them knew Thompson and his reputation, and none of them doubted he was about to impose stricter law enforcement on Austin. They stared straight ahead, shoulders squared, waiting to be dismissed. Dennville glanced at Thompson.

"Anything else, Marshal?"

"That's all for now, Sergeant. I'd like to see you and Allen in my office."

Thompson moved to a private office at the rear of the squad room. When he entered, he stopped just inside the door, clearly surprised. A handsome walnut desk, polished to a sheen and obviously new, was positioned before the window. Behind it was a tall judge's chair, crafted in oxblood leather, and equally new. Dennville paused in the doorway.

"Courtesy of the mayor," he said. "He thought the city could afford a new desk for the new marshal."

"Well, Sergeant, he sure picked a beauty."

Thompson took a seat in the oxblood chair. He ran a hand across the gloss of the desktop, and smiled in appreciation. Then, glancing up, he saw Allen standing behind Dennville. He motioned them into the office.

"I'll give it to you straight," he said, fixing Allen with a hard stare. "You're a liar and a perjurer, and a disgrace to the uniform. You're fired, as of right now."

"You've got no right," Allen said lamely. "Creary forced me to testify against you. I was just following orders."

"So here's your last order. Put your badge on this desk and make yourself scarce. You're off the force."

"You're gonna be sorry, Mr. Big Shot."

Thompson rose from his chair. "I won't ask you again. Hand over the badge."

Allen swallowed, his Adam's apple bobbing up and down. He unpinned the badge from his tunic and carefully placed it on the shiny desk. His eyes black with hatred, he turned and walked out the door. Thompson looked at Dennville.

"Any objections?"

"Not from me," the sergeant said. "You've made yourself an enemy, though. He's a regular little weasel."

"To hell with him," Thompson said dismissively. "Before the day's out, I'll make lots of enemies. So will you."

"How so?"

"I've always respected you, Sergeant. From all I've seen, you're on the square and you get the job done. Are you up to some rough work?"

Dennville looked quizzical. "What sort of rough work?"

"We're going to put out the word in Guy Town."

"And what's the word?"

"Don't step over the line . . . ever."

Guy Town was a world apart. A circus of sorts, it was a place where grown men came to play. Some were attracted by the gambling, and others by women. Whiskey simply fueled the merriment.

Early that afternoon Thompson and Dennville proceeded along Cypress Street. They were both known to the sporting crowd, though Thompson rarely ventured into Guy Town. Dennville, on the other hand, was there on a nightly basis, enforcing a rough brand of justice. He was intolerant of drunks and rowdies, and often led the police into fist-swinging melees common to the red-light district. He was considered an artist with a billy club.

Thompson in a police uniform was a sight that drew stares. Having denounced the sporting crowd during the elections, he was now looked upon as a Judas. For years, though he was an uptown gambler, he had been regarded as one of the fraternity. But his campaign for law and order and his election as marshal, had put him on the opposite side of the fence. Worse yet, he'd exposed the payoffs from dives, and threatened the established order of vice. Things would never be the same in Guy Town.

The sporting crowd was no great mystery to Thompson. Essentially they were outcasts, preying on the unwary and the gullible with no more scruples than an alley cat. Within the fraternity there were petty squabbles and jealousies, and incessant bickering for position in the hierarchy. Yet there was solidarity as well, for they saw themselves as a small band pitted against the world. Their ranks were forever closed to outsiders.

Thompson's plan was simplicity itself. There was a pecking order in the sporting crowd, with some more influential than others. However independent, gamblers, saloonkeepers, and whorehouse madams looked to their own for leadership. For the most part, those with the most successful operations assumed a dominant role in the hierarchy. The place to start, Thompson informed Dennville, was at the top of the heap. Their first stop was the Lone Star Gaming Parlor.

The owner was Ned Parker. A heavyset man, he operated one of the roughest dives in town. His dealers were skilled sharpers, and the object of the drill was to fleece the customers without getting caught too often. Anyone who objected was dealt with swiftly and harshly by the bruisers who worked for Parker. Until a week ago, he had been a paying client of Marshal Ed Creary. His crooked games had never drawn police scrutiny.

The Lone Star was a large boxlike room devoted solely to gaming. A long bar traversed one wall, and on the opposite side were faro and twenty-one layouts, and two dice tables. Everyone in the room paused as Thompson and Dennville came through the door, and walked directly to an office at the rear of the bar. They entered without being announced.

Ned Parker was seated behind a desk. The stub of a cigar was wedged in the corner of his mouth, and the chair creaked as he leaned forward. His beady eyes flashed with anger. "You boys oughta learn to knock."

Dennville closed the door. Thompson crossed to the desk and stopped. "Ned, I'm here with bad news," he said with a faint smile. "I was sworn in just this morning."

"So what?" Parker said, puffing a cloud of smoke. "You think I'm impressed with your fancy uniform?"

"You will be before I leave. I've come to put you on notice."

"Notice of what?"

"The rules have changed," Thompson said. "I don't take payoffs and you're through running crooked games. Break the rules and I'll close you down."

"Don't make me laugh," Parker retorted. "You'd have to shut down every joint in Guy Town."

"No, you're wrong there, Ned. The others will fall in line when I close your doors."

"I thought you were handing out all that horseshit to get yourself elected. Are you on the level?"

"Take me at my word," Thompson said evenly. "One complaint about crooked cards and I'll slap a padlock on this place. You wouldn't like it in jail."

Parker munched his cigar. "You've been a sporting man your whole goddamn life. You tellin' me you suddenly got religion?"

"I was a gambler," Thompson said, ignoring the gibe. "I was never a crook."

"I ought to sue you for slander."

"You wouldn't win that one, either. Get straight and stay straight. That's the message."

"What about the other joints?" Parker demanded. "You deliverin' the same message to them."

Thompson smiled. "You'll deliver it for me, Ned."

"Why would I do a fool thing like that?"

"To protect yourself and the Lone Star. Why give them the edge when your games are straight?"

"I haven't said I've bought the sermon myself."

"Then you'd better start wearing warm clothes. I'm told it gets downright frosty in the city jail."

Thompson left him to ponder the thought. The next stop was a parlor house on the corner of Cedar and Colorado. The bordello was operated by Blanche Dumont, herself an institution in Guy Town. Her career spanned two decades, and her house was the most elegant in the district. The other madams considered her the virtuoso of the flesh trade.

The reception room was decorated in French Rococo, with silk damask draperies and a massive crystal chandelier. The girls were voluptuous and genteel, and a pearly-toothed black man coaxed the latest tunes from a sparkling white piano. Blanche Dumont, who was built like a pouter pigeon, wore a gown that barely restrained her breastworks. She greeted Thompson with coquettish trepidation.

"Marshal Thompson," she said, her bosom heaving. "And my dear friend, Sergeant Dennville. I do so hope this is a social call."

"Afraid not, Blanche," Thompson replied pleasantly. "We're here on official business."

"Oh, that sounds so . . . dire."

"Not if you give me a little cooperation. I'm here to ask a favor."

"Aren't you the charmer?" she said with a coy smile. "How could I refuse a gentleman anything?"

Thompson suppressed a laugh. "Blanche, I want you to use your influence with the other madams. Deliver a friendly warning."

"Oh, dear me . . . a warning?"

"Tell them I won't tolerate any high jinks. I expect them to run orderly houses and stop rolling drunks. Anybody who crosses me will be on the next train out of town."

"Well, I'll try," she said, fluttering her eyelashes. "Of course, I can't promise anything. Some of the ladies are . . . indiscreet."

"You're a persuasive woman," Thompson said. "I depend on you to convince them, and no diddling around. Let's get the word out by tonight."

"You are the insistent one, aren't you?"

"I treat my friends right, Blanche. You help me and I'll help you. Do we understand one another?"

"Oh, goodness yes, perfectly."

Outside, a wintry sun was tilting westward. Dennville shook his head as they turned toward Congress Avenue. He laughed a low, chuffing laugh.

"You've got a way with the ladies, Marshal. All the whores will be talking tonight."

Thompson chuckled. "I'd say we've done a good day's work."

"And I'd give a nickel to hear what the sporting crowd says."

"I just suspect it'd singe our ears."

They walked off through the streets of Guy Town.

NINETEEN

"I really think you should go."

"Katie, I'd feel like a hypocrite."

"You're a public official now. You have a responsibility to set an example."

"The roof would probably collapse when I walked in the door. God doesn't look kindly on heathens."

"Oh, that's monstrous!"

Catherine turned from the mirror. They were in the bedroom, and she'd worked herself into a snit. She was dressed for Sunday morning church services, and her color was high. For all her cajolery, Thompson refused to budge, dodging every argument with maddening equanimity. She thought he was shortsighted and obstinate.

"Honestly, Benjamin!" she said waspishly. "You're so exasperating sometimes."

Thompson knew he was in trouble. She never called him by his full name unless she was in a temper. He tried to shrug it off with a smile, watching as she gathered a cabriolet bonnet and pinned it atop her hair. She wore a satin Princess Polonaise dress, very much in vogue, and complimentary to her figure. He gave her a slow once-over.

"You're looking mighty pretty today. I always liked you in purple."

"Magenta!" she corrected him sharply. "And don't you dare try to flatter me. I won't be patronized."

"Guess I'm in the doghouse, huh? All because of a little thing like church."

"What am I going to tell Reverend Jones? I promised him you would attend services today."

Reverend Clarence Jones was pastor of the First Methodist Church. His prominence in the community was magnified by his position as chairman of the Austin Ministers Association. His devotion to universal brotherhood was such that even the Baptists spoke kindly of him.

"Whoa now, Nellie," Thompson said suspiciously. "Why would you be talking about me with Preacher Jones?"

"You needn't be crude," she said, fussing with her hat. "You could at least call him 'Reverend.'"

"And you needn't try to slip off the hook. Since when have I become a topic of discussion with a preacher?"

"Since you became marshal, if you must know. You've been in office a week, and people are already starting to say nice things about you. Reverend Jones made a point of asking me if you would attend services."

"Did he?" Thompson said gruffly. "After he did his damnedest to get me defeated in the election. The man's got brass, I'll give him that."

Catherine sighed. "You might give him the benefit of the doubt. Perhaps he realizes he made a mistake."

"Was that what he said?"

"Well, no, not just in those words. But he said he'd been hearing good things about you."

"Yeah?" Thompson inquired skeptically. "Like what?"

"You know," she murmured, trying to say it without saying it. "How you've made things better . . . downtown."

"You're talking about whores and such? Guy Town?"

"No one uses those terms in polite society."

"Katie, I'm the city marshal, remember? I don't have a lot of dealings with polite society."

"Well, anyway, you've made an impression on the right people. I'm sure they realize they misjudged you."

Thompson's first week on the job had been notable by its relative calm. His detractors fully expected him to shoot someone, leave the streets littered with bodies. Instead, a lull seemed to have settled over Guy Town, even the rowdies wary of clashing with the police. The word slowly got around that Thompson had issued a stern warning to the sporting crowd.

"Won't you reconsider?" Catherine asked. "I mean, after all, Reverend Jones did ask for you. Doesn't that tell you something?"

"Maybe too much," Thompson said dryly. "Jones and the rest of the preachers want to start a reform movement. I won't let myself get drawn into it."

"Ben, for goodness' sake listen to yourself. Do you really think the reverend has ulterior motives?"

"I think preachers are just like anyone else. They'll play along to get along—and get what they want."

"Now you're starting to sound cynical."

"No, just practical."

"Bobby and I will be late for church. I have to go."

"I'll see you off."

Thompson was dressed in his uniform. He'd planned to stop by the office, even though it was Sunday, and check on the men. He strapped his gun on over his tunic, and followed her out the door. She led the way downstairs.

Bobby was waiting in the hall. His hair was slicked back, and he wore a brown herringbone suit with a matching cap and checkered bow tie. He looked around as they came down the stairs, and a moonlike grin spread over his face. He seemed to squirm with excitement.

"I knew Ma would talk you into it. Boy, won't Reverend Jones be surprised!"

"Not today, son," Thompson said. "I've got business that needs tending."

"Aww, darnit all, Pa! I wanted everybody at church to see you in your new uniform."

"Maybe we'll do it another time. Today's not a good day."

"Yeah, but all the guys'll be there. I was countin' on it, Pa!"

"You heard your father," Catherine broke in. "We'll just have to go without him. It can't be helped."

"What'll I tell the guys?"

"Tell them your father was called away by duty."

Thompson took a woolen shawl from the coatrack and draped it over Catherine's shoulders. She gave him a sheepish smile, aware that her conspiracy with the boy had been uncovered. He grinned, squeezing her arm, and she kissed him on the cheek. As he opened the door, Bobby jumped back with surprise. Clell Miller, one of the police officers, stood with his hand raised to knock.

"Sorry about that, Marshal. Didn't mean to scare nobody."

"No harm done," Thompson said. "What can I do for you?"

Catherine slipped past them. "We have to run or we'll be late. Come along, Bobby."

The boy reluctantly followed his mother out the door. As they went down the front steps, Thompson looked back at Miller. "What's the problem, Clell?"

"Sergeant Dennville sent me to fetch you. We've got a disturbance at Dora Kelly's house."

"What sort of disturbance?"

"One of her whores stiffed a customer. The sarge figured you'd want to know."

"Clell, he figured exactly right. Let's go."

Sergeant Dennville was seated at his desk in the squad room. A man who looked to be in his early twenties was slumped in a nearby chair. His left eye was a rainbow of purple and black.

Dennville glanced around when Thompson and Miller came through the door. He rose from behind his desk as they crossed the room, his expression one of sober amusement. He motioned to the young man.

" 'Morning, Marshal," he said. "This gentleman is Amos Barber. He'd like to file a complaint."

The young man got to his feet. His left eye was almost swollen shut, discolored from the eyebrow to the cheekbone. He nodded with a hangdog look of shame. "Sorry to get you out on a Sunday, Marshal."

"Don't worry about it," Thompson said. "That's quite a shiner you've got there. Who slugged you?"

"The bouncer at Dora Kelly's place. I wanted my money back and we got in a big argument. She finally sicced him on me."

"You wanted your money back from Dora Kelly?"

"No, the girl," Barber said. "Her name was Frankie."

"Frankie Howard," Dennville added. "She's one of Dora's whores."

Thompson nodded. "How did the girl come by your money, Mr. Barber?"

"Well—" Barber hesitated, averting his gaze. "She got me drunk and I spent the night in her room. When I woke up this morning, my wallet was empty. She robbed me."

"And that's when the trouble started?"

"All hell broke loose. I called her a thief and she called me a liar, and Dora Kelly sicced her bouncer on me. Threw me out of the place."

"How much money did you lose?"

"Everything I had in my wallet—eighteen dollars."

"We can recover your money," Thompson said. "But you'll have to testify against the girl in court. Are you willing to press charges?"

"Court?" Barber winced, clearly uncomfortable. "Will my name get put in the papers? I can't afford to lose my job."

"Where do you work?"

"I'm a teller at the First National Bank. Mr. Wooldridge wouldn't stand still for one of his employees being caught in a—parlor house. He'd fire me on the spot."

"Yeah, he's the sanctimonious sort, isn't he?"

"Marshal, he's hell on wheels when it comes to Guy Town. I'm a single man, but that wouldn't even matter. He'd still give me the boot."

Thompson considered a moment. He thought it ironic that Alexander Wooldridge was even remotely involved with a whorehouse robbery. His first instinct was to let it appear in the newspapers, and embarrass the man who had scorned him during the elections. But his responsibility was to the law, and somehow ensuring that the young bank teller wasn't made the scapegoat. He looked at Barber.

"Maybe there's a way to keep it out of court. You'll still have to file a complaint."

"Anything you say, Marshal," Barber quickly agreed. "Just so it doesn't get in the papers."

"You wait here," Thompson said. "Officer Miller will keep you company. Sergeant Dennville, you come with me."

"Yes, sir."

A short while later Thompson and Dennville entered the bordello operated by Dora Kelly. As they came through the door, a hulking bruiser of a man stopped them in the hallway. He was stoutly built, with mean eyes and the flattened nose of a prizefighter. He barred their path into the parlor.

"We're closed," he said in a surly voice. "Come back tomorrow."

"Stand aside," Thompson ordered. "I'm here to see Dora Kelly."

"She ain't seein' nobody today."

"Save yourself some grief, tough guy. Out of my way."

"You don't scare me, Thompson. What'll I get, a night in jail? Fuck off."

Thompson hardly seemed to move. The Colt appeared in his hand and he laid the barrel across the bouncer's skull with a mushy *thunk*. Stunned, the man wobbled backward, trying to raise his clenched fists, and Thompson struck him again. He went down, out cold.

Dora Kelly stormed across the parlor. She was a lumpy woman, with henna-dyed hair, and the look of a harridan. Her eyes burned with fury.

"You sorry bastard!" she screeched. "What d'you mean hittin' Sam like that!"

"You're under arrest, Dora." Thompson holstered his pistol, stepping over the bouncer. "You and one of your girls, Frankie Howard."

"You kiss my fat ass, Ben Thompson. Arrest for what?"

"Larceny, robbery, and running a bunco game. And felonious assault on the young fellow your goon worked over this morning."

"That's a pack of lies!" she fumed. "You won't never make it stick."

Thompson grinned. "We'll let the judge decide who's telling the truth. I calculate you ought to get five years, maybe ten."

"Wait a minute now, don't get crazy on me. I'll square it with the kid, even double his money. Give him free nookie the rest of his life. How's that?"

"You should have listened to Blanche Dumont. She warned everybody I wouldn't tolerate rough stuff."

"C'mon, have a heart for chrissakes!"

"Here's the only deal you'll get," Thompson said. "You and Frankie be on the evening train for Dallas. Otherwise, you're headed for prison."

"Jesus Christ!" she bellowed. "You're runnin' me out of town?"

"Dora, you're closed down as of right now. I'll have this place padlocked before the sun sets. You're through in Austin."

"You goddamn shitheel! Who gives you the right to play God?"

"I'm done talking," Thompson said sharply. "Catch a train or go to jail. What's your pleasure?"

"Some choice," she snapped. "I'll catch the train."

"Couple of other things."

"Christ, what now?"

"Take your friend along." Thompson said, jerking a thumb at the bouncer. "I want him out of Austin."

"Sam goes wherever I go. What's the other thing?"

"I'll have the eighteen dollars you took off young Mr. Barber."

She pulled a wad of cash from the pocket of her housecoat. After peeling off several bills, she slapped them into his hand. Her features were set in an angry scowl.

"I hope you burn in hell."

"Don't miss your train, Dora."

Thompson stepped over the bouncer, who was leaking blood on the carpet. He went through the hallway and out the door, followed by Dennville. On the street, they walked toward the corner in silence. Dennville finally gave him a curious sidewise look.

"You're better with a pistol than I am a billy club. Where'd you learn that trick?"

"In the Kansas cowtowns," Thompson said. "Bat Masterson calls it 'buffaloing' a man."

"Neat work," Dennville said with admiration. "Same goes for Dora, too. We're better rid of her."

"You might say Dora was an object lesson."

"What's an object lesson?"

"A demonstration that we're serious."

"Nobody's ever gonna doubt that."

Thompson was pleased with the morning's work. He thought the story would be all over the sporting district by nightfall. A story with a moral.

Get straight or get out of town.

TWENTY

The story quickly made the rounds. All over Guy Town, madams and cardsharps realized that Thompson was in dead earnest. Anyone who bent the law was certain to become acquainted with the city jail. A serious infraction would likely result in a one-way train ticket.

On Monday, the newspapers offered differing versions of the incident. The *Statesman* dryly reported that Marshal Thompson had "exported Dora Kelly and one of her lady boarders to climes farther north." The *Republican* commented that "Our new marshal now operates a kangaroo court, with himself as judge and jury." No one questioned he would skirt the letter of the law when it suited his notion of justice.

By the following Saturday, the sporting crowd was of mixed emotions. On the one hand, Thompson rejected any alliance with the reformers, whose goal was nothing less than the abolition of Guy Town. On the other, he enforced his own moral code with harsh measures, rigidly intolerant of anything that smacked of underhanded schemes. He upheld the right of men to gamble, carouse, and fornicate within certain bounds. He punished anyone who stepped across the line.

Thompson normally went home for supper. He found that the hours of a lawman were somewhat similar to those of a gambler. All forms of crime, from simple burglary to armed robbery, were more prevalent once the sun went down. Not surprisingly, he'd discovered that Saturday was the busiest night of the week for a peace officer. Saturday was payday for workingmen, and with money in their pockets, Saturday night was their night to howl. He skipped supper at home to tend to business.

On Saturday, November 20, he was seated in his office. He'd returned around six o'clock from an early supper in a nearby café. Sergeant Lon Dennville was now at supper, and Clell Miller was manning the squad room. There were five officers on the streets, with four of those assigned to patrol Guy Town. Later, Thompson and Dennville would tour the sporting district, appearing unannounced in gaming dives and saloons. Their presence generally served to put the rowdier element on notice.

Over the past two weeks Thompson had become fast friends with Lon Dennville. Their relationship was still one of chief lawman and second in command; but an easy trust now existed between them. Dennville, little by little, had opened up and revealed how the department had operated before the election. Ed Creary, he noted, had kept to the office, rarely venturing onto the streets, particularly on a Saturday night. He'd made it a practice to show up after a troublesome situation had been quelled. Usually just in time to provide a quote for the newspapers.

Thompson was hardly surprised. His assessment of the former marshal had always been that of a man who left the dirty work to others, and took the credit. Nor was he overly amazed when Dennville explained how the system of payoffs from the dives had operated. Carl Allen made the weekly collections, and Creary ordered the other men on the force to overlook irregularities and crooked games. The men detested Creary, with the exception of Allen, and their honesty had never been put to the test. Creary kept all of the graft for himself, with a token payment to Allen.

Thompson once asked Dennville why he hadn't quit the force. Dennville explained that he had a wife and three children, and political corruption was no reason for them to go hungry. He'd signed on as a policeman seven years ago, serving under four different city marshals in that time. Slowly, by steering clear of politics, he had worked his way through the ranks, finally being promoted to sergeant. Out of the four marshals, Creary was the only crook and Dennville had turned a blind eye to the payoffs. He thought Creary would never be elected to a second term.

Still, reflecting on the past two weeks, Thompson was somewhat less sanguine. Without hard proof, the mayor and the city council would never have turned on Creary. To indict the man they had supported for office, particularly on the basis of rumor, would have been to indict themselves. When Thompson decided to run for election, they'd found a solution that made them look good with the voters. Otherwise, Ed Creary might be sitting in the marshal's office tonight.

Dennville rapped on the door. "Not interrupting anything, am I?"

"Nothing monumental," Thompson said. "I was thinking about Ed Creary."

"What about him?"

"How the election could have gone the other way. It was my word against his about the payoffs. There was no proof."

"There was no evidence," Dennville amended. "The sporting crowd knew it, and they're the worst gossips in the world. That was enough for the voters."

Thompson lit a cheroot. "Good thing, too," he said, exhaling smoke. "Otherwise I'd be dealing poker tonight."

"Guess where Creary is tonight?"

"You sound like you know something I don't."

"The Lone Star," Dennville said soberly. "Ned Parker hired him to ride shotgun on the gaming operation. How's that for a joke?"

"Pretty sad," Thompson observed. "Creary's got no taste for trouble. Why would Parker hire him?"

"Parker's bouncers can handle any trouble. I think Creary's just window-dressing."

"I don't follow you, Lon."

"Former marshal, defender of the law, all that stuff. A testimonial that the games at the Lone Star are straight."

"That won't wash," Thompson said. "We just agreed everybody knows Creary was accepting payoffs. Why would anyone take his word on straight games?"

Dennville shrugged. "Maybe any window-dressing's better than none at all. Maybe Parker hired him out of charity. I haven't got the answer myself."

There was a protracted moment of silence. Thompson stared off into space, puffing thoughtfully on his cheroot. He knew Ned Parker to be a cagey operator, slick and shrewd. A man who never acted without purpose.

"Maybe we're missing the message," he said at length. "What if Parker wanted to show the sporting crowd he's not impressed with me or my badge? What better way than to hire Ed Creary?"

"Yeah, I suppose," Dennville said doubtfully. "But we'd still close him down if he's running crooked games. What's the point?"

"Parker's always got something up his sleeve. What you see isn't necessarily what you get."

"So what do we do?"

Thompson stood. "Let's head on down to Guy Town."

"We were anyway," Dennville said. "Do I hear the wheels turning? You got something in mind, Marshal?"

"You check out a few saloons, and I'll stop by the Lone Star. Just to pay my regards."

"Are you talking about Parker or Creary?"

"I'll know when I get there."

The Lone Star was packed. On a Saturday night men from throughout Travis County traveled to Guy Town. Their pilgrimage was in pursuit of women, liquor, and games of chance. The sporting crowd invariably sent them home with hangovers and empty pockets, no wiser for the experience. The dives were always mobbed on payday.

Thompson walked through the door shortly after seven o'clock. The evening was off to a fast start, with men ganged three deep at the bar. The gaming layouts were crowded as well, knots of men chasing fortune with more abandon than skill. A whoop of laughter went up as someone rolled a winner at a dice table.

All around the room, men turned as Thompson moved past the gaming layouts. His uniform drew attention, and his name was known throughout the county. The election, and his campaign to bring honest gambling to Guy Town, had won him many friends. Few men understood how the games were rigged, but every man wanted a fair shake. His election as marshal was widely applauded.

Halfway through the crowd, Thompson paused and watched the action at a twenty-one layout. The dealer was aware of his scrutiny, and nervously dealt a hand around the board. His apparent interest in twenty-one was actually a dodge, for his attention was focused on a faro layout at the next table. Out of the corner of his eye, he watched the dealer finish out an entire deck of cards. He detected no sleight-of-hand.

Ed Creary was standing at the end of the bar. He watched Thompson while Thompson pretended to watch the twenty-one game. His eyes were guarded as Thompson turned away and moved on through the crowd, pausing briefly at one of the dice tables. He suspected the purpose of the visit was not gambling; but rather his newly announced position with the Lone Star. He tried to appear indifferent when Thompson approached the bar.

"Well, Mr. Creary," Thompson said expansively. "I understand you've found gainful employment. How's it going?"

"No complaints," Creary said stiffly. "So far, it beats politics."

"I wasn't aware you had any experience at gambling. How'd you come to land the job?"

"Are you asking out of personal curiosity?"

Thompson made an offhand gesture. "Just like to keep tabs on who's who in Guy Town."

"I'm the house manager," Creary told him. "Not that it's any of your business."

"Last time we met you were hot under the collar. Sounds like you're still carrying a grudge."

"Take it any way you want. I don't owe you an explanation."

"Not as long as you obey the law."

The door to the office opened, Ned Parker looked from one to the other, his expression cloudy. He nodded to Thompson. "What brings you around, Marshal?"

"Thought I'd give you a pat on the back," Thompson said with some irony. "From the looks of things, you're operating on the square. How's it feel to be legit?"

"Nobody ever said I wasn't."

"Nobody except me. But like they say, that's water under the bridge. You're on the right track, Ned."

"Glad you approve," Parker remarked. "Anything else on your mind?"

"No, just that I see you've hired Mr. Creary. You'll make a good team."

"Why don't I believe you mean that?"

"You're a suspicious man, Ned."

"Marshal!"

Gabe Ewing, one of the city policemen, pushed through the crowd. His mouth hung open, revealing a gold tooth, and he was breathing heavily. He skidded to a halt.

"Sergeant Dennville wants you muy pronto! There's a brawl over at the Cosmopolitan."

"Anybody hurt?"

"Will be unless they're stopped. Gawddamn cowboys got into it with the railroad men."

"Let's go."

Thompson hurried toward the door. Outside, Ewing followed him at a fast clip, angling across the street. The Cosmopolitan, far less elegant than its name, was a hangout for railroad workers. Ewing quickly explained that a bunch of drunken cowhands had invaded the saloon, apparently looking for a fight. The railroad men jumped to defend their territory.

Downstreet, Thompson stopped before the open doors of the Cosmopolitan. Dennville and three policemen were busting heads with their nightsticks, trying to wedge a path into the melee. The saloon was a wreck, tables and chairs upturned, and the backbar mirror shattered. Cowhands and railroad workers pounded away in a slugfest, grunting and cursing in a riotous donnybrook. The floor was littered with dazed and bloodied men.

Thompson stepped through the doors. He pulled his pistol, holding it overhead, and fired three shots into the ceiling. The roar of the Colt bracketed off the walls, the echo deafening in the confined quarters of the room. Everything abruptly stopped, men frozen with their arms cocked to throw a punch and others locked in a stilled wrestling match. The combatants stared toward the door, slowly separating, their eyes fixed on the uniformed man with a gun. A leaden silence settled over the saloon.

"Fun's over!" Thompson shouted, wagging the snout of his pistol. "You boys back off and stand easy. *Now.*"

Warily, their eyes on the gun, the men broke apart. The cowhands congregated near the bar, assisting their fallen comrades to their feet. The railroad workers collected their own wounded and gathered along the opposite wall. They stood loosely bunched, staring daggers at one another, reduced to bloodied silence. Not a man among them was unscathed.

Dennville walked forward. "Wish I'd thought of a gun. You damn sure got their attention."

"What happened?" Thompson asked.

"You know cowboys," Dennville said with disgust. "Saturday night's a complete loss unless they find a fight. They busted in here, just itching for trouble."

"What about the railroad men?"

"They didn't have much choice in the matter. It was a fight or run."

Thompson looked at the cowhands. "You boys are under arrest and let's not hear any back talk. Everybody outside . . . right now."

Dennville and his men spread out along the bar. They herded the cowboys, fourteen in number, through the front doors. A few minutes later they had them formed in columns of twos, somewhat like a squad of battered soldiers. They stood slump-shouldered in the center of the street.

"Hold on a goddamn minute!"

A large, gangly man came hurrying up the sidewalk. He was stuffing his shirt in his trousers, breathing hard. He slammed to a halt before Thompson.

"What's going on here, Marshal?"

"Who are you?"

"Floyd Ollinger," the man said. "I own the Circle O spread outside Round Rock. These are my boys."

Thompson nodded. "You look like you got caught with your pants down, Mr. Ollinger."

"Well, hell, I was over at Blanche Dumont's house. Somebody busted in and told me my boys was in a fix."

"Your boys are headed for jail."

"What's the charge?"

"Drunk and disorderly, breach of peace, and resisting arrest. I'll likely think of something else by the time we get them locked up."

Ollinger groaned. "Ain't there some way besides jail, Marshal? I'd gladly pay for any damages."

"No, sir, no other way," Thompson said. "Austin is the state capital, not a cowtown. You ought to teach your boys the difference."

Dennville marched the squad of cowhands toward Congress Avenue. Thompson nodded curtly to the rancher and walked off behind the column. A reporter was standing at curbside, scribbling furiously in his notepad. He had his story for the night in Guy Town.

The *Statesman* ran it in the Sunday morning edition. A bold headline was centered below the fold on the front page.

CITY MARSHAL DECLARES
AUSTIN NOT A COWTOWN;
ARRESTS COWBOY TOUGHS

TWENTY-ONE

On Tuesday morning Thompson left the house around nine o'clock. He was attired in a Prince Albert suit and stovepipe hat, with a fur-collared chesterfield topcoat. He walked toward the streetcar stop at the corner.

The sky was overcast, dingy clouds drifting on a sharp northerly breeze. Yet he was in a chipper mood, his stride brisk and his shoulders squared. Over breakfast, he'd read a report in the *Statesman* on the Saturday night incident in Guy Town. The fourteen cowhands had been held in jail until their hearing yesterday morning in city court. Judge Horace Warren had fined them fifty dollars each and assessed a thousand dollars in damages.

Floyd Ollinger, the rancher who employed them, had paid heavily for a night on the town. The *Statesman* reported that he had shelled out almost two thousand dollars, including court costs, to secure the release of his crew. Thompson had received congratulations from the mayor, the sheriff, and a brief but laudatory note from the state house. Governor Oran Roberts commended him on a job well done, and his knack for the succinct phrase. Austin was indeed no longer a cowtown!

In celebration, Thompson had given himself the day off. Since being sworn in, slightly more than two weeks ago, he'd gone into the office every day, including Sundays. He felt he deserved a break, and in any event, he was on call in case of an emergency. Dennville was fully capable of handling routine matters, and knew where to reach him if he were needed. He had let personal affairs slide since taking office, and he couldn't put it off any longer. He planned to check the books at the Iron Front.

Downtown, he stepped off the streetcar at Mulberry and Congress Avenue. People were by now accustomed to seeing him in uniform, and he drew bemused stares from by-passers as he proceeded along the street. A few minutes later he entered the Iron Front and found the usual morning ritual already under way. The bartenders were busy stocking shelves for the noon hour rush, and a handyman was wiping down the gaming tables with a clean, damp cloth. Joe Richter was seated at the desk in the office.

"Ben!" He got to his feet with a wide grin and an effusive handshake. "I never see you anymore—except in the newspapers."

"My wife says the same thing," Thompson observed amiably. "I spend most of my time these days in Guy Town."

"Yeah, I read the *Statesman*. That was some free-for-all Saturday night. Sounds like you and your police were really outnumbered."

"Well, like the fly walking across the mirror said: It all depends on how you look at it. We had them surrounded, Joe."

Richter chuckled. "I notice you're not in uniform. Don't tell me you're playing hooky?"

"Took the day off," Thompson said. "Thought I'd have a look at the books. How are we doing?"

"By golly, Ben, I hate to toot my own horn. But things are downright zippy, and that's a fact. We're already ahead of last year."

"I should've made you a partner before now."

"Hey, better late than never. I've got no complaints."

Thompson found nothing to quibble about either. Richter got him seated at the desk and left him alone to inspect the bookkeeping ledgers. He spent an hour running figures, and finally sat back with a mild look of wonder. The date was November 23, and the Iron Front was ahead of last year by almost $12,000. All that with still a month to go before the end of the year. He told himself it was an early Christmas.

"Where's the sonovabitch that calls himself City Marshal?"

Thompson looked up with a scowl. The man in the doorway was strikingly handsome, with wavy straw-colored hair and eyes like steel-blue agates. He wore a fringed buckskin jacket and an ivory Stetson, with a brace of pistols snugged tight in a buscadero rig. The jingle-bobs on his spurs chimed musically as he stepped into the office. Thompson broke out in laughter.

"King Fisher!" he said, clasping the other man's hand. "How long's it been?"

"A year, maybe two or three. I heard these idjits up here elected you marshal. Figgered I had to see it with my own eyes."

"You came all the way to Austin for that?"

"Naw," Fisher said with a sly smile. "Got myself appointed deputy sheriff of Uvalde County. How's that for laughs?"

"I think God played a joke on somebody."

"What the hell, every dog gets his day."

King Fisher was an unlikely lawman. A rancher, his spread was near the town of Eagle Pass, some two hundred miles southwest of Austin. His checkered life had made him a legend of sorts along the border with Old Mexico. He was known to have killed seven men in gunfights, and he'd been arrested several times on charges of rustling and murder. Yet he had been acquitted in the most sensational trials ever held in Uvalde County.

Thompson considered Fisher one of his closest friends. In their wilder years, they had gambled up and down the border, on both sides of the Rio Grande. When Thompson went on to the boomtowns, traveling the gamblers' circuit, Fisher established a ranch outside Eagle Pass. He'd prospered, marrying his childhood sweetheart, and fathered four daughters. But he was still marked as a dangerous man, quick to take insult. Thompson had often thought they were peas from the same pod. And now they both wore badges.

"So what brings a big lawman like yourself to Austin?"

"Delivered a prisoner," Fisher said. "Some dimdot robbed a bank in Fort Worth and hightailed it for the border. We caught him in Piedras Negras."

"Did you now?" Thompson said, arching an eyebrow. "I seem to recall Piedras Negras is on the other side of the river. How'd you square that with the Mexicans?"

Fisher grinned. "I've got a deal with the chili peppers. They look the other way when I cross the river and nobody gets hurt. Works out real good."

"Why didn't you take your prisoner on to Fort Worth?"

"Well, you can just imagine, the Rangers got their bowels in an uproar when they heard the news. This half-assed bandit outruns 'em and outsmarts 'em, and I nail him without a hitch. They wired orders to drop him off here."

Thompson sobered. "I remember you never had much use for the Rangers. Small wonder they got bent out of shape."

Captain Lee Hall, among other Rangers, had arrested Fisher over the years. Every time, he'd managed to slip out of their net by convincing a jury he was an upstanding citizen. The Rangers thought of him as the one who got away.

"I've quit worryin' about the Rangers," Fisher said breezily. "Let 'em tend to their knittin' and I'll tend to mine."

"Will you be in town for a while?"

"Got in on the mornin' train and I'm headed back on the afternoon train. Jack Harris invited me to stop off in San Antone."

"Don't play cards with him," Thompson warned. "He's too slick by half."

Fisher looked surprised. "I figgered you and him would've patched things up by now. You still on the prod?"

"I'm not one to forget a man who rooks me. Trouble was, I couldn't prove it."

Harris owned a gambling hall and variety theater in San Antonio. A year ago, on a visit there, Thompson had gotten into a dispute with Harris over cards. He was still embittered by the experience.

"You ought to kiss and make up," Fisher said jokingly. "I'll tell him to send you a love letter."

"That'll be the day," Thompson said, waving it off. "Look here, why don't I treat you to a steak for lunch? Then I'll put you on your train."

"Hell, I never turn down a free meal. We'll kick around old times."

"Like the time that señorita's old man invited you to a shotgun wedding?"

"Jumpin' Jesus, don't remind me!"

Their laughter carried into the club as they walked from the office. Thompson's chipper mood was brightened even more by the appearance of an old friend. A friend from what was now the good old days.

They swapped stories over thick steaks charred blood-red in the center.

Early that evening the men began wandering into the Iron Front. Mayor Wheeler and James Shipe were the first to arrive, followed in short order by the law partners, Luther Edwards and Jack Walton. Will Cullen, the liquor wholesaler, came in a little after eight.

The men gathered in the private room at the rear of the club. Their weekly poker game, revived shortly after the elections, was no great secret. Thompson gambled nowhere else, and he felt he'd upheld his promise to the voters. The game, in his opinion, was a social affair, more recreation than gambling. He had to work at not winning.

A cider glow from the overhead lamp lighted the table. The walls, paneled in dark hardwood, gave the room a certain elegance, and a sideboard was stocked with liquor. The men took their customary chairs after pouring themselves a drink, ready for an evening of friendly rivalry. James Shipe, since he was a banker, acted as the game's banker. He exchanged chips for cash.

Thompson shuffled, his hands deftly working the cards. He dealt around the board, flipping the cards face-up on the table. The first man to catch an ace would have the opening deal, and tonight that was Luther Edwards. He called five-card stud, again shuffling the cards, and allowed Wheeler, who was seated on his right, to cut the deck. The men anted a dollar.

"Damnedest thing," Cullen said as he peeked at his hole card. "I've gotten used to seeing Ben around town in his uniform. He looks like somebody else in a suit and tie."

"King bets three." Walton, who was high on the board, tossed in three chips. "Now that you mention it, I prefer the uniform. It gives him an air of . . . dignity."

"Look who's talking," Thompson retorted, calling the bet. "Maybe we ought to require lawyers to wear uniforms. You boys could use some dignity."

"Ouch!" Walton said, pulling a face. "I think I got hoisted on my own petard."

Shipe folded his hand. "Don't let him kid you, Ben. You're doing a fine job and everybody here knows it. You're the talk of the town."

"And the newspapers," Wheeler said, dropping chips into the pot. "Even the *Republican* can't find fault with the police department. That in itself is an achievement."

"Have to raise," Edwards said. "Bump it three."

Everyone paused to inspect his hand. He had a jack showing, and he gave them a crafty smile. Cullen folded his cards. "Just goes to show you about lawyers. Dealt himself a pair of jacks."

"Luther likes to bluff," Walton said, throwing in a handful of chips. "Your three and raise you five."

"I'm convinced." Thompson turned his up card face-down. "I doubt you're both bluffing."

Wheeler studied on it a moment. Then, with a reluctant sigh, he dropped out. Edwards and Walton, the two attorneys, were the only ones left in the hand. They played the next three cards, betting and raising, enjoying themselves immensely. At the end, Walton turned up a king high, still certain his partner was bluffing. Edwards won it with a pair of jacks.

"How 'bout them apples!" he crowed. "Dealt myself a winner."

"Your time's coming," Walton joshed him. "I'll get you before the night's over."

Thompson watched the byplay with amused interest. He knew their style of poker, and he'd read them and their cards from the outset. Edwards was a conservative player, who rarely bluffed. By contrast, Walton regularly bet and raised on the come, chasing a winning hand. He thought it fortunate that their livelihood was derived from the practice of law. Poker was not their game.

Cullen began shuffling the cards. Shipe, who was seated to Thompson's left, glanced around. "That was quite a story in the *Statesman*. Judge Warren really stuck it to those cowboys."

"Hooray and hallelujah!" Wheeler cackled. "That two thousand went straight into the city treasury. At this rate, Austin may have its first surplus in years." He laughed humorously. "Keep those fines coming, Ben."

"Take it easy on crime, though," Walton said with mock concern. "You're liable to put us lawyers out of business."

"The governor thinks different," Thompson said. "I got a real nice note from him yesterday."

"What—" Wheeler blurted out. "You got a note from Oran Roberts?"

"Just a few lines about those cowboys. He said something like 'a job well done.' "

"I'll be a monkey's uncle," Wheeler muttered. "Nobody in City Hall ever got a note from Oran Roberts. You're the first."

Edwards chortled out loud. "You're just a bunch of bureaucrats. Ben's jailing rowdies and posting whores out of town. The governor knows who deserves credit."

"Don't make too much of it," Thompson interjected. "I told you, it was a little note. Maybe ten lines."

"That's not the point," Wheeler said. "Oran Roberts is a skinflint with compliments. Consider it high praise."

"Whatever you say," Thompson said, uncomfortable with the attention. "We sort of got off track here, gents. Let's play poker."

Cullen called five-card draw. A sizeable pot developed, and Shipe won it with three fours. The game shifted back and forth throughout the evening, with no heavy winner. But between hands, the talk was of the note from Governor Oran Roberts. No one thought it anything less than remarkable.

By the end of the evening Thompson was worn out with the talk. He was gratified by the esteem of men he respected, particularly these men. But he felt himself too much in the limelight, and purposely folded several strong hands. There was room for more than one winner among friends.

He managed to lose a hundred for the night.

TWENTY-TWO

A tawny sun flooded the land. The sky was clear and there was a crisp wind out of the north. The warmth of the sunlight took the bite out of the air.

Lute Walker drove a farm wagon south toward Austin. Seated beside him was his wife, Selma, wrapped in a woolen greatcoat against the morning chill. Their team of horses, a roan and a blaze-faced sorrel, puffed frosty snorts with every breath. Winter was upon the hilly countryside.

The Walkers were black landholders. Their farm was located some ten miles northeast of Austin, along Bluebonnet Creek. They were in their forties, married for nearly seventeen years, and to their great regret, childless. Selma was barren.

Every Saturday the Walkers drove into town. Like farmers from all over Travis County, they came to town once a week to stock provisions and visit with their friends. These brief trips were especially rewarding for the Walkers; their few friends were widely scattered around the county. They were the only colored people on Bluebonnet Creek.

Today's trip was even more meaningful. It was the first Saturday in December, and there were plans to be made for the Christmas season. Every year a special service was held at the Evangelical Baptist Church of Austin, the largest black church in the county. People drove for miles to attend a pageant celebrating the birth of Jesus.

Lute and Selma were former slaves. Following the Civil War, when they were freed, their first act was to enter into wedlock. Then, quickly departing a cotton plantation in Eastern Texas, they traveled west in search of the Promised Land. The Union government offered them forty acres and a mule to start them on the path to freedom. They settled in the hill country outside Austin.

Those were unusual times for freedmen in Texas. The summer of '65, the Union Army of Occupation took charge of the state with an iron hand. Union commanders held the power of life and death; their word was law, without appeal or mitigation. The verdict of a military tribunal was final, and former Confederates were treated to harsh justice. Black men, for the first time in their lives, were equal before the law.

Carpetbaggers swarmed into Texas from the North. Loyal Unionists, northern born, they occupied the civil posts vacated by the rule of occupation. Next came the scalawags, southern-born turncoats, swearing allegiance to the Union in return for a license to steal. Between them they held every government office of importance, from governor to county judge. Their dictates were enforced by the bayonets of federal troops.

Yet it all ended in March 1870. Texas was readmitted to the Union, and the occupation forces went on to other duties. Carpetbaggers and scalawags were turned out of office, and native Texans once more governed the Lone Star State. For black freedmen, it was as though the clock had been set back to bleaker times. They were reduced to second-class citizens, denied the vote; no longer equal before the law. They were niggers again.

Lute and Selma Walker nonetheless prospered. By watching every nickel, they were able to purchase another forty acres from a disenchanted freedman. The land was bountiful, and while they would never be wealthy, they were comfortable. Devout Christians, they gave thanks at Christmas by providing for the less fortunate. Their meeting today with Reverend Titus Lacy was for that very reason. No needy family would go wanting on the day Christ was born.

Halfway into town the steady drum of hoofbeats sounded to their rear. Lute Walker looked over his shoulder and his brow squinched in a tight frown. Two riders, cowhands from the Box B Ranch, were rapidly gaining on the wagon. One was Clint Buchanan, a burly man with a mean streak and a hair-trigger temper. The other was Ross Taylor, tall and lanky, no less loutish than his partner. They were known to Walker, and best avoided. He glanced at his wife.

"Keep your mouth shut," he warned. "Don't pay no 'tention to what they say. Let me do the talkin'."

Selma sniffed. "I got no truck with white trash."

"You mind me now, woman!"

The cowhands reined in alongside the wagon.

Buchanan leaned forward on his saddlehorn. "Well, looky who we got here. Where you headed, Rufus?"

"Jes' into town," Walker said, gripping the reins tightly. "Got things to do."

"High and mighty, ain't you?" Buchanan growled. "Never a 'yes, sir' or a 'no, sir' or any other kind of sir.' You're talkin' to a white man, boy."

"Whyn't you jes' let us be, Mistuh Buchanan? We don't want no trouble with you folks."

"Hell, you're the one causin' all the trouble. Ain't that right, Ross?"

"Damn sure a fact," Taylor agreed. "What we got here is a coon that don't know his place."

Ethan Bullock, owner of the Box B, had been trying to buy Walker's farm for years. He loathed the idea of a black man farming eighty acres that abutted the southern quadrant of his rangeland. Neither the offer of money nor petty acts of harassment had altered the situation. He routinely encouraged his men to bedevil the Walkers.

"Helluva note," Buchanan said in a surly voice. "You oughta show a little respect, Rufus. Nobody likes a smart-ass coon."

Selma Walker jerked around. "Git on away from here, white trash. Go on, *git*!"

"You hear that?" Buchanan bellowed. "Sorry bitch called us white trash."

Taylor flushed. "I never could stand an uppity nigger. We gonna take that, Buck?"

Buchanan pulled his pistol. "Stop that gawddamn wagon! Do it or I'll plug you."

Walker hauled back on the reins. Buchanan and Taylor, waving their pistols, forced the couple to dismount from the wagon. Then, while Buchanan covered them, Taylor jumped into the wagon and drove off. They stood watching their wagon and team disappear down the road.

Buchanan rode away, leading Taylor's horse. He called back over his shoulder. "So long for now, black-bird!"

"Lordy," Walker muttered, fixing his wife with a look. "Told you to mind your mouth."

"I don't take nothin' off no white trash!"

"Well, you done done it now, woman."

Lute and Selma Walker trudged off toward Austin.

Thompson was seated in his office. He'd just returned from the noon meal and he felt comfortably stuffed. So far it had been relatively quiet for a Saturday, with only one incident in Guy Town. He knew that would change by nightfall.

The sound of voices drifted in from the squad room. He heard the deep rumble of a man's voice and the strident tones of a woman in some distress. A moment later Sergeant Dennville appeared in the doorway with a black couple. He ushered them into the office.

"Marshal Thompson," he said, motioning them forward, "this is Mr. and Mrs. Walker. Thought you ought to hear their story. They've been robbed."

"Come right in, folks," Thompson said, indicating chairs before his desk. "Have a seat and tell me what happened."

"Thank you kindly." Selma Walker seated herself and her husband took the other chair. "We been walkin' more'n three hours. I'm plumb wore out."

"I wouldn't wonder," Thompson said sympathetically. "Whereabouts were you robbed?"

Lute Walker cleared his throat. "'Bout five miles out on the Phlugerville Road. Took our wagon and team."

"What about your money?"

"No, suh, Marshal, they wasn't after money. Them boys jes' set on makin' trouble."

"Why would they do that?"

"'Cause they trash!" Selma Walker said hotly. "Ol' man Bullock all the time sic 'em on us. Wasn't the first time."

"Ethan Bullock, the rancher?" Thompson asked. "Are you saying you know these men?"

"We knows 'em," Walker intoned heavily. "Couple of cowhands what works for the Box B. Clint Buchanan and Ross Taylor."

"So they've hoorahed you before?"

"Couldn't hardly count the times. Bullock wants our land and we ain't gonna sell. He jes' keeps on pushin' and pushin'."

Thompson despised a bully. He could never tolerate the strong using force to intimidate the weak. The fact that the Walkers were colored only made it worse. There was no practical way for them to fight a white man. The times were against them.

"We'll find these men," Thompson promised. "Would you be willing to testify in court? That's the only way we can bring charges."

"We surely will," Selma Walker affirmed. "The likes of them belongs in jail."

Walker looked concerned. "What about our wagon and team, Marshal? We ain't fixed to buy another."

"We'll do our best, Mr. Walker. You have my word on it."

"Lordy mercy," the woman said, turning to her husband. "How we gonna git home, Lute? I cain't walk no more."

"Don't you worry," Walker assured her. "Reverend Lacy find us a way home. We *be fine*."

Thompson rose. "Let me know where you'll be, Mr. Walker. Just in case we find your wagon."

"We come back here before we leave town. I appreciates all you done, Marshal."

"No thanks necessary, Mr. Walker. Glad to be of service."

Dennville showed them out of the office. He returned a moment later. "I was thinking maybe we should notify the sheriff. They were robbed outside the city limits."

"Good idea," Thompson said. "Send Miller over to the courthouse. Tell Sheriff Horner we're working on it."

"How do you want it handled?"

"I'd like you to take a tour of Guy Town. It's Saturday, and those cowboys probably headed for the nearest saloon. Or maybe one of the whorehouses. Try to get a line on them."

Dennville nodded. "Do you want them arrested?"

"No," Thompson said firmly. "Way it sounds, we've got ourselves a couple of hardcases. Come get me if you find them."

"You think they'll fight?"

"Lon, I never try to second-guess cowboys. They're apt to do anything."

"I'll go have a look around."

Dennville turned out of the doorway. Thompson lit a cheroot and leaned back in his chair. He puffed a wad of smoke, reflecting on the Walkers and their long hike into town. No one deserved to be treated that roughly.

He thought the men responsible belonged on a rock pile.

* * *

The whorehouse was located on Live Oak Street. A favorite with cowboys, it was three blocks west of the stockyards. The girls, priced to please, were two dollars a pop.

Directly across the street was a saloon. Dennville waited inside by a fly-blown window, watching the bordello. Tied to a sturdy rack outside the house were four saddle horses and a team hitched to a farm wagon. The team matched the description given to him by the Walkers.

Upstreet he saw Thompson round the corner with Gabe Ewing. He'd sent Ewing, one of the officers on the day shift, to notify the marshal. As they walked toward the saloon, he moved to the door and stepped outside. He jerked a thumb at the whorehouse as they halted on the curb.

"Our boys are over there," he said. "I went around to the back door and talked with Sallie Dagget, the madam. She identified them as Clint Buchanan and Ross Taylor."

Thompson stared across the street. "You'd think they would've ditched the wagon and team. Wonder what was in their minds?"

"Well, like you said, never try to second-guess cowboys. Maybe they figured black folks wouldn't report a robbery."

"How many men in the house?"

"Just four," Dennville replied. "When I talked with Sallie, they were all upstairs with girls. That was about thirty minutes ago."

"So they could be downstairs by now."

"I'd say that's a safe bet."

Thompson nodded to Ewing. "Gabe, I want you to cover the back door. We'll come through the front and try to take them without a fight. Watch yourself if they make a run for the alley."

"I'll be waitin' if they do, Marshal."

Ewing hurried toward the corner. Thompson gave him five minutes, then led Dennville across the street. They entered the front door into an alcove that opened onto the parlor. Two girls, dressed in filmy housecoats, were drinking with two men at a small bar along the opposite wall. An older woman, seated on a sofa by the window, looked around at Dennville. Her head bobbed imperceptibly at the two men.

"Everybody stand easy," Thompson said in a stern voice. "Clint Buchanan? Ross Taylor?"

"That's us," Buchanan said brusquely. "What about it?"

"You're under arrest for robbery of a wagon and team."

"You gotta be shittin' me. We took that wagon off ol' Tarbaby Walker. Wasn't nothin' but a joke."

"Your joke misfired," Thompson told him. "Armed robbery's a prison offense. Drop your gun belts."

"No goddamn way!" Buchanan snarled. "I ain't gonna be arrested over no nigger."

"Me neither," Taylor said, backing away. "You just leave us the hell be."

"Hold it," Thompson ordered. "Don't do anything stupid."

"We ain't ascared of you, Thompson."

"Drop your guns—*now*."

Buchanan ducked low behind the bar. Taylor grabbed one of the girls, an arm around her neck, using her as a shield. Thompson drew his pistol, his attention fixed on the bar. Dennville advanced on the girl and Taylor, gun in hand.

Buchanan popped up from behind the bar. He eared the hammer on his Colt in a metallic whirr, and fired. The slug nicked the doorjamb in a spray of splinters and flecked paint. Thompson feathered the trigger and Buchanan's head exploded in a mist of brains and bone matter. He dropped as though struck by a thunderbolt.

The girl squirmed aside, kicking Taylor in the leg. He yelped, clawing at his holster, and brought his six-gun level. Dennville, pistol extended at arm's length, shot him in the chest. A bright dot stained his shirtfront and he stumbled backward, legs tangled. He pitched to the floor on his back.

Sallie Daggett fainted. She slumped sideways on the sofa, her mouth ajar. One of the girls froze, her eyes blank, and the other sank to her knees, head buried in her hands. The acrid stench of gunsmoke, permeated with the odor of blood and death, filled the room. No one moved.

Dennville slowly lowered his pistol. He stared at the dead men with a look of numbed shock. His face was knotted with revulsion.

"Jesus," he said quietly. "They knew they couldn't win. Why'd they fight?"

Thompson grunted. "Some men won't be convinced."

"Convinced of what?"

"Not to get killed."

TWENTY-THREE

On Monday morning, Thompson arrived at the office early. He was carrying copies of the *Statesman* and the *Republican*, which he hadn't taken time to read at breakfast. The shooting was headlined in each of the papers.

Dennville and the other officers greeted him as he moved through the squad room. The graveyard shift was being relieved by the day shift, and half the force was momentarily present. The men watched with guarded respect as he went through the door of his office.

Their attitude toward Dennville had altered as well. Until Saturday, the sergeant had never killed a man in the line of duty. Like most police officers, he'd rarely had occasion to pull a gun, relying instead on a nightstick. Yet he had acquitted himself well in the shootout, and the men treated him with newfound respect. He was something of a celebrity in the squad room.

Thompson took a seat behind his desk. After lighting a cheroot, he unfolded the *Statesman*, the date on the masthead December 6. He'd purposely avoided reading the article at breakfast, wary of further exciting Bobby. The youngster was already bursting with pride that his father had killed a man while wearing the badge of city marshal. The article was less sensational than Thompson had expected.

A straightforward accounting of the gunfight was first presented. The paper called it an unfortunate incident, brought on by two unruly cowboys already wanted for robbery. There was a brief report of how the cowboys had stolen a wagon and team at gunpoint from an unarmed colored man and his wife. Thompson and Dennville were commended for their courage under fire and their devotion to duty. The article went on with accolades for the police department.

Austin had never been more orderly. Since the election, our community had enjoyed one of the dullest months in police circles in a long time, all due to stricter law enforcement. Every law-abiding citizen should consider it a worthy tribute to City Marshal Ben Thompson and his officers.

Underscoring the point, the article then related statistics from the police blotter. For the past month, there had been no murders or assaults, and only one burglary within the city limits. The offenses were minor in nature, ranging from vagrancy and intoxication to keeping a disorderly house and disturbing the peace. All told, the number of arrests totaled only seventy-seven, a further reflection on the efficiency of the new city marshal. The article ended on a laudatory note.

Thompson next turned to the *Republican*. George Harris, the editor, was at some pains to stress Saturday's gunfight. His article dwelled on the virtual certainty of violence and bloodshed when a "shootist" occupied the office of city marshal. Yet, once he'd vented his spleen, he reluctantly admitted the overall drop in the crime rate. He attributed this to a general fear of Thompson, rather than efficient police work. Still, he was unable to distort what remained the central fact. Austin's streets were safer under the new marshal.

All in all, Thompson was satisfied with the coverage. He'd fully expected Harris to again raise the specter of a "shootist" wearing a badge. But when he put aside the *Republican*, he thought it had cost the editor dearly to recognize in print the reduction in crime. The article contained little in the way of praise, and that in itself was hardly surprising. He was nonetheless pleased with the token acknowledgment of a job well done. Hard facts were difficult to ignore.

Dennville rapped on the door. "You've got a visitor— Alexander Wooldridge."

"I'll be damned," Thompson said, somewhat startled. "Show him in, Lon."

A moment later Wooldridge entered the office. His normally stern expression seemed somehow tempered. "Good morning, Marshal," he said evenly. "I trust I'm not intruding."

"Not at all," Thompson replied, motioning him to a chair. "What can I do for you, Mr. Wooldridge?"

The banker got himself seated. "I've read those articles," he said, nodding at the newspapers on the desk. "I'm here to make a confession."

"Confession?"

"Thompson, I've always considered myself a

forthright man. I want you to know that I now believe I misjudged you."

"Did you?" Thompson said, unwilling to let him off the hook. "Are you talking about me, personally, or my work as a peace officer?"

Wooldridge shifted uncomfortably in his chair. "I opposed your election for what I considered sound reasons. I see now that my concerns were misplaced. You've done an excellent job."

"I have to admit I'm curious, Mr. Wooldridge. Why the sudden change of heart?"

"Simply put, I was wrong. Austin has benefited by your election to office. I felt obligated to say as much."

"How about this?" Thompson said, tapping the *Republican* with his finger. "George Harris claims I'm still a 'shootist' with a badge. Doesn't that bother you?"

"Not greatly," Wooldridge observed. "You once said to me that you'd never shot a man who hadn't fired on you first. The death of those cowboys was regrettable, very sad indeed. But I now take your point."

"That's good to hear, and I appreciate the sentiment. I know it wasn't easy for you to come here."

"I never allow pride to stand in the way of principle. You deserved an apology."

"Let's just say all's well that ends well."

"One other thing." Wooldridge hesitated, his features solemn. "I'm in your debt for that unsavory affair with Amos Barber. Your discretion saved me a good deal of embarrassment."

The name rang a bell. Thompson abruptly remembered the young bank teller who had been robbed and beaten in a whorehouse. His brow arched in question.

"How'd you find out about Amos Barber?"

"There's little in Austin I don't know about."

"Did you fire him?"

"Nooo," Wooldridge said slowly. "But I daresay Mr. Barber won't be visiting Guy Town again. In a manner of speaking, he's seen the light."

"I'm glad to hear it," Thompson said. "He just got in with some bad company. No harm done."

"Yes, thanks to you, Marshal."

Wooldridge got to his feet. They exchanged a handshake and the banker walked toward the door. Thompson dropped back into his chair, still somewhat surprised by the unannounced visit. Dennville entered the office.

"Just call me nosy," he said. "What the deuce did he want?"

"Absolution."

"For what?"

"Deceit and deception."

"Who'd he deceive?"

Thompson smiled. "Himself."

There was another surprise awaiting Thompson that evening. Bobby met him at the door when he came home for supper. The boy was jumping with excitement.

"Uncle Billy's here!" he yelled. "He brought me some real Mexican spurs!"

Catherine and Billy were seated in the parlor. Thompson moved across the room as his brother rose from the sofa. Billy wrung his hand with a broad grin, inspecting the uniform. He cocked one eye in a wry look.

"I didn't hear any music," he said jocularly. "Where'd you leave your band?"

Thompson laughed. "You're looking at the latest thing in police uniforms. Designed it myself."

"You could've fooled me. You're tricked out fine enough to lead a parade."

"Pa! Pa!" Bobby demanded. "Lookit here!"

The youngster proudly displayed a pair of Mexican spurs. The shanks and heel bands were in bright silver, engraved with an intricate leafy pattern. The hand-tooled leather straps were decorated with silver conchas, and the rowels resembled spiked buzzsaws. Bobby's eyes danced with merriment.

"You ever see anything like that, Pa? Uncle Billy brought 'em all the way from Mexico."

"They're dandy, all right," Thompson said, properly impressed. "We'll have to get you some fancy boots."

"And a horse!" the boy whooped. "Will you get me a horse, too, Pa?"

"I'll have to think about that. A horse is a big responsibility."

"Awww, criminy, Pa! What's boots and spurs without a horse? Pleeeze!"

Catherine rose from her chair. "Let's leave your father and Uncle Billy to talk. You can help me with supper."

"C'mon, Ma." Bobby's face fell. "Lemme stay with them."

"You heard me, young man. No back talk."

"Yes 'um."

The boy put on a woebegone expression. He followed his mother through the dining room, still carrying the spurs. Billy watched after them a moment, slowly shaking his head. He grinned.

"Guess we know who rules the house. Katie don't take no sass."

"She's a caution," Thompson said, seating himself in an armchair. "Where'd you get the spurs?"

"Took 'em off a dead Mexican."

"You killed a Mexican?"

"Just joshing," Billy said with a lopsided smile. "'Course, I can't say the same for you, Mar-*shal*. Heard about them cowboys the minute I stepped off the train."

"Couple of damn fools," Thompson said gruffly. "I gave them every chance to surrender. They made a fight of it."

"Well, cowboys never had a lick of sense. Otherwise they wouldn't be cowboys."

"Those two sure fit the ticket."

Billy looked at him. "How's it feel to be a lawdog?"

"Have to say I like it," Thompson admitted. "Wearing a badge has its own rewards. I sleep good at night."

"You always was good at whatever you did. Even if it is a strange line of work for a Thompson."

"Are you still shamed to have a lawman in the family?"

"Hell, I don't tell nobody," Billy said with a glint of amusement in his eyes. "You think I want to get booted out of the sporting crowd?"

"Always got a snappy comeback," Thompson said amiably. "So what brings you to Austin?"

"Lost my taste for the riverboats. Damn things just go back and forth, back and forth."

"Don't try to kid an old kidder. You've got another dose of itchy feet, don't you? Where are you headed now?"

"Leadville," Billy said. "Figured I needed a change of scenery."

"From the Rio Grande to the Rockies? Yeah, I'd say that's a change."

"You know the gamblin' man's motto—follow the money."

Leadville was located deep in the Colorado Rockies. A strike of unsurpassed magnitude made it the silver capital of the world. The population now exceeded forty thousand and the monthly payroll of $800,000 was the largest of any mining camp in the West. There were reportedly two hundred gaming parlors, all operating seven days a week.

"Whyn't you come along?" Billy said. "Chuck that badge and get back to the sportin' life. We'll have ourselves a whale of a time."

"You're a bad influence," Thompson said with mock solemnity. "I've got a police force to run and a town to look after. Austin couldn't get along without me."

"God, listen to the man! I see you've learned to toot your own horn. Hope your hat still fits."

"Don't worry yourself on my account. You're the one who needs a keeper."

"Here we go again," Billy hooted. "I get along just fine, thank you all the same. Nobody's yet clipped my wings."

"Christmas isn't far off," Thompson said. "Why don't you stay over till after the New Year? You'll find plenty of poker games right here."

"Never give up, do you? I'll have to pass on the invite. Gotta keep movin'."

"You'll freeze your butt off in the Rockies. There's probably ten feet of snow."

"So there's nothin' to do but gamble till springtime. What more could a man ask?"

Catherine served a sumptuous pot roast for supper. Over a second serving, Billy entertained them with tales of the El Dorado called Leadville. He told them, swearing he had it on good authority, that $100,000,000 in ore was taken from the mines each year. Bobby listened, entranced and wide-eyed, all the way through dessert. He went to bed clutching his Mexican spurs.

Later, in their bedroom, Catherine asked Thompson if the tales were really true. He assured her that Billy was only exaggerating by five or ten million. Then, as he began undressing, he recounted the morning visit by Alexander Wooldridge. He considered it a good omen for the future.

"Way I see it," he concluded, "Wooldridge will support me in next year's election. I'm all but guaranteed a second term."

"Why of course you are!" she exclaimed. "With or without Wooldridge, you're certain to win. You're the best marshal Austin ever had. Everyone says so."

"Not everyone, but close enough. I might end up wearing a badge a good while."

"You'll wear it as long as you want it. I just know you will."

Thompson went to sleep a contented man. His one concern was his brother, who seemed infused with gypsy blood. Yet he understood the pull of wanderlust. The lure of the sporting life.

He sometimes dreamt of the old days.

TWENTY-FOUR

Austin basked beneath a mellow January sun. The sky was clear all the way to the horizon, just a hint of winter in the air. Friday morning crowds, encouraged by a break in the weather, filled the streets.

Thompson emerged from City Hall at noon. He stood for a moment, surveying the street, watching the press of shoppers move along the sidewalks. After several days of cold drizzle, the warm sun had brought people jamming into the business district. He idly wondered how long the good weather would last.

A week ago Austin had ushered in 1882. The crowds today somehow reminded him of the revelers on New Year's Eve. He'd kept the entire police force on duty that night, with most of them assigned to Guy Town. By midnight, the city jail had been overflowing with boisterous drunks and scrappy cowhands. He was relieved that New Year's came only once a year.

Never introspective, Thompson was nonetheless an astute observer. As a gambler, he'd read men's faces, their actions and mannerisms, at a card table. He was vaguely aware that he now employed somewhat the same technique on a crowded street, or whenever he inspected a Guy Town dive. Hardly two months as a peace officer, and yet he viewed the world from a different perspective. He looked at people with the eye of a lawman.

"Surveying your kingdom, Marshal?"

Thompson turned at the sound of the voice. He saw John Walton coming down the steps of City Hall. The attorney was carrying a leather briefcase, his features amused. He motioned out into the street.

"You look like a general inspecting his troops. What do you see out there?"

"Law-abiding citizens," Thompson said with an ironic smile. "Just the sort to put you lawyers out of business."

"Never happen," Walton retorted. "We've been defending the innocent since Roman times. Julius Caesar would've gotten off with a good lawyer."

"So who'd you get off today, counselor? I take it you've just come from court."

"Yes, another morning under the memorable jurisprudence of Judge Warren. He makes up the law as he goes along."

"Don't let him hear that," Thompson advised. "Was your client anyone I know?"

Walton looked rueful. "Your men caught him burgling the Beach Street Pharmacy. Ollie Crawford."

"Otherwise known as the dumbest thief in Travis County. He was rifling the cash drawer in the dark of night—with a lighted candle."

"I regret to say Ollie's no mental giant. Defending him requires an innovative legal argument."

"I'll bet it did," Thompson said. "What was your defense?"

"Mental impairment," Walton replied with a straight face. "I argued that a burglar who works with a candle falls under the legal definition of lunacy. I pled for a short, and hopefully instructive, stay in the mental asylum."

"How did that go over with the judge?"

"I'm delighted to say he bought it."

"You're joking," Thompson said dubiously. "He sentenced Crawford to the asylum?"

Walton beamed. "He said, and I quote: 'Anyone that stupid had to be crazy.' He gave him six months."

"I'll be damned. You're even cagier than I thought, John. Not to mention devious."

"Duplicity is the trademark of a criminal attorney. Although I don't get to practice my trade much these days. You've scared off all my clients."

"Just doing my job."

That statement hardly told the tale. After two months in office, Thompson had reduced the crime rate to an all-time low. The burglary by Ollie Crawford was the only serious offense in the last thirty days. Guy Town was relatively quiet, and hard cases routinely bypassed Austin. No one wanted to incur the displeasure of the city marshal.

"Tell you what," Walton said with some levity. "You're bad for business, but I'm the forgiving sort. What say I spring for lunch?"

"You're on," Thompson agreed. "How about Delmonico's?"

"Sounds good to me."

Thompson led the way up Mesquite Street. Delmo-nico's was something less than its name, a café of solid fare and low prices. But it was handy for the noonday meal, only a half block away, and frequented by the City Hall crowd. The Blue Plate Special was twenty cents.

Upstreet, Thompson pulled open the door. Then, as he was about to wave Walton through, he noticed a commotion from the direction of Congress Avenue. He looked closer and saw Gabe Ewing scattering people right and left as he sprinted along the sidewalk. The policeman skidded to a halt.

"Fire!" he bellowed. "Marshal, the capitol's on fire. Look there!"

Thompson turned toward Congress Avenue. State House Square opened off the near corner, and the cap-itol dome was visible in the distance. The buildings across the street blocked his view of the capitol itself; but he saw clouds of thick, black smoke spiraling sky-ward. He grabbed Ewing's arm.

"Did you sound the fire alarm?"

"They're on the way," Ewing said, bobbing his head. "Figured I oughta come get you."

"Head back to the office," Thompson ordered. "Tell Dennville to roust out the night shift and call in the pa-trol from Guy Town. I want every man on the force, pronto. Get moving!"

Ewing took off for City Hall. Thompson, with Wal-ton at his side, ran toward Congress Avenue. When they rounded the corner, they saw the capitol sheathed in roiling flames. The fire appeared to have started on the ground floor, and then spread rapidly to the upper sto-ries. Dense black smoke all but obscured the dome.

Thompson's first reaction was that it looked worse than it actually was. The state house was constructed of limestone blocks, and the building had always seemed impervious to fire. But as he looked closer, he saw that the inside of the capitol was a raging inferno. The interior walls were constructed of wood, most of them heavily paneled, and the rooms ignited like kindling. The three-story structure was quickly engulfed in flame.

From downtown, he heard the clang of a fire bell. He turned as the horse-drawn engine hurtled northward on Congress Avenue. A dozen or more firemen clung to the engine, their long coats flapping, hard-crowned helmets covering their heads. The driver brought the engine to a grinding halt, sawing at the reins, barely able to control the horses. The engine rocked to a stop at the corner of Mesquite and Congress Avenue. The capitol building was almost a hundred yards across the square.

Fully a thousand people lined the streets surrounding the state house grounds. The capitol had been evacuated, and buildings around the square quickly emptied as frightened shoppers hurried outside. Thompson was aware of more people crowding onto the square, drawn by the sight of the capitol wreathed in flames. Angry shouts attracted his attention and he spotted Dennville bulling a path through the throng. The onlookers gave way reluctantly, jostling and shoving, their eyes fixed on the fire. The sergeant finally broke clear, trailed by four policeman. He halted in front of Thompson.

"We're it for now," he said. "I sent somebody to fetch the night watch."

"Here's what we'll do," Thompson told him. "Post one man to patrol each side of the square. I want those people kept back from the fire."

"Four men aren't much for that job."

"They're all we've got. When the others show up, put them where they're needed most. You roam the square and jump on trouble spots."

Dennville gazed out at the crowds. "Some of those people won't want to move. They're here to see the fireworks."

"Use your nightsticks," Thompson commanded. "Bust their knees if they won't cooperate. Just keep them back on the sidewalk."

"Where will you be?"

"Over by the fire engine. I'll take care of the crowd there myself. Let's get moving."

Dennville rushed off with Ewing and the other officers. Thompson, still trailed by Walton, walked to the southwest corner of the square. The firemen were frantically attaching hoses to water hydrants on opposite sides of the street. Onlookers were ganged close around, watching the operation with ghoulish interest. Thompson waded into their ranks.

"Get back!" he shouted roughly. "Give these men room to work. Off the street!"

The crowd edged back onto the sidewalk. One man was slow to move, and Thompson took him by the collar. He lifted the man on tiptoe and danced him to the curb. The spectators broke out laughing as he dropped the man in the gutter.

"You folks stay clear!" he called out. "Let the firemen do their job."

The firemen began reeling off hoses from the engine. A man was stationed at each of the hydrants, waiting with a single-headed lug wrench. Within a matter of moments, the hoses were played out to their full length. The lines were still some fifty yards shy of the capitol building.

The fire chief rapped out an order. At each of the hydrants, the men cranked their wrenches, throwing open the valves. The hoses swelled, undulating with the rush of water, and the firemen wrestling the nozzles braced themselves. A jet of water burst from the hoses with a sharp *pop*.

The water arched in a rainbow under the noonday sun. The firemen planted their feet, raising the nozzles, trying to direct the stream onto the fire. But their hoses were stretched taut, and they were still fifty yards from the capitol building. The water pressure from the hydrants was inadequate for the distance.

The firemen struggled valiantly, muscling the hoses forward another foot or so. Yet the hydrant pressure was simply too low to hurl a forceful stream into the middle of the square. By the time the water reached the fire, it diminished into a weak spray, and turned to steam as it made contact with the flames. The firemen were reduced to little more than spectators.

Thompson, like the crowds lining the square, watched with a look of disbelief. For the first time, he noted a congregation of government officials gathered on the opposite corner. Among them were Governor Oran Roberts, Sheriff Frank Horner, several state legislators, and Mayor Wheeler. He saw Harry Burke, the fire chief, rushing toward them with an expression of impotent rage. He hurried across the street.

"I warned you!" Burke shouted, halting before the governor. "I told you we needed fire hydrants on the capitol grounds. Now you see what happens!"

Governor Roberts was a man of distinguished bearing. His features flushed at the verbal assault. "Talk to these gentlemen," he said, motioning to the gaggle of legislators. "I requested funding and they tabled the bill. They felt it was an unnecessary expenditure."

"Unnecessary!" Burke roared. "Look where your penny-pinching got us. We're gonna lose the capitol."

"Lower your voice," Governor Roberts said coldly. "The fault lies with the legislature, and I will so inform the press. I refuse to debate the matter on a street corner."

Thompson stepped forward. "Governor, there's plenty of time to fix the blame. We've got a bigger problem right now."

"Do we?" Roberts said, staring at him. "What might that be, Marshal?"

"We'd better start worrying about the businesses around the square. We're liable to lose half the town if that fire spreads."

A northwesterly breeze was scattering sparks and firebrands across the southern side of the square. The Governor was silent a moment, assessing the situation with newfound concern. He looked back at Thompson.

"You're absolutely right, Marshal. What do you suggest?"

"Let's get a bucket brigade formed," Thompson said without hesitation. "Start dousing the buildings on the south side of the square. Keep the fire engine where it is for now."

"Excellent idea," Roberts agreed, nodding to the officials gathered around. "Marshal Thompson is acting on my authority, gentlemen. Give him whatever assistance he needs."

Thompson began issuing orders. He told Burke to turn the fire hoses on the buildings at the lower end of the square. Then, after drafting Sheriff Horner and his deputies into service, he sent them off to organize a bucket brigade. He next signaled Dennville, who now had a full complement of police working the crowds. He instructed the sergeant to clear the street around Congress Avenue.

There was something in Thompson's voice that brooked no argument. The men hurried off to their assigned tasks like soldiers rushing into battle. A moment later the dome of the capitol buckled in a screeching, volcanic roar. The oval structure settled inward upon itself, and then collapsed, demolishing the third story. The debris rumbled downward, wiping out the second story, and crashed into the ground floor. Cinders and sparks leaped skyward.

A searing blast of heat shot out around the square. Then, in the next instant, the southern wall of the capitol toppled over in a thunderous firestorm of limestone blocks. Tongues of flame lapped at the rubble, and fiery timbers flashed a brilliant orange, consumed within the smoky pyre. There was one last flare, bright as the sun, then the ruins leveled in a glowing bed of coals. The breeze, stiffening to a wind, quickly fanned the embers.

An eerie hush fell over the square. The crowds jamming the streets stood like rows of sunlit sculpture, shocked beyond speech, staring at the rubble. Thompson's voice abruptly broke the silence, belting out orders in shouted commands. The police and the firemen, as though awakened from a trance, were galvanized to action. Dennville led the police in clearing Congress Avenue, and sheriff's deputies began forming bucket brigades with volunteers from the crowd. Thompson seemed everywhere at once.

Governor Roberts, looking on, nodded in approval.

He turned to Wheeler. "Mr. Mayor, I admire a man who knows how to take charge. I think Austin has found itself a marshal."

"No question about it," Wheeler said proudly. "Ben has a natural gift for leadership. He'll go far."

"I'll depend on you and Marshal Thompson when we start rebuilding the capitol. Once construction begins, the square will require constant policing."

"You can count on us, Governor. Whatever it takes, Ben will handle it."

"After today, I'm confident he will. Just look at how those men jump!"

Thompson barked out a command. The firemen directed their hoses onto the roofs of business concerns at the south end of the square. He then turned his attention to the bucket brigade.

Not a man among them doubted who was in charge.

TWENTY-FIVE

The ruins of the capitol were being cleared by workmen. A crew of some fifty laborers loaded rubble onto wagons, which carted the debris to a site outside town. The cleanup operation was now into its fifth day.

Thompson stepped off the streetcar at Mesquite and Congress Avenue. A two-story frame structure occupied the southwest corner of the state house grounds. Hurriedly constructed, the building had been hammered together and whitewashed over the previous weekend. For the immediate future, it would serve as the capitol.

Pete O'Rourke, foreman of the work crew, stood at the southern end of the square. He motioned a wagon loaded with rubble onto the street, and started to turn away. Then, spotting Thompson, he walked forward with a broad smile. He knuckled the brim of his hat.

"Mornin' to you, Marshal," he said pleasantly. "Looks to be a fair day."

"That it does," Thompson replied. "How's it going, Pete?"

"I'd have to say we're makin' headway. 'Course, as you can see, it's a terrible mess. We'll be at it awhile."

"How long before you'll have it cleared?"

"Couple o' weeks or thereabouts," O'Rourke said, gesturing to the charred skeleton of the capitol. "We still hafta raze them walls and haul off all that gawddamn limestone. It's a ball-buster, Marshal."

"You'll earn your pay," Thompson agreed. "I can't say I envy you the job."

"Well, somebody's gotta tear it down before they build it back. That's the way of things."

The governor had convened an emergency session of the legislature on Saturday, the day after the fire. The lawmakers met in the Knights of Pythias Building, and shortly before sundown they had put together a deal for a new capitol. By Monday, the governor had contracted with a syndicate of construction companies to build an even grander state house. The syndicate, in exchange for three million acres of state land, would construct an edifice of quarried granite. The capitol, like a mythical phoenix, would rise from the ashes.

"Imagine," O'Rourke said with wonder. "A year from now we'll have ourselves a brand new capitol. Granite, no less!"

"Pete, I just suspect it'll be a sight."

Thompson nodded, about to walk on, when he saw Governor Roberts emerge from the temporary state house. The governor was accompanied by Enoch Langley, the leading architect in Austin. They started toward the ruins of the capitol, and then Roberts caught sight of Thompson on the street corner. He turned with a friendly wave.

"Good morning, Marshal," he called out. "Always on the job, I see."

Thompson laughed. "Governor, you caught me playing hooky. I'm running late today."

"You don't fool anyone. I'll wager you were on the streets till the wee hours."

"Yes, sir, that's the safest bet in town."

"Keep up the good work, Marshal."

Roberts and the architect moved off across the square. Thompson nodded to O'Rourke and proceeded east on Mesquite, toward City Hall. The friendly exchange was yet another indication of how his stock had risen since the day of the fire. The governor had praised his actions in both the *Statesman* and the *Republican,* calling him "Austin's indispensable man." He secretly savored the label, though he tried to downplay it with others. There was talk that he had a promising future in politics.

A few minutes later he entered the squad room. The change of shifts had just taken place, and some of the day patrol were still collecting their gear. Last night, shortly after midnight, Thompson had led a raid on a parlor house, and he nodded to the men on the graveyard shift. Dennville, who looked fresh as a daisy, was seated at his desk. He got to his feet.

"Marshal," he said with a wry smile. "Those whores are set for court at ten o'clock. You want me to handle it?"

"Good idea, Sergeant," Thompson observed. "You're looking perky this morning. How the devil do you do it?"

"Lots of strong black coffee. Works everytime."

"I'll have to remember that."

"There's a telegram on your desk. The boy delivered it just after I came on duty."

"Thanks, Lon."

Thompson walked to his office. He hooked his cap on a coatrack and took a seat in the oxblood chair behind his desk. He tore open the telegram and glanced at the bottom of the form. The message was from Allan Pinkerton, head of the Pinkerton Detective Agency. He quickly scanned the contents.

> *Urgently request your assistance. Carl Wilson, fugitive on murder warrant Kansas City, believed hiding in San Antonio. Reliable reports indicate Wilson under protection of San Antonio authorities. Fugitive white male, age twenty-nine, dark hair, height five seven, weight one hundred forty. Offer one thousand dollars for apprehension. Please confirm acceptance of assignment by telegraph.*

Thompson's immediate reaction was one of surprise. Then, unable to suppress a surge of pride, he felt highly flattered. The Pinkertons, headquartered in Chicago, were renowned manhunters, retained by government agencies and private corporations. Allan Pinkerton, founder of the agency, had devised the original "Rogues' Gallery," with detailed descriptions of criminals throughout America. Among their celebrated cases, the Pinkertons had been retained to apprehend such outlaws as Jesse James and Sam Bass. The agency routinely worked with enforcement officers across the country.

Thompson stuffed the telegram in his pocket. He moved through the squad room, letting himself out the door, and walked down the hall. Sueann Mabry looked up from her desk as he entered the waiting room of the mayor's office. He motioned her down, and without being announced, proceeded directly to the mayor's inner sanctum. Wheeler, who was poring over a stack of correspondence, glanced up with a curious expression. He put the letters aside.

"Good morning, Ben," he said. "I've been expecting you."

"Then you're a first-class mind reader. I only just decided to come talk with you."

"Something important, is it?"

"See for yourself."

Thompson handed him the telegram. Wheeler read it through, nodding slowly to himself. His mouth pursed in thought, and he looked up with a sober gaze. He returned the telegram to Thompson.

"I received one myself."

"From Allan Pinkerton?"

"None other."

Wheeler took a telegraph form from his desk. He passed it across to Thompson and sat back in his chair. His eyes narrowed as Thompson scanned the contents, then read it again. The message spoke for itself.

We are most impressed with law enforcement record of City Marshal Ben Thompson. Request you authorize his assistance in apprehension of fugitive last reported in San Antonio. Your cooperation in this matter highly appreciated.

"I'll be damned," Thompson said in a bemused voice. "Wonder how they found out about me, anyway? I've only been on the job a couple of months."

"How about that article in the *Police Gazette*?"

Wheeler asked. "Those two cowboys being killed attracted quite a bit of attention."

"It's not exactly the first time I made the *Police Gazette*."

"Yes, but you're a law officer now."

"Well, maybe that's the difference."

"I'm a little at a loss," Wheeler remarked. "How would Pinkerton know the San Antonio police are protecting this man Wilson? Where would he get that information?"

"No big secret there," Thompson said. "The city marshal and the sheriff are both crooked as a dog's hind leg. Have been for years."

"You know that for a personal fact?"

"Let's just say I know San Antonio. I spent some time there when I was a gambling man."

"All the same—" Wheeler hesitated, considering. "Why wouldn't Pinkerton contact the Rangers? They have statewide arrest powers."

"Think about it a minute," Thompson said. "The Rangers aren't much on cooperating with detective agencies. They got pretty well singed over that Sam Bass business. Pinkerton almost stole their thunder."

"You mean they were working at odds on the same case?"

"Yeah, it was nip and tuck for a while. The Texas & Pacific hired the Pinkertons to hunt down Bass, and they almost pulled it off. You might say the Rangers took offense at being bypassed."

"Even so," Wheeler wondered aloud. "Why doesn't Pinkerton send his own agents after this Wilson fellow?"

"I wouldn't hazard a guess," Thompson said. "Maybe

they don't feel welcome in Texas anymore. Fact is, he offered me the assignment."

"You couldn't accept it in your capacity as city marshal."

"Then I'll do it on my own. I'm due some time off anyhow."

"I don't understand," Wheeler said with a puzzled frown. "Why would you want to get involved with the Pinkertons? You've made your name as a lawman."

Thompson nodded. "Tom, I guess it's nothing but asinine pride. I'd like to catch myself a murderer."

"That's it, another feather in your cap?"

"I didn't say it made sense. I'm just keen for the idea."

"What about the police department? You have obligations here."

"Things are pretty quiet these days. Lon Dennville's a good man. He can handle it."

"How long will you be gone?"

"I figure a couple of days at the most. Either I'll catch the fellow or I won't."

"What if I ordered you not to go?"

"Are you?"

"No," Wheeler said with an air of resignation. "You never were one for taking orders. But I still think it's a foolish stunt. You've got nothing to gain."

Thompson smiled. "There's always the reward."

"You're not doing it for the money."

"I won't tell anybody if you don't."

"When do you plan to leave?"

"I'll catch the evening train."

"Well, for whatever it's worth, I wish you luck."

Not quite an hour later Thompson walked into the house on University Avenue. Catherine hurried into the parlor from the sewing room, clearly amazed to find him home in the middle of the morning. She knew from the look on his face that he was bursting with news. Her smile was quizzical.

"You look like you just swallowed the canary. What's going on?"

"I got a wire from the Pinkertons. Allan Pinkerton himself."

"The detective agency?" she said, now thoroughly bewildered. "Why would they contact you?"

"Pinkerton offered me an assignment," Thompson said. "He wants me to locate a man in San Antonio."

"I assume you're talking about a criminal."

"The wire said he's a fugitive."

"A fugitive from what?"

"Not too many details," Thompson said casually. "Way it sounds, he murdered somebody in Kansas City."

"Oh, is that all?" she said with a mocking laugh. "A fugitive murderer who's visiting San Antonio. And you're supposed to locate him."

"And take him into custody."

"Yes, of course, that too."

"Katie, don't make too much of it. Lawmen take people into custody all the time."

"Honestly!" she said in exasperation. "You are the marshal of Austin, Ben Thompson. What earthly business do you have running off to San Antonio?"

Thompson shrugged. "Tom Wheeler wanted to know the same thing. I told him it was dumb pride, and that's the best answer I've got. Pinkerton asked and I'm going."

Catherine sensed that it was something more than

pride. In two months, he had all but tamed Guy Town, and forcibly persuaded the sporting crowd to walk the straight and narrow. He was bored and looking for excitement, some greater challenge. A new world to conquer.

And yet . . .

The thought of San Antonio bothered her for another reason. Her voice took on a note of concern. "I want you to promise me something."

"I'll try," Thompson said. "What've you got in mind?"

"I want your promise you'll stay away from Jack Harris. Will you do that for me?"

"Katie, I'm going there to arrest a fugitive. I've got no business with Harris."

"I asked for your promise."

Thompson was reluctant to give his word. His dispute with Harris was a long-standing one. In late 1880, while visiting San Antonio, he'd spent an evening in Harris's establishment. A faro game turned ugly when he accused the dealer of cheating and Harris took it as a personal affront. For a moment, gunplay seemed inevitable.

City Marshal Phil Shardon hastily intervened. Thompson was wary of trouble with the law, and he agreed to leave the club. Still, he'd denounced Harris for operating crooked games, and their antagonism lingered on following the incident. Even now, over a year later, he was leery of making promises about Jack Harris. He was accountable for himself, but not his enemies.

"Tell you what," he said lightly, looking at Catherine. "You've got my word I won't go hunting trouble. How's that?"

"I suppose it's better than nothing. I just wish you weren't going to San Antonio."

"You worry too much about things. I'll be fine."

She had some dark premonition it wasn't true.

TWENTY-SIX

———◦◦◦———

The train arrived late in San Antonio. Thompson stepped off the lead coach shortly before midnight, carrying a small valise. He was dressed in civilian clothes, with his badge tucked into his vest pocket. He took a hired carriage uptown.

The Menger Hotel was located on a broad plaza. The night clerk assigned him a room on the second floor, and he crossed the lobby to the stairs. By the time he got undressed, he was bushed, weary from a long day and a long train ride. Yet, after turning down the lamp, he paused a moment by the window. The Alamo was visible beneath the silvery light of a sky brilliant with stars.

Thompson, like all Texans, felt the emotional tug of the Alamo. There, in 1836, a small band of dauntless men had fallen before the might of Santa Anna's army. But for their sacrifice, all of Texas might yet be the northern province of Mexico. Staring out the window, he was reminded that honorable men often found immortality in an honorable death. He went to sleep thinking about the defenders of the Alamo. And honor.

The next morning Thompson crossed the plaza at about ten o'clock. He was rested from a night's sleep, and felt his vigor restored by a leisurely breakfast. The town was situated along the San Antonio River, and with the advent of the railroad, it had become a center of commerce and trade. The plaza was bustling with activity, but even so, the pace was somehow slower, almost indolent, compared to Austin. He often thought there was still a good bit of Old Mexico in the town by the river.

Across the way, he entered the city marshal's office. Another time, under different circumstances, he would have avoided paying a call on the marshal. All lawmen in San Antonio were obligated to Jack Harris, who controlled the vote in the sporting district. The bad blood that existed between him and Harris virtually assured an adversarial relationship with local officers. Yet he needed the marshal's cooperation, rather than interference and meddling. He cautioned himself to play the cards as dealt.

Phil Shardon was a fleshy man with a bristly mustache. His sullen manner indicated that he still remembered Thompson's last visit to town. "Heard you got elected marshal," he said. "Not too choosy up Austin way, are they?"

Thompson ignored the jibe. "I'm not here to swap insults. I have official business in San Antonio."

"What sort of business is that?"

"The Pinkertons retained me to apprehend a fugitive. He's wanted for murder."

"This fugitive got a name?"

"Carl Wilson."

Shardon blinked, a telltale giveaway. "Never heard of him," he said. "'Fraid I can't help you, Thompson."

"I don't want your help," Thompson informed him. "I want to give you some advice."

"Advice about what?"

"Take care that Wilson's not warned I'm in town. I'd be sorely troubled to hear he'd skipped out."

"Told you I don't know him," Shardon said in a surly tone. "You tryin' to call me a liar?"

Thompson stared at him. "I'm telling you to sit on your thumb till I have Wilson in custody. Otherwise you'll answer to me."

"Your badge don't mean shit here."

"I'm not talking about the law."

"That sounds like a threat."

"It is."

Shardon started out of his chair. Then, looking closer, he saw something in Thompson's eyes that gave him pause. He sat back.

"Do whatever you gotta do and get the hell out of my town. I don't take kindly to threats."

"Just remember what I said about Wilson. No tipoffs."

"I heard you the first time."

"Thanks for your cooperation, Marshal."

Thompson walked out of the office. He preferred persuasion to threats, but there'd been no choice. On the street, he told himself that the price of Shardon's silence had been fear. He knew he'd won when the lawman's look betrayed a loss of nerve. Satisfied, he turned toward the sporting district.

The Vaudeville Theater & Gaming Parlor was on the corner of Commerce and Soledad. Jack Harris was the proprietor, but he rarely put in an appearance before noontime. Thompson went there instead looking for Will Simms, an old friend who owed him a favor. Some years ago he'd hired Simms as a dealer at the Iron Front and taught him the trade. Simms later moved to San Antonio and caught on as house manager at the Vaudeville Theater. Their friendship had survived the altercation with Harris.

Simms, like all house managers, was responsible for getting the club into operation by late morning. When Thompson came in, he was checking liquor stock with one of the bartenders. He happened to glance in the backbar mirror, and his face suddenly went chalky. He dropped his inventory pad on the bar and hurried across the room. His eyes were round as marbles.

"Ben!" he said in a shaky voice. "What the hell are you doing here?"

"I'm here to see you," Thompson replied. "Something wrong with that?"

"Damn right there is! I thought you would've heard by now. Jack posted you out of this place."

"You mean Harris won't allow me in the club?"

"It's worse than that," Simms said. "He swore he'd shoot you if you ever came in here again. He keeps a shotgun behind the bar."

Thompson's eyes went hard. "Nobody tells me how to come and go. That includes Jack Harris."

"For old time's sake, I'm asking you to take your trade elsewhere. I don't want to see either of you shot."

"I'll tend to Harris later. All I want now is some information."

"What sort of information?"

"I'm tracking a man wanted for murder. His name is Carl Wilson."

Simms looked blank. "Doesn't ring any bells."

"Maybe he's using an alias," Thompson said. "He's about your height, muscular build, dark hair, late twenties. Someone new to town."

"Well, I'm not—"

"Someone eager to buy drinks for Phil Shardon."

A flicker of recognition passed over Simms's features. Then just as quickly, it was replaced by a guarded look. "I don't want any trouble with the law, Ben. Don't put me on the spot."

"Shardon won't bother you," Thompson said with conviction. "I came to an understanding with him not ten minutes ago. He took himself out of the game."

"You're sure about that?"

"It's the straight goods, Will."

"Charlie White," Simms said. "That's the name your man's using. He hit town sometime last week. Likes the dice table."

"Any idea where he's staying?"

"A dump just down the street. The Commerce Hotel."

"I owe you one, Will."

"Ben."

"Yeah?"

"Don't come back here again and we'll be square. Okay?"

"I'll think about it."

"I'd sooner have your word."

"See you around, Will."

"Sweet Jesus."

* * *

The Commerce Hotel was halfway down the block. The lobby was spartan—creaky wood floors and one tattered sofa placed before the front window. Thompson closed the door behind him and crossed to the registration desk. He nodded to the clerk.

"I'm looking for a friend of mine. I believe he's staying with you."

"Yes, sir, and the name?"

"Charles White."

"You're in luck," the clerk said, glancing past him. "There's Mr. White now."

Thompson turned from the desk. He saw a man in a rumpled suit descend the stairs and move toward the door. The description was a match for the one supplied by the Pinkertons, but he wanted to be certain. He quickly crossed the lobby.

"Hello, Carl."

The man broke stride. His shoulders stiffened and he looked around. "You talking to me?"

"Police officer." Thompson flashed his badge with his left hand. "I have an outstanding warrant on you, Mr. Wilson. You're under arrest."

"There's been some sort of mistake. My name's White. Charles White."

"Save it for the judge, Carl. Put your hands behind your head."

"I'm telling you—"

Wilson, like a magician, tried for misdirection. He broke off in midsentence and his hand snaked inside his coat. Thompson was a beat faster, popping the Colt from his shoulder holster. He thumbed the hammer.

"Don't get yourself killed, Carl. Bring that gun out real slow—and drop it."

A frozen moment slipped past as Wilson debated his chances. Then, careful of any sudden movement, he eased a stubby bulldog revolver from his waistband. He dropped it on the floor.

"Turn around," Thompson ordered. "Hands behind your head."

"How'd you find me?"

"A tip from the Pinkertons."

"Dirty bastards!"

"Walk ahead of me, Carl. No monkey business."

Thompson marched him uptown. On the plaza, by-passers hurriedly moved aside as they turned into the marshal's office. Shardon was seated behind his desk, his expression glum. He avoided Wilson's eyes.

"Got a prisoner for you," Thompson said. "Lock him up nice and tight till the extradition hearing. He's headed back to Kansas."

"You don't have to tell me my business."

"I'm wiring the Pinkertons he's now in your custody. Take care he doesn't escape."

"What the hell's that mean?" Shardon demanded. "I've never yet lost a prisoner."

"A word to the wise," Thompson said flatly. "You turn him loose and I'll come looking for you. Got it?"

"Don't try to bullyrag me, Thompson. I'm tired of your goddamn threats!"

"Think of it as a prophecy."

"You playing God now?"

"No, just the messenger."

Thompson walked out of the office. He crossed the plaza to his hotel, where he borrowed pen and paper from the desk clerk. After composing a wire to Allan Pinkerton, he tipped a bellman to take it to the telegraph operator at the depot. He thought the wise thing would be to send it himself, and catch the next train out of town. Instead, he went up to his room.

The Alamo was awash in sunlight. He stood at the window, reflecting again on honor and honorable men. The smart move, he told himself, would be to forget Jack Harris, ignore the insult. But then, almost certainly, the word would spread that he'd tucked tail and run, lost his nerve. Honor dictated that he at least make an appearance at the Vaudeville Theater. A couple of drinks, no more, then leave. A quick in and out.

Just long enough to thumb his nose at Harris.

The Vaudeville Theater & Gaming Parlor was ablaze with light. A crescent-shaped bar occupied the center of the main room, with gaming tables along the walls. The theater was at the rear, through an arched doorway, footlights spilling out over the stage. The first show of the evening opened with a team of acrobats.

There were two doors into the establishment. One was just off the corner of Commerce, and the other off the corner of Soledad. Thompson walked through the Commerce Street door shortly after seven o'clock. He'd waited until evening, when the place was packed, to make his appearance. He moved directly to the bar.

A bartender nodded a greeting. "What's your pleasure?"

"Whiskey," Thompson said, glancing at the gaming tables. "Jack Harris around?"

"Haven't seen him tonight."

"Doesn't he usually show up before now?"

"Ask Mr. Simms. He'll know."

Will Simms rushed forward from the entrance to the theater. He appeared agitated, his features flushed. "Ben, for chrissake! I thought you'd left town."

"Not yet," Thompson said. "Where's Harris?"

"I talked him into staying home till later. Word's out you turned that Wilson fellow over to the marshal. I figured you would've caught a train by now."

"Will, here's the way it works. I'll have a drink and wait for Harris to show. He has to understand I won't be barred from a public place. His or anyone else's."

"You're asking for trouble," Simms said earnestly. "The minute he walks in here and sees you, he'll start a fight. You've got to believe me."

"I'm not looking for a fight," Thompson assured him. "I just won't be barred by the likes of Jack Harris."

"Listen, let me try to smooth things over. You go wait outside and I'll collar Jack the second he walks in. Maybe we can patch things up some way or another."

"You think there's any chance he'll listen to reason?"

"Hell, Ben, it's worth a try. Just give me a little time."

Thompson was silent a moment. "All right," he finally said. "We'll play it your way. But I won't wait all night."

Simms walked him to the Commerce Street door. "I'll come get you as quick as I can. Jack ought to be here any minute."

"Tell him what I said, Will. I won't be barred."

"I'll do my damnedest."

Thompson went out the door. Simms walked to the opposite door, moving onto the sidewalk. He hoped to intercept Harris, who lived west of the club and usually came to work by way of Soledad Street. He kept darting glances back through the barroom to the door on Commerce. He wasn't sure how long Thompson would wait.

Outside, Thompson tossed the stub of a cheroot into the gutter. He patted his pockets, surprised to find he was out of smokes, and turned downstreet. A few doors down, he entered a cigar store, which stayed open during the evening hours. He bought a half-dozen cheroots, a brand imported from Mexico, and stuffed all but one into the inside pocket of his suit jacket. He lit up as he went through the door.

On the street again, he walked back toward the vaudeville house. As he approached, he noted a crush of men shouldering their way out the door onto Commerce. Their features were apprehensive, oddly alarmed, and he heard one of them say, "Harris has got a gun." He dropped the cheroot, blocked a moment by men rushing past, and then hurried forward. The door was open and he saw most of the crowd in the barroom scattering for cover. Jack Harris rounded the far end of the bar with a double-barreled shotgun.

Simms tried to stop him. "Jack, I'm begging you," he pleaded. "We can settle it if you'll just talk to Ben. Don't do this!"

"Out of my way," Harris shouted in a rough voice. "I'm through talking with that son-of-a-bitch. He wants a fight, he'll get it."

"I'm telling you he doesn't want a fight."

"Then he should've stayed out of my place!"

Thompson stepped into the doorway, his pistol drawn. "Ditch the shotgun, Harris. I'm not looking for trouble."

"You've found it!" Harris yelled, his features contorted. "Nobody calls me a sharper."

"Then you shouldn't run crooked games."

"Goddamn you to hell!"

Harris brushed Simms aside. He raised the shotgun, earing back both hammers, and brought it to his shoulder. Thompson leveled his Colt, staring over the sights, and fired. Harris staggered, a starburst of blood dotting his shirtfront, and tried to right the scattergun. His eyes were crazed.

Thompson fired two shots in quick succession. The slugs struck Harris just over the sternum, not a handspan apart. He reeled sideways in a nerveless dance, dropping the shotgun, and slammed into the bar. His legs gave way and he collapsed, overturning a spittoon. His foot drummed the floor in an afterspasm of death.

A sudden pall of silence fell over the room. The crowd waited in a stilled tableau, their eyes locked on Thompson. He moved just inside the doorway, placing his back to the wall. His gaze swept the startled faces, the Colt at his side. He looked at Simms.

"Will, go get the sheriff. Tell him I won't surrender to Shardon."

"I got it," Simms said in a rattled voice. "You'll surrender to him but not the marshal."

"Tell him to come right along."

"I'll tell him, Ben."

Simms took off running for the plaza.

TWENTY-SEVEN

The courtroom was mobbed. Friends of the deceased, most of them members of the sporting crowd, turned out in force. They were in an ugly mood, and extra sheriff's deputies were stationed by the doors. The atmosphere was electric with tension.

The benches were jammed as well by the general public. The sensational nature of the killing drew people who had never before entered a courtroom. They were there for a look at the most famous shootist in the state of Texas. The fact that he was now a lawman merely whetted their curiosity.

Three days ago, on Friday afternoon, a coroner's jury had been impaneled. Thompson, who was being held in the county jail, had testified in his own behalf. He was represented by John Walton, who had been summoned from Austin the night of the shooting. The coroner's jury had ruled death by homicide in the demise of Jack Harris.

By Monday morning, the newspapers were demanding a speedy trial. For some years, Harris had been a power in local politics, routinely delivering the vote of the sporting crowd in any election. He was a popular figure as well, operating a vaudeville house that was all but an institution in San Antonio. The newspapers urged the swift and certain conviction of his killer.

Shortly before ten o'clock, Thompson entered the courtroom from a door behind the jury box. He was escorted by Sheriff Dave McCall, and his appearance brought a restive murmur from the crowd. A weekend in jail had left his suit in need of pressing, but he was freshly shaved, his eyes alert and confident. He joined Walton at the defense table.

"Good morning, Ben," Walton said. "Are they treating you all right?"

"Well enough," Thompson replied as the sheriff walked off. "I wouldn't recommend the accommodations."

"No guarantees, but I think you've spent your last night in jail. Our case has improved over the weekend."

"What happened?"

"I had a long talk with Will Simms last night. He's come around to our way of thinking."

On Friday, at the coroner's inquest, Simms had been the state's chief witness. He testified that Thompson had provoked the shooting, ignoring repeated warnings to stay away from the vaudeville house. Under cross-examination, he proved to be a hostile witness, evasive in his answers as to details about the actual gunfight. His testimony virtually assured a ruling of homicide.

"That's a switch," Thompson said. "What changed his mind?"

Walton chuckled. "Well, first, I appealed to friendship. You might say that got me nowhere fast. He really does blame you for Harris's death."

"So what brought him around?"

"I told him there was no guarantee you would be convicted. Then, not all that subtly, I suggested he didn't want you as an enemy."

Thompson smiled. "You're a shifty one, John. Doesn't the law frown on threatening witnesses?"

"Who threatened anyone?" Walton said wryly. "I prefer to think of it as the carrot and the stick. Simms opted for the carrot."

"Let's hope he's got the gumption for it. Lots of people in this town would like to see my neck stretched. They'll put the heat on him to stick with his story."

"I suspect he fears you more than he does them. That's always an inducement to tell the truth."

"We'll find out," Thompson allowed. "Did you send my wire to Catherine?"

"Just as you instructed." Walton took a telegram from his briefcase. "Hers came in early this morning."

Sheriff McCall refused to permit delivery of telegrams to the jail. Thompson's only means of communication with Catherine was through his attorney. Over the last three days they had exchanged several messages. He quickly scanned today's reply.

My Dearest, trust in God during your ordeal. Bobby and I are with you in spirit, and we know you will return home safely. We await your good news.

Your loving wife,
Catherine

Thompson folded the telegram. As he tucked it into his pocket, he told himself God could always use a little help. He trusted Walton's veiled threat to Will Simms far more than he did divine intervention. There was something to be said for the persuasive effects of fear.

"All rise!"

The bailiff's command brought the spectators to their feet. Judge George Noonan, who presided over the District court, entered from his chambers at the rear of the room. He mounted the bench, seated himself in a high-backed chair, and took out his spectacles. He nodded to the bailiff.

"This court is now in session," the bailiff dutifully responded. "The docket concerns the matter of the State versus Benjamin F. Thompson. Be seated!"

The crowd resumed their seats. Judge Noonan adjusted his spectacles, waiting for everyone to get settled. He was an imposing man, with salt-and-pepper hair and sharp features. His eyes were magnified behind the glasses, and his look left no doubt as to who was in charge. He addressed the courtroom in an orotund voice.

"This is a preliminary hearing to determine if Mr. Thompson will be bound over for trial. Are you gentlemen ready to proceed?"

Fred Cocke, the prosecutor for Bexar County, got to his feet. "The State is prepared, Your Honor."

"The defense is prepared," Walton echoed. "And may I say it's an honor to be in your courtroom, Judge Noonan."

"Save it for your closing argument, counselor. Call your first witness, Mr. Cocke."

Sheriff McCall was the lead witness. Under Cocke's

guidance, he testified that he'd arrived at the vaudeville house some twenty minutes after the shooting. He went on to relate that Jack Harris—"dead as a doornail"—was found on the floor beside the bar. Thompson, he noted, was still on the premises and readily admitted to the killing. He concluded by stating he had taken Thompson into custody.

Walton rose for cross-examination. "Sheriff McCall, did Mr. Thompson attempt to flee the scene—at any time?"

"No, he was there when I got there."

"As a matter of fact, he sent someone to fetch you. Isn't that correct?"

"That's right."

"And he voluntarily surrendered his gun to you—didn't he?"

"Yes, he did."

"And he voluntarily surrendered *himself* to you—didn't he?"

McCall shrugged. "Yeah, I suppose he did."

"No further questions, Your Honor."

Thompson watched the sheriff walk to the other side of the room. His attention was diverted when he saw City Marshal Phil Shardon seated in the front row of spectators. He idly wondered if extradition papers had been filed on Carl Wilson, alias Charles White. But then, on second thought, he decided that was a matter for the Pinkertons. He had problems of his own.

Doctor Anton Herff, the county coroner, was called to the stand. Upon arriving at the vaudeville house, he testified, he had examined the deceased. The cause of death was gunshot wounds, one high on the breastbone and two through the heart. He offered the opinion that death was almost instantaneous and remarked again on the massive damage to the heart. He seemed impressed with Thompson's accuracy.

Walton kept his chair. "We have no questions of this witness, Your Honor."

Leo Sneed, one of the bartenders at the vaudeville house, next took the oath. His hair was freshly greased and parted in the middle, and his handlebar mustache appeared coated with wax. Prosecutor Cocke approached the stand.

"You were tending bar January thirteenth, the night of the shooting?"

"Yessir."

"You served the defendant a drink, isn't that so?"

"Yessir, I surely did."

"In the course of which," Cocke elaborated, "you overheard a conversation between the defendant and one Will Simms, an employee of the establishment. Would you kindly relate the gist of that conversation for the court?"

Sneed cleared his throat. "Mr. Simms all but begged Thompson to leave the place. Told him just being there was bound to cause trouble."

"What was Thompson's response?"

"Well, he got real hot under the collar. Said he wouldn't be banned by anybody—especially Mr. Harris."

"What happened then?"

"Thompson went out and directly Mr. Harris come in the other door. Mr. Simms told him Thompson was outside and Mr. Harris looked scared for his life. He grabbed a shotgun from behind the bar."

Cocke led him through the sequence of events. Sneed testified that Thompson burst into the barroom without warning and shot Harris dead. He stated that he had no recollection of an exchange of words before Thompson opened fire. He went on to say that Harris never fired the shotgun. Cocke walked away with a smug look.

"I have nothing more, Your Honor."

"Mr. Sneed," Walton said, moving to the stand. "Where were you when the shooting started? When the shots were actually fired?"

"Well—"

"Isn't it true that you ducked beneath the bar?"

"Yeah, I reckon I did."

"And you didn't see who shot whom or when, did you?"

"No, not just exactly."

"Nor did you hear the warning issued by Mr. Thompson to Mr. Harris. You were too frightened to hear anything—weren't you?"

Sneed swallowed hard. "I was mighty scared, that's a fact."

"Thank you for your candor, Mr. Sneed."

The state's final witness was Will Simms. After swearing the oath, he seated himself, clearly uncomfortable. Cocke prompted him through a recitation of events immediately prior to the shooting. Then, pausing for dramatic effect, Cocke shook his finger in the air.

"You *pleaded* with the defendant to leave in peace. Not to provoke an altercation. Correct?"

"Yes."

"You warned the deceased that Thompson would not accept being barred from the establishment. That he would force the issue. Isn't that so?"

"I tried my best."

"And yet the defendant stormed back into the barroom—acting in cold blood!—and shot Jack Harris dead. Isn't that what happened?"

"No."

"What?" Cocke thought he'd heard wrong. "What did you say?"

Simms fidgeted nervously. He was all too aware of the puzzled stares directed his way from the sporting crowd. "I said 'no.' "

"No? No what?"

"Thompson warned Harris to drop the shotgun. He told him plain as anything he didn't want a fight."

"Well, Mr. Simms, that's patently ridiculous. You testified in the coroner's inquest that no such thing happened."

"I didn't testify one way or the other. I just didn't say it."

"And now—suddenly!—you're changing your story?"

"I'm not changing anything," Simms said, squirming in his chair. "I'm telling you the way it was."

"Your Honor!" Cocke exploded, turning to the bench. "This man has impeached *himself.* He's lying!"

Judge Noonan frowned querulously. "He's your witness, Mr. Cocke."

"I demand that he be charged with perjury. I demand it!"

"Another day, another time," Judge Noonan informed him. "Get on with your questions."

Cocke stalked back to the prosecution table. "I'm through with this—this perjurer."

"I have a couple of questions," Walton said, crossing to the witness stand. "Mr. Simms, did Jack Harris raise his shotgun and point it with deadly intent at Ben Thompson?"

"I'm sorry to say he did," Simms admitted. "He swore he'd kill Ben if he ever set foot in the place again."

"And did Mr. Thompson attempt to avoid a fight? Did he try to talk Harris out of it—before he fired?"

"Yes, he did."

"So to put a point on it, Mr. Thompson acted in defense of his own life. Is that correct?"

"I wish he'd never come back to the club. But, yeah, that's the way it worked out."

Fred Cocke, his eyes rimmed with disgust, rested the case for the prosecution. Under the law, there was no obligation for Thompson to testify in his own defense. Walton nonetheless called him to the stand. He went straight to the point.

"Mr. Thompson, did you seek an altercation with Jack Harris?"

"No, I did not."

"Was it your intent to provoke him when you went to the vaudeville house on the night of January thirteenth?"

"I went there because no man can be barred from a public place. I wasn't looking for trouble."

"And you didn't draw your gun until he started toward the door with a shotgun. Isn't that true?"

"That's the whole truth of it."

"And as a last resort—when all else failed—you fired in protection of your own life . . . didn't you?"

Thompson nodded. "I regret there was no other way."

"Thank you." Walton turned from the stand. "Your witness, Mr. Cocke."

Cocke snorted derisively. "I have no questions for your mankiller."

"The defense rests, Your Honor."

Judge Noonan ordered closing arguments. Cocke railed on, his voice an octave too high, damning perjurers and holier-than-thou mankillers, and slick defense lawyers. Walton reviewed the case in a calm, dispassionate manner, and asked that the facts be allowed to speak for themselves. After he finished, the judge announced that it would serve no purpose to delay his decision. He ruled it a case of justifiable homicide.

The courtroom went from shocked silence to a drumming uproar. Harsh mutters of protest turned to angry catcalls and shouts of outrage. Several members of the sporting crowd surged toward the balustrade separating the spectator section from the front of the courtroom. Deputies waded into the throng, and Sheriff McCall moved to block the center aisle. The situation seemed on the verge of riot.

Judge Noonan rose from his chair. He furiously wielded his gavel, every whack resounding with the report of a cannon. He finally hammered the jostling crowd into silence. His eyes were fierce.

"You men stand back!" he thundered. "I will not tolerate disruption in my courtroom. Anyone who opens his mouth will be held in contempt and thrown in jail. Clear that aisle!"

The men mobbed around the balustrade slowly backed off. Deputies bulled a path through the crowd, and formed a tight wedge blocking the center aisle. Sheriff McCall turned and walked quickly to the defense table. Will Simms, terrified for his own life, vaulted the railing and followed along. The lawman glowered at Thompson.

"You'd best clear out," he said. "That bunch would as soon lynch you as not. I won't have it in my town."

Thompson nodded. "What time's the next train?"

"Half past two. I'll put you on it myself."

"I want my pistol back."

"You'll have your damned gun." McCall jerked a

thumb at Simms. "Take your weasel with you. His life's not worth a plugged nickel around here."

"How about it, Will?" Thompson asked. "Want to come along?"

Simms grinned weakly. "Austin sounds mighty good to me."

Sheriff McCall led them to the door at the back of the courtroom. Walton and Simms brought up the rear, and a fresh outburst of angered curses followed them through the door. Thompson appeared stoic, but he was inwardly saddened, at odds with himself. A thought persisted in some dark corner of his mind.

He'd won the battle but lost the war.

TWENTY-EIGHT

—◁◁◁◁|∫|▷▷▷▷—

The train chuffed to a halt shortly after ten o'clock. Austin lay cloaked in mealy darkness, the depot lights like a beacon in the night. A bitter wind whipped down out of the northwest.

Thompson stepped off the observation deck of the rear passenger coach. Walton and Simms followed him across the platform and through the deserted station-house. Outside, on Cypress Street, one carriage for hire waited at curbside. After Thompson gave the driver instructions, they climbed aboard. The carriage rolled off toward the center of town.

The men sat wrapped in brittle silence. All the way from San Antonio, Thompson had been moody and withdrawn, his thoughts turned inward. He stared out of the carriage now, his features dappled in the glow of streetlights along Congress Avenue. He seemed singularly downcast for a man who had escaped from the shadow of the gallows. He was clearly brooding on something too personal for words.

Uptown, the carriage stopped at the Austin Hotel. Simms, who had fled San Antonio with the clothes on his back, opened the door. His mood was no less bleak than Thompson's, for he'd left behind a good job and a future full of promise. His face was squinched and tight as he stepped down from the carriage. He looked back at Thompson.

"Hope you've got a job for me at the Iron Front. I'd hate to wind up at some joint in Guy Town."

"Don't concern yourself," Thompson assured him. "You put your neck on the line, and I'm not one to forget a friend. We'll work something out."

"I'll see you tomorrow, then?"

"You can bank on it, Will."

The carriage pulled away from the curb. Thompson was silent a moment, staring out the window as the driver circled around to Congress Avenue. Then, his mood seemingly broken, he turned to Walton. His mouth quirked in a faint smile.

"John, you saved my bacon," he said. "I want you to know I'm grateful. Damned grateful."

Walton waved it off. "What the hell, that's what lawyers are for. I was just doing my job."

"No, it was more than that. If you hadn't turned Simms around, I would've been shaking hands with the Devil. They had me slated for the hangman."

"All's well that ends well. I'm glad things went our way."

Thompson merely nodded. "You send me a stiff bill for services rendered. You earned it."

"Any lawyer appreciates a generous client."

"Just put me at the head of your list."

Thompson dropped him off at his home on Chestnut Street. A few minutes later the carriage drew to a halt outside the house on Elm. After paying the driver, Thompson started up the walkway to the porch. He'd wired Catherine before departing San Antonio, and he wasn't surprised by the light burning in the parlor window. He knew she would be waiting.

Catherine met him at the door. "Oh God, Ben!" she cried, slipping into his embrace. "Don't you ever go away again!"

"I think I'm home to stay awhile."

"Are you all right? I practically fainted when I got your telegram. They won't bring any more charges?"

"No, it's over," Thompson said. "I'm a free man."

"I prayed and prayed. You can't imagine how hard I prayed."

"Somebody up there must have heard you. Where's Bobby?"

"I sent him to bed." She waited while he hooked his coat and hat on the halltree. "He tried to stay awake, but he kept dozing off. He's wild to see you."

"Tomorrow's time enough."

Something in his voice seemed to her strangely subdued. She followed him into the parlor, seating herself on the sofa as he slumped into his chair. In the light of the lamp, she saw that his features were gaunt, oddly morose. He appeared anything but a man who had been exonerated just that day of murder. She searched his face with a quizzical expression.

"What's wrong?" she said softly. "You look so—I don't know—so down in the dumps. Shouldn't we be celebrating?"

"There's nothing to celebrate." Thompson scrubbed

his whiskery jawline. "I went to San Antonio and damn near got myself hanged. I'm not exactly proud of it."

"Yes, but you were freed. You weren't at fault."

"Katie, don't you see, I killed a man. A sworn law officer and I killed a man in a personal fight. I'm just not cut out to wear a badge."

"That's not true," she said quickly. "You've done a marvelous job. Everyone says so."

"No," Thompson said in a weary voice. "I shouldn't have run for marshal. It was the biggest mistake of my life."

"Why on earth would you think that?"

"I haven't thought about anything else. All the way back from San Antonio it kept eating at me. I am who I am, Katie. Nothing's going to change."

"You're talking about yourself . . . aren't you?"

"On the train tonight I figured it out. A lawman has to put personal things aside. But I've never been able to overlook an insult. You can't teach an old dog new tricks."

She sensed he felt he'd dishonored the badge, his oath of office. "You've made up your mind, haven't you?"

"Yeah, I have," Thompson said flatly. "What happened with Jack Harris just proved it could happen again. I'm going to resign as marshal."

She leaned forward, touched his arm. "Why not sleep on it? You might feel different in the morning."

"Tomorrow or the next day wouldn't matter. The fact is, I wasn't meant to be a lawman. I know that now."

She desperately wanted to believe he was wrong. But in her heart she knew he'd looked deep within himself and found the truth. The only truth.

His personal code of honor was more important than the badge.

Dear Mr. Mayor,

    I hereby tender my resignation as marshal of the City of Austin. Consider the resignation effective immediately, or as soon as a successor can be appointed. I endorse Sergeant Lon Dennville most highly for the position of city marshal. He is an honorable man and a distinguished peace officer.

Your obedient servant,
Ben Thompson

Thompson delivered his resignation to the mayor early the next morning. Tom Wheeler was at first stunned, and then argued strenuously that the resignation was not acceptable. He finally persuaded Thompson to hold off until the city council be convened in emergency session. The aldermen began trooping into City Hall late that morning.

Lon Dennville was flabbergasted. Like everyone else in Austin, he'd read the newspaper reports of Thompson's problems in San Antonio. He knew something was seriously wrong when Thompson walked into the squad room dressed in civilian clothes. Yet he was shocked to learn that only moments before Thompson had tendered his resignation. He was even more amazed that Thompson had recommended him for the job.

"I don't want it," Dennville protested. "I couldn't' fill your shoes and we both know it. The whole thing's crazy."

"You underestimate yourself," Thompson informed him. "You've played second fiddle long enough, and now's the time to move up. You'll make a fine marshal."

"Dammit, Ben, you're the one that was elected. Nobody wants me in the job."

"Take the appointment and make the most of it. Next time they'll elect you."

"I still think it's nuts."

"Life's a lot like poker, Lon. Play the cards you're dealt."

Their discussion ended shortly before eleven o'clock. Thompson was summoned to the City Council conference room, down the hall from the mayor's office. He found Wheeler and the aldermen seated around a long table, all of them solemn as owls. They eyed his Prince Albert suit with looks of trepidation.

Earlier that morning, when he was dressing, Thompson had considered donning his police uniform. But then, with hardly a moment's thought, he'd left it hanging in the armoire. He felt it only fitting to retire the uniform with the badge. What was past was past.

"Listen to me now, Ben," Wheeler said, motioning him to a chair. "We've put it to a vote, and it's unanimous. We refuse to accept your resignation."

Thompson knuckled his mustache. "Tom, it's not like you've got a choice in the matter. I've resigned and that's that. It's official."

"Let me put in a word." Wayne Latham, the alderman for Guy Town, sat forward in his chair. "Marshal Thompson, as you'll recall, I opposed your election to office. But today, I've voted with these gentlemen." He nodded around the table. "We want you to stay on."

"Damn right!" Wally Peterman, who represented the First Ward, waved his arms. "So you killed some no-account in San Antonio. So what? Who cares!"

"I do," Thompson said soberly. "Alexander Wooldridge got it right during the election. He told the voters a 'shootist' shouldn't be allowed to wear a badge. I'm sorry to say I proved his point."

"That's old hat," Peterman countered. "You were cleared of that business in San Antonio. We need you here in Austin."

Thompson wagged his head. "What you need is a professional peace officer. Lon Dennville's the man for the job."

"You're wrong," Wheeler persisted. "Everybody in this room—the people of Austin!—want you. We're asking you to stay."

"Gentlemen, I appreciate your vote of confidence. But I guess I'll have to decline. Some things just aren't in the cards."

Thompson shook hands around the table. Then, with a final nod to Wheeler, he walked out of the room. He felt a momentary sense of pride that Wheeler and the aldermen had tried to argue him into staying on. But in the next instant, he knew he'd done the right thing— Austin would get the marshal it deserved.

On the way out of City Hall, he met Ed Creary coming through the door. The man he'd defeated in the election seemed more presentable than usual. He was dressed in a freshly pressed suit and he radiated confidence. His mouth creased in a sardonic grin.

"Well, Thompson," he said in a gloating voice. "The word's out you were forced to resign. Good news travels fast."

"I wasn't forced into anything," Thompson said. "I resigned for my own reasons."

"Likely story! You shouldn't go around shooting

people. Not on your own time, anyway. Doesn't look good."

"What's it to you one way or another?"

"What else?" Creary retorted. "Austin has to have a new marshal and I'm here to present my case. I've got an idea the city council will jump at the chance."

Thompson grunted. "They'd probably get railroaded out of town. You're too crooked for the job."

"You ought to learn to watch your mouth. I might just call you out."

"Go ahead, call me out."

Creary's hand edged toward the inside of his suit jacket. The move was hesitant, somehow tentative, but all the excuse Thompson needed. He popped the Colt from his shoulder holster and lashed out in a shadowy blur. The barrel struck Creary across the forehead in a splatt of blood and his hat went flying. His eyes rolled back in his head and he wilted at the knees. He dropped in a bloodied heap on the sidewalk.

A woman rounded the corner and stopped with a gasp. She looked from Thompson to the fallen man, and back again. "Ma'am," Thompson said, tipping his top hat. "You'll have to excuse the disturbance. I've been wanting to do that for a long time."

She glanced down at the sidewalk. "Isn't that Ed Creary?"

"Yes, ma'am, it is for a fact."

"Well, then, I say high time, Marshal Thompson."

"Former marshal, ma'am, but you're exactly right. High time."

Some ten minutes later Thompson walked through the door of the Iron Front. The noon hour was approaching and the bartenders were busy stocking shelves. Joe

Richter stood talking at the bar with Will Simms. The bartenders paused, greeting Thompson, and Richter hurried forward. He pumped Thompson's arm.

"By God, it's good to see you, Ben. You gave us a scare what with that business down in San Antonio."

Thompson laughed. "Had a good lawyer and an eyewitness. Will, here, was my ace in the hole."

"We were just talking about it," Richter said. "Will tells me you offered to put him back on the payroll."

"Joe, that's not the half of it."

Thompson briefly explained that he'd resigned as marshal. Before they could recover from the shock, he launched into a whole new plan for the future. He intended to buy the building next door, an older mercantile that was rapidly losing ground to the stores uptown. The building would be gutted and refurbished, and transformed into a variety theater. Will Simms would manage the operation.

"Last night it came to me," he went on. "There's money to be made in the show business, and Will's the perfect man for the job. Not to mention it'll draw even bigger crowds to the Iron Front."

"We'll be swamped!" Richter agreed heartily. "After the show, where else would they go? Right here!"

"Joe, that's the whole idea. We'll corner the market in Austin."

Richter and Simms fell to discussing how the Iron Front and the variety theater would work in tandem. Simms was wild-eyed with enthusiasm, already planning how he would stage the hottest vaudeville extravaganza in Texas. He'd bring in Eddie Foy, the great comedian, and Lola Montana, the exotic dancer. Maybe even Lillie Langtry, the toast of New York!

Thompson listened with appreciative interest. They

were both good men, and he knew they would make it a resounding success. Yet, even as they rambled on, his gaze was drawn to the poker tables at the rear of the room. A vagrant thought surfaced in his mind, and he wondered that he'd ever run for public office. For a time, goaded by some wayward ambition, he had pretended to be a lawman. The folly of it seemed to him now beyond reason.

There was, in the end, a sense of having come full circle. He was who he was—a gambler—and a damned good one. Perhaps the best who ever traveled the cowtowns and mining camps of the frontier. A sporting man with the nerve to bet it all on a single card.

One thought triggered another. He turned to Richter. "Spread the word to the high rollers. I'm open for business."

Richter appeared surprised. "You want a game tonight?"

"Tonight and every night, Joe. I'm back in action."

Thompson laughed with the wonder of it all. Old times or new times, it was the best of times. For he was where he belonged.

A gambling man with the world to win.